Praise for *To Kill a Man*

'A strikingly good thriller with a contemporary feel'
Daily Mail

'A thrilling and involving mystery that provides a masterclass on
American politics, but also has a real human story at its heart'
Sunday Express

'An absorbing and timely thriller'
Irish Independent

'Completely gripping and original. Sam Bourne puts
female anger, vengeance and power at the centre of his
latest and most exciting novel'
Hadley Freeman

'A compulsive, zeitgeisty tale of gender politics and social
media manipulation. The perfect post-#MeToo thriller –
I gobbled it up'
Louise Candlish

'A pacey, intelligent thriller set in the treacherous world
of Trump-era politics . . . Recommended'
Jewish Chronicle

'This, then, is a topical #MeToo novel, and Bourne
skilfully and absorbingly links Winthrop to
other victims of male violence'
Sunday Times

To Kill a Man

Also by Sam Bourne

The Righteous Men
The Last Testament
The Final Reckoning
The Chosen One
Pantheon
To Kill the President
To Kill the Truth

As Jonathan Freedland

Bring Home the Revolution
Jacob's Gift
The 3rd Woman

To Kill a Man

SAM BOURNE

Quercus

First published in Great Britain in 2020 by Quercus
This paperback edition published in 2021

Quercus Editions Ltd
Carmelite House
50 Victoria Embankment
London EC4Y 0DZ

An Hachette UK company

A CIP catalogue record for this book is available
from the British Library

PB ISBN 978 1 78747 496 3

10 9 8 7 6 5 4 3 2 1

Typeset by CC Book Production
Printed and bound in Great Britain by Clays Ltd, Elcograf S.p.A.

MIX
Paper from
responsible sources
FSC
www.fsc.org
FSC® C104740

Papers used by Quercus are from well-managed forests and other responsible sources.

For Sarah – the woman in my life

MONDAY

Chapter 1

Washington, DC

Later she would tell the police she knew it was a man. She would say the sound of a footstep just before midnight, the heaviness of its tread, left her in no doubt that a man was inside her home.

She would tell them she had been at her desk most of the evening, working away on a document. She would explain that it was 'a closing memorandum for the committee', adding in her formal statement the official name of both the case and the committee. Not that it was necessary. The detectives knew who she was. She had served as lead counsel to the House intelligence committee during those televised hearings that had riveted the nation, conducting the most dramatic cross-examinations, briefing the media on camera just afterwards and building a cult following in the process. In Washington, and on cable TV, Natasha Winthrop had become a semi-celebrity. There was talk of a run for high office, even the very highest.

She also told the police what was less well-known: that while she had become a hero to those who despised the current president, she had simultaneously aroused a matching level of passion among those who loved him. She showed the detectives some of the tweets that had come her way, including a couple that had arrived earlier that day: *Choke, bitch* was one, *Hey whore why aren't you dead yet* was another.

She told the police she was used to noises in the night. They were the proof that it wasn't just real-estate hype: her home in Georgetown really was a colonial-era house, one that creaked and groaned with memories. But this sound, together with the softer one that came after it, had left no room for doubt. The second noise seemed more cautious, anxious not to repeat the mistake of the first. It contained human deliberation, taking care to disguise itself, aware of its own implications – though she used different words when talking to the police. It was nearer too, no question about it. And obviously, unambiguously, it belonged to a man.

Her statement said it was only a few seconds later that a man was standing before her, framed in the doorway of her study on the ground floor. She told the detectives that he seemed to pause, as if making an assessment. He was dressed all in black: boots, dark jeans, close-fitting winter jacket. His face was covered by a ski mask, with only his eyes visible. She said that his eyes had stared at her and that she had stared back at him. It was probably no more than a second, but that meeting of their eyes felt interminable. He took a long look into her, as if searching for something.

She'd wanted to move, but could not. She was frozen, her arms and legs as much as her throat. And what was strangest was that in that second, he seemed frozen too. Paralyzed somehow. Two people staring at each other, facing the void.

But then the moment was over. In two swift strides, he marched into the room. Very deliberate steps, as if coming in to collect something. She told the police that, for a fleeting second, she'd wondered if this were a robbery. If he was there to steal one of her files. Or, more likely, her computer. Given her work, it would hardly have been shocking: there were plenty of people who'd have been glad to know what she knew.

In both her first, unofficial interview with a police officer and in her signed statement, she mentioned that she had prepared for this eventuality. After the break-in at the firm, she'd had a panic button installed, linked to a private security company. There were two: one by the bed, one in the kitchen. But none in her study. Which meant she'd have to get past him and out of this room.

But before she'd had a chance to move, he was close enough to push her over. The flat palm of his hand on her left shoulder and she was down. And then he was on top of her. She told the detectives that this seemed a practised movement, almost a technique. She thought at the time: he's done this before.

Then he tore at her clothes. One hand stayed on her shoulder, the other began to tug at her belt and at her zip. She was writhing, but it was no good. The strength of him was too much.

She described how he used his knees to keep her pinned down, one of them pressing so hard into her hip she thought it would crack. He was so close, she could smell him. The damp of outside was on his clothes, that wet-dog smell of wool soaked in the rain.

In her statement, she described how he kept the ski mask on throughout, so she had only his eyes to go on. Her impression was that he was neither young nor old, but somewhere in between. Perhaps a few years older than her. Say thirty-eight or thirty-nine. She thought she saw, perhaps when the mask slipped, that his hair was dark and that he had stubble on his cheeks.

Later she would do her best to describe what the police kept referring to as 'the struggle', though that seemed the wrong word. She remembered that her free hand, her right hand, rose several times to push at his face. Not to remove his mask but to hurt him. She remembered him flinching and her nails catching his neck. They scratched him, deep enough for her to feel the flesh break, a tearing sensation that surprised her.

'That's good,' she heard him murmur. 'I like that.'

She told the detectives that when she heard him say that, a surge of nausea had rolled through her.

She tried to abbreviate her account of what happened next, though the police pressed her for details. How he used his knees to keep her immobilized, how his fingers tugged and pulled at her jeans, how his breath was on her face. Where exactly he put his fingers. How many. What he did.

When she tried to explain how she responded, to give an account of her thought process, she stumbled. The best she could manage was to say that there was no thought, that thought was not the right word. That none of this happened in her head. That her body took the decision for her.

Wriggling to escape from him, she raised her back just enough to lift herself off the ground. (She told the detectives that she wondered if he had allowed her this move, because it meant her body was closer, and therefore more accessible, to him; that he might have taken it to imply some kind of acquiescence or even – heaven forbid – pleasure, as if she were arching her back to meet him. The thought appalled her. But it also struck her as useful.)

His breath was heavier and faster now, his focus on – and, yes, she accepted this was an odd word, but it was the one that came to mind – his *invasion* of her was total. He seemed to pay no attention to what her right arm was doing, within touching distance of the top of the desk. He did not notice that her fingers were clawing at it, desperately scratching at the surface.

Soon her fingers reached higher until they found the edge of her laptop. She knew that she was close.

Still locked in place by his superior strength, her hand finally found what it was looking for: the hard, cool metal texture of the heaviest object on the desk. No bigger than a fist, it was a small and not especially striking bust of Cicero. Her statement explained that it was a gift from a former boyfriend, bought from one of those kitsch souvenir shops on a work trip to Rome a year ago. (*To Natasha: Behold, a great advocate of yesterday – for a great advocate of today.*)

She did not hesitate, she did not plan. Instead, with no thought at all, she gripped the bust in her hand, making sure she was holding

7

it tight, then slowly lowered it until her fist was directly level with his temple. He didn't see. He was too focused on himself.

A pause for a fraction of a second as she retracted her hand, and then, like the release of a catapult, she let it fire back as hard as she could, smashing directly into the side of his head, the metal of the statue colliding with the bone of his skull.

The sound it made was loud, but it was quieter than the silence that followed. A sudden silence, after the noise of struggle and breath and writhing and pain, a silence that filled the room and the rest of the house.

His head fell forward straight away, his face landing on hers. She felt her skin turn moist, slick. She told the police that she initially assumed it was his blood.

Slowly, she let her fingers uncurl, so that the bust fell out of her hand. She tried to wriggle out, but he was still on her, a deadweight. Her face was getting wetter. She used her free hand to dab at her skin and when she looked at her fingers she saw that the wetness was clear, like warm water. She told the police that a memory returned of a murder case she had tried a few years earlier. She knew what this was: cerebrospinal fluid. Seconds earlier it had been cushioning this man's brain inside his skull. Now it was all over her. According to her police statement, this was the moment she understood that the man was dead and that she had killed him.

She told the police that it had taken some effort to get his body off her, that the weight had seemed to get heavier, the flesh more inert. She'd had to use her arms, her knees, her core, until, at last, she'd felt the corpse roll off her, landing on its back. It was then that she noticed the damp patch on the bunched material of his pants and saw that he had been unable to contain himself.

In her written testimony, Natasha Winthrop testified that it was only then that she'd pulled off the ski mask and looked upon the man's face. She did not add that it was only then that she truly understood what she had done.

Chapter 2

Washington, DC

'Maggie, how the devil are you?'

'I'm good, Senator. I'm good. How about you? You OK?'

'You betcha, Maggie! You bet your life. Come on now. Take a seat. Right here. That's it. Great. So let me take a good look at you. It's been a while, right?'

Maggie Costello could feel her jaws and cheekbones taking up that most traditional of Washington formations: the rictus grin. She knew she ought to smile, that it was expected of her. Part of that obligation was presumed gratitude. Here she was, getting face time, a one-to-one, a breakfast-time meeting – albeit without breakfast – with the frontrunner for her party's presidential nomination, a man recognized across the world and widely loved in America (at least by those on her side of the political aisle). Seventy years old, having served for the best part of half a century in Washington, Senator Tom Harrison was a veritable legend. Of course she should be grateful: the man could well be the next President of the United States and *he* had asked to see *her*, not the other way around. That dynamic was so rare, she was meant to be savouring it, delighting in it. If Washington was a jungle, and by God it felt sweaty and foetid enough at times, this was that precious moment when the alpha gorilla dips his head in your direction. So yes, she certainly should be bloody smiling.

She kept that up while Harrison worked his magic. Without so much as a note in front of him, he was telling her the highlights of her résumé: the work she'd done as a former White House operative under both of the last presidents – serving one willingly, the other anything but. He ticked off each achievement, chiefly the disasters she had averted, not because he thought she might have forgotten what she'd been doing these last few years – though, let's face it, there were men in this town who would indeed mansplain your own CV to you, given half a chance – but because he wanted her to know that he knew.

'I gotta say, Maggie. You're a heroine of mine. I mean that.' He patted his heart and shook his head, as if overcome with the sincerity of his feelings. 'I mean, what you did with the whole book-burning thing? Goddamn, that was something. And that's even before we get to the way you exposed the president and the—'

'Thank you, Senator.'

'No! It's we who should be thanking *you*. My God, what you did for the American people. For the world! It's huge, Maggie. Huge. From the bottom of my heart.'

'Thank you.'

'But – and I hope this makes you happy – I don't want to talk about all the fire-fighting, troubleshooting stuff you do, even though, don't get me wrong, you do it so well. No one better in this town. No one. Bar none! And I've been around a while, Maggie, I don't mind saying. *Bar none*, Maggie.' He fixed her with his longest, most earnest look. In the end, it was she who had to look away.

'But that's not why I brought you here. I don't need a firefighter on my team.' And then, with that little chuckle in the voice as familiar to any American as the sound of their own doorbell, 'I don't plan on starting too many fires.'

'OK.'

'Well, not those kind of fires! You know what I mean, Maggie. Because,' and on that last word his voice did a little sing-song, doing the work of a drumroll, 'I remember what brought you to this town.'

'Really?' she said, fighting the urge to add, *Because I don't.*

'Oh yes, Maggie. I go back a long way. And I remember that you were hired by a certain occupant of the Oval Office as a *foreign policy* specialist, correct me if I'm wrong. Oh yes, you see,' he was tapping his temple, 'don't believe what you read in the *New York Times*, all that "more senior than senator" bullshit. I still got the best memory in the business. And so I remember: you were brought into that administration because of what you'd done in the Middle East. Maggie Costello, peacemaker.'

'That was a long time ago.'

'Not that long ago. Woman your age, nothing's that long ago. What are you, thirty-three? Thirty-four? My staff are giving me evil looks. What? It's illegal to mention a woman's age now?

Give me a break. Craig, get me a soda or something. Maggie, am I wrong?'

'About my age or about Jerusalem?'

'Jerusalem. That's what you do, right? Diplomacy, mediation, background in NGOs, United Nations? That's your thing.'

'It was.'

'Because, believe me, we are going to have some major crap to clear up if we get this crowd out. And I mean, C-R-A-P. The mess these people have made all over the world, with our friends, with our *allies*? You don't need me to tell you. You read the news; you know. Jeez, Louise.'

Despite herself, Maggie could feel her head growing lighter, as if a warm mist was filling her brain, as if it might start floating. It'd been so long since anyone had regarded her as anything more than a handler of crises, she barely knew how to respond. Surely, this was what she wanted, to be treated as more than a glorified 911 service, to be viewed as a person of expertise?

'So you're envisioning a role in the national security team, is that right?' She was forcing her voice to hold steady. 'And obviously we take nothing for granted, but, if you win, either State or NSC?'

'As you say, nothing for granted, Maggie. *Nuh-thing*. No measuring the drapes on this campaign. That's a rule. Complacency kills you in this game. *Kills* you. We take nothing for granted until my hand is on that Bible and I'm swearing the oath – and not even then! Ellen's rolling her eyes at me now. Sorry, Maggie. Some of them have heard that one before. But I mean it. No complacency.'

'Sure. But part of the national security team?'

'What's that?'

'Me. My role. I'd be part of the national security team.'

'That's how I see you. You're tough, Maggie. That's what everyone says. That's us, eh, Maggie? Fighting Irish. My great-grandfather on my mother's side. Donegal. Did I tell you I visited there a few years ago, back when I was chairing Foreign Relations? They rolled out the red carpet, I can tell you. "The prodigal son returns." You get all that when you go back home? Course you do! You're a rock star. Don't be modest.'

Maggie hesitated, a pause that was so familiar to her. On the one hand, she didn't want to labour the point, she didn't want to seem pedantic, or boringly literal, or too demanding. And on the other, she knew a politician's non-answer when she heard one. *That's how I see you* was not the same as *Yes*.

'So that's a yes? A designated member of the national security team?'

Harrison let out a small sigh, then quickly restored himself, giving her a flash of those brilliant white teeth, which seemed to have had a fresh bleaching, doubtless for the upcoming campaign. 'Look, my preference would be to give you as much scope as possible. Free rein.' He crinkled his face. 'I don't want to tie you down with a narrow little title. Put limits on you. You're too big for that.'

She smiled, reminded that in Washington a compliment was to be approached warily. It was almost always a diversionary tactic or consolation prize, a signal that you had missed out on the real thing.

'You want to keep me free for other things.'

'I want you to have authority across the campaign.'

'In case something blows up perhaps.'

'Exactly. You've got it.'

'So a troubleshooter.'

'Yes! I mean, no. Not at all.'

'It's OK. If that's what you'd like me to do, you can just say.'

'No, not at all. That's not how . . . though of course . . . Look, you got me all tongue-tied here. I bet you hear that from a lot of guys, don'tcha! No, seriously, Maggie. I value your expertise in the foreign policy area. I really do. But, sure, if we hit some turbulence – and my plan is very much for that *not* to happen, believe me – but if we fly into some bumpy air, I'd want to turn to my most trusted navigation officer. Which could well be you. Maggie, I'm only telling you what you already know. Talk to anyone in this town and they'll tell you. "You find yourself in a hole, you want Maggie Costello right next to you – because, God darn it, she'll get you out."'

After that, there was some more chat about the shape of the race, how he'd already locked up the key endorsements and how, knock on wood, things were looking just great. He checked that she was a full US citizen, despite the Irish thing. Maggie confirmed that, yes, she had become a citizen years ago, and that she'd been given FBI clearance to work in previous administrations, so working for the next one should present no problem. They both smiled at the confidence – not complacency, mind – of that.

At no point, Maggie noticed, did the president-to-be mention his vision for the country over the next four years, or sketch out a policy programme, either foreign or domestic. The closest he came was that reference to the janitorial burden that would rest on whoever came next, clearing up the mess left, and added to daily, by the current incumbent. Which, given the havoc and ruin of the last few years, struck Maggie as fair enough. Just undoing all that damage was a sufficient mission.

Aides were coming in and out throughout and now one lingered at the door with a tight expression that said, *I mean it this time: you really have to finish.* Harrison got to his feet, repressing a little groan at the effort, shook Maggie's hand and headed towards the door. Maggie had just bent down, reaching into her handbag, when she jolted. She could feel two hands on her shoulders, giving a squeeze that made her jump. A second later there was breath in her ear and Harrison's voice as he whispered: 'Can't wait to have you on board.'

Reflexively, she stiffened and, equally instinctively, tucked in her bottom, as if to prevent a grab or smack of her buttocks. It didn't come, but her body had prepared for it. By the time she looked over her shoulder, the politician was out the door, a flutter of aides around him, including, she now noticed, several women, at least two of them in their twenties.

Can't wait to have you on board. In a way, innocuous. Sort of thing a male boss might say to flatter any soon-to-be employee, man or woman. On board, part of the team, joining the gang. But said that way, in a whisper, nuzzled into her ear, it had another sound. Something about that construction: *Can't wait to have you.* In that voice, and because the remark was addressed only to her, deliberately out of earshot of the rest of the team, even the 'on board' sounded sexual, as if it were a euphemism for something else. On board, on bed, in bed. *Can't wait to have you.*

These thoughts galloped ahead of each other, while she stood, frozen, in the meeting room. Her face was hot; she was blushing. And then came the realization that she had said nothing – that she had stood mute, uttering not a word, not even a sound, of protest – and, with that, came anger. Not chiefly at him, the would-be, even likely, next US president, but at herself. How could she have not said anything? Why had she let him do that grabbing, pseudo-massage thing? What message had she sent to those two young women in his retinue? Hadn't she, by her silence, told them there was nothing they could do, that resistance was impossible, that they just had to take it? If even she, an accomplished Washington player with a reputation of her own, could not push back, what possible hope did they have?

And then, as she gathered up her bag and headed for the door, the backlash began. Maybe she was getting this out of proportion. It was a friendly gesture. A little shoulder massage; hardly the end of the world. And he's an old guy, from a different time. When he was coming up, that's just how men were; no one ever told him it was wrong. Besides, people like their politicians to be warm and human, don't they? Aren't we always complaining if they're too robotic, too managerial, too professorial? What he did was not that different to a pat on the back and an encouraging word: *Good to have you with us.* Get over it.

In the lift down, she let both voices slug it out until, by the time she was back outside and on the street, her chief thought was disbelief that here she was, yet again, having this internal argument. How many times had she been through this in her career, in her *life*? The tiny little gesture or remark that left you feeling unsettled, even shaken, but not so uncomfortable that you did anything about it. The episode that sat in that grey area, leaving you with no clear idea what to do.

She hailed a cab and was about to thumb out an email to the campaign chief of staff saying thanks, but no thanks. She thought better of it. Too quick: if she did that, they'd assume it was a reaction to what just happened. That itself would turn it into a thing. And right now she didn't want it to be a thing. Not least because Tom Harrison might win the election and she might need to eat lunch in this town again.

Instead she opened up a WhatsApp message from her sister that had arrived nearly an hour earlier, while she was in the meeting. All it said was *Wow*. Attached was a video that Maggie had already seen, because it had been widely shared since late the previous week. But the fact that Liz had wanted to pass it on struck Maggie all the same. Though Maggie would never say it to her face, her sister served as a one-woman focus group for Maggie, a reliable spokesperson for the real world. A teacher and mother of two living in Atlanta, Liz had never seen the Beltway, let alone lived within it. That fact had helped form an operating principle in Maggie's mind, one that had come to seem like an iron law of political science: if something – a candidate's message or a political scandal – had reached Liz, then it had truly cut through.

Maggie clicked on the video again, making this the fourth time. She wanted to watch it through her sister's eyes, curious to see what Liz had seen in it. It was a forty-two-second video clip that, her phone informed her, had now been viewed two million times. It featured a woman in her mid-thirties, with short, dark hair and piercing green eyes. Maggie could see the comments posted underneath, including one from a journalist who had been among the first to share it, with these words:

If our politics is broken, and it is, then maybe we need to look beyond conventional politics and politicians. Maybe it's time to pick someone fresh and untainted. Someone who can inspire, and is a real human being. Someone like Natasha Winthrop.

Chapter 3

Washington, DC, a few hours earlier

After she dialled 911, Natasha Winthrop barely moved. She stood for minute after minute in her study, staring down at the inert body on the floor. The sight of it froze her.

If anything, the horror seemed greater now than when he'd been alive. Then at least she'd had adrenalin powering through her system. Now it was receding, leaving behind pure terror. She could not take her eyes off the man at her feet, his eyes wide open. It was the strangest feeling: she was alone in the house, but not fully alone. She was with *him*.

The voice of rational thought, the inner voice that ordinarily she trusted most, was telling her that 'he' was now an 'it'. That this corpse no longer posed a threat, that it could not do her any harm. But she was not listening to that voice. She could barely hear it. It was drowned out by the sheer fear pumping through her veins.

The fear had multiple components. Fear of a dead body, most

certainly. Perhaps, she thought, if she had done more criminal law, handled more murders, she might have become inured to such a sight years ago. But for her, the mere presence of a corpse was utterly horrifying. There was also that fundamental fear of an intruder in the house, right here in this room. That terror had not receded simply because the intruder was dead. There was still the fear of what he had wanted to do to her, of what he had begun to do to her. His face was still there. She could look at it.

Twice she imagined that he would somehow strike at her again, as if this state of inertia were temporary, as if he would rouse himself and resume. Perhaps it was a trick, to make her lower her guard. Maybe it was part of the thrill for him, playing dead like this.

In a strange way, she didn't believe she had killed him. He was a big, violent man. He was monstrous. It made no sense to imagine that she had overwhelmed him. Yes, she was fit; she could run 10k without too much trouble. She was relatively tall. But the idea that she could overpower a man like this, overpower and *kill* a man like this, how could such a thing be possible? There must be some other explanation, some other outcome yet to be revealed.

She stayed like that, immobilized for what felt like hours. She stirred only when she became aware of the damp on her shirt, where he had left his mark on her. She had the strongest urge to get it off, immediately, to rid herself of it. She began to undo the buttons, to wriggle out of it.

And then the rational voice, the lawyer's voice, intervened and told her to hold on. She needed to stay just as she was. She was not to change a single thing. She needed the police to find the shirt on her, unaltered and . . . uncontaminated. She would need to show them what had happened. This was evidence. This was proof.

A memory came back to her, of a colleague who later became a friend telling a group of other female lawyers about rape cases. She'd told them that plenty of rapists exhibited sexual dysfunction. Either they couldn't get an erection or, if they could, they were prone to premature ejaculation. 'The weird thing is, they don't seem to care,' her friend explained to the group, who were listening rapt. 'For them, penetration is not the main event.' Apparently, the big thrill came later, when they masturbated over the memory of what had happened: in particular, when they recalled the state of terror of their victim. That was the real turn-on. Natasha remembered that conversation and shuddered.

And then it came, the loud thud. A single sound. *There's someone else here*, she thought. She held still. She was waiting for a second noise, the creak on an upstairs floorboard that would reveal the direction of travel. Then she would know for certain who was here and how close he was.

When it came, the noise was solid and steady. Repeated three times. But it came from the wrong place. It seemed to come from outside.

It took her a long moment – maybe ten or fifteen seconds – to realize that what she had heard was, in fact, a knock on the door. It was when that thought had registered, after travelling at a fraction of the normal speed, that the knocking sound came again. There was a voice too. 'Miss Winthorpe? Miss Winthorpe, can you hear me? It's the police.'

After that, the adrenalin receded further still. Until then, she understood, she had been in a heightened state of awareness, noticing everything. She pictured herself as an animal, every hair on its skin raised, its nostrils twitching, every nerve ending attuned to even the tiniest sound or smell or signal. But now that there was another person in the house – there to help – she lowered her guard and allowed the adrenalin tide to go out. The result was utter exhaustion.

She watched as a succession of different people arrived, the house becoming fuller. She couldn't take in their names and they struggled with hers, as always. 'It's Winthrop,' she heard herself say several times. 'Not Winthorpe, Winthrop.'

One thing she noticed, though, from the start: a confusion on their faces that told her that this was, from a policing point of view, an awkwardly complicated situation. She saw it in the pair of officers who came to the house first: two young women, one African-American, the other a Latina and both heavily armed. They seemed unsure how to approach her. Should they adopt the sympathetic voice they'd doubtless learned in training, reserved for when handling victims of rape and sexual assault? Should they be sitting her down, offering her a cup of coffee and taking her hand? Or should they be formal and wary, given that they were dealing with a woman apparently responsible for the corpse lying on the floor?

They resolved the dilemma by saying almost nothing. Not to Natasha anyway. Instead, they spoke into their radios, talking to 'despatch' and a variety of others through the crackling static. They watched her though: careful to be sure she didn't touch anything and didn't go anywhere.

Before long the house was bustling with people, some of them in full forensic gear: all latex gloves and paper shoes. As if they were about to go into surgery. Natasha was ushered out of the room. But the body – he – was still there.

In among all the various detectives and senior officers, there was one woman whose specific task was to look after Natasha. Her name was Sandra, and she introduced herself as the 'chaperone', though someone else referred to her as a Sexual Offences Investigative Techniques officer. Efficient and capable, but with a voice that was appropriately soft, she explained what needed to happen, one step at a time, often ending a sentence with 'Can you do that for me?' and 'Is that all right, Natasha?'

First, she took her to the bedroom, so that she could change clothes, slowly and with great care. Once Natasha had taken off an item, Sandra would place it inside its own clear, plastic bag, with a zip lock. She wore latex gloves. She explained that every item might contain a tiny speck of DNA that would be used to identify the 'assailant'. That was the word she used. Slowly Natasha understood that, when it came to the assault on her, the crime scene was not the downstairs study – the crime scene was her body.

Ordinarily, the notion of undressing – and undressing fully – in front of a stranger would have thrown her. (Although not as much as it would throw some women: if you've lived with five other girls in the dormitory of a Massachusetts private boarding school, privacy becomes rather a relative concept.) But she was too numb to hesitate.

At one point, Natasha asked if she could use the bathroom.

'I know it's really difficult, but it'll be better if you can hold on just a bit longer, until you have a chance to be examined by the doctor,' Sandra said. 'Can you do that for me?' She was talking to Natasha as if she were seven years old. Normally that would bring a firm slapdown. But now Natasha did what she was told, slowly and in a daze. As if she had flicked the switch on herself marked 'low power mode'.

Eventually, and now wearing loose sweatpants and a baggy fleece, she was led back downstairs. It was transformed: areas marked off with tape; officers in white forensic suits; and the sound of constant chatter on police radios. Natasha sat where Sandra indicated she was allowed to sit.

She couldn't say how much time passed. It might have been minutes, it might have been hours. She could see that her own movements, her own cognition of what was going on around her, had slowed down. She seemed to be buffering. And yet one thing caught her eye.

She saw two police officers, one of the two women who had arrived first along with a senior detective, locked in conversation. She was briefing him, reading from her notebook. The detective was nodding, taking in what she was saying.

Perhaps it was her line of work, but Natasha was adept at reading situations like this. In court, it was always useful if you could intuit when someone was hearing information that was new or sensitive. And that was what she could see now. Instantly, and no matter how fogged her brain was with shock, she could tell that this exchange between the two officers was not routine. The young woman was telling her superior something important and unexpected. That much was written on both their faces. The detective's eyes were registering first surprise, then interest, then a kind of satisfaction, as if he'd been proven right on a key point.

At that moment Natasha was certain that the police had found something. And, without knowing how or why or what that was, she knew it made them suspect that she had not told them the whole story.

Chapter 4

Washington, DC, Headquarters, Metropolitan Police Department

The 07.45 morning meeting was chaired by the man known universally, by critics, colleagues and perhaps even his immediate family, as Ratface. His formal title was Assistant Chief of Police of the Metropolitan Police Department for Washington, DC (Investigative Services), but to everyone inside this room, he was Ratface. The nickname was not cryptic or allusive, but literal: he looked like a rodent.

Usually this meeting was dull, a read-out from the department's seven district commanders, updating the group on ongoing inquiries and any new cases that had arisen overnight. Each of the seven would read out a roll-call of cases in a shopping-list monotone that suggested every item was routine and required no further discussion. The purpose of this meeting was oversight, so, naturally, the aim of everyone attending was to ensure they escaped with as little oversight of their own work as possible. Ideally, none.

The commander for the Fourth District had finished her list –
announcing that the investigation into the suspected arson
attack on a community centre, conducted with their colleagues
in the Fire and Emergency Medical Services Department, was
'advancing as before', which was taken to mean 'without progress' – when her counterpart for the Second District, which
included the Georgetown neighbourhood, cleared his throat.

Ratface took that as his cue to move his chair forward, noisily.
He leaned in, his body language signalling extra interest. The
district commander looked up, noticed the move and reached
for a pen, scribbling on his list. Veterans of the 07.45 suspected
he had hastily adjusted his running order.

Accordingly, he began: 'Georgetown: suspected sexual assault
of white female, thirty-six, resulting in death of assailant. Victim
underwent medical examination overnight and will be questioned this morning. Dupont Circle: mugging and stabbing—'

'Hold up.' Ratface blocked the attempt to move on. 'Can we
have a name on the victim, please?'

Reluctantly, the commander answered. 'Natasha Winthrop.'

The room greeted that news with a combination of gasps, a
whistled exhalation and, from one senior officer, a declaration
of 'Jesus fuck'.

'Full report please,' Ratface said.

There followed a brief account of the night's events, punctuated with some head-shaking disbelief both at the notion that a
young, female lawyer had killed a man with her bare hands and
that the lawyer in question was one fast becoming a national
figure.

'Who's in charge?' asked Ratface. He was told that since the incident had happened out of hours, the specialist homicide unit could not be called immediately. Two officers of the local district, backed by a specialist in sexual assault, were handling it.

Ratface grimaced. He bit down on his pen, staring at the table as, so his colleagues presumed, he made the political calculation of what did or did not best serve his ambition to become Chief of Police of the nation's capital – the same calculation, in other words, he made every minute of every working day, evenings and weekends. Eventually, he spoke.

'As we all know, this individual' – he meant Natasha Winthrop – 'has a high profile. There will be tight scrutiny of every aspect of our conduct. Press, social media. The feminist community, in particular, will be quick to judge how we handle a case of sexual assault.'

'We put a foot wrong and we'll have the OPC over us like a fucking rash,' a colleague chipped in (perhaps in revolt at the prissiness of *feminist community*). Natasha Winthrop had fought a few cases involving the Office of Police Complaints, and the nodding that followed this remark suggested the colleague had a point. Natasha had once been the go-to lawyer for those who represented people screwed over, beaten up or even killed by the police. Everyone in the room understood: it would not be smart to screw over Natasha Winthrop.

Ratface chewed his pen a bit more, then gave the order. 'Current officers are to stand down. This needs to be handled at commander level. Reporting directly and daily to me.'

Chapter 5

Washington, DC, a few hours earlier

Natasha Winthrop prided herself on her sense of direction, her spatial awareness and her memory for landmarks. Together they ensured she was rarely lost. But as of this moment, they had abandoned her.

At first, she told herself it was because it was dark, or because this was an unfamiliar part of the city, in the southwest quadrant that she barely knew, or because she was not driving but rather was a passenger, in the back seat of a police car, seated next to a watchful Sandra. But every now and then the more likely explanation barged its way into her thoughts: not that long ago she had been the victim of a violent sexual assault and she had killed a man. No wonder she had no idea where she was.

The one thing she noticed as they moved through empty roads were the signs for the hospital. She couldn't have told you which one, but that was where they were heading. She noticed that, once they pulled in, they drove past the regular entrance and parked by a side entry, unmarked and away from the main building.

She had visited places like this long ago, back when she handled cases of this kind, though she hadn't done many. She recognized the same heroic effort to pretend it was something else, to soften the atmosphere: floral prints on the walls, little scented bags of potpourri. The futile effort to pretend you'd come in for a massage rather than a forensic examination, as if this were a hotel spa rather than a police-cum-medical facility.

Sandra led her into what she said was the Initial Room. Two chairs facing each other, a low coffee table, more bland art on the walls. Natasha looked around, noticing that all the surfaces were plastic: even the seats were wipe-clean. Of course. This was a sterile space, designed to prevent any contamination of evidence. The evidence being, once again, Natasha and her body.

Sandra stepped out. But she was still audible, from down the corridor. Natasha couldn't make out the words; just Sandra's voice and the short, intermittent replies of another woman. Not quite hushed, but unmistakably an exchange of sensitive information. Was she briefing the doctor who was about to do the examination? Or was this more talk of whatever it was the police had seen at the house, with its implied accusation? Natasha detected the same uncertainty she had picked up earlier: these people didn't know whether to treat her as a victim of a sexual assault or a suspect in a homicide.

A moment later the doctor – longish, greying hair; kindly face – was there, explaining the sequence. That she would examine Natasha's body. That the process might take some time, because they had to be sure to miss nothing. And that Natasha was to say if anything made her uncomfortable and that they would take a break. She stressed that Natasha was in charge here and nothing would happen that Natasha did not want to happen. Natasha understood what the doctor was doing – she could almost see the page in the training manual, warning police and medical staff of the dangers of inflicting on victims a second violation. But she wondered if they were being extra careful. Under 'Occupation' she had, after all, entered the single word 'Attorney'.

Natasha lay on the examination couch with her eyes closed, telling herself that this was no different from a visit to a gynae-cologist. Letting the doctor do what she needed to do: take the swabs, examine, study, probe. She could tell when the woman paused, when she lingered for a moment. What had she seen? A scratch? A thumbprint, perhaps, where the man had pressed hard on Natasha's flesh?

Natasha's eyes stayed closed while the examination went on, for hours it seemed. She sent herself away while the doctor worked, a technique she had learned long ago. The trick was to launch herself into the sky, to float above the moment and separate herself from it: a self-induced out-of-body experience. But it wasn't easy.

Eventually, the examination was over. They offered Natasha the option of going to stay with a friend or remaining and show-ering 'here in the facility'. Returning to her own house was not 'a possibility at this stage, ma'am'. It was a crime scene they wanted left undisturbed. Natasha muttered something about 'getting back on the horse', worried that if she left it too long she might never want to sleep in that house again. But the officer looked at her blankly, waiting for an answer to the two options offered. Natasha said she would stay and shower, 'right away, please'. She had been itching to cleanse herself the second it had happened; she could still feel his . . . fluid on her skin, or at least the memory of it. She wanted it gone.

The shower was long but devoid of pleasure or relief. She scrubbed herself hard, but at no point did she feel like she was becoming clean. She only stopped when the water began to turn cold.

She slept for a couple of exhausted, restless hours on a hard, narrow mattress that resembled the examination couch. There were no overt nightmares. Instead, she woke every twenty minutes or so, with a start; once she even gasped. It was the recollection on waking, fresh each time, of what had happened a few hours earlier. For a split-second, there would be a brief hope that it had all been a mistake, that she had imagined it. But that would vanish as soon as it had arrived, chased away by the realization that this was no dream. It was real.

Every so often, a picture would come into her head. Unbidden, she saw that newly dead body. The damp clothing. The face.

A few hours later, there was more activity outside, more whispers. And within a few minutes, Natasha Winthrop found herself in an interview suite, facing two detectives, a man and a woman. The woman – white, late forties, dark hair, grey at the roots – introduced herself as Marcia Chester. Her face was lined, and seemed to be covered in a very fine dust, perhaps foundation, applied the previous day. She looked tired, but in a way that suggested the fatigue was structural: a life of hard work and

SAM BOURNE

constant stress. Natasha had known plenty of women like that; she smiled what she hoped was a smile of solidarity and empathy, one woman to another. The detective didn't reciprocate, but kept turning the pages in the file open on the desk in front of her.

The man was younger: black, wearing spectacles, bookish rather than hipster. He identified himself as Adrian Allen.

Chester began, confirming that she was the more senior. She asked Natasha to state her name, date of birth, address. She said that she was tape recording the interview.

'Can you tell us what happened last night at your home address?'

Perhaps it was the demands of being asked a direct question, the reminder it brought of her professional life. But at that prompt, Natasha cleared her throat and clicked into gear. She willed herself to shake off the sluggish, out-of-body disconnection of before. Now she described what happened, as precisely and clearly as she could. She spoke confidently, knowing what her questioners wanted and determined to be a good, useful witness. She was no longer buffering.

It helped that she knew how regular members of the public could be frustrating when giving a legal statement, repeating themselves, being vague, missing out crucial parts of the story, elaborating on things that were irrelevant, getting the timing of events wrong. Natasha Winthrop wanted the police to see that she was not like that, that she was a fellow professional.

But when it came to describing the moment she saw her attacker in the doorway, her voice gave her away. She trembled. And the sound of her own voice wobbling seemed to act as a cue. By the

34

time she'd got to the end, her cheeks were wet. She reached for a tissue on the table in front of her.

'Can I go back one step?' It was the man.

'Yes.'

'You say he appeared in your doorway at midnight.'

'Yes, around then. Give or take.'

'You're not sure?'

'No, I am sure. I remember the clock on my computer. It said eleven fifty-nine pm.'

'So you *are* sure.' It was the woman speaking.

'Yes. I'm sure.'

'So why did you say "give or take"?'

'I meant, I don't know the exact minute he appeared in the doorway. But I checked the time on my computer when I first heard a noise in the house. Which would have been only a minute or two before that.'

'All right.' Chester turned back to another page in the file. 'You have a chain on your front door, am I right?'

'That's right.'

'But it wasn't broken.'

'I'm sorry?'

'It's not broken. See?' She held up a close-up photograph of Natasha's front door, the chain dangling down as always. 'It's all in one piece.'

'I hadn't put it on.'

'OK,' said Allen, as if ready to move on.

'Why not?' It was Chester, not yet satisfied.

'I hadn't locked up yet.'

'But it was midnight. Is that your normal practice, to be alone in your house in the dead of night with your front door unlocked like that?'

'But it wasn't the dead of night. It was the evening.'

'You said it was midnight.'

'I mean it *had been* the evening. I had been working through the evening. At the end of the evening, after an evening's work, I planned to lock up, turn off the lights and go to bed.'

'All right. If you say so.'

'I do say so. What are you getting at?'

Now Allen spoke. 'Nothing at all, Ms Winthrop. We're just trying to get everything straight in our minds, no loose ends.' He smiled.

Chester resumed. 'You weren't expecting someone that night?'

'No.'

'Not your partner perhaps?'

'No.' Natasha paused, unsure how much to give away. 'I'm single.'

'You hadn't kept the chain undone because you were expecting someone to come over?'

'No.'

Chester turned another page, as if unimpressed or, at the very least, uninterested. Natasha, instinctively searching for a sympathetic face, glanced over at Allen. He offered a tight smile.

'All right,' Chester said, as if ready to take another tack. 'And the man who attacked you. You're absolutely sure you'd never seen him before?'

'I've told you, he was wearing a mask. I didn't see his face fully until it was over.'

'Sure, but when you did. Absolutely the first time you'd seen him?'

'Absolutely.'

'Not known to you at all?'

'No.'

'You weren't expecting him to come over?'

That put a crack in Natasha's resolve to be the calm, capable witness and professional equal of this woman.

'"Come over"? *Come over.* Do you not understand what happened to me? This man tried to *rape* me. You're making this sound like some kind of social call.'

'Please, Ms Winthrop.' Allen, stepping in. 'My colleague and I are just trying to make sure we've dotted every i and crossed every t. We're just being thorough.'

'And you believe in being thorough, don't you?' It was Chester.

'What?'

'We've spoken to your neighbours.' It was a statement rather than a question.

'Yes?'

Allen chipped in, 'They're all very concerned for you, as you can imagine.'

'But d'you know what's strange? What struck me as strange, anyway.' Chester fixed her gaze on Natasha for a long minute, inviting her to answer, a hint of a smile on her face.

'No, I don't know. What?'

'None of them heard a scream.'

'I'm sorry?'

'None of them heard anything at all, in fact. No sound of a

break-in. That's OK. He might have been a pro, got his way in without making too much of a ruckus. They can do that, the good ones. But not a sound out of you. Not a peep.'

The male detective was looking at Natasha, his face still friendly – or friendlier than Chester's, at any rate – but he was doing nothing to hold his colleague back. Natasha was aware that he was watching her, gauging her reaction, scrutinizing her face. Chester carried on:

'And it was weirdly hot last night, wasn't it? Like, crazy for this time of year. We had the air-con cranked up, I can tell you. And you had the window open. In your home office, I mean. That kind of night.' She was looking at her colleague, as if seeking his endorsement on this point. 'So if you had made a sound, somebody would have heard it. Wouldn't they, the neighbours? A woman screaming.'

'I did, I'm sure . . . I wanted to, but I couldn't . . .'

Allen said, 'I understand.'

'Just, you'd think, a strange man appears out of nowhere, in your doorway, just like that, standing there, in your home office – well, most women I know would let out an almighty scream, don't you think so, Detective Allen?'

'But I . . .'

'I mean, you couldn't help yourself, could you? Just the surprise.'

'I've told you. I was so shocked, I couldn't scream. I mean, I gasped but no—'

'Which is why I was asking, you know, left field and all, but was this perhaps someone you did know after all?'

'No, it was not. I'd never seen him before.'

'Not once? Never ever?'

Why it should be that phrase in particular that did it, Natasha couldn't say. But the nursery rhyme condescension of those two words – *never ever* – somehow made her snap back into herself. Her professional self.

'I know what you're implying here and it's completely unacceptable. I've been the victim of a horrific crime. I was defending myself from attack.'

It was Allen who replied. 'No one's implying anything, Ms Winthrop. Not at all.'

'Oh no? By suggesting I might have known my—'

'Not *suggesting*,' he said. 'Asking.'

'Even when I've already told you several times, exactly—'

'We're just trying to be absolutely sure of the facts. To go through every detail.'

Then, as an aside, Chester added with a curl of sarcasm: 'Following the rules and procedures.'

There was silence then, as she absorbed what this woman had said and as, perhaps, Allen did the same. Natasha understood. She looked back at Chester.

'Is there some kind of problem here?'

'None at all.'

'Is this about my professional work?'

'Let's get back to last night. You said—'

'Is that it? Is this about the committee? Or are you expressing resentment of my past involvement in complaints against the police? Is that what this is about?'

'You said the assailant was a man you'd never—'

'Hold on. I think we ought to get this cleared up. Just because I have represented people who were mistreated by the—'

'Ms Winthrop.' It was Allen, stepping in. 'Please. Let me reassure you. My colleague and I are determined to do the most thorough job we can. She meant nothing else. Just that we are going to do everything properly and thoroughly.'

And with that, Natasha was sure she saw him shoot a look, more of a glare really, at the senior officer: part scolding, part imploring. Translated it would have read: *I thought we talked about this.*

There was silence for a moment. Allen understood, even if Chester did not, that they were dealing with an attorney who did not tend to take prisoners. They could not risk her claiming there was so much as a hint of prejudice in their handling of her case.

But Natasha could see: she was no fool, this Chester. All the transcript would show was a commitment to 'following the rules and procedures'. Who could object to that? Her sarcasm would remain silent and unseen on the page.

The door opened and a young woman, a uniformed police officer, came in, passing a note to Chester. The detective read it, then passed it to Allen. The young woman left, saying nothing.

With no change in her expression, Chester spoke again. 'Can I go back to this business about the door?' She didn't wait for an answer. 'We'll obviously have forensics take a thorough look, but at first glance – to the naked eye – there's no sign of forced entry.'

'I don't know how—'

'Which is fine. Like I say, a hundred ways to catch a turtle, if you know what you're doing. Which this man might, for all we know.'

'Look, I've—'

'But the thing is, there's the neighbours. As I've said. They say – well, one of them says anyway – that they're pretty sure they saw the door open at around midnight last night. Man was taking the garbage out, apparently. Likes his routine, he says. Does it every Sunday night at around the same time: midnight. Apparently. So he steps out and sees a man at the entrance to your place, at the top of the stoop. Sees him go in, door opening for him.'

'The door *opening* for him? I don't understand. How would—'

'Oh, don't worry about that. It can look like that. You jimmy a door, if you're a pro, it can look like you're just turning a key. Skilled, these guys.'

'Very skilled.' It was Allen. His shoulders were down. He looked relieved that things were back on track, that Chester was behaving herself.

'I see.'

'No, that's not what worries me,' Chester resumed. 'It's more this.' She tapped on the piece of paper on the table in front of her, using her forefinger. The sheet was face down, just in case Natasha Winthrop was one of those people who could read a document upside down. Which she was.

'What is that?'

'This is a report on the CCTV covering your home and a few others. Expensive neighbourhood, private security; well covered by cameras. We don't have all the pictures in yet. But this is what we got from the security firm this morning.'

'And what does it say?'

'It says that the footage shows a male, face obscured by a ski mask or similar, entering your premises at eleven fifty-nine last night. It shows that he entered by the front door. No apparent use of force.'

'Apparent being the key word,' said Natasha.

'Yup. Absolutely right. Apparent. But it also says that the CCTV image shows what appears to be the outline of a person opening the door. It's indistinct, but the report is quite clear. There seems to be someone letting this man in. And, given what you've told us, Ms Winthrop, the only person that could possibly be is you.'

Chapter 6

Washington, DC

The flaw with these crack-of-dawn Washington meetings, Maggie reflected, not for the first time, was: what were you meant to do afterwards? Fine, if you had a regular job. Then you simply went to your office as if nothing had happened, pitching up no later than you would on a regular day. Sometimes earlier, in fact; at least in Maggie's case. Even after all these years in DC, she was still not used to the world of breakfast meetings at 6.30am, the world of coming off an overnight flight and heading straight into the office, the world of being at your desk soon after dawn – all of it driven by a work ethic so puritanical it would have shamed the witchburners of Salem. None of it made any sense to Maggie. On the few occasions when she had to surrender, and allow the incursion of an appointment into what should have been her sleeping hours, she had arrived at work afterwards feeling uncharacteristically virtuous. *Look who's at their desk before nine: how about that?*

But these days, it was odd. She was no longer on anyone's books, not expected anywhere. So after that session with Senator Tom Harrison, she was released back into the wild. True, she'd hardly had her feet up since leaving the White House, drawn into defusing serial crises here, there and everywhere, but for now there was no clock she was meant to punch, no place she was meant to be. Uri was not around. Lord knows they'd had their false starts over the years, including a long spell apart, but this was not one of those: instead her boyfriend was in India, shooting the documentary that had consumed him for months. He would be away for another fortnight. Which meant she was, for now, living a life she had barely known in this city: a single woman in Washington, whose time was her own.

In celebration of the fact, she decided to give herself a rare treat and sit down for a delayed breakfast at the Tabard Inn on 17th and N. After the weirdness of that meeting with Harrison, the dark interiors and English country hotel vibe felt like a necessary balm.

She found a corner table and, despite a vague sense that she should keep it analogue by reading the abandoned copy of the *Washington Post* on her table, habit made her pull out her phone.

She barely looked at the emails, including a follow-up from her contact in Harrison's office:

Hey, that went GREAT! Huge enthusiasm at this end. Lots of big hires being rolled out today and tomorrow (including a very cool get). Know the senator psyched to announce your name in that first wave. Good for us (momentum, buzz) and good for you – founder-member, present-at-the-creation. Say yes and we'll fix everything ASAP. Say yes!

Maggie swiped the email app away and went straight to Twitter. The first tweet she saw puzzled her. It was from a journalist who was a talking head regular on cable TV:

Am hearing attorney Natasha Winthrop was violently attacked last night – and killed her attacker. More details later.

That had already been retweeted nine hundred and twenty-three times by the time Maggie saw it, even though it had been up less than twenty minutes. Often the retweets came with a single word of mini-commentary – *Whoa* or *Jesus* – and, in one case, the emoji for a pair of eyes in gawp mode.

Maggie scrolled through to see that the story was spreading fast. A *Saturday Night Live* star had posted it with the message:

Always knew Winthrop was badass.

In reply, another comedian, a woman whose public radio spots had spun off into a hugely successful podcast, wrote:

That's the kind of lawyer *I* want.

Maggie now put 'Winthrop' in the search window and the screen filled up. The tweets seemed to be coming in every second, more and more of them. *New tweets available.*

There was one from CNN:

DC Police confirm lawyer Natasha Winthrop violently attacked in her home last night – apparently killing her assailant.

That triggered a new wave, bigger than the first. Besides the initial reaction of shock – *OMG* was a concise favourite – there was the occasional new thought. A former congressman, on the left of the Democratic Party, tweeted:

Winthrop involved in some of the most controversial terror cases of the last three years. Possible link?

Next was a tweet from a legal advocacy group that had represented terror suspects held at Guantanamo Bay. They'd been a regular *Fox News* target, branded a glorified jihadist front. Winthrop had worked with them on a couple of cases. The tweet featured a picture on the steps of DC Federal Court, a group whose hands were linked and held aloft, apparently celebrating a ruling in their favour. Winthrop was second from the left, beaming.

#Solidarity with Natasha Winthrop, fighter for justice

And now, inevitably, came the Twitter scolding and guilt-tripping. A female blogger for *Slate* said:

Can I remind people that we are talking here about a woman who has just undergone a violent assault and a terrible trauma?

Next came the ombudsman of a high-minded newspaper:

A warning that this case could come to trial. The more journalists and others speculate, the harder it will be to ensure that trial will be fair.

But the one that seemed to have caught fire, its retweet numbers clicking upward in real time, as Maggie watched, was from a name she did not immediately recognize.

Natasha Winthrop fought back. #Heroine

The profile picture didn't help: it was a book jacket. Maggie clicked on it and read the one-line bio with surprise:

Carmelita Tang is a Political Analyst for Fox & Friends. Her book — You Just Don't Get It! — is out now #TakeBackOurCountry

Now Maggie scrolled through the retweets and saw that almost all of them were from the same crowd: avowed supporters of the incumbent president, whose Twitter handles featured strings of emojis and initials to signal their devotion. Several included the image of a gun, to telegraph their belief in the Second Amendment. More than a few had replied to Tang's original message, adding their own endorsement for Winthrop's action, sometimes accompanied with a barbed attack on Winthrop herself:

Now even the libtards get it. #2A

Or:

Like we always said, a conservative is just a liberal who's been mugged. Or violently attacked in their own home. #2A

Or:

Now do you get it?

That, Maggie marvelled, was quite an achievement. The free-Guantanamo and NRA crowds on the same side? That didn't happen often. Winthrop had managed to unite Fox News and NPR, gun nuts and feminists, which in a country fighting a near-constant culture war took some doing. Maggie thought back to that bit of video that had been in circulation in the hours before this story broke, and the tweet that came with it:

If our politics is broken, and it is, then maybe we need to look beyond conventional politics and politicians. Maybe it's time to pick someone fresh and untainted. Someone who can inspire, and is a real human being. Someone like Natasha Winthrop.

Chapter 7

Greg Carter fiddled with the camera – actually a phone – one last time, trying to get it straight on the tripod. Once again, he silently cursed the amateurishness of this arrangement. If the whole point was to simulate the conditions of a TV debate, then surely that should mean simulating the conditions of a TV studio – lights, big bulky cameras, floor managers, the works. This campaign could surely afford it. But Doug Teller, the campaign manager, had been insistent. Full debate prep was coming in a few weeks; until then, the focus was on content, working up lines and themes. For that, two lecterns and an iPhone were sufficient.

That was especially true for this session, hastily arranged and at Greg's suggestion. The plan was to wargame what was still a hypothetical scenario at this stage: the addition of a novice and entirely untested rival to the field at the very last moment, just days before the deadline for contenders formally to register their candidacy. Greg had wanted to do it for weeks, as soon as that appearance at the hearings had started generating buzz. Doug hadn't disagreed exactly, but it hadn't been a priority. Which was why this overnight development in Georgetown was not wholly unwelcome, at least to Greg. It had signalled to both Doug Teller and the candidate himself that their Political Director was no slouch, that Greg Carter's instincts might be worth heeding right away, rather than waiting until they were vindicated by events. Greg had seized on the opening – who knew how long it would last? – and proposed they do the session immediately. Which meant doing it right here, in one of the small meeting rooms in the DC office, the circular table pushed into a corner to make room for the two makeshift podiums.

A moment later and Tom Harrison was in the room, entourage in tow, a cellphone clamped to his ear.

'—you betcha.' A pause. 'I would love that. You know how much Betsy and I love that ranch of yours. Let me get my people to look at the schedule. And Ron? I can't thank you enough for your generosity. I mean it. I won't forget it – and nor will the American people.' The phone went back inside the breast pocket, Harrison's smile disappearing along with it. The candidate then fixed his gaze on Carter.

'All right, Greg. You got me for about ten minutes.'

'OK. Great. The plan is to game out a match-up against—'

'Winthrop. I know that. How do you want to do it?'

'I thought I'd be the moderator and I've asked Ellen to play Natasha Winthrop.' Ellen Stone had only just walked in the room, a trailing member of the retinue that was all but glued to the candidate.

'Greg, isn't it you who normally plays the opponent?'

'I have done so far, that's true. But I'm not sure an African-American male is going to get you in the zone for facing off against a thirty-something white woman.'

'I don't know, Greg, you're a pretty good actor.' Despite a flash of those whitened teeth, the line conveyed exasperation rather than friendliness. The senator didn't like these drills, that much was obvious, at least to Greg. He wasn't sure Doug had picked up the signals.

A moment later Harrison had taken his place behind the lectern. 'OK, shoot.'

Greg sat himself on a hard, plastic chair equidistant between the two 'candidates', only one of them fully play-acting. The image on the phone would be of his back forming the apex of a triangle, just as it would be on TV. Although, of course, if Winthrop were to enter the race, she would be one of nearly a dozen contenders, lined up like gameshow contestants. Still, unrealistic as it might be, the one-on-one, mano-a-mano format suited Greg's purposes better. It would be more clarifying.

He straightened his papers and cleared his throat. In his peripheral vision, he saw Doug Teller let himself into the room and take up a position at the back, joining about half a dozen aides, strategists and the resident pollster.

'If I could start with you, Senator Harrison. You'll have seen in the news that Natasha Winthrop was forced to defend herself from an attacker in her own home. What will you do to fight crime in this country?'

Harrison flashed a smile warmly towards Ellen.

'No smiling: she was raped.' It was Doug, heckling from the back. Harrison reshaped his face into a look of anguished concern.

'Can I begin by saying how proud I am to be sharing a stage alongside such a brave young woman.'

'Patronizing.' Doug again.

'Let me begin by welcoming Natasha Winthrop to this debate stage and indeed to this race. Our democratic process is stronger when more people step up and take part.'

No interruption from Doug, which everyone in the room, Harrison included, took as endorsement. The candidate went on.

'Like many Americans, I was horrified when I learned what happened to Miss Winthrop.'

'Miss? What is this, 1950?' Doug's silence had lasted less than fifteen seconds.

'Actually, I think that's quite good.' It was the pollster, like Doug a battle-hardened Washington operative in his mid-fifties – and therefore one of the few who dared talk back to him. 'Older voters, south, Midwest – sounds respectful. And subtly reminds everyone she isn't married.'

'Hmm. We'll test it. Go with "Natasha" for now, Senator. Sounds elite. Kind of foreign.'

Harrison cleared his throat and re-set himself. 'What happened to Natasha shouldn't be happening in America. Americans should be safe in their own homes.' He turned away from Greg to face Ellen. 'And what you did was tough. It was brave. It took courage. Heck, I'd have a good mind to make you Secretary of Defense.'

'I'm not running to be Secretary of Defense, Senator Harrison.

I'm running to be President of the United States.' Ellen looked as surprised by her rejoinder as everyone else in the room.

'Ouch.'

'Zing.'

'Oh, come on,' Harrison said, stepping back from the lectern. 'That was a compliment.'

'But you saw how she came back at you. It sounded like you were patronizing her.'

'She's a lawyer who was in college until five minutes ago, and I'm saying she's tough enough to head the US military. You don't think that's a compliment?' With upturned palms and by way of an appeal, he looked towards the women at the back, clustered between Doug and the pollster. 'Right?'

None would meet his eye; two were looking at Doug, as if waiting for his cue. Written on their faces was the uncertainty that always bedevilled the mid-ranking employee of a political campaign: who exactly was their boss? Was it their day-to-day superior, the campaign manager who hired them and who gave them the small boosts and opportunities that might shape their careers? Or was it the candidate they were paid to get elected? It was rare for those two to come into conflict but, when they did, the result was usually paralysis.

'What if I try something else?' the senator said. 'Something warmer, more personal. What if I make this a human moment?'

With that, he stepped out from behind his lectern and approached Ellen. 'Natasha, I want to say, from the bottom of my heart, how sorry I am – and how sorry all Americans should be—'

'No, no, no. No way.'

There was a chorus from the women at the back. The voices merged, but Greg picked out 'creepy', 'stalker' and 'invading personal space'. Greg watched the senator retreat to his place. He imagined what the video would look like: old man, young woman. Optics: horrific.

In the silence that followed, and even though he'd have been the first to say that they needed to be guided by the expert voices of women in this area, Greg decided to weigh in. He was reluctant and not just because of his gender. If it were up to him, they'd all keep quiet until afterwards. Let Harrison do his thing, then analyze it later, watching the video. But Doug was in charge and patience was not quite his style.

'Look,' Greg said, 'the senator has to praise her. If he doesn't, he looks churlish. Maybe even a bit rattled. She's being hailed everywhere as a hero, including by moderates. They're his people; he needs to signal that he gets it. Maybe not with the Defense Secretary thing, but somehow.'

'All right,' Harrison said. 'What would you suggest?'

Now one of the women at the back spoke. Kara, number two in the comms team. 'Ideally, you praise her but you do it in such a way that it plants doubts.'

'Like what?'

'Like, maybe she's a hothead. You know, her temper's out of control.'

'OK,' said Doug. 'Let's try that.'

Greg began asking his question again, but the senator silenced him with a wave of the hand, preferring to plunge straight into his new answer.

'What you did was tough. But in this job, when you're President of the United States, sometimes toughness is not enough. Sometimes, you have to show restraint. Sometimes, you have to know when to hold back.'

'Are you suggesting I should have held back and let that man rape me, Senator?'

Harrison stepped away from the podium again. 'Jesus Christ, I can't win against this woman. Whatever I say to her, it's wrong. She'll kill me up there.'

'Maybe literally.' It was the pollster.

Only Doug dared laugh, before regrouping. 'All right,' he said. 'I think we can see there is a Dukakis-sized hole in the ground here, which we are being invited to walk right into.'

Greg, who had turned around, could see a couple of blank faces among his younger colleagues. Now Doug clocked them too.

'Oh, for fuck's sake, it's not *that* long ago. And if you don't remember it, go watch it on fucking YouTube. "Governor Dukakis: if you saw your wife Kitty raped and killed before your eyes, would you still oppose the death penalty for her killer?" Dukakis gives some wonk answer about recidivism rates or some shit, whereas—'

'Whereas, the right answer,' said Harrison with a smile, taking the baton from Doug and, better yet, now glimpsing the finish line that he was to aim for, 'the right answer was: "If I saw my wife raped and killed in front of me, I'd grab the man responsible and I'd rip his throat out with my bare hands. I'd hang him by his ankles and then I'd slice an artery and watch him bleed to death, as slowly and painfully as possible. But this isn't about me.

This is about the authority of the state and our system. And the state and our system have to be *better* than me. Which is why the death penalty isn't the answer."'

'Love that. Every time.'

'So,' Harrison continued, his confidence renewed, 'what I'd say to your question, Greg, is this. What Natasha Winthrop did that night took great guts. But women shouldn't have to rely on their guts, or their own bare hands, to defend themselves. Not every woman could do what she did. Not every woman should *have* to do what she did. That's what we should do for each other, as a country. That's what our police should be for. And that's what has gone wrong under this terrible president.'

Greg could feel the atmosphere behind him had changed, that Doug and the rest were all but ready to applaud. All the same, he went in with the follow-up that he believed any TV moderator worth their salt would ask.

'Are you saying, Senator Harrison, that you think it was wrong that Natasha Winthrop took the law into her own hands?'

'I'm saying, Greg, that she should never have been left in the position where that was her only chance. I could say that I'd prefer she had never taken the law into her own hands but that's not—'

'And have *you*, sir?'

'Have I what?'

'Ever taken the law into your own hands?'

'I grew up in a tough neighbourhood, Greg. Chicago was a tough town. Sometimes, in the schoolyard, you had to stand up to a guy, let him know he couldn't push you around and—'

Ellen interrupted, gripping the lectern tight. 'And sometimes, Senator, you have to defend yourself against a man who has his hands around your throat and means to kill you. I've been there. I know.'

Harrison stood there, silent. After a beat, he threw a look in Teller's direction which Greg at first took to be a protest, but which he soon realized was something more desperate. Senator Tom Harrison, presumed frontrunner for his party's nomination for the White House, was asking for help. He, like everyone else in the room, was beginning to understand that if Natasha Winthrop entered the race, then what he had said a few moments ago might just be the truth.

I can't win against this woman.

Chapter 8

Washington, DC

Those words from Chester – *the only person that could possibly be is you* – caused the temperature to drop. Natasha Winthrop stiffened, aware that there had been a shift. The earlier jabs in her direction had been mere feints, their intent denied as soon as they had been thrown. But this was a direct punch, explicit and unambiguous.

The two detectives collected up their papers, returning them to the stiff paper file that sat on the desk in front of them: the universal sign that the meeting was over.

'Hold on,' Natasha was saying. 'I need to see this CCTV image. There's been a mistake. I didn't let anyone into the house. I was in my study the whole time, exactly as I've told you. You need to show me this picture you have.'

'We don't have that at this time,' said Chester, deploying a stock bit of bureaucratese in a way Natasha took as a deliberate taunt.

'You just referred to it a second ago,' Natasha said, incredulous,

58

a finger stabbing at the table where the mysterious sheet of paper had lain, face down, a moment earlier.

'That was a *report* of the CCTV footage.' Chester smiled a tight little smile. 'All appropriate information will be shared in due course.' Another smile. 'Now, talking of information, Miss Winthrop: in a case like this, it would be routine for us to examine your smartphone.'

'Well, that's completely out of the question.'

'To rule out any connection between you and the deceased.'

'That phone contains all my contacts with my clients. It's privileged information.'

'I see that and of course you're under no compulsion to provide it to us.'

'Well, that's that then.'

'At this stage. But as things develop, we will do whatever is necessary to access the information we need.'

Allen was nodding, as if still trying to make nice. Natasha wondered if it was force of habit: good cop was his default setting. 'Just to rule things out,' he said.

'Well, we can tackle that situation when it arises,' Natasha said. 'But for now, the answer is no. And I'd like your notes to record that my sole and stated reason is the protection of attorney-client confidentiality. And to record my adamant, total rejection of the claim that I let this man into my house.'

'Understood,' he said. Chester remained mute, simply staring hard at Natasha for a good fifteen seconds, before eventually tucking her documents under her arm – no text showing – and heading out.

A guard came in, to usher Natasha to a 'holding suite'. Once there, she sat alone, on a single, hard plastic chair, under the eye of not one but two surveillance cameras, positioned unabashedly in the corners. She let out a long, deep sigh. The image that came into her mind was of that man, lying dead on her floor, his bodily fluids all over both of them.

She opened up her phone, flicked it out of airplane mode and felt it come to life in her hand. Buzzing and trembling as the inbox filled up and the texts, WhatsApps and DMs arrived. She skimmed them – the good wishes from friends, the offers of help from former colleagues, the tweets from strangers – and she had the same feeling she'd had about two weeks earlier, when her televised performance at the committee had suddenly become a sensation. This was the second time this month that she had felt herself buried in an online avalanche.

She moved away from her mentions to look at the general newsfeed, and at first she assumed she'd failed to press the button properly: this string of tweets was about her too.

Breaking: DC Police still holding Natasha Winthrop after questioning her for more than an hour this morning.

So that was out. Somebody inside this building, inside DC Police at any rate, was not just leaking the details of this inquiry, they were supplying live, play-by-play commentary. She searched for 'Winthrop' and 'CCTV': still nothing. 'Winthrop' and 'footage'. Not yet.

Instead, all she could see were different versions of – and reactions to – the news that she was still being questioned. There seemed to be hundreds of them, flooding in every second. And most seemed to be using the same hashtag. #Heroine.

The older messages were praising her as some kind of vigilante. And the people doing it were so odd: writers for the *National Review*; pundits from *The Blaze*; cheerleaders for the president. All those right-wingers who normally hated her were suddenly lauding her as a poster girl for self-defence. Many of them seemed to think she had shot her attacker.

The best defence against a bad man with a gun is a good *woman* with a gun. #Heroine

But the fresher messages expressed less admiration for her than hostility towards the police. At the milder end there was mere impatience, hoping that DC Police would soon end 'this ordeal', calling on the department, first, to issue a statement that Natasha had been attacked and that she had killed in self-defence and, second, to allow her to go free. A distinguished book reviewer for the *New Yorker* tweeted:

The longer this goes on, the more it adds to the anguish Natasha Winthrop has already had to suffer. Enough.

A young writer for *The Nation* weighed in:

Every hour DC Police keep #Natasha under this cloud of suspicion, the more it looks like a vendetta #settlingscores #waronterror #civilliberties

And a woman who had set up a website dedicated to monitoring sexual harassment posted this:

Imagine if a man had knocked out a violent attacker. Everyone would be praising him as a hero. But naturally a woman is viewed with suspicion.

A former US congressman, Republican, had tweeted just two minutes earlier:

Every American has the right to defend their home with all necessary force. The police have nothing to investigate.

And then, right before her eyes, she saw it change. A tweet from the local CBS affiliate:

Breaking: Police investigating CCTV footage, apparently showing Winthrop letting assailant into her home.

She closed her eyes, like a sailor who knows a fifty-foot wave is about to crash onto the deck. She didn't need to see any more. She knew what was coming. Soon it would be: *Police suspect Winthrop may have known her attacker.* And eventually: *Police believe Winthrop knew her victim.*

She leaned back, letting her head rest against the breeze-block wall. Her eyes remained closed.

It's possible she fell asleep, if only for a few seconds, because she started when she heard the beep of the door being clicked open.

'Natasha!'

Even the way he said the word irritated her. The faux pity, like a parent addressing a toddler who'd fallen over: *Look at you, poor thing!* The cheek of it grated on her, considering – and she knew this was a petty thought, especially at a time like this – he was below her in the hierarchy of those who served the committee. He was the mere spokesperson, while she had been the senior counsel. Three years her junior, and yet here he was: Dad come to bail out the teenager who'd been hauled in for speeding.

Or perhaps, she acknowledged to herself in the same second, her irritation at the sight of Dan Benson had a simpler explanation. Namely, she didn't trust him.

'I can't believe you've been going through this alone,' he said, flicking his hair away from his forehead as he pulled up a chair alongside her.

'Well, they offered me a lawyer. But I figured, hey, I've got that covered.'

'Sure, but I mean, just in terms of *emotional support*, Natasha.' He bit his lower lip and fixed her with a look of earnest concern, the man who prides himself on his sensitivity to women, the man who posts a clenched-fist emoji of solidarity on International Women's Day. 'Natasha, no woman should be alone at a time like this.'

'That's really kind, Dan.' She began thinking through the angles. 'Was this the chairman's idea?'

'Very much so, of course. Now, tell me, how can I get you home?'

So, the chairman. Made sense, and not only because he was

Benson's patron. Of all the members of the House committee, the chairman had been the one most obviously rattled by Natasha's sudden media exposure. He'd had a presidential bid of his own to nurture; these hearings were meant to be his launch pad. And then his damned *counsel* sucks up all the ink and grabs all the airtime. That was not how things were meant to work. Had he seen #Heroine trending and despatched his bag-carrier to ensure Natasha was suitably and swiftly contained?

'I'm not allowed to go home. Crime scene.'

'You're coming to my apartment. Shower, sleep, eat. Whatever you need.'

Dan Benson's home might well have been the last place on earth she wanted to go – second only, perhaps, to the home of his boss – but she understood that she was short of alternatives. She had friends she could call, but the explanations, the hassle, the wait. No, it made more sense to accept this offer and get out of here right now.

There were forms to fill in, and more delays, but eventually Natasha Winthrop was in a cab threading her way to Dan Benson's apartment block near Cleveland Park. Her willpower was strong and she didn't so much as glance at Twitter. But her phone buzzed all the same: journalists mainly, along with a few friends and legal contacts. The former suggested she call back, so that she could tell her 'side of the story'. The latter offered help, a move clearly, though tacitly, prompted by the report of video footage that purportedly showed her letting her assailant into her home. Benson was talking, but she wasn't listening. Occasionally she murmured a noise of assent or comprehension but she knew that her eyes had glazed over. She was elsewhere. She was staring at her memory of that man – standing in her house, framed in the doorway, in that suspended second before he moved towards her.

What brought her back was the sight of a truck, its satellite dish extended and its ears pricked up, parked on the corner of Benson's street. For the briefest of seconds, she told herself it might be something else. Maybe even a coincidence.

But as she got closer, it was obvious. The WJLA livery on the side announced it as belonging to a news crew for Channel 7 and the side door swung open to reveal a bank of screens and a technician already at work. As the cab got closer, she saw two more sat-trucks, their dishes cocked, primed for broadcast. And there, next to what she assumed was Dan's building, a little knot of snappers and reporters, with one, two, three, four TV cameras.

'Christ,' Dan said. 'A goat-fuck.'

Instantly, Natasha knew he was lying. The feigned surprise wasn't fooling anybody; not her, anyway. How else had the press known to come here? She had told no one she was heading to Benson's, save for one other colleague from the law firm who had offered to come collect her from police headquarters. Oh, and a friend who had made the same offer. Actually two friends. But who would they have told?

'No can park,' the driver was saying over his shoulder, gesturing at the street, where it seemed every space had been filled by the press corps.

'All right,' Dan replied, his eyes darting. 'Just slow down.'

Natasha pictured herself and Benson emerging from the taxi,

how it would look on the news. The pair of them jostled, questions barked out, trying to make their way to the entrance. The visual implication to the casual viewer that they – she – had done something wrong. Why else would she be hunted like this? To her surprise, she found time to consider one other cause for alarm: people were bound to see those pictures of her and Dan and conclude they were a couple.

She looked over at Benson, his eyes on the sidewalk, his fingers on the door handle as the car slowed down, a parachutist by the hatch waiting for the right moment to jump. She noticed that in his other hand Dan held his house key between thumb and forefinger, ready to be deployed. He was thinking ahead, avoiding a protracted moment of fumbling while the cameras clicked away at more than a dozen frames per second. (It struck Natasha that the true professional, used to this situation, would have had someone already positioned inside the apartment building, waiting on the other side of the door, ready to open it and usher them in.)

Natasha looked at Dan. Her eyes conveyed that she was expecting him to handle this, to be the expert. *This is your trade. You're meant to know what to do.*

The taxi was slow enough that someone in the cluster of reporters and photographers and camera operators spotted Natasha behind the car window and in less than a second they all had: they'd wheeled round and their lenses were already trained on the kerbside passenger door. To Natasha, they looked like a single, panting animal, with two dozen eyes – all staring towards her.

'We'll just get out calmly and walk towards the front door as calmly and normally as we can. As if we're just getting out of a cab and calmly heading home. And sombre, obviously. No smiles. Other than that, nice and easy. Calm.'

Natasha thought: anyone who can't stop talking about being calm is almost certainly panicking.

Benson handed the driver a twenty, and Natasha could feel the beast on the other side of the glass, its multiple eyes trained on her as she remained inside that cramped space. It was waiting, hungry – somehow it seemed reckless to make the beast wait. She had a sense that even a second's delay would be seen as weakness, would make its hackles rise, make it likelier to pounce. Dan opened the door, and began to step out.

The first thing that hit her was the din. The cameras clicking, the jostling and, above all, the shouting. So much louder when it was right in your face, so much louder than it looked on TV. She had witnessed a so-called goat-fuck a few times, on the steps of various courtrooms, of course, and, just a couple of weeks ago, outside the US Capitol following the hearings. But to be at the centre of it in the wild, to be on the receiving end of it on a residential street: that was something else entirely.

The shouting did not let up. Mostly it was a loud chorus of 'Natasha!' as if every photographer in there was a long-lost friend, urging her to look their way, punctuated by the occasional, 'Hey, dude, out of my shot!' or, more directly, 'Out of my fucking way!' Someone must have made the mistake of treading on a foot or, worse, jogging the elbow of a camera-holding arm, because Natasha heard two men in unison brand a third a 'cunt'.

All of this occurred in a single second, rising in volume the instant Natasha put a single foot on the sidewalk. She heard it before she saw any of it, from the collective click of two dozen shutters, illuminated by the sudden concentration of lights aimed squarely at her.

Benson put a hand on her elbow and guided her towards the entrance. The press pack formed a gauntlet, naturally dividing themselves into an impromptu honour guard, on both sides of what was now a path from the kerb.

Natasha was struck by the self-policing nature of it, as if there were an invisible line that no one dared cross. Some collective instinct within the beast led to the clearing of a path along which the quarry – Natasha – was allowed to proceed. No one jumped in front of her or Benson; no one obstructed their route to the door.

But the path did narrow, as reporters on both sides of it leaned in, shoving their microphones directly under Natasha's face. She was looking down, which she knew was a mistake: it looked too guilty. Or maybe it would come across as respectfully sombre. Who the hell knew?

Benson still had his hand on her elbow, trying to steer her through. The questions all came at once, each one tangling with the other until they were all but indecipherable. She picked out: 'What happened, Natasha?' 'Did you kill him?' And, though she wouldn't swear to it, 'Did you use excessive force?'

The path in front had narrowed to a small opening. The Red Sea was closing. The two sides had converged. Not yet at the door, she would have to push through. The gap was so narrow, she and Benson were now moving in single file, with him in front. Her back felt dangerously exposed. She imagined a hand on it, giving her a shove, bringing her to the floor. She had a flash memory of that man standing in the doorway, his eyes eager.

She could hear Dan saying, 'Excuse me' and 'Come on, guys, let us pass.'

Finally, they were at the door. The questions were still coming, bellowed from behind. The photographers' chorus of 'Natasha! Natasha!' did not let up.

Natasha could see that Benson had kept his key gripped between his thumb and forefinger, held up and ahead of him, as if it would slice the obstacles in their way, like the blade of an ice-breaker. And then, a moment or two later, they were inside.

The noise faded a bit, but Natasha could still hear them taking pictures. The white brightness of the TV lights was still visible through the glass of the entrance lobby. But she felt like she had reached safe harbour, all the same.

Dan ignored the elevator and went to a side door, which led to a staircase. Two flights and they were in his apartment. Wood floors, a couple of tastefully framed prints, some books. Soulless and empty, it screamed single-in-Washington. Benson closed the curtains, a precaution, he explained later, against the prying, airborne eye of a drone camera.

He then fell into a sofa. 'Jesus Christ,' he said, his palm against his forehead. He looked exhausted from the ordeal outside. Natasha, however, stood still, all but frozen.

'Come on, Natasha. Sit down.'

She ignored his request, and looked instead at her phone. She wasn't going to check the news or social media. Instead, she was going to send a message to someone she had never met, who she knew of only by reputation. But everything that had just happened convinced her she now had no choice. She needed Maggie Costello.

Chapter 9

Washington, DC

As Maggie waited by the elevators in the underground car park, a small wheelie suitcase at her side, she reflected that this was a double first. Never before had any politician she worked for – she would never use the word 'client' – asked her to bring over a pair of her own jeans, perhaps a skirt, a couple of tops and a supply of fresh underwear. And never before had she been drafted in by a possible presidential candidate who was simultaneously a rape victim and murder suspect, with just over a week to clear her name before it would be too late to enter the race at all: the filing deadline to get on the ballot paper was only eight days away.

As she waited for the elevator to reach level minus three, Maggie took another look at the text that had arrived an hour earlier.

> *My name is Natasha Winthrop. I know of your work and have admired it from afar. You have a reputation for being able to solve any*

*and every crisis and for being a fierce defender of what's right. That's
precisely what I need at this moment. Will you help me?*

Maggie had given a non-committal answer, suggesting that
they meet. Winthrop had replied with a message that made
Maggie smile.

*That would be ideal. The trouble is, I'm at the home of a colleague
who I don't *entirely* trust, unable to go back to my own house and
wearing clothes I'd dearly like to burn. So, and I know it's a bit
early to be asking this, but is there any chance you could bring me
something to wear? And without putting a plant on the balcony, as
it were, I'm afraid I'm going to have to give you rather convoluted
instructions for how we might see each other.*

Maggie had read the message twice, unsure if she believed it.
The poise, the dry humour, the casual Watergate reference: there
weren't many in DC who talked like that, not in a town where
lean efficiency was prized above elan. But hadn't this woman just
been through a life-changing trauma? Maggie wondered if she
was being tricked.

Still, she had gone to the underground car park on M Street all
the same, following the instructions that arrived in a subsequent
text. She had punched the numbers into the keypad by one door,
and then did the same at the next. And now here she was, staring
at the sign above the elevator door, willing it to come soon. She
had bad memories of underground car parks.

She glanced at her phone one more time, at the search page

generated by typing in the words 'Natasha Winthrop'. There were dozens of items prompted by Winthrop's breakout moment during and after the hearings: mini-profiles, celebrity tweets (including several women declaring a 'girl crush' on 'the fierce attorney who just ripped into the administration'), analyses, memes, the works. But before that, surprisingly little.

Winthrop had been quoted in news accounts of some of the court cases she had fought, Guantanamo and the like, and the statements attributed to her were sharp and pointed – 'An injustice is still an injustice, even when it takes place so far away we can't see it' – but none revealed anything much about her. There was a small piece in *Washingtonian*, which noted that Winthrop had been spotted stepping out with the new head of the Kennedy Center before expressing a sneaking admiration for the lawyer's heels. Otherwise, the best source was a story that had appeared in the style section of the *Washington Post*, in their gossipy 'One to Watch' series.

Natasha Winthrop is making waves, and no, that's not a reference to her skill with a jib and a boom (though Chesapeake types agree she is quite the sailor). Legal eagles say she's rising fast, the former Supreme Court clerk tipped for a place on that bench herself one day, and perhaps sooner rather than later. With forty still on the distant horizon, the Boston Brahmin has brought a touch of old line class to DC, the Winthrops being one of that vanishingly rare species, a true, straight-off-the-Mayflower family whose blood runs true blue. WASPier than a buzzing hornet, the Oxford-educated former Rhodes Scholar is smart, well-bred and—dare we say it?—gorgeous. Still single, she's been linked to some of the capital's most eligible bachelors, but so far this is one WASP who refuses to be caught . . .

Maggie recalled her own appearance in the 'One to Watch' slot, back when she worked for the president who, as Tom Harrison had reminded her, brought her to DC in the first place. She too had been hailed for her sudden appearance close to the top of the Washington tree, with a lip-licking reference to her looks. Something about 'long, auburn hair, the color of a Dublin autumn' and, predictably, the mandatory mention of 'Irish eyes'. Still, the one impression that emerged from this skimmiest of skim searches was that Winthrop had not sought media attention. What Maggie had pulled up was the bare minimum of coverage for someone in Winthrop's position, given her caseload and the issues it touched on. It was about the same volume Maggie herself had generated, which was as little as humanly possible.

The elevator had arrived, taking Maggie from the bowels of this corporate building up to the third-floor offices of Gonzales Associates. The firm was well-known to Maggie, as it was to every viewer of MSNBC and reader of *The Nation*: it was the go-to law firm for progressive causes, regularly teaming up with the American Civil Liberties Union to represent some hopeless and apparently lost cause. The original Gonzales was long dead now, but he had set the tone from the start, defending the Black Panthers in a string of civil disobedience and direct action cases. Recently the Gonzales roster had included a class action lawsuit on behalf of the entire population of Puerto Rico, suing the United States federal government for both neglect and racist

discrimination. The administration's failure to respond ade-
quately to the last natural disaster to pummel the island was at
the centre of the case.

The doors opened and Maggie was confronted immediately by
a familiar face: Natasha Winthrop waiting for her in the lobby.

Winthrop extended a hand and smiled widely. 'Really good
of you to have come, Maggie. I've heard so much about you.'
Maggie took her hand and smiled back.

Winthrop looked like her photographs – tall, slim, her dark
hair closely cropped and almost boyish – but instantly Maggie
saw something else that usually eluded the camera lens. It was the
glow of her eyes. They were an exquisite green, positively sparkling with intelligence. Even in that first greeting, they hinted at a
comic knowingness, as if fully cognisant of the absurdity of this
and every other situation. It seemed such an odd fit for a woman
who had just been involved in a double act of deadly violence,
both as victim and perpetrator.

Maggie's first thought was, *How on earth does this woman look this
good, after everything she's been through?*

'Come on in,' Winthrop said, using her swipe card to let herself
through the office door, where the reception desk was unattended.
They walked past an open-plan area that was also empty, past several
glass-doored offices, two of which were occupied, even at this late
hour. In one of them a man looked up as the two women passed, but
he seemed immersed in his work, white AirPods clamped into his
ears, so Maggie was unsure if he'd even registered what he'd seen.

Eventually they were at a door where the name 'Natasha
Winthrop' was etched into the glass – small and discreet rather

than showy. They went in, Natasha gesturing for Maggie to take the two-seater sofa, while she flopped into a matching chair. Together the two pieces of furniture formed an L-shape, so that they were only a foot or two apart.

'Maggie, I cannot tell you what a *relief* it is that you're here. The actual Maggie Costello, for heaven's sake. I feel like the cavalry's arrived.'

'Well, I'm only glad—'

'As soon as this *nightmare* began, I knew I'd need your help. But I just *assumed* you'd be abroad – in Jerusalem or Damascus or Tehran or heaven knows where, putting the world to rights, saving our collective skin. So when I sent up that little emergency flare, I had no expectation whatsoever you'd be able to answer it. But here you are. I am *beyond* grateful.'

Just as the newspaper photographs had failed to do justice to her eyes, so the brief, viral video clips had failed to capture Natasha Winthrop's voice and, specifically, her accent. In all her years living in DC, Maggie was not sure she had heard anything like it. The cadences were familiar enough, but only when coming out of the mouth of upper-class English folk. (A type Maggie had encountered often enough during her first job, with an NGO in Africa: the aid world was crawling with posh Brits.) But an American who talked this way, outside of Katherine Hepburn in *The Philadelphia Story*? Maggie suspected Natasha Winthrop was the very first.

'I should warn you. I'm not normally one of those Washington types who spends an hour talking about themselves and then says how interesting it was to meet you.'

Maggie smiled in recognition.

'But this is not a normal situation.'

'No.'

'I'm aware that I'm not functioning at full capacity. There should probably be a health warning after – I'm not sure what to call it – an *experience* like this: "Do not drive or operate heavy machinery." Or make major decisions.'

'You should take some time.'

'Of course I should.' Natasha looked down, her head at an angle, as if fascinated by a spot on the ground to the left of her feet. She scratched the hair by her temple. 'The trouble is, there is no time.' There was a beat or two of silence. 'So I am going to have to break my usual habit and be one of those appalling Washington people, I'm afraid.'

'Not at all. You should tell me what's going on.'

Natasha cleared her throat, both to punctuate the moment but also, it seemed to Maggie, to gird herself and to compart-mentalize – to put her recent 'experience' to one side. Maggie recognized that move because she had made it herself often.

'To put it simply,' Natasha began, 'your reputation is as the number one solver of political problems – crises, even – in this city. Well, that's what I need, Maggie. You see, I thought I had a legal problem, but I now understand, as of this evening, that I have a political problem.'

'Political? But you're not a politician.'

Winthrop sat a few inches back in her chair, and gave Maggie a dazzling smile. Of admiration, mainly. They both knew Maggie was playing naive, and they both knew Maggie was angling to hear her answer.

'This is political in the following ways. One, DC Police and I—'

'Have history.'

'Exactly. So whether that makes them want to treat me better or worse than a regular person, I'm not yet sure. But it will colour their response in some way or other.'

'Has it already? Coloured their response, I mean?'

'We'll get to that. Second, there has been some obviously *absurd* speculation about me as a presidential candidate. It doesn't matter whether or not I would even consider such a thing—'

'Politician's answer.'

'"I have no plans at this time," she said, adopting the cheesy rhythms of a generic US candidate. They both smiled. 'But genuinely, it's ridiculous. It's the last thing I'd want to do. Dealing with this level of attention, all the time? Complete nightmare. I'm a lawyer: I have my cases, I have my clients. I want to be able to do my work for them, in peace.'

'I can feel a "but" coming.'

'But what I've realized is that it's entirely irrelevant whether I would even *dream* of running. What matters is—'

'People in your party think you might.'

'Yes indeed.'

'And that will colour *their* responses.'

'Precisely. It already has.'

'Which is why the chairman of the House intelligence committee sent his top operative to act as your minder.'

'Benson, yes.' Natasha made the slightest quizzical expression, curious as to how Maggie knew about that. Maggie held up her phone, the all-purpose answer to how anyone knew anything these days. 'It was good of him to give me safe harbour for a few hours. But it goes without saying that it'd be *idiotic* for me to trust him.'

'Is his boss running?'

'He certainly wanted to. But even if he isn't, he's close to Senator Harrison, and probably fancies that he might prosper under a Harrison administration.'

'So he doesn't want you bursting on the scene and sucking up all the oxygen.'

'Like I said, it's all perfectly absurd. And of course, third, a case like this – man attacks woman, woman kills man – was always going to be political, whoever I was.'

Another smile passed between them, acknowledgement of the truth Natasha had voiced and the fact that both recognized it. Then Natasha leapt to her feet, startled. 'You must forgive me. I have been *appallingly* rude.' She was now behind her desk, searching for something at knee level. 'I've not offered you anything to drink.'

'I'm fine.'

'Not even a Scotch?'

Maggie hesitated. She was meant to say no. 'What Scotch have you got?'

'I've got a ridiculously expensive bottle of Talisker single malt.'

Another beat of hesitation. 'You must have known I was coming.'

Winthrop poured two glasses – no ice, drop of water – handed one to Maggie and then returned to her seat. Maggie watched as Natasha took a first sip, her eyes closed. Maggie suspected she was not savouring the taste so much as allowing in the exhaustion.

'My first assumption was that I could handle this myself. I'm a lawyer and quite a good one, if that isn't an awful thing to say. Homicide cases are not my specialist area, but I have colleagues here and elsewhere who could help me. But this morning's events have altered my view.'

'Tell me about the police interview. You said that you felt that your, um, history had coloured their response to you. What happened?'

'After a while, you learn how these people operate. They were terribly fixated on the idea that I might have opened the front door to my assailant and ushered him into my home. Which is, of course, a perfectly natural line of inquiry, albeit one that is wholly false in this case. But what I have learned is that, to a detective, facts are divided into two distinct sets. They're either confirming or contradictory of their operating hypothesis. If they're the former, then great: more evidence to support the hypothesis. But if they're the latter, also no problem: they can be absorbed into the hypothesis. They are reshaped as the exception that proves the rule.'

'And is that how they treated this CCTV footage of you opening the door, as the exception that proves the rule?'

'No. The opposite. Once they started talking, I understood that their theory of the case was the reverse of what I had been telling them. They don't believe I acted in self-defence, they don't believe my account at all. They believe that I killed this man for whatever reason and that I invented some story to explain it. The emergence of this supposed video footage – which, by the way, neither I nor anyone else has seen and which either does not exist or has been entirely misinterpreted – fits their hypothesis perfectly. Which is that I am a liar. Or fantasist. Or both.'

Maggie sipped slowly from the glass. She felt the hit of the taste on her tongue, then the warmth of the burn as it moved through her mouth and into her throat. She closed her eyes for a second, enjoying the sensory blast, then opened them again, suddenly conscious of Winthrop's eyes on her. Drinking was different for her these days, after all she'd learned. Now it came with a pang of self-reproach that had never troubled her before. She didn't want to be her mother's daughter.

She straightened in her chair and said, 'And did you?'

'Did I what?'

'Did you open the door to that man?'

'No, I did not. I was in my study the whole time. The first I saw of him was when he appeared in the doorway to that room. But, as I say, that's not the point I'm trying to make.'

'Your point is that the police's starting assumption is that you're guilty till proven innocent.'

Winthrop took a swig and nodded.

'And that should obviously inform your strategy. But I still don't see why that can't be a legal strategy. Why can't you deal with this as a lawyer?'

Natasha held the glass to her lips as she smiled broadly, revealing a set of perfect white teeth as her eyes brightened. 'You mean, why do I need you?'

'I suppose.' Maggie looked down at her glass and back up again. 'Yes.'

'Because of that starting assumption, Maggie. What's the reason for that? Why have they set out on this case wanting me to be guilty of murder, rather than a victim of a violent sexual assault and attempted rape?'

'Because you've fought them and won. The Guantanamo cases.'

'Couple of corruption ones, too. But those are symptoms, not cause. What's the cause?'

'Because while the Chief of Police was handpicked by the mayor, the rank and file tend to tilt pretty rightward and you're the socialist, libtard enemy within.'

Natasha leaned back and nodded. 'I think so, yes.'

'And are they right?'

'Right? About my politics?'

Maggie put her glass down. 'Are they?'

'I was raised with immense privilege, Maggie. Expensive school, expensive college, no debts. My home was so big and gorgeous, we had our own stables and I didn't just have my own pony, I had my own *horse*. Several horses, in fact. It was a life of *ludicrous* privilege. I now live in a beautiful, tasteful home in Georgetown, in Washington, DC, which, even though I may never want to set foot in that house again, is in one of the smarter neighbourhoods in the capital city of what is both the richest country in the world and the richest country there has ever been in the history of our planet. *Ludicrous* privilege.

'My most recent job was advising a committee whose members belong to a body that can spend billions and billions of dollars in an instant. They just have to press a button on their desks: aye or nay. I watched these people, Maggie, and – believe me – there are not many contenders for the Nobel Prize among them. These are not the finest brains. And yet, just by raising their hands or pressing that little button, they can buy an airplane or a ship that costs hundreds of millions of dollars. They can make a tiny tweak to the tax code that puts yet more millions into the pockets of people – usually their donors – who already have so, so much. Maggie, these are people who have homes with twenty-five bed-rooms, along with a second or third house in Montana or Florida or Vermont, and an apartment in London or Paris or both for the occasional weekend shopping trip. And climate-controlled closets for their suits. And another for their shoes.

'And meanwhile, you can go out that door,' she raised her right hand, 'and walk ten paces and you will find a man shaking a paper cup for pennies. Because he is hungry and thirsty. Because he literally does not have enough food to eat tonight. He might well have served in the military, where he saw such horrors that he couldn't sleep at night even if he did have a bed. Which he doesn't.

'And you can walk maybe ten minutes more and you'll be in a neighbourhood where it'll be normal to find ten people sharing two rooms – grandma and six kids in a room the size of my en suite bathroom – where there's a little girl whose belly is rum-bling, because she too has had nothing to eat, who has nowhere to sit down, let alone a space to do her homework or, God forbid, read a book. There'll be mould creeping up the walls, damp that will get into her lungs and give her a bronchial infection. But she won't go to the doctor, because her family can't pay the bills. And what tiny help they once got from the government is no longer there, because the president decided to "play to his base" and cut the food stamps programme.

'I desperately want that to change. I would love kids like that little girl to have a library that's open and has actual books in it or a school whose roof is not leaking and a hospital that's there when they're sick, even if they don't have a dime in their pocket. I'd like the air to be clean and the rivers not to have barrels of toxic shit dumped into them, and for us to stop choking every glorious sea creature in the ocean with so much plastic their guts look like the contents of a trash can. I want us to stop cooking the planet and stop the ice melting and stop dropping bombs on people who are far away, and stop calling people who flee their homes out of desperate fear "invaders" or "aliens", but instead offer them the helping hand we would want if we were in their shoes. I want the world to be kind. For us to shout at each other a little less and to smile a little more. I'm sure we can do it. We're rich enough. We're smart enough. We just have to want to do it. And I want to do it.'

Maggie's tiny intake of breath was too quiet to count as a gasp, but a gasp was what it was. She realized she had been holding her breath as Natasha Winthrop spoke, afraid to break the moment. It was involuntary. She did not think about anything except the words the woman in front of her was saying and the woman saying them. She was mesmerized.

Only now that Natasha had stopped talking did Maggie's conscious brain start formulating thoughts. *Jeez, she would make one helluva candidate.* And then: *Is that a rehearsed speech? Has she said those words a hundred times before? Because it didn't sound like it. Or is she just very good?*

A memory returned to Maggie, or more precisely a feeling. It was that unmistakable quickening of the pulse she had felt when she'd first been called to Washington a decade or so earlier – summoned there by the man who insisted that idealism and realism were not incompatible foes, but allies just waiting to be fused together. The first time she met that man, tramping around Iowa, she had been struck by his commitment, his principles and his basic humanity. Despite everything, including her loathing of all things Washington, she had allowed him to persuade her to join his presidential campaign and, when he won, to come with him to the White House. She had, said her friends – including the man who would become her direct boss, mentor and friend, Stu Goldstein – 'been seduced'.

She'd laughed that off at the time: there never was anything like that between her and the former president, not even a hint of it. (That man would never have inflicted on any woman the unsolicited shoulder squeeze Maggie had endured that morning.) And yet 'seduced' was the right word. A candidate had to do more than persuade a would-be aide – or voter, for that matter – of the merits of their arguments. They had to strike a chord that resided not in the brain, but somewhere between the heart and the gut. Maggie had had that feeling at the State Fair in Iowa a decade ago. She had it again now.

And by God, she needed it. Everyone did. Politics had been so desperate for so long, one awful outcome after another, in this country and almost anywhere you cared to name: the good guys on a losing streak and all the wrong people in control. Even the *notion* of finding someone with talent, charisma and their heart in the right place was thrilling in its novelty. Maggie, her former White House colleagues, the people she knew and loved, her sister Liz, they all felt the same aching lack – the absence of someone to believe in. The absence, corny as it might sound, of hope.

'I understand,' Maggie said at last. 'And I want to help.'

Natasha gave a smile that somehow demanded of Maggie further elaboration.

'I'm on board. Whatever you need to get through this.'

Natasha Winthrop was reaching across for a handshake when there was a strong buzzing sound, her phone vibrating between them. The screen was face up and Natasha was so distracted by it, she immediately and instinctively diverted her right hand away from Maggie's to pick it up. She glanced at it and said only, 'Christ.'

Now Maggie's phone buzzed too, several times in succession. More messages began to buzz into Winthrop's phone. There was the low chirrup of landlines as phones in the outer office started to ring, joined by Natasha's direct line in this room.

Maggie took one look at her screen and instantly understood why everyone suddenly wanted to hear the voice of Natasha Winthrop.

She opened up the first message, a news alert from CNN:

Breaking: DC Police say man killed overnight in alleged attack on Washington lawyer Natasha Winthrop was the wanted rapist and suspected murderer Jeffrey Todd.

85

Chapter 10

Long Island, New York, three weeks earlier

The woman was much younger than the man. They were separated by more than four decades. They were also separated at work by not just a few rungs but the entire corporate ladder. The man was the head of the news division while the woman was in the first year of an entry-level job. So when the man asked the woman to help him work through programme proposals for the coming season, the woman did not feel she could say no. Even when the man explained that this was work that fell outside regular hours and was best done at his beach house.

The woman was wary, but also conscious that this was an opportunity. Some of the woman's more experienced colleagues hinted that they too had been given similar opportunities when they were starting out and it was clear that they had taken them, even if they were now reluctant to say much more. She registered that it was only women who tended to have been singled out in this way, but she decided that that was no more than a reflection of the demographics of the television news industry at this level.

The man picked her up at the nearest station. He wore jeans and drove his own car. They reached the house in ten minutes, and the man immediately showed the woman where she would be working. It was a stand-alone guest house, complete with its own bathroom, small kitchen and view of the ocean. The shelves were covered with awards, trophies and statuettes, as well as photographs of the man with famous personalities associated with film and television. The man called this house 'the cottage'.

The woman worked for several hours on her own, while the man remained in the main house. Later she saw the man going for a run along the beach. On his way back, the man stopped and knocked on her door. The man did not wait for the woman to reply, but walked right in. The man was flushed and sweating. He told the woman he wanted her to come with him to the main house, so that he could show her the next tranche of work to be done. The woman was apprehensive, but did not feel she could say no.

The man led her into his office. At its centre was an enormous glass desk. In front of it were picture windows so close to the water you could see the surf of the waves. On the shelves were yet more awards – Peabody, Emmy, Grierson – as well as photographs of the man with presidents, prime ministers, two kings, a queen and a pope.

The woman was looking at these pictures when she realized the man was no longer at her side. He had walked through a second door that led into a bathroom. The woman could hear the sound of a shower running. The man had left the bathroom door ajar.

The man called the woman's name. She pretended not to hear him, focusing instead on the documents piled on the desk which he had mentioned as the basis of her next task. But he called her name again and then again.

The woman replied that she was working. But the man called out that he could not hear her. The woman approached the bathroom door, so that she could be sure to be heard.

With her back to the opening, so that she could not see inside, the woman repeated that she was getting on with the work he had asked her to do. Again, the man said he could not hear her.

The woman turned her head, just enough, she hoped, to ensure her voice would carry. But the shower was not what she expected. Instead of containing a glass cubicle two or three yards away, this was a wet room – a single, unbounded space. So when the woman turned, she caught a glimpse of the man at the centre of it. He was facing towards the door. He was naked and he was soaping himself, even as he called out her name. His eyes were shut.

The woman turned away in less than a second and returned to the desk. The woman told herself that she had seen nothing, that the moment was too fleeting, that perhaps it was only her imagination.

In the seconds that followed, the woman shuffled the papers several times, trying to focus on the work she had been given.

A minute later the man came out of the bathroom. Because her head was down, focused only on the papers on the desk, the woman did not hear or see him emerge. She did not see that he was wearing only a bathrobe, white and open, with no cord tied at the waist.

It meant that the woman jolted with surprise when she saw the man suddenly appear next to her, his penis, exposed and erect, a matter of inches from her face.

The woman flinched and turned away. The man said, 'I was calling you. Didn't you hear me?'

'No,' she said. 'I was just here doing my work.' Only now, hearing her own voice, did the woman realize that she was weeping.

'Ah, baby. Don't cry,' the man said softly, and she wondered if he was about to be gentle. Instead, while he continued to whisper, 'Don't cry, baby,' he grabbed a fistful of her hair, tugging at the base of her scalp. She heard herself yelp.

The woman felt the man grip her head with both hands, holding it so tightly that she couldn't turn it in any direction. She thought of her phone just a few inches away, on the desk where she had placed it a moment ago. She could not use it to escape or to summon help. It was out of reach. Instead she stared into the phone's unblinking eye, braced herself and hoped that what she had heard was true.

Chapter 11

Washington, DC

There's badass and then there's kaboom. #IStandWithNatasha

Paging Marvel. You just got yourself a new Avenger. #IStandWithNatasha

'Legally speaking, the issues confronting Natasha Winthrop have not altered. But the political context of this case has altered dramatically.' Good thread

Whatever evidence the DC Police have against Winthrop, they can put it in a file, tie it with a ribbon and forget about it. There is not a jury in America that would convict her for killing a serial rapist and wanted murderer. #IStandWithNatasha

The two of them, Maggie and Natasha, had not moved from their seats. Instead, they sat there, with their phones in their hands, as the world came to them. The reaction time between the naming of the dead man and the hailing of Winthrop as a modern-day hero was breathtakingly short. What might have once taken weeks or days was now the business of seconds, as public opinion remoulded itself before their eyes. The first shift, triggered by the CCTV story casting Winthrop as a liar and, perhaps, much worse, was now entirely reversed. She had slayed a dragon, exacting revenge on behalf of all womankind.

Maggie could not stop scrolling. A man had broken into the home of a woman, bent on attacking her. She had fought back and killed that man – unaware that the man she had killed was a murderous rapist on the run. It was the stuff of legend. A myth was building, right now, in real time. Maggie could feel it taking shape between her fingers.

The phones were still ringing, but Natasha's was no longer buzzing. She had turned it off. She was resting her chin on her fist and thinking. Maggie spoke first.

'Something tells me that DC Police won't be rushing you back in for questioning any time soon.'

Winthrop didn't move. Her gaze remained fixed on a spot on the carpet.

Maggie began to collect her things. She was about to say something – 'Well, that may be the shortest assignment of my career' – but thought better of it. Of course, Winthrop was subdued. She now understood that the man who had made his way into her house, who had had his hands all over her body, who had pressed her to the ground and violated her, that that man was someone capable of the most extreme violence. Natasha

Winthrop now understood that she had had a brush with death and, Maggie knew well, the natural response to that was not only relief.

Now Maggie stood at the door to the office, the cacophony of phones chiming louder than ever. 'I'll be going,' she said quietly.

That stirred Natasha out of her thoughts. 'Oh no, I am sorry. I do that occasionally, I'm afraid: one of my "trances", Great-Aunt Peggy used to call it.'

'Great-Aunt Peggy?'

'The lady who brought me up. After my parents—'

'Christ, yes. Sorry. Of course. That was inept of me.' Maggie had read that on Wikipedia and should have remembered it: Winthrop's parents had been killed in a car crash when she was a teenager, leaving her to be brought up by an aunt. It had happened in Germany, where her father had been serving with the US Air Force. 'I'm sorry.'

'Not at all. No Peggy to pick me up on it now, of course. Probably fallen into the most appalling habits.'

'Really?'

'Died a few years ago, I'm afraid.'

'I'm so sorry.'

'Thank you. I do miss her *terribly* though, as you can imagine.' Natasha was now on her feet, the two of them walking towards the reception desk. 'It's been wonderful to talk. Thank you so much for coming by.'

'It was my pleasure. Really. I'm glad everything's working out.'

'Well, fate does seem to have dealt us rather a twist.'

'The police should be out of your hair now. But if you need anything, you know where I am.'

'I do, Maggie. Thank you.'

'And Natasha?'

'Yes?'

'If you do decide to run for office, I can help with that too. You should think about it.'

'I'm not sure about that. America's a very conservative country.'

'But the way you put it in there, the way you talked: you'd be surprised how many people would—'

'No, I don't mean what I stand for. I mean what just happened to me. Is America ready to accept a woman who's been raped as their president?' An ironic smile crossed her lips. 'I suspect they'd rather not have to think about it.'

Maggie persisted. 'If you change your mind, call me. You know the deadline to register as a candidate is a week tomorrow. After that, you can't get on the ballot paper. There's not much time.'

Natasha extended a hand with another smile, signalling that it was time to part. 'I'm grateful, Maggie. Really.'

TUESDAY

Chapter 12

Ratface had had to give up his solo spot at the head of the table. He now shared that space with another, his chair placed a deferential inch behind hers, just to remove any doubt. She being Carol Ward Tucker, Chief of Police.

'Thank you, colleagues,' she began, her voice the firm, nononsense timbre of a school principal, one that carried an unspoken warning: *Don't even think of messing with me. I worked twice as hard as any white woman to get here and four times as hard as any white man.* The men in this room were terrified of her, starting with Ratface.

'Assistant Chief Hussey has briefed me on the Winthrop case. I am fully up to speed. I would say only this. No officer on this force should draw the mistaken conclusion that, in light of recent developments relating to the identity of the dead man found in the Winthrop property, our interest in resolving this matter has somehow terminated. It has not. I do not want the people of this city believing they can kill people in their houses with impunity,

97

so long as those they kill have a sufficiently ugly history. That's not how it works. We are part of the criminal justice system. Each of those words matter. We bring *criminals* to *justice*. And we have a *system* to do it. A system. We do not condone, explicitly or implicitly, vigilante action, no matter how justified that action might look to the people we serve. Is that clear?'

There was a recalcitrant murmur, akin to a morning greeting from the sixth grade.

'With that in mind, I want to make clear that we will pursue this case with our usual vigour. If a crime has been committed, we will find the evidence and lay it before a court of law. Whether that is a crime that should be punished and, if so, whether severely or leniently, will be a decision for the courts. Not for us. Our job is simply to find the evidence, wherever it may lead. If we find that two crimes have been committed, one by the dead man and another by the woman who killed him, we shall establish the evidence pertaining to both of them. Is that clear?'

Another murmur of affirmation, louder this time.

'One final thing, colleagues. Do I need to emphasize how little I care that the woman at the centre of this case is well-known? Do I need to spell out that we do our jobs, without fear or favour, that we follow the evidence, wherever it may lead? To put it more directly, is there a need for me to make plain that I give precisely zero fucks that this woman is a celebrity on cable news, that she has an adversarial history with this department, that she may have political ambitions which could make the "optics" of this case "uncomfortable"? The best way we can "play" this politically, either for the police department or – should this be on anyone's mind at this time –' and here there was the tiniest, almost imperceptible movement of the eyes towards Ratface – 'for our own ambitions and careers, is not to play this politically at all.'

She placed her palms down on the table, as if preparing to push away her chair, and let out a small, tight smile, signalling that the speech was over. 'In conclusion, then, my fellow police officers: get to the bottom of what happened in that townhouse in Georgetown as if it were a crack-house in Anacostia. And here's the three-word version for anybody who tends to zone out when a woman talks too long: Do. Your. Jobs.'

Chapter 13

TMZ Update: Twist in Vigilante Tale

Badass legal legend Natasha Winthrop — the DC hotshot lawyer who whacked her rapist — may have some tricky questions to answer. The #IStandWithNatasha heroine won millions of admirers when police announced that the attacker she'd killed in self-defense in the early hours of Monday morning was none other than Jeffrey Todd, wanted for a suspected murder and a string of rapes across several states. All signs pointed to the dropping of charges against the glamorous Washington attorney, who's been dubbed a role model for the #girlsfightback movement.

But our sources say trouble is brewing for Winthrop. Her browsing history has emerged and it's not pretty. She's been on a ton of dating sites, all of them firmly in the NSFW category. Put it this way, this is not your mom's Tinder. She was a regular at BDSMdate.com as well as fetish sites Fetlife and Fetster, KinkCulture and even Perversions. com. Word is, she was looking to hook up with those who like their sex rough, offering herself as a sub for a male dom.

Winthrop wouldn't be the first celeb with a taste for the dark side, but detectives are said to be taking a very close look at evidence that the legal eagle was on the lookout for those who shared a very niche taste: rape fantasies. Our moles in the DC copshop are wondering if there might be more to the Winthrop story than first met the eye, asking if the rising star lawyer all over political TV in the last month during those wall-to-wall, must-see congressional hearings has been telling the truth, the whole truth and nothing but the truth. Remember those early reports that security cameras showed Winthrop opening the front door to her attacker, even though she is reported to have said the man busted his way in? Yup, we thought you did . . .

Maggie scrolled down, looking for an update, but that was it. That's all they had. She pushed back out of her chair and headed to the kitchen, reflexively reaching for the shelf above the counter before remembering that she had deliberately moved the Ardbeg from here – relocating the whisky to a high, hard-to-reach cupboard in the bedroom. Not quite the same as pouring it down the sink – that would be a criminal waste – but a gesture in that direction. This way, she reasoned, she would have a glass only when she really needed it, rather than simply out of habit. She would have to make a decision. She glanced at her watch: too early.

Her first instinct was to tell herself that this story must be false. She knew from direct and still painful experience that wholly invented stories did make their way online. There was no reason for her to assume that this was any different.

She checked herself. Actually, there were three good reasons. First, those references to 'our moles in the DC copshop': pretty bold to insert those if this was pure invention. Second, while this site was not exactly the *New York Times*, it was rarely flat wrong. It had scooped the world on a couple of big celebrity moments – reporting star deaths was a specialism – and, by its own standards, had a reputation to defend. Third, Maggie was aware of confirmation bias, and knew she was hardly immune from the desire to seek out or accept evidence which supported what she already felt. It struck her now as confirmation of something else: that her subconscious was rooting for Natasha Winthrop. It – she – was resistant to anything that dented that faith.

Interesting, Maggie thought, trying to affect a detachment from her own feelings. They had only just met and for little more than half an hour. And yet here she was, already acting like an online true believer, ready to dismiss any uncomfortable facts as fake news. Christ, it happened so fast.

Maggie dipped into what had once felt like the stream of social media, but which these days resembled a flash flood or, more often, an open sewer. One feminist activist had linked to a *Guardian* piece:

Natasha Winthrop's sexual preferences are no one's business but hers. She's still a hero.

That had been tweeted out by a flurry of other women, along with a few young, bearded men, under the hashtag #IStillStandWithNatasha, each of them jostling to show that there was no sexual preference that could faze them. Several mentioned witches and witchhunts, with this message from a writer of experimental novels typical:

Since the dawn of time, men have tried to punish women for their sexuality. Well, sexuality is no crime. The only crime here was the attack on Natasha Winthrop by Jeffrey Todd and those seeking to make excuses for it.

What Maggie couldn't help but notice was the voices that were now silent. Earlier, when Winthrop was the woman who had defended herself against a serial rapist, every right-thinking blue-tick on Twitter was eager to declare that they stood with Natasha: TV anchors and pundits, a couple of pop stars and Instagram clean-living gurus, some well-loved Hollywood actors, several of the younger generation of congresswomen. They had all been happy to #StandWithNatasha. Now, they were keeping their counsel, waiting to see how this played out.

And despite that spirited call in the *Guardian*, it wasn't because they disapproved of Winthrop's alleged interest in rough sex (though that would certainly have persuaded most of the politicians and family-friendly actors to keep their distance). No, the worry was the one that few online were daring to spell out. It was the same worry prompted by yesterday's reports of the CCTV footage.

What if Natasha Winthrop had not just admitted her assailant into her home, as the police claimed that video footage showed, but invited him there? What if she had scoured some of the darker edges of the BDSM world to find a man who would stage a rape against her? The thought was disturbing; Maggie shuddered at the idea of it. Nor could she square it with the woman she had met and enjoyed meeting last night. She could barely compute such a thing.

Still, as Uri often liked to say, 'Who are we to gaze into the human heart?' People were complicated, human sexuality endlessly so. If that's what Natasha Winthrop liked, sure, it would finish her off politically and, doubtless, professionally too. There would be no way back from it. But it didn't change what had happened to her. The man had clearly crossed whatever line he and Natasha had agreed; what had begun as consensual sex had turned into actual rape; she had defended herself and that man, a violent criminal, was dead. The facts remained the facts.

No, Maggie thought. That would not fly, and certainly not with the police. For one reason above all. It meant Natasha had not told the whole truth. She'd claimed the man's presence in her apartment was a shock that came out of nowhere. If she had – in whatever elaborately coded way – summoned him to her home, then she had to disclose that. The police would now disbelieve every word Natasha Winthrop said to them. Natasha's only defence would be embarrassment: she was simply too ashamed to admit to her sexual kink, and had sought to keep it private. Maggie could hear her saying it. *Given that the sexual act at that moment was not consensual, given that I believed my life and safety to be in danger, the claim of self-defence still stands. Legally, this information is irrelevant.* No, it would not fly.

Maggie looked out of the window. She wasn't high enough to have a view of the city, just a flavour of these few streets around Dupont Circle. How many other people were doing what she was doing, at this very moment? Gobbling up every word of the Winthrop story; Googling 'staged rape'; visiting Perversions.com when their partner was not looking.

Hold on, she thought. This is precisely what Marcia Chester and her team were hoping for. It was such a classic move: leak the incriminating evidence, try the case in the court of public opinion. It had to be the police who had done it, and this had to be the reason.

Let's say every word in that story was true. Let's say that Natasha was indeed an enthusiast for that kind of sex. That didn't necessarily explain what had happened with Todd. The two could be wholly unconnected. It might be a complete coincidence that a rapist had entered the home of a woman who had an interest in rape. Or the two facts could be related, but in a way that didn't incriminate Natasha: her address might have been known to others who shared that interest, and then somehow found its way to Todd. Nothing in what was reported of that browsing history proved that Winthrop had opened her door, literally or in any other way, to Jeffrey Todd.

No. This was a dirty trick and, by police standards, not an original one.

Maggie reached for her phone and sent Natasha a text:

I'm on the case.

Next she scrolled through her contacts to find the name of a man who knew how this game was played. She thumbed out the words:

I need your help.

Chapter 14

Washington, DC

He'd been promoted six months ago, so that Jake Haynes now headed up his paper's investigative team in Washington. For most people, that would mean getting to see him at such short notice would be next to impossible. But, as Jake had explained on the phone, 'You're not most people, Maggie.'

She couldn't argue. In her closing days at the White House, when she was a holdover from the team of the president she had revered and worked instead for the president she abhorred, she had handed Jake the story of the year. No one ever knew she was his source and, perhaps for that reason, neither of them ever said out loud what they both knew to be true: that he owed his promotion to her.

So he paid her back a different way. Instead of the rumpled, on-deadline impatience that used to be his default response to Maggie – and remained so for everyone else – he now reacted to her name appearing on his phone by answering within one ring and with an eagerness disguised as warmth.

'If it isn't Maggie Costello! What can I do for you, Maggie?'

'Oh, hi there, Jake. I haven't called you at a bad time?'

'No such thing with you, Maggie. No such thing.' She heard him lower his voice, as if speaking to the room he was in. 'I'll catch up with you guys later. I need to take this.' So he was in a meeting, probably hosting it, given his position. And he was stepping out to talk to her.

'Thanks, Jake. It's about Natasha Winthrop.'

'Sheesh, I got whiplash just *following* that story. One minute, it's *Death Wish*, the next it's *Fifty Shades of Grey*. You working for her?'

'I'm helping her out.'

'That's the first thing I've heard that makes me think she might have a shot at the White House. If she's smart enough to hire Maggie Costello . . .'

'About this browsing history thing, I was just wondering—'

'That came to us first actually.'

'Really?'

'Yeah, one of my colleagues. Covers Capitol Hill. There when he got in this morning. We discussed it, decided it wasn't for us.'

'Really?' Instantly, she regretted her tone. She'd sounded incredulous, as if unable to believe Jake had passed on that story. She'd known enough journalists to appreciate her own mistake: no fear gripped them more tightly than the fear they'd missed a story. She rowed back fast. 'I mean, surely you didn't even need to discuss it. It's tabloid crap, isn't it?'

'That's what we thought,' he said, though he sounded unconvinced by her reversal. 'Uncertainty over provenance, authenticity. Privacy issues. Use of encrypted, personal data. And the whole thing just didn't, I don't know, smell right.'

'The sex stuff?'

'Sorta. I wasn't comfortable with it.'

Maggie remembered that Jake had, more than once in their dealings over the years, reminded her that the *Times* was a 'family newspaper'. She imagined what he would have made of the whips, chains and butt plugs that featured on BDSM.com.

'I'd be very interested in hearing more about that, Jake. In seeing anything that might shed light on the, like you said, provenance of the material. Could we meet?'

There was a pause as he took in what she had said. The key words were 'seeing' and 'meet'.

An hour later, they were in their usual rendezvous point: the food court of Union Station. Reliably, constantly heaving, it was an easy place to sit unnoticed – far enough away from the usual watering holes favoured by Washington types. And Maggie still loved that high, domed ceiling. Union Station, even in its relatively recent, restored incarnation, was one of the few buildings in America that at least felt old. Compared to Europe, it was a new-build. By American standards, it was Stonehenge.

Jake was already there when she arrived, having found a table outside Shake Shack. He stood up, his jacket less creased and a smidgeon more expensive than in the old days, gave Maggie an awkward embrace, resettled his glasses on the bridge of his nose, gestured for her to sit down, then indicated the two cardboard coffees in front of him. 'I took the liberty of ordering for you.'

She took a sip. 'So, Jake. The story came to the *Times* first.'

'I don't know that we were *first*. But before TMZ. Fact that it surfaced there makes me think lotsa folks came to the same decision we did.'

'The *Post*?'

'Right. It wasn't there, was it? Or on TV. Not even Drudge.'

'Why do you think that is?'

Jake leaned back, stretching out at his elbows as if using an unseen chest expander. Back when he'd been a beat reporter, covering the intelligence agencies, Jake Haynes had always struck Maggie as crabbed somehow, a neurotic ball, waiting to crank out the next story. Now that he was the boss, he had filled out a bit. As if he could take his time, even relax a little.

'Not for use, Maggie, but I think New York just felt a little nervous going after, you know—'

'A woman?'

'A woman who had been *raped*. Excuse me, a *high-profile* woman who had been raped. Who may be a candidate for president. Who, if she was – and even if she isn't – has a following among a very particular demographic.'

'Young, progressive women who think the *Times* is too centrist, too male and terminally unwoke?'

Jake smiled. 'That's what I never understood with you, Maggie. Why ask the question when you *always* know the answer?'

'Not always, Jake. Like in this case, I have a question I can't answer.'

'Which is?'

'Who leaked you Natasha Winthrop's browser records?'

'You know I can't tell you that.'

'I know.'

'And I also don't know the answer.'

'Really?'

'Really.'

'I can't tell whether I should believe you.'

'You should because, one, I'm a nice guy.' He smiled, a feeble attempt at sweetness, all but fluttering his eyelashes. 'Two, you are the one person in Washington that I really would not dare to shit.'

'Because I'm too valuable a source.'

'That, and because you'll find me out. But I haven't got to three yet.'

'Sorry. Three.'

'And, three, none of us knows who leaked this material. Totally anonymous drop. That's one of the reasons we were nervous, actually. You know me. I'm old school. I like to see the whites of their eyes. I don't mind being manipulated. I just—'

'"—like to know *why* I'm being manipulated."'

'You've heard me say that before?'

'Once or twice.'

'Huh.'

'So this came to you, what, via Signal or Telegram or something?'

'Actually, no. That was old school too. Well, kind of modern old school.'

Maggie furrowed her brow. Jake leaned down, to one side, and into his bag. 'It came like this.'

He produced a USB drive, a memory stick, and laid it on the

table. It had no distinguishing marks, just the brand name of the manufacturer.

'Can I have this?'

'No, Maggie, you cannot have this. Jeez.'

'But, it's been published now. What difference would—'

'Because that is material about a public figure submitted in confidence to the *New York Times*. You are working for said public figure. I hand that over to you – and therefore to her – what kind of precedent is that? Besides, she – you – may have ways to work out the identity of the source from that drive.'

'Have you? Worked out the source?'

'No.'

'Have you tried?'

'I gave it to the tech guys to look over, but once we made the decision not to run the story, we took it no further.'

Maggie turned the drive over in her hands before pushing it back across the table, allowing Jake to pick it up and put it in his breast pocket.

'Anything else on there?' she asked. 'Of interest, I mean. Old documents, anything else about Natasha Winthrop?'

'Nothing. They'd been thorough. The drive was clean. Unused. All it had was the search history for a specific period. Last four weeks. Tons of legal stuff; material relating to the hearings, obviously. Some shopping. Lots of email. And the, you know, dating sites.'

'And were they all in that same, what's the word? That same vein?'

'Yes, they were. TMZ rendered the story accurately.'

'All dominance, bondage—'

'The main sites were all in that vein, yes. But the searches zeroed in on this specific sub-category, you might call it.'

'Rough sex?'

'And rape. Yes.'

'And was there any direct contact between her and—'

'Apparently it was just searching and browsing. I didn't review all the material myself, but the reporter who it was sent to said that it was just, you know, swiping back and forth. Kind of like window shopping.'

'Nothing more direct? Between Natasha Winthrop and—'

'Nothing like that, no.' He paused, as if waiting for one more question. Maggie tried to read his face.

'You say the drive was "sent to" a reporter. You mean it was "sent" sent? In the mail?'

Now Jake Haynes smiled, as if Maggie had solved the puzzle he had set her.

'Did it come just like that? In an envelope?'

He nodded. 'Like I said, old school.'

'And do you still have the envelope?'

'As it happens . . .' he said, bending down once more into his bag. He came out with a small, padded brown envelope. He moved it across the table.

Maggie looked at the address label on the front: typewritten, from a printer. She turned it over. No return address. She turned it back over, clocking Jake's smile of anticipation. Finally she looked at the postmark. In an instant she understood his excitement.

There, clear and unmistakable, was printed the origin of this parcel. Two words that instantly set a thousand wheels turning in Maggie's mind.

Langley, Virginia.

Chapter 15

London, two weeks earlier

At first, the woman found it exciting. Like the noise, the heat, the steam, the sweat and the constant, vein-bulging pressure, the shouting and swearing issuing from the two men in charge – the head chef, whose name was above the door, and his faithful sidekick, the manager – struck her as confirmation that she had arrived. Wasn't this how a professional kitchen was meant to look and sound?

That helped her shrug it off, initially at least. The yelling in someone's face – the 'hairdryer treatment', the other kitchen staff called it – was surely no more than proof of the passion and intensity necessary to run a top-flight restaurant. The same went for that time the chef threw a small, but heavy, pan at the head of one of the girls who, like her, was on work experience. Perhaps because it missed its target, none of the other 'workies' even talked about it.

The woman noticed a pattern. If one of the younger men in

the kitchen made a mistake, there'd be a quiet word in the ear. But if she or one of the other women messed up by, say, holding a dessert plate in such a way that the blood-red coulis ran and left a visible trace on the rim, then it'd be an instant hairdryer.

Once, shortly after closing time on a Saturday evening, at close to one am, the woman was tasked with cleaning the floors. She registered that it was the third time that week that she had been given that job. She noted that the young man who had started work experience the same day she had had not been asked to do it even once. She did not say anything. Instead, she squeezed out the mop and set to work, telling herself that such chores were all part of what she was here to learn: mastery of the kitchen.

After she had mopped and scrubbed and cleaned, she heard the restaurant manager approaching. She was glad, thinking he would see how hard she had worked.

He glanced down at the floor and said, 'No. Not good enough.'

The woman assumed he was joking, that any minute now he would say: 'Just kidding. Nice job. See you in the morning.' The floor was spotless.

The man, seeing her smile, said, 'Not nearly good enough. Do it again.'

'What?'

'You heard me. Do it again. Here, I'll give you a hand.' He extended a foot to the bucket of filthy water and, with one expertly aimed kick, knocked the whole thing over. The woman watched as the grey, foetid liquid spread its filth across the surface that she had spent the last forty minutes bringing to a shine.

The woman decided that it was a test, one that she would not fail. She would not cry. Instead, she picked up the now-empty bucket, went to the tap, filled it up and started again. She did not fall into bed that night until well past three am.

After that, the woman resolved to stay inside a protective armour of her own making. She would not listen to either the chef or the manager, unless they were talking directly to her, and she would screen out everything but their specific instructions.

So when she heard the chef refer to grapeseed oil as rapeseed oil, putting undue emphasis on the first syllable, she made it float out of her mind as soon as it floated in. The woman also did that, though it took more effort, when she caught the manager complaining that a chicken breast was 'drier than an eight-year-old's snatch'.

The woman tried to adopt the same approach when one of the two men would squeeze past her in the kitchen, putting a lingering hand on her back or her bottom. Or when one of the pastry chefs got pregnant and carried on working until she was in her eighth month, and the head chef kept asking if she was lactating yet, because – and these were his words – he wanted her to pump her breast milk into a bottle 'so I can drink it'. The pastry chef pretended she hadn't heard that remark and left the room. Which meant she didn't hear her boss turn to the restaurant manager for a long disquisition on the nature of sex with a pregnant woman.

One night the restaurant was closed for a private function and the woman was carrying a tray of fried oysters, accompanied by caviar crème fraiche and served in large spoons. The head chef called her over to where he was holding court with a group of

VIP guests, all men. He promptly picked up one of the spoons and shoved it in the woman's mouth. She found herself gagging and saw that the chef was grinning. The woman understood then that that was the point. That was the thrill. He could force himself down the throat of a young woman and she couldn't do a thing about it.

Not long afterwards, the woman talked about her situation with a university friend who was already doing a paid job at a law firm. The friend's first response was obvious: 'Why don't you complain?'

The woman explained that that was hardly an option. There was no HR department, no line manager, just the two men themselves. If she said anything, she'd be out. And she needed this on her CV; she would need them to write her a reference.

They discussed the one senior woman in the kitchen. 'Why don't you talk to her?'

But that too was not an option. 'I don't know what happened there, or what they've got on her, but she totally covers for them.'

And so she said nothing. Right up until the day the head chef went further, as the woman always feared he would. Thanks to that conversation with her friend, the novice lawyer – who had discussed the situation with an older colleague – she was prepared.

It happened at night, after closing time. Not mopping the floor this time, but when she was putting chairs on tables. She did as she told herself she would. When the moment came, when he moved towards her, she glanced towards the heavens, putting her faith in the only thing she believed might help her.

Chapter 16

Washington, DC

Langley, Virginia.

Maggie was focused on those two words, squinting hard at them as if they might, just through the power of her gaze, yield their secrets.

She was back at her kitchen table, the screen of her laptop filled with an image of the small, padded brown envelope that Jake Haynes had, like a magician, produced from his bag. He hadn't let her take the envelope away, though naturally Maggie had asked. He had drawn a line regarding the journalistic ethics of protecting the anonymity of a source, deciding that while showing Maggie how the information had reached his office skirted close to that line, surrendering the evidence would have crossed it. Maggie could just about work out that logic, not least by framing it the way Jake would have done: how would this look as a paragraph in the *Washington Post? In a statement, the* New York Times *confirmed that Mr Haynes handed some of the material to a former White House official . . .*

So she didn't blame him for refusing her request. But nor did she blame herself for taking, when he'd gone to get a refill of coffee, a couple of discreet photos with her phone, just for her own reference.

Langley, Virginia.

She tried to think through the options methodically. *Start with the obvious, and work your way out from there.* That was the advice, often repeated, of her mentor, Stuart Goldstein, whenever an event had multiple possible explanations. So: start with the obvious.

Someone at the Central Intelligence Agency in Langley, Virginia, wanted to take down Natasha Winthrop. What's more, they did not care if it were – or perhaps actively hoped it to be – known that the CIA desired that outcome. A Langley postmark: you might as well take out an ad.

Which raised the second possibility. That someone wanted to implicate the CIA. Quite heavy-handed, but that might not matter. Which nodded to a sub-possibility: that the prime objective was to divert attention away from the real source. In which case, posting it from Langley would count as a blunt, but effective, decoy.

She looked again at the photo. The envelope was covered with stamps, rather than franked. That meant the sender had avoided visiting a post office, or using home mailing software, both of which would have left a trace. Basic precautions.

Maggie got up and began to pace. Start with the CIA scenario. Why would anyone in that agency care about Natasha Winthrop? She knew what they'd say on Twitter: that this was an establishment plot to destroy a woman who threatened their interests, a potential president who challenged the powers that be. As for the giveaway postmark, what would the online natterers say about that? That the deep state was now so arrogant, it was all but giving the finger to democratic norms: it positively wanted the America sheeple to know who was boss.

Did Maggie buy any of that? A year or so ago, her answer would have been an emphatic, laughing no. The very idea was ridiculous. But now, in the era of a president who made jokes-not-jokes about installing himself in the Oval Office for life, who treated the Attorney-General as his own personal lawyer and regarded the Department of Justice as a gang of heavies to be set on his enemies, why not? Once it would have been outlandish to imagine a sitting president deploying the CIA against a political rival. These days, and given everything Maggie had seen from this White House, it was wholly conceivable.

On the other hand, and for related reasons, there were enough people around ready to believe such a thing that it made for a highly convenient alibi. What if the leaker had not been taking orders from the man in the White House, but from one of the crowded pack of contenders on the other side of the partisan divide, all of them jostling for the right to take him on? Popping that USB stick in a parcel marked Langley, Virginia, simultane-ously kneecapped a rival – one who had novelty and excitement on her side – and handed the progressive base an immediate vil-lain, all in one go. Yes, it was crude, but these days crude worked. Nuance got lost; nuance was for losers.

That still left several other unanswered questions. How did the source, whoever it was, come to have these computer records?

Had the police obtained them in the last few hours, as part of their investigation into Winthrop? It could have been them who wanted them made public, prosecuting their case against Natasha before the jury of public opinion, especially, perhaps, after the revelation of the dead man's identity had turned her into a hero. The timing wasn't quite right though: Todd was named on Monday evening, while this envelope had been mailed earlier that day.

Maggie examined the postmark again, just to be sure. The stamp looked real enough, but she thought of Liz, her computer geek sister, and the miracles her high school students were able to pull off, twisting and moulding photographs to look any way they wanted. Might the apparently inky stamp be a digital fake? Maybe.

Either way, the police surely had easier, swifter and more direct ways of releasing information than shopping a memory stick around Washington news desks and doing it by snail mail. Or was this the work of a single, partisan detective, who had passed the records to a Capitol Hill contact, confident that politics would do the rest? Another thought struck. Perhaps the police had nothing to do with it. Ideologically driven folk worked in phone companies and internet service providers too.

Still on her feet, she was back at the kitchen table. She pecked at a few keys on the keyboard and brought up the TMZ story detailing Natasha's search history. All this focus on how the records might or might not have surfaced was, Maggie understood, so much displacement activity. It enabled her not to look at the picture the records painted, of a woman whose sexual interests apparently shaded beyond play-acting dominance and submission into something much darker. If these records were accurate, Natasha Winthrop had sought out sexual violence. Whether that was the pretence of it, the simulation of it, or the thing itself, Maggie had no way of knowing.

And yet, without that knowledge, she could take this no further. Winthrop might have believed herself to be playing a sex game, while her attacker was bent on inflicting grave harm. Had Natasha misunderstood him that night? Or had he misunderstood her? There was only one way to find out.

Chapter 17

'That's OK, if you want to finish up while we start, that's no problem at all. That's good pizza, right? One of the perks of the job, my friends.

'So, why don't I get this party started? As I mentioned, I'm Alex, I'll be your facilitator tonight. I hate that word too – I see you, Sharon! – but all it means is, I'll be the one asking the questions, just kind of moving the ball along. Key thing you gotta know is, I don't have any opinions at all. I'm serious! What I mean is, if I ask you about a thing, that's not because *I* think that thing or that I want *you* to think that thing. It really is just a question. All right? And this is not *Jeopardy*, OK: there are no right or wrong answers. I really want to stress that: no right or wrong answers. Whatever you say is valid, because it's your opinion. That's why we've brought you here, and given you pizza and Coke – and Diet Coke too, Lauren, don't say we don't look after you guys! Because we want you to feel relaxed and because –

genuinely – we really value what you say. Your opinion is what we want to hear. Don't worry about what other people think, or what I think, just say what *you* think. Yeah? Are we good? All right. Opening topic – remember, no "good" or "bad" answers – where do you guys get your news?'

Dan Benson looked up from his phone and through the glass: glass on his side, a mirror on theirs. He had witnessed a hundred of these in his old job, maybe more. And he knew the right pose to strike was jaded DC professional, dragged out to some motel in Nowheresville, Flyover Country, against his will. But – big but – the truth was, he was an addict. He *loved* focus groups, way more than was healthy. For him, it was the closest he ever got to being a reporter out on the campaign trail, trekking through the hog farms of Iowa or the snows of New Hampshire, talking to real-life, actual voters, taking the pulse of the American people. Except you didn't have to schlep around in muddy boots, shivering in the cold outside a Dairy Queen or a Wendy's, approaching total strangers like a homeless person (except weirder, since you had a notebook in your hand), because you were indoors, cosy and safe on the other side of that mirror, observing but unobserved. He *loved* it.

Focus grouping had been one of his core duties in his last job, the one he had walked away from just twenty-four hours ago. A 'defection', political Twitter had called it. Benson had been re-reading some of those tweets again just now, albeit in his 'lurker' account, the anonymous one he maintained for precisely this purpose – liking and bookmarking in a manner impossible under his own name. The story had broken (with a little help from his own fair hand) via an Axios reporter, and had set the tone for the rest of the coverage:

INBOX: Top Steele staffer defects to Harrison campaign. Hiring of Dan Benson, longtime aide to House Intelligence Chairman, confirms Harrison winning the money/endorsement/talent game. Prediction: Steele ain't running. And if he was, he ain't now.

Most of it was positive and, crucially, all of it was clueless as to the timing. Most Hill reporters simply assumed that Dan had started working for Harrison the moment his move had been announced, not before. That assumption was helpful. The last thing he needed was for people to start working back through his schedule, realizing what he was doing and who he was with during his last day on the chairman's payroll . . .

Now, though, he had put his phone away and was staring hard through the glass. In the past, when he had done focus groups for Steele or for senate colleagues on the judiciary committee, usually to test out the favourables/unfavourables on a Supreme Court nomination, things would stall right at the start. The facilitator would hold up a picture, saying, 'Can anyone tell me who this is?' and there'd be a circle of blank faces as they contemplated a judge they'd never heard of. Not this time.

Every single person in that room was nodding in recognition at the picture of Natasha Winthrop. Benson made a mental note: *Don't ever let that photograph make it within one thousand miles of one of our ads.* It looked like the cover of *People* magazine, Winthrop's teeth white and dazzling, her eyes and earrings sparkling, the hair short, dark and perfect.

One of the focus groupers was speaking. A white man, early fifties, assertive – always the first to speak, in Dan's experience. '. . . don't normally watch those things, I'm more of a *Monday Night Football* guy, but she was something else. She lit the place up.'

A black woman in her thirties, who had identified herself earlier as a dental nurse, agreed. 'My son was laughing at me, 'cause I kept wanting to put C-SPAN on.' The others laughed warmly, several of the women nodding. 'Those hearings were electric. The way she tore into all those – excuse me for saying it – but all those men, just showing them up like that. Sheesh.'

So far, so familiar. Benson had seen the polling data; he didn't need to be told that Winthrop's performance as the lead inquisitor for Steele's committee had made her a star. Still, seeing the data on a laptop screen was one thing. Hearing it from actual human beings, live and unprompted, was something else. Not for the first time, he wondered if his boss – his new boss – could ever defeat such a candidate, should it come to that. Or was Senator Tom Harrison fated to be yet another establishment frontrunner steamrollered by a national phenomenon?

The facilitator had moved on to recent events. 'Now the person we're talking about was in the news recently. Anyone want to tell me why?'

'She killed that evil rapist with her bare hands.' It was the dental nurse, quick as a flash. The others were agreeing.

The moderator was looking around the room, trying to draw

out those who had so far said nothing. He lighted on Eleanor, a white, retired schoolteacher. 'What did you think about all that, Eleanor?'

The woman paused, as if weighing up her desire to speak against the propriety of doing so. She pursed her lips slightly, a gesture that instantly encouraged Benson. She cleared her throat.

'I know they want us to believe she killed that man in self-defence and all that. But I don't know. It just don't sit right with me.'

'What don't sit right?' It was the nurse, not the moderator.

'What happened. In her house.' A pause. 'And before.'

Dan leaned forward, his face just inches from the glass.

Alex, the facilitator, broke the brief silence. 'What happened before, Eleanor?'

'I don't know whether I like to talk about such things. I'm surprised the rest of you don't bring it up. Y'all saw it as well as I did.'

'Oh, OK, OK.' The white guy. 'You're talking about those dating sites.'

'If that's what they call them.' Eleanor's arms were now firmly folded. 'I don't think it was a date she was looking for. Least not a date as I understand the word. I think she was looking for sex. Unnatural sex.'

'That don't mean he got a right to *rape* her.' The nurse thumped the table as she spoke.

'I never said he had.'

'So what are you saying then?'

'I'm saying that . . . what I'm saying is that, there's more to this than meets the eye. That's all.'

The nurse folded her own arms now, to match her antagonist,

then did a quarter-turn, showing Eleanor her shoulder. But, Dan noticed, the rest of the group, or at least those who had kept quiet, seemed to side with Eleanor. They didn't want to do so out loud; perhaps they were worried about adopting a socially unacceptable position in public. (And, by God, if Dan hadn't seen that phenomenon at work before.) And yet their gut instinct was suspicion. Natasha Winthrop was gorgeous, exciting and TV gold. They were thrilled to watch her. But that didn't mean they trusted her.

Dan Benson sat back in his seat, letting it rock on its hind legs. Here, at last, was something he could work with.

WEDNESDAY

Chapter 18

Cape Cod, Massachusetts

Maggie had only to close her eyes and she was back in Ireland. A deep breath through her nostrils, and it was Saturday afternoon on the beach at Sandymount, the air cool, its scent combined with the spray of the waves. The spell did not end even when she opened her eyes to see Cape Cod, Massachusetts, and the mighty Atlantic rather than Dublin Bay and the Irish Sea. The only difference between now and then was that in those days she could run around, seemingly for hours, without ever feeling a hint of strain; now she could hear herself panting.

No such trouble for Natasha, she couldn't help but notice, who was now a good fifteen yards ahead. Maggie suspected the idea had been for the two of them to take a run together, chatting away as they jogged along the beach. But Maggie could run or she could talk: she could not do both. Perhaps Natasha, able to speak steadily even as she pounded along the shore, found it awkward, being together in silence like that. Or maybe she found it frustrating, having to keep her speed down to allow Maggie to keep up. Either way, Natasha was now surging ahead, a trim, taut figure that testified to someone who knew how to run. The sight brought back a set of feelings Maggie thought she had left behind in adolescence: jealousy, admiration, pleasure, inadequacy, desire, all jumbled together in a strange, vaguely unsettling stew.

If she'd have known it would have been like this, she'd never have said yes. If Natasha had baldly invited her to come running in Cape Cod, she would of course have said no. But it hadn't happened quite like that.

Instead, after Maggie had paced around her apartment a few more times, she had sent Winthrop a message:

We need to talk.

A reply had come seconds later.

We do.

Maggie suggested they meet at Winthrop's office. Natasha said no, she no longer considered her office 'secure', which Maggie took to mean that it was no longer leakproof, rather than unsafe. Maggie was thumbing out some alternative venues, including her own apartment, when the phone started ringing. It was Natasha's voice, against the hum of traffic. She was driving, she said, already on her way northward. It would be a nine-hour drive: 'Just the thing to clear my head.'

Maggie urged her to turn around, this very moment. It was

madness to leave DC. It would look like an admission of guilt. Natasha needed to be in town to put out a response to the phone records, and to strategize next steps. Going to ground now would look awful, confirmation that the story was indeed as bad as it looked, if not worse; so bad in fact that Natasha Winthrop dared not show her face. And that was before you even got to the legal implications, given that the police were bound to press hard on this new line of inquiry. What if the police demanded to bring Natasha in for more questioning, as was highly likely, only to find the subject of their inquiry had absconded?

Natasha had laughed at that. 'No one's absconding. I'm not fleeing the country. I'm not defecting to *Moscow*.' She urged Maggie to calm down, get some sleep and then catch the early shuttle to Boston the next day. Natasha would pick her up at the ferry terminal in Provincetown. 'Oh, and bring sturdy shoes,' she said, before hanging up.

And that's what had happened, though it had taken a while for them to meet up. Maggie paced around MacMillan Wharf for several minutes before they found each other. For one thing, Natasha had arrived in a beaten-up vintage Saab that seemed designed to elude attention. Maggie had all but ignored it, assuming it to be abandoned. Even when she squinted inside, she had looked away. The woman in the car looked old, with a full head of silver hair.

But then a window had been wound down, a waving hand had emerged and Maggie had crossed the street to take a closer look. Once she was near enough, the old woman had said firmly, 'Get in', and the voice confirmed it. It was Natasha Winthrop.

Once they'd driven off, she pulled off the silver hair-do and chucked it onto the back seat. 'The one great advantage of this boy's haircut of mine. A wig just *slides* right on it. Fantastically convenient.'

'You mean, this is not the first time you've gone out in disguise?'

'Only since the hearings. It became tedious. I couldn't go to Safeway; everyone wanted a stop-and-chat. But when I popped that thing on, I could whisk round in ten minutes. I fear this is something that awaits us, Maggie: there is nothing more invisible than an *older woman.*' She held up her hands in the manner of a monster from a horror movie, as if the very notion of a woman over the age of fifty was terrifying. 'I'm rather looking forward to it in a way. Imagine the things you could do if no one noticed you were there.'

Maggie found herself smiling, involuntarily. She had given Natasha that little lecture about not looking like a fugitive, and here she was all but wearing camouflage.

Maggie kept smiling, probably inanely, as Natasha powered along Route 6 in fourth gear, the Saab as heavy as a submarine. Something about Winthrop's brio, her aristocratic confidence, her cavalier disregard for the usual proprieties was energizing. Maggie had met plenty of men like that – again, they were copiously represented among the Oxbridge boys in the press, diplomatic and NGO corps in Africa – but their upper-crust insouciance, their casualness and, above all, their sense of entitlement had always left her cold. Somehow, though, Winthrop was different.

The obvious explanation was that she was a woman, who, no matter how well-born, would have had to fight hard to get to where she was now. Still, that was only part of it. The larger explanation, Maggie knew, was harder to pin down. It was located somewhere in that gleam in Natasha's eye, the playful, conspiratorial hint that there was a joke to be had and that both she and Maggie were in on it. Maggie might not know it yet, but she would, in time. Or at least that was the promise hinted at by that look in Natasha's eyes.

Soon they were off the main road, turning down a winding lane through woods and past lakes – or 'ponds', as Natasha called them. The houses were becoming larger and more infrequent. Eventually, there was a small turning, and a narrower lane. It took Maggie a moment to realize that they were on private property, that the fields and lawns on both sides were all part of a single estate. The lane finally widened out into a sweeping gravel driveway and before them stood a wide, old house, its roof slate-grey, its window frames a clean, brilliant white, its bricks a weathered reddish-brown, so weathered that Maggie knew that she was not looking at mere colonial-style but the thing itself. The house formed an L-shape, with a mighty, aged American beech tree in the front lawn. Natasha came to a stop, pulled on the handbrake and said, 'Here we are then. Home.'

Maggie got out of the car, but said nothing. It wasn't so much the scale of the house – she had been in more than enough McMansions, including the homes of multiple party donors in the affluent suburbs of Chicago or Philadelphia, to know that size and taste were often in inverse proportion – but its solidity, its rootedness. Such places were so rare in America that it briefly floored her. The Winthrops, Maggie knew, were one of the original Boston Brahmin families, that handful who could trace their roots to the very first colonists to set foot in the New World, those who had arrived dreaming of a new England. Here was the proof.

'We often get that,' Natasha said, smiling widely at Maggie's dumbstruck silence. 'Pilgrim's Cove is a magical place. Come inside.'

The name should have been the clue, but it hardly prepared her for what came next. Natasha pushed open the wide, solid front door and they were in a hallway. But beyond that, and opened up, was a living room whose back wall was formed of a series of tall glass doors, looking out to the sparkling blue of the ocean. The house backed right onto the beach.

'Jesus,' Maggie said. It was the first word she had uttered.

'So now you know why I was prepared to drive through the night to get here. Maggie, I do not exaggerate when I say that every *second* away from this place feels like an unconscionable waste.'

An older woman had appeared, greeted instantly with a warm hug by Natasha. For a moment, Maggie wondered if this was Great-Aunt Peggy, before remembering that the woman who had brought up the young, orphaned Natasha had herself died. Maggie was used to thinking that no one in the world had a smaller family than she did: just Liz really. But this woman, Natasha Winthrop, had no one. Despite all her glamour and success, Maggie felt sorry for her.

'Maggie, this is Molly. She's a dear, dear friend who also happens to look after this *impossible* house. Molly, this is my good friend Maggie Costello – am I saying that right? "Cos*tello*", is that right, Maggie? That would be so Washington for me to be mispronouncing your name this whole time.'

'Not at all. In Ireland we tend to say "*Costello*", you know, with the weight on the first syllable, but literally no one here ever—'

'Well, *Costello* it is. *Costello*. *Costello*.'

'There's no need. I'm not one of those—'

'I absolutely insist. So, Molly. Meet Maggie *Costello*.'

They shook hands, both smiling at the awkwardness of it, both aware that they were moons and Natasha was the sun.

'So. A swim, Maggie? In the ocean? To cool off from that horrid journey. Icy at this time of year, I know, but *so* invigorating. Or shall we lend you some,' and here she gave a conspiratorial wink to Molly, simultaneously injecting a note of intrigue into her voice that was almost lascivious '. . . running kit?'

And so Maggie had succumbed, accepted a pair of Natasha's old sneakers – fancier than anything Maggie owned – and followed her along the path through the trees and to the beach. Before she knew it she was out here, the sound of the surf in her ears, the air misted with spray, the light a prism of colours, the autumn sun a rebuke to the clammy offices, chiming phones and constant clamour they had left behind in Washington, DC.

After perhaps forty minutes, and to Maggie's relief, they headed back to the house at walking pace. En route, Natasha pointed out the cove where smugglers had brought liquor to the Cape during Prohibition, hauling barrels of Scotch ashore in the dead of night. 'I always thought that that whisky must have tasted especially good,' she said. 'Forbidden fruit and all that.'

Next she guided them behind the sand dunes and onto a trail through the woods, stopping to show Maggie the trees she remembered from her childhood. They stopped at the hollow where Natasha had once curled up and hid for hours, with only a copy of *To Kill a Mockingbird* for company. 'I think I probably decided to become a lawyer inside this very tree.'

Eventually, they wended their way back to the estate, a gardener advancing with a tray of tall, cold glasses to mark their return.

'This is the bit that makes it all worth it,' Natasha said as she passed Maggie a glass. Only when Maggie brought it to her lips did she realize that this was not a tumbler of fizzy water, ice and lemon but an enormous gin and tonic. They clinked glasses and Natasha said, 'To getting it right.'

A moment later, the tour resumed, as Natasha pointed out the vegetable garden, the croquet lawn and the grass tennis courts. The place was ridiculously gorgeous.

'So this was your childhood,' Maggie said.

'Not my *entire* childhood. I spent most of it in Germany, of course. On the base. Even once I'd moved back, I only ever summered here. The rest of the year I was in boarding school. But, yes, those were magical times. Extraordinarily privileged.'

'If you run for president, you'll need to explain this to people somehow.'

'Maggie, I've told you. That is *such* nonsense.' A pause. 'If I ever had to explain myself, I'd just tell the truth. I was born into great privilege, but I'd give every last piece of it back to have what most people take for granted.'

Maggie knew what Natasha meant, but she wanted to hear it. She waited, keeping her gaze on Natasha, who spoke eventually.

'There's no one left now. Everyone else has gone. It's just me and the sea.'

'I tell you one thing that surprised me.'

'Yes.'

'One little detail that I was not expecting at all.'

'Go on.'

'I will. But first: a refill.'

They were in the room Natasha referred to as the 'small kitchen', though the description was comically inaccurate. It was a room generous enough to hold a thick, gnarly farmhouse table, a fireplace wide enough to stand in, as well as a heavy, oil-fired range. Maggie suspected that this room had once functioned as the servants' kitchen, though she hadn't dared ask. She had played the awestruck sightseer enough for one day.

After the run on the beach and the drinks in the garden, Maggie had cleared her throat to initiate the talk they needed to have. She would begin with the phone records, and move on to the Langley postmark – or withhold that fact, depending – and then make her demands. She had rehearsed the speech in her mind on the flight up here: *Natasha, I cannot even begin to do an effective job for you unless I have all the facts. If you want me to help you, you have to trust me.*

But Natasha had hushed her, insisting they each take a shower and then talk over dinner. She had despatched Molly to show Maggie her room – towels on the bed, stunning view of the ocean – and then disappeared into the 'library', which Maggie assumed was an office. That worried her: surely they needed to talk before Natasha started making calls.

She had tried again over dinner. But Natasha had raised her palm in protest, joking that she had her own 'due diligence' to exercise. She wanted to know everything about Maggie. How and why she had left Dublin; about her first job with an NGO, and how that had led Maggie to serve as an improbably young mediator between armed factions in the Congo war; the secondment to the UN, followed by ad hoc work for the US State Department, including in the Middle East, and the eventual move to DC. She was especially fascinated to hear about Maggie's brief stint as a couples' counsellor, deploying her mediation skills between warring spouses rather than armed factions. ('You'd be amazed how similar the work is,' Maggie had said. 'First job is to find out the red lines, then work back from there.') Then Natasha wanted to know what it was like to be a foreigner in America, about taking US citizenship, about whether Maggie felt Irish or American or both or neither. She wanted to glean every detail about life on the campaign team of their party's last successful presidential candidate, her eyes bright as she lapped up the stories of Maggie's spell in his inner circle in the White House. And then she listened, head resting on her right fist, her face a picture of sympathy, as Maggie described the torrid period she had spent working for his successor, as a holdover in the early days of the current administration. Maggie recounted the craziness that had unfolded there and her role in it – 'However bad you imagine it was, it was so much worse' – and everything that had happened since.

Throughout, Maggie tried to bring Natasha back to the business in hand. 'Enough about me,' she would say. 'Much as I love talking about myself, we really must . . .' but Natasha would not be diverted. 'If we are to work closely together, I need to know who you are,' she said. 'If I am to put my life in your hands, then I need to take a good look at those hands.'

And so, Maggie had answered her questions and, truth be told, she had enjoyed it. How many times had she done the reverse, listening as a man delivered a monologue about his life and times? Uri was an exception: he was a listener as well as a talker. It was one of the things she loved about him. But most of the time, in Washington especially, Maggie was the one asking the questions, offering an encouraging nod of the head, murmuring her understanding and appreciation: the perfect audience. Now it was Natasha who was in the stalls, granting Maggie the stage. Even when Maggie sought out Natasha's opinion on an issue, she would speak – often passionately, sometimes movingly – but she would also listen. Maggie had watched a lot of politicians in her time, up close. But she couldn't think of another who listened the way this woman listened.

Still, once Molly had come in to clear away the plates and they had moved to a pair of armchairs, Maggie was adamant.

'We need to talk about this,' she said, holding up her phone. 'You've left this story unanswered for nearly twenty-four hours. That's a disaster, in terms of both the politics and the law. You don't need me to tell you about the police inquiry: this is obviously going to be their number one lead. I don't know what you could have done, maybe nothing, but they've had the field to themselves for a full day. As for the politics: fucking horrendous.'

'Is it?'

'You've seen what people are saying.'

'Actually, I haven't. When I come up here, I try to turn off Twitter. Detox.'

'Right.' Maggie collected herself. 'I mean, that's admirable. But . . . Jesus. You're in the middle of a Category Five hurricane, and you don't even look?'

'Calmest place to be in a hurricane. And no, I don't look.'

'Good. Keep it that way.'

'I will.'

'But take it from me—'

'Will do.'

'It's ugly.'

'OK.'

'And we're now twenty-four hours behind. Also, though you keep saying you're absolutely positively definitely not running, if by any chance you changed your mind, you'd need to register your candidacy in precisely six days. So these are—' She heard Stuart's voice, sardonic in these situations. 'Sub-optimal conditions.'

'I know, Maggie. And I'm sorry. But I needed time to think.'

'OK. So you've had time and now you need to talk. To me. You need to tell me—'

'I know. That's what I've decided, too.'

'—everything. Because otherwise this can't work.'

'I came to the same conclusion. While we were out running.'

'What conclusion?'

'I just had to get there in my own time. To tell you.'

Maggie went quiet. Goldstein's first rule of conversation and especially interrogation: *Silence is golden*. Natasha got out of her seat, whisky glass still in hand.

'First thing to say: the story is true.'

Maggie said nothing.

'The browsing history. It's an accurate history of my internet use and searches.'

Maggie exhaled sharply. Not in relief, but in the manner of a weightlifter girding herself for a heavy load.

'I did look on those dating sites. BDSMdate, Perversions, Kink, whatever they're called. I looked through them all. Very thoroughly.'

'OK.' Maggie could hear the tone in her own voice, the strained patience. She sounded as if she were addressing someone holding a firearm, urging them to put down the gun.

'I had been doing it for a while. Whoever has those records will have more. The police will see that.'

'All right.' *Let's do this nice and slow.*

'We could say that I'm into it. That I have a thing for rough sex. That I wanted to meet men who would play out a rape fantasy with me, who would burst into my home and pretend to rape me. We could say that.' A beat. 'If you think there would be any advantage in it.'

'I can't imagine there'd be huge advantage in that, to be honest, Natasha, no.'

'Depends what the alternative explanation is, doesn't it?'

That stopped Maggie. She paused for one moment, then another, then another. 'Let's forget what's advantageous and what isn't. We'll come to that. For now, the only question is: what's the truth?'

Natasha drained her glass, pulled herself up to full height, gave her head a slight shake, as if she had just splashed cold water on her face, and said: 'I was using those sites to lure Jeffrey Todd to my home.'

Chapter 19

Cape Cod, Massachusetts

'What?'

'That's why I was on those sites. I was looking for him. With a view to engaging in a deliberate act of entrapment. I wanted him to come to my home and attempt a rape. I would then have the evidence to convict him, once and for all.'

'I don't underst—'

'What don't you understand?'

'Any of it. All of it.' Maggie could hear the irritation in her own voice. For a split-second she imagined trying to explain this to someone else or, heaven forbid, the public. 'You wanted this man to come and rape you, so that you could catch him red-handed in the act of rape? How did you know that . . . I mean, how did you find . . .'

'OK, I'll back up.' Natasha went over to the fireplace, where a couple of logs were giving a soft, warming heat, just enough to take the edge off an autumn evening in an old house. She picked up a poker and gave the logs an unnecessary prod. Maggie watched her, trying to square the information she had just received with the legal counsel in front of her, who had won squeals of adoration from the cable TV commentariat a couple of weeks earlier, setting off a round of feverish presidential speculation. The two hardly seemed to compute.

Natasha topped up her glass, did the same for Maggie, and returned to her chair. 'Before I came to Washington, I was in the DA's office in Manhattan, as you know. Everything came through that office: murder, assault, theft. Sexual violence wasn't my area, but I took an interest. I had a very formidable colleague who specialized in rape. At the team meetings, she would talk often about the extraordinary difficulties in getting results in such cases: as I'm sure you know, the statistics are jaw-dropping. Guess what percentage of rape cases in this country leads to an arrest.'

Maggie waited for the answer, realizing only when Natasha raised her eyebrows that it was she who was meant to supply it.

'I don't know.' She thought of a number, then, knowing that the stat was going to be awful, she halved it. 'Thirty per cent? Twenty?'

'Somewhere between five and six per cent.'

'No.'

'Yes! And how many rape cases do you think end in a conviction?'

'I don't know.'

'Less than one per cent. Nought point seven per cent, to be exact. And not even all of those go to jail. That's just one in every one hundred and forty-three cases. Which means one hundred and forty-two rapes happen without a man ever being held to account.'

'Jesus.'

'It's quite something, isn't it? My colleague's case file was full of the most appalling stories, Maggie. You can't imagine. People who had suffered prolonged, brutal sexual violence. At the hands of husbands, fathers, step-fathers, boyfriends, uncles, co-workers, bosses, first dates, *fifth* dates, clients, customers, strangers, friends, *priests* – you name it.

'And of course, most of these cases had gone nowhere. Because that's what always happens. On the rare occasions when a man *is* arrested – remember, just five or six in every hundred – most of those never even get referred to a prosecutor, let alone to court. Police say there just isn't enough there. And if by some miracle the case does make it to trial, then the chances are high that it'll end in an acquittal. Which means the vast majority – more than ninety-nine out of every hundred rapes – get off.

'Countless reasons for that, of course. My colleague would go into all of them, chapter and verse: the myths that exist about rape, the things people – police, jurors, *prosecutors*, for heaven's sake – believe. You know: "Look how that woman was dressed, she was asking for it." Or: "She'd been drinking, she was asking for it." Or: "She once watched porn, she was asking for it." Or: "It's only rape if she's black and blue all over." Or: "It's only rape if it's done by a stranger." You'd be amazed at how all this stuff persists.

'But the biggest problem is the obvious one: there are never any witnesses. Except the victim, of course. "He said, she said."'

'So you thought you'd change that. Lure a rapist into trying his luck against a lawyer who was ready.'

'Yes. I mean, not quite. We're running ahead. Can we go back to the DA's office?'

'All right. The DA's office.' Maggie drained the last drops of whisky from her glass.

'I became rather fascinated with my colleague's case file. Obsessed would be too strong a word, but I was curious. As I mentioned, it wasn't my own area of law – by then, I was beginning to take an interest in public administration, Guantanamo and so on, some human rights law – but I would keep an eye on it. And Caroline liked to have someone she could vent to, at the end of a long day. Feet on the desk. Glass of vodka for her, whisky for me.' Natasha looked at Maggie with a smile that was impossible not to reciprocate.

'Anyway, there was one name that recurred in the file. He'd been arrested in one jurisdiction and released for lack of evidence; then his name popped up a few months later, somewhere else. Pure luck that Caroline learned of the second case, which was in New Jersey. Or not luck, exactly: a diligent cop. Both went to trial which, given the stats we discussed, is quite something: it means he was either the most *extraordinarily* unlucky chap ever to walk the face of the earth or a rather prolific rapist. Statistically, he'd have needed to commit one hundred and ninety rapes just to be *arrested* twice, let alone come to trial.

'Needless to say, he was acquitted in both cases. He did get sent to jail once. Not for rape, though, even though that's what they hauled him in for originally. He was convicted on a lesser charge of battery: I suspect the prosecution just took whatever they could get. Lucky for him, that meant he was never on any sex-offender register.'

'Except for Caroline's files.'

Natasha smiled. 'I suppose so. Her files were probably the most comprehensive around.' She seemed to be forming another thought which she kept to herself. Another sip of whisky. 'The point, Maggie, is that this man had essentially evaded justice for *years*. It was clear that he was a serial menace to women, acting with unfettered freedom.'

'But you worked in the DA's office years ago, right?'

'Yes, several years ago. But I stayed in touch with Caroline. The occasional vodka.' That smile again. 'I knew he was still at large.'

Maggie nodded, encouraging Natasha to return to the story.

'It might have been after one of those conversations, but I remember thinking that the only way we'll ever get these men is if we have cast-iron evidence. I mean, even then it won't be guaranteed. Still, a rapist's worst nightmare would be to attack a woman like me. Because a lawyer would know how to collect the incontrovertible evidence.'

'Like what?'

'Well, there's obviously the DNA and so forth. But audio and video is what I had in mind.'

'Video?'

Natasha nodded, her lips glued tightly together.

Maggie hesitated, unsure what she was being told. Quietly, she said: 'And is there . . . video?'

'We're getting ahead of ourselves again. The key moment came a few months ago, when I hit on the notion of entrapment. I found whatever I could about Todd, including police reports of cases where they suspected but could not prove his involvement. You have to realize, Maggie, that thanks to DNA evidence, police in at least three states had been looking for him for several months. He was the prime suspect in at least four rapes and one homicide. He was on the FBI's "wanted" list. But he'd gone to ground.'

'So you had to flush him out.'

'The files made clear that he had a modus operandi. That he used dating sites. That's how he found his victims and how he got access to them.'

'Always BDSM sites?'

'He used a whole range. "Suddenly Single" for divorcees and widows. "The Heart is Sacred" for Christians. He was on so many. But, yeah, he was on those ones too. And it made sense to do it there.'

'Why?'

'Because this was needle-in-a-haystack stuff. I needed to target him specifically. And the one thing I knew about him was that he was a rapist.'

'Those things are all anonymous, right?'

'Sure.'

'So how did you know it was him?'

'Oh, that wasn't so hard. Part of the country, approximate age. Oh, and he used his initials as part of his username.'

'You're kidding.'

'I'm not. Some of these men are wickedly manipulative and cunning. And others are just not very bright.'

'So once you were sure it was him, it was a matter of creating a fake ID and persona for yourself and then, what? Inviting him to come into your home and . . . force himself on you?'

'Please, Maggie. This is already so difficult.'

'I'm sorry.'

'We were in touch via encrypted message. I gave him the time and place. I had it all planned. I would have hidden cameras, audio recording equipment and – of course – personal security guards, all standing by. He would be caught and the evidence against him would be unarguable.'

'But if you'd entrapped him, it wouldn't count, would it? Legally, I mean.'

'I'd thought of that. I had only consented to the *pretence* of rape. The moment I signalled that I wanted it to stop, he had to stop. If he didn't stop, then it ceased to be a pretence. It would become a crime at that moment.'

'And you'd have the proof. Video, audio, CCTV, the lot.'

'Exactly.'

'So, and I know this will sound a bit obvious but . . . where is it? Where's the proof?'

Natasha's shoulders slumped and she let out a long sigh. For the first time since Maggie had come to this extraordinary house, Natasha Winthrop looked vulnerable and oddly lonely. After a long pause, she said finally, 'Because, Maggie, my terribly clever plan went wrong. It went horribly, fatally wrong.'

Chapter 20

Stockholm, Sweden, one week earlier

Could she send another text, or would that be annoying? She'd thumb it out and see how it looked. The woman had sent two already, in the last half hour, and the reply to the second had come markedly slower than the reply to the first, so maybe that was a sign – one of those little cues that, in her working life, she was so good at picking up. But in this area, it was so much harder to keep her distance, to sound cool and detached. She knew it sounded needy, that it was almost certainly counter-productive, that the risk was high that it would trigger that sullen response she dreaded: the withdrawal of affection. But still, she needed to know. She typed out the words and looked at them on the screen.

> *Hi there! Just wanted to check, before I disappear into this meeting.*
> *Did it work? Does he look sleepy? You're a star, thanks v v much.*
> *Let me know!!*

Even she could see the double exclamation mark reeked of desperation. And yet, how else to keep it light? An emoji? Maybe an emoji. The last babysitter used them all the time, but then when the woman used them in response she'd made a grimace, as if the woman had brought in a terrible smell. Maybe this one would feel the same way. No point trying to pretend you were on the same level as these girls. They were younger and prettier than you were and – crucial point – they had all the power. At this moment, she had the woman's little boy in her hands – was probably bathing him right now – and so you did whatever it took to keep them happy. If that meant no emojis and a couple of desperate exclamation marks, then so be it.

She pressed send, hoping that the nanny would show mercy and, rather than wait, fire a short, reassuring message back. Ideally it would read: *Lucas enjoyed his supper, is now nice and clean and sleepy. Every now and again he looks at a picture of his mummy and smiles. Not like he's pining for you, but because he loves you.*

Yes, that would be perfect. Why couldn't Maja just do that? Send a message telling her that her baby boy was happy without her, though of course not so happy that he didn't miss her. Why not send that, Maja? And why not send it *right now*.

The woman looked at the clock. Just after seven pm. The office was empty, the city through the windows twinkling in the dark. Usually there'd be at least a few partners, real and aspiring, toiling away, but there was an 'off-site' tomorrow, and they were all having dinner tonight in a spa resort. The woman had chosen to stay behind so that she could get back to Lucas, but the timing also suited her. She needed to meet Granqvist and, since he had insisted on total discretion, an empty office was as good a place as any.

When it came to the sending of desperate texts, August Granqvist had shown far less restraint than the woman had with her babysitter. He had been bombarding her for at least twenty-four hours, hinting that his place in the cabinet was at stake. His financial arrangements, supposedly tidied up and placed in a blind trust when he'd taken ministerial office, were exercising him. The clear implication was that the newspapers had seen something and were about to make trouble. The woman's guess was that he wanted to make hasty amends, yet was also aware that any housekeeping he performed now could itself look suspicious. Politicians always got themselves into these pickles, where not to act risked embarrassing exposure but to act risked an accusation of cover-up. Tonight she would be asked to find some golden path between the rock and the hard place.

A beep. The woman grabbed at the phone. Not the babysitter. Granqvist.

I'm approaching the back entrance. Can you meet me?

Fair enough. The woman understood that it wouldn't look great if a government minister were seen pacing around, waiting to consult his lawyer. Out of hours too. She checked her phone again, kept it with her and went to let him in.

Five minutes later and they were in the managing partner's office – he'd told the woman she could use it to go through her proposed plan of action. She laid it out calmly, eschewing the laptop she normally favoured for such presentations. (It would spook Granqvist if he thought any documents existed.) Instead she relied on a yellow legal pad and a ballpoint pen. Old school.

The plan involved retrospective divestment, with disclosure not required until the end of the tax year. The beauty of it was that it didn't need his signature. The woman could do it for him. Which meant he could look reporters in the eye and say, 'I have nothing to do with the investment decisions conducted on my behalf and executed by my lawyers.' The retrospective element meant they could plausibly imply that Granqvist (or his advisers) had dumped these dodgy investments ages ago and for sound financial reasons, rather than that they'd got rid of them today because they'd suddenly hit the news.

Once she'd explained it and answered the last of his questions, he fell back in his chair and let out an almighty roar, his fist pumping the air, like a football coach whose team has scored an injury-time winner: *YES!*

He took off his jacket, ripped off his tie and reached into his briefcase from where, like a cruise ship magician, he produced a bottle of Bollinger. 'Let's celebrate,' he said, rushing out to the water cooler to bring back two plastic cups.

'I really ought to be getting back to my son,' the woman explained, packing away her papers.

'I insist! You don't know the relief I am feeling right now. And that's all down to you. One glass.'

The woman looked at her watch. If she left now she might be just in time to do Lucas's last bedtime story. And yet this office – the boss's office – was a reminder that August Granqvist was one of the firm's most influential clients. The last thing she needed was him firing off a dissatisfied customer note to the managing partner. 'One glass,' she said.

'Sit, sit,' he said, gesturing at the couch. The transformation from worried, needy client to dominant male had taken no more than a minute. He was now playing the generous host, filling the space of the room with his presence. As she'd feared, he now sat himself alongside, rather than opposite, her.

'So how come they've left you holding the fort, eh? Don't tell me you're not only the firm's most beautiful lawyer, but also the one who runs the show? I wouldn't put it past you. I'll tell Anders: he needs to watch his back!'

The woman laughed and took a deep swig of champagne. Not because she wanted it, but to fulfil her one-glass obligation as quickly as possible. That proved to be a mistake.

'Ooh, she's eager, this one,' Granqvist said, stretching across to top up her glass. 'I can never resist a woman who drinks like a man!'

The woman gestured her refusal, but he wouldn't hear of it. She pulled her glass away just as he began tipping the bottle, but it was too late, Bollinger spilled onto her skirt, foaming and soaking the fabric. She tried to spring to her feet, but his hand got there first, rubbing her thigh as if to wipe away the drink.

'Please, there's no need—' she began, but the touch of her leg had triggered something in him and, in an instant, his face was in hers, his tongue on her lips, licking at her. She recoiled, but as she moved away his hand gripped her thigh and then, less than a second later, it was up between her legs, reaching for her underwear.

All of that had happened in a couple of seconds, no more. The speed of it shocked her, so that she could barely let out a sound. Suddenly, she could hear a noise by the door and she imagined he had somehow kicked it shut, or had thrown off his shoes, ready to press himself on her fully. She closed her eyes, involuntarily scrunching up her face in expectation of the worst.

Which meant she could not explain the yelp she heard, a howl of male pain as Granqvist leapt off her, clutching his eyes. She looked to see that a third person was in the room: Elsa, a senior colleague, clutching a can of pepper spray which she had discharged into Granqvist's face.

'Are you OK?' Elsa was asking, and it took a moment for the woman to understand that she was asking the question of her. She stammered some kind of reply, but Elsa was not listening. She was using the boss's desk phone to call the police. 'I'd like to report a sexual assault,' she was saying. 'No, I am not the victim. I am a witness. Yes. That's right, an eyewitness to a sexual assault. I have the perpetrator right here.'

Only then did the woman see that Granqvist was on the floor, the heel of Elsa's shoe on his neck. With her other hand, she was still holding the pepper spray ready to be fired in the man's face if he dared move so much as a muscle.

Chapter 21

Cape Cod, Massachusetts

'You mean, because you killed him?'

'Oh no. It went wrong long before that.'

Natasha was back on her feet, pacing. She seemed nervous, agitated even. And yet, it was also clear that her current state was only temporary, that it existed on the surface. Underneath, and Maggie had been struck by this the first time they met – even, truth be told, when she'd first seen that viral video clip of Natasha at the senate hearings – there was a steadiness. As if all that she had gone through – the attempted rape, the life-and-death struggle, the killing, the police interrogation and now a public, sexual shaming – as if all that could not shake the core of her, which was solid.

To her surprise, Maggie found herself thinking of the man whose presidential campaign she had joined all those years ago: he'd had that same quality. Voters found it reassuring, soothing even. *Everything's going to shit, the economy's in freefall, the planet's burning up, but this guy seems pretty Zen – and if he's calm, well, maybe I don't need to panic.* Like a captain sounding unfazed on the PA even when the plane was flipping around like a hooked trout. That was a big part of the former president's appeal; it helped get him to the White House. Maybe it would do the same for Natasha Winthrop.

'I should have seen it coming really,' Natasha said. 'In retrospect it's obvious. We agreed a day and a time and he came on a different day and at a different time. I mean, why wouldn't he do that? I'd told him that I wanted to play out a rape scenario, and so he decided to make it a bit more real. I wouldn't be *pretending* to be caught by surprise. I would actually be caught by surprise. Maybe that made it more exciting for him. Or maybe he didn't care, he just wanted my address so he could come and rape me. I don't know.'

'But it meant you weren't prepared.'

'That's right. I hadn't set up any of the cameras or recording equipment. I didn't have anyone there. It was a complete disaster.'

'So how did you know it was him?'

'What?'

'When he finally came into your room. Your study. How could you be sure it wasn't just some random intruder?'

'Oh I see.' She seemed to hesitate for a second. 'I'd seen pictures of him, remember. From the police files. He was wearing a ski mask, but the height, the build, the eyes: it all matched.' She paused again, hovering near the fireplace. 'Funny thing is, now that I think about it, I never doubted it was him. The moment I heard a sound in the house. Of course it was him.'

'And he knew how to get in.'

'Sure. I'd given him instructions, hadn't I?'

'Right. And is there a record of those instructions, including the proposed date and time? Because that would show that he had caught you by surprise.'

'We communicated by Signal. All messages set to "disappear". They evaporate within an hour. Well, they certainly did at my end.'

'But maybe not his.'

'I don't know. No doubt the police will find out soon enough.'

'Though if they had found them, I suspect we'd already know about it. Maybe they're hard to retrieve. But those messages would confirm your story. That you invited him into your home. There'd be no doubt about it.'

'In order to trap him, Maggie. With a view to bringing him to justice.'

'And is there anything that would confirm that that was your plan? Did you mention it to any one?'

Natasha shook her head.

'Why the hell not? Jesus, Natasha, isn't that basic?'

For just a moment, Natasha replied with a look that cut right through Maggie, a glare of pure ice. And then it was gone, as quickly as it had arrived, Natasha's face restored to its previous shape: warm, open, curious. It all took less than a second, so brief Maggie wondered if she had imagined it. But the chill on Maggie's skin lingered, the sense that she had glimpsed something that could not now be unglimpsed.

She pressed on, as if nothing had happened. 'What about the security guys, the ones you were planning to have on standby?'

'I hadn't fixed that up yet. I was going to.'

'OK,' Maggie said, trying to hide her disbelief. Not of Natasha's story, but of her stupidity. She was such a smart woman, why hadn't she taken even those basic precautions? Without any proof of her intention, her plan, this would look like a straightforward, premeditated murder: she had lured a man to her home to kill him.

And yet, Maggie now understood, that was not how she herself saw it. She was furious at Natasha's failure to leave a trail of supporting evidence not because she did not believe her but because she *did*. Almost without noticing it happen, she had accepted Winthrop's account. It rang true. Not least because, crazy as it might sound – and it sounded deranged – there was no other possible explanation for why Natasha Winthrop would have arranged to have a wanted rapist and killer come to her home.

'But it was such a risk,' Maggie said eventually. 'You were taking a huge risk. You knew this man was dangerous. Extremely dangerous. Yet you sought him out. Even if he had come when he was meant to come, and you had some guys hiding in the basement, he posed a direct threat to your life. I just don't—'

'Get it? I know. I can see how it looks. Successful lawyer, huge career in front of her. It must seem lunatic to you, Maggie.'

An image of one of her sister's text shorthands flashed in front of her: NGL. *Not gonna lie.*

'But I had been fixated on all this for so long.'

'On Todd, you mean?'

'No, even before that. On this *problem*. The files in the office. Case after case of rape, reported but no charges, no trial, no conviction. The statistics, Maggie: I'd see them in state after state. Fifteen thousand rapes, one hundred convictions. You can't ignore it. The rape of women has, in effect, been decriminalized. If a crime goes unpunished, to what extent is it still a crime?'

'I'm not sure you can—'

'No, I mean it. If society essentially shrugs its shoulders at a certain act, then it is signalling that it has made a decision. And the decision in our society is that, most of the time, a man is permitted to force a woman to have sex with him. It is tolerated. Like smoking weed at home. Or hitting eighty on the interstate. Technically a crime, but not really. Once conviction rates reach *less than one per cent*, that tells you we've made up our mind. This is no longer a crime. Do this, and ninety-nine times out of a hundred, nothing will happen to you. You'll be fine. You'll get away with it. What man wouldn't play those odds?'

'So you decided to take the law into your own hands?'

'No. The opposite.'

Maggie must have made a quizzical face, because Natasha's response was fierce.

'The *opposite*. I wasn't trying to be some kind of vigilante, Maggie. I didn't set out to kill this dreadful man. That's the last thing I wanted. I wanted to *catch* him, in the commission of a crime, and then bring him to justice. It's very important you understand that, Maggie. Very important to me.' Her clear green eyes, alert and sharp, drilled hard into Maggie's. 'The security men who I had planned to have in attendance would have been there partly to protect me, but mainly to serve as witnesses. I wanted to build a case against this man, who would then face trial and, if convicted, go to jail. That was always the intention.'

Maggie nodded, chastened.

'I messed it up terribly, Maggie, that much is obvious. What I did was very stupid. Maybe it was wrong too. But what I've told you is the truth.'

THURSDAY

Chapter 22

Now, remember, if you're in the neighbourhood, why not stop by? It's real simple, just come on up to Forty-Eighth and Sixth Avenue, around eight o'clock, and the first one hundred folks in line will qualify for the brand new merch that we're giving away—

Merch? You are just so down with the kids, Steve.

What? Oh I get it. Merchandise. Is that better? Katie wants me to say 'merchandise'. But seriously, come on by, and you can have your pick of the merchandise *— is that OK? Prefer it that way?*

I liked merch too. It sounded cool.

Your pick of the merch just released by the president's re-election campaign. T-shirts, bumper stickers, key rings and of course—

Your red baseball caps.

That's right.

They are looking good.

They really are. Lots of top-quality stuff for you, as the campaign to re-elect the president hits its stride. We had our exclusive first look at the new logo on the show on Tuesday, and now, if you're in New York City, why not come by—

Love the new logo.

It's great. So come say hello to us here at Fox & Friends, *Forty-Eighth and Sixth, any time after eight o'clock.*

Brian, what have you got for us?

Lots of breaking news overnight, Katie. The big story coming out of London, England. Or at least from the website that we still think is based there. From that renegade website that leaked so many classified, top-secret documents from the basement of a London embassy, comes a new trove of leaked information about potential presidential candidate Natasha Winthrop—

Sheesh. That one just keeps on giving—

This is just an incredible story. These latest leaks: an exchange of encrypted messages between Winthrop and, get this, Jeffrey Todd. You heard that right: the so-called victim in contact with her alleged attacker, the man she killed in her home just four nights ago. Joining us now in Washington, senior political correspondent, Griff Marsh. Griff?

You better believe it, Steve, Katie, Brian. Bombshell leaks overnight, suggesting dialogue between the dead man and his killer, would-be presidential candidate Natasha Winthrop. You'll remember we talked on the show earlier this week about Winthrop, lead counsel in those crucial hearings in Congress – lot of liberal buzz about her as a potential nominee to challenge the president in the fall.

She claimed to have fended off an intruder, killing him in self-defence. Two days ago, it emerged that she was a habitual user of dating sites – I'm not going to say what kind at this hour of the morning. Lots of families watching. But let's just say Winthrop was a user of extreme and controversial dating sites that cast doubt on

*her original account of what happened. Now, Steve, Katie, Brian —
these leaked messages out of London show Winthrop and Todd were
talking directly to each other. On one occasion, just six days before
the incident, she wrote—*

Let's get that up on screen—

*Here we go. Her words to him. 'I'm not going to tell you which
door will be unlocked. You'll have to work that out for yourself.'*

*His reply: 'You don't need to tell me anything. If I want to get
in, I'll get in.'*

*These are her words again: 'We have to agree on a time. I can't
rule out the risk of being observed or interrupted, unless we fix a
time.'*

Gee, Griff, are we talking about some kind of collusion here?

*Lots of questions to be answered, Brian. Was this some kind of
— and I apologize to families watching — but was this some kind
of sex game that went wrong? Or was Natasha Winthrop luring
Jeffrey Todd to her home on false pretences, if you will? Questions
detectives are going to want answered as the day goes on. Whatever
the answers, it appears Winthrop's initial account was not the whole
truth. Remember police sources telling* Fox & Friends, *Winthrop
first claimed she had* no knowledge *of this man, that this man was a
complete stranger, that this attack came out of the blue. That account
is very hard to square with this latest dump of encrypted messages
between Winthrop and her victim. Steve, Katie, Brian?*

*All right, Griff Marsh there for us in Washington, DC. Welcome
to Thursday, hope you're up, hope you're dressed. Up next: vaping.
Is it racist? That's what students in Portland, Oregon would have
you believe. That story, next.*

Maggie muted the TV and glanced instead at her phone. The story had broken less than an hour ago, and Twitter was already obsessed with little else. Natasha still had some defenders, most of them feminist writers and activists who insisted that Winthrop's sexual interests were her own business — *If edge play is her thing, I could care less* — and that it made no difference whatsoever if she knew her victim. *On the contrary, all this confirms is that this was a rape like most rapes. It's a Hollywood myth, loaded with misogyny, that rape is only 'real' when it's committed by a stranger.* But, Maggie noticed, the retweet rate, once a wave, was now a trickle. Not so many wanted to #StandWithNatasha now.

And what did Maggie herself think? She'd had hours to think about that, including during the long journey back from Cape Cod. Yet when her sister had called her a few minutes ago to ask about arrangements for Thanksgiving and the subject had come up, Maggie had been unable to give a straight answer.

Liz never had any idea who her sister worked for. That was an iron rule for Maggie. Not to protect her clients' confidentiality — fuck that, as Liz would say — but for Liz's sake. And the sake of her children. Whatever danger might come Maggie's way, Liz and the boys were bound to be safer if they knew nothing.

Even so, Liz had been following the Winthrop story, which, in her capacity as an unofficial one-woman public opinion sample, once again confirmed to Maggie that it had cut through: if Liz brought up a topic unprompted, chances were high that that topic was on Middle America's mind. Most of what obsessed DC passed her by. But occasionally, her sister was gripped or outraged or moved by a news event, and that was as reliable as any poll as to what signal was breaking through amid all the noise. It wasn't failsafe, but as a guide to what mattered to purple-state America – those suburban, pragmatic, comfortable-rather-than-affluent Americans who swung elections – Liz supplied high-quality intel.

'So go on. Is she guilty or innocent?'

'What do you think?'

'What do *I* think? Who gives a fuck what I think? I teach computer science in middle school. You're the big-time Washington insider. Go on, Mags. What's the goss?'

'I'm not sure. How does she come across to you? Do you like her?'

'I thought she was a right stuck-up cow at first. That weird accent. Like she was English or something.'

'But?'

'I don't know. I heard her talking about all the people who've been shafted by this president – you know, that clip they keep showing – and she's obviously a fucking brainbox—'

'Definitely.'

'But that's not what I liked. She seemed properly angry about it, do you know what I mean? Not bullshit, politician angry, but like an actual person. That thing about kids who grow up knowing that no matter how hard they work, no matter how good they are, they're never going to be able to get out, never escape – that life is never going to get better.'

'Four walls and bars on the window.'

'Right! That bit. Seriously, I have kids in my class and that's exactly what it's like for them. I mean, *exactly*. The whole

American dream, social mobility crap – these kids would literally stare at you blank in the face if you talked about that to them. It just doesn't compute.'

'Because they don't have—'

'Because if they go to college, they'll have crazy debt for years. And their parents don't have any money. They're spending what they have on doctors' bills or medicine or looking after Grandma. Like she said, "They can't get—"'

'"Their head above water, let alone take a breath."'

They said the line together. Liz didn't hesitate. She knew it word-for-word. Maggie imagined Stuart's reaction to a politician who wasn't the president being quoted by a schoolteacher in suburban Georgia: he'd be beside himself.

'So go on. You must have heard something; you always know what's going on. Did she or didn't she?'

'Did she or didn't she what?'

'Oh, for fuck's sake, Mags. Did she kill him?'

'Yes. No one denies that.'

'You know what I mean! Did she, you know, *deliberately* kill the guy? Like, set out to—'

'Liz, isn't that Callum calling you? Isn't that his voice?'

'You are such a bitch. Just tell me. Was this whole thing—'

'He sounds like he really needs you. Laters, Liz.'

'Proper bitch.'

Maggie looked at the phone again now. Her sister thought she was holding back – whether out of discretion or to wind her sister up – but actually it was much simpler than that. That conversation had confirmed it. In fact it had confirmed two things. Natasha Winthrop had the potential to be the real deal, a once-in-a-generation candidate, and that Maggie Costello did not, in her heart of hearts, know whether or not she was a cold-blooded murderer.

She had gone over their conversation a dozen times in her head, reconstructing the crackling fire, the freshly caught fish, the expensive wine, the warm tiredness in her legs after the run along the shore. She bought the argument Natasha had marshalled: she had been as persuasive about the failings of the criminal justice system when it came to sexual violence as she had been about child poverty. But there was one question that tugged at Maggie and wouldn't let go.

Why him?

OK, so Natasha had become incensed at the way women were repeatedly abused not just by men but by the law. (The less-than-one-per-cent figure was now drilled into Maggie's brain.) She could see how Natasha might have been driven, in despair, to take direct action; not so much taking the law into her own hands as dragging it by its lapels so that it would be forced to see who Todd was and what he had done.

But there were hundreds of men she could have picked. Why this one?

Natasha had said she'd been looking through those files of her colleague, that this case had leapt out. It's true that, if the news reports were right, Todd had been a prolific, vicious rapist. Of course Natasha would have been appalled to read the details of his crimes, and outraged to see that he'd paid no price for committing them.

And yet such outrage would, ultimately, have been abstract, wouldn't it? Of course, Natasha would have been disgusted by the idea that this man could get away with such wickedness. Maggie would have felt the same way. Any woman would. (She thought of Uri and corrected herself: plenty of men too.) But to be so determined that he face justice that Natasha was ready to lure him into her own home, to have security guards on hand: no one would take a risk like that for a purely abstract principle, would they?

No one normal, no. But Natasha Winthrop was not normal, was she? She was exceptional. That much was obvious. The intellect, the charisma, the drive. Maybe a one-in-a-million person like her would do something crazy, inviting a random rapist into her home to bring him to justice. Maggie had come to Washington to work for a truly extraordinary person, the man who had become president what felt like a lifetime ago. She had learned that such men and such women do things that no one else would even—

Her phone vibrated. A news alert from the *Washington Post*.

Breaking: DC lawyer and political rising star Natasha Winthrop arrested for the murder of Jeffrey Todd.

Chapter 23

The killer left a trail. It ended in his own death
By Gabrielle Sanchez, **Washington Post Staff Writer**

He was new in town, a young man working as an apprentice mechanic who made fast friends. He hung out with kids his own age who, unlike him, had stayed on in school. He was invited to their parties. And it was at one of those that a high school student three years his junior lodged a complaint against him, alleging that at a weekend party he had cornered her in a bedroom, pinning her on a bed, and that he had "pressed himself against her". She said that another boy had witnessed the incident, that he had been cheering the young man on, laughing as he did so.

The young man in question was Jeffrey Todd, who would be found dead twenty years later in the home of Washington rising star and putative presidential hopeful, Natasha Winthrop, allegedly killed in the act of attempted rape.

The then principal of the high school in Glasgow, Kentucky, Norma Curley, told the Post *that that second student had denied the girl's account and that Todd's parents had stood steadfastly behind their son, insisting on his innocence. The girl, who could not be reached by the* Washington Post, *eventually withdrew her complaint when it emerged that she had "had a beer" at the party.*

But that episode is only one of several dark memories of Todd offered by friends, family members, employers, lawyers and law enforcement officials in interviews conducted by the Washington Post. *Together they form a picture of a violent, troubled man first charged with rape two decades ago and accused but never convicted of crimes of sexual violence on multiple occasions since. It's a story which has shaken the DC establishment, but also sheds light on the vagaries of the criminal justice system and on a corner of American life blighted by poverty, opioid addiction and neglect.*

The storefronts have been shuttered in Glasgow, Kentucky for so long, the locals have forgotten what they used to be. "I want to say, that was a liquor store," says former warehouse manager, Tanya Frye, pointing at a shop now sealed behind a rusting sheet of perforated metal, itself covered in graffiti tags. "And I'm pretty sure that was the hardware store. Or maybe the video store?" She walks through an area that, she says, has "been like this forever," agreeing with a reporter's suggestion that it could be the set of a post-apocalypse zombie movie. There's a sound of crunching plastic beneath her feet. She looks down to see a discarded syringe. Nearby is a used condom.

It was here, in this town of trailer parks, food stamps and broken windows—that statistics record as one of the poorest in America— that Todd got his first job after his apprenticeship sputtered into failure. He became a packer at the warehouse. "He was shifting

TO KILL A MAN

stock, simple as that," says Frye. "Straight out of high school, strong, willing to work. He was OK."

Todd had only been doing the job six weeks, when a female employee approached Frye. "She asked to speak to me privately in the office. She closed the door and said, 'Jeffrey raped me.'" The employee, who did not respond to the Post's requests for comment, said that Todd had forced her into a sexual act in his car, parked in a deserted lot nearby. "She went to the police. She had DNA evidence, if you know what I mean."

Todd insisted that any sexual intimacy between them had been consensual. The pair had been seen earlier that evening at Rumors, the local bar, playing pool, and that had been enough to cast doubt on her story. The District Attorney for the area decided not to prosecute. In a written statement to the Post, the DA's office said: "While it is not our policy to speak about individual cases, especially when many years have passed, we would stress that resources are finite. Our duty to the people of Kentucky is to ensure their tax dollars are not wasted pursuing action that, in our professional judgment, would be extremely unlikely to end in conviction."

So began a pattern for Todd, who drifted from job to job—bartender, taxi driver, hospital orderly, school janitor—across Kentucky, Tennessee, Missouri and Oklahoma. The Washington Post has discovered that on at least half a dozen occasions, Todd was the subject of rape allegations that never reached a courtroom, usually on grounds of insufficient evidence. Law enforcement sources have told the Post that they believe that there may be many more.

In one case, prosecutors believed they had sufficient evidence. Four years ago, Todd was tried in Tulsa for the sexual assault and battery *of Juanita Bock. The DNA evidence was conclusive, and Todd's lawyers conceded that he and Bock had had sexual intercourse. In testimony, Todd did not deny that he had pinned Bock down during sex or that he had gripped her by the throat, leaving dark bruising around her neck, or that he had penetrated her using a series of objects.*

But, they argued, this had all been done with Bock's consent. Critical for his case was that Bock had waited nearly a week before reporting the attack and that she had sent him text messages a few days after the incident which made no mention of it.

Maggie skimmed through the next few paragraphs, which gave more details of Todd's chequered employment history, including how he had been fired repeatedly for aggressive or unacceptable behaviour. There was a reference to the death of his parents a few years earlier, but that was not what she was looking for. It came a sentence later.

A turning point occurred nearly a year ago, when a twenty-nine-year-old legal secretary was found dead in Bowling Green, Kentucky. The post-mortem examination confirmed that she had been the victim of a violent sexual assault, with asphyxiation given as the cause of death. The DNA evidence left no doubt: it matched perfectly DNA samples associated with a man who had been held in police custody many times before, repeatedly accused of sexual violence. Detectives were certain: the killer was Jeffrey Todd.

An immediate warrant for his arrest was issued, his details circulated among police departments in five states and eventually nationwide. "We thought it would be easy, that we'd pick him up in a day or two," said Detective Mike Crump, who worked the case. But Todd had gone to ground. The last known sighting was on the very day the dead woman was reported missing. "Seems Todd understood that this time we had him, that he wouldn't get away with this one," said Crump. "His only option was to go on the run."

He evaded local police, he evaded the FBI. Jeffrey Todd seemed to have vanished into thin air until last Sunday, when he was found dead on the floor in the home of Natasha Winthrop.

Without thinking, Maggie moved her cursor over that last line and highlighted it. She then put the pen she'd been holding – she'd never mastered the art of reading without a pen in her hand – back between her lips. She was desperate for a smoke, but didn't want to break the moment of concentration. Wisps of thought were forming and she feared they might slip away.

No one else had been able to find Todd, not even the FBI. Yet somehow Natasha had drawn him out, into the daylight. How had she done it?

Or had she not done it at all? Natasha thought she had entrapped Todd, but what if that was only how it was meant to look? What if Todd had been placed right in front of her, allowing her to believe she was reeling him in when, in reality, it was she who had been trapped – duped into making contact with a killer who would not be caught, but would kill again? Or was the trick even more devious, a plot hatched by someone who either wanted Natasha to be killed or to kill in an act of self-defence they knew could be made to look like murder? Who was the cat here, and who was the mouse?

Chapter 24

Washington, DC

Natasha had warned her. As she had handed Maggie her keys, along with a set of entry codes and computer passwords, she had warned that there was no time when the office of a top law firm was guaranteed to be empty.

'It's a bit of a macho thing,' she had said. 'Lawyers like to show off their stamina. You head home at one am and someone will ask why you're having an early night.'

Which meant that as Maggie punched in the numbers, using the same underground entrance she had used three nights ago, she had no idea if she would be able to work discreetly and alone, or whether she'd have someone over her shoulder. Maggie had asked Natasha if she trusted her colleagues. The answer had not been wholly reassuring: 'I think so.'

The elevator had arrived at the third floor. As the doors opened, the reception area was in darkness. Maggie stepped forward, a motion that was sufficient to activate the lights. It illuminated the open-plan office, which revealed itself as unoccupied: just the odd peeping light of computers on standby and laptops on charge.

Maggie headed to Natasha's office; the door was unlocked. She pushed it open and waited for the automatic lights to come on. A second later, she remembered that Natasha had mentioned that too. 'I'm afraid I disabled the automatic lights thing: just couldn't *bear* that awful fluorescent glare.'

So Maggie pawed her way across the desk, reaching for the light, a beautiful, vintage Anglepoise lamp whose switch required physical effort, which it rewarded with a satisfying clunk. Once it came on, Maggie recalled the surprise, and slight pleasure, she had felt when she walked in for that first meeting with Natasha. She had been expecting a neat, even paper-free wooden surface, cleared and sorted, confirming that Natasha Winthrop had reached the summit of the legal profession before the age of forty because she had an orderly, rational and disciplined mind.

Instead, Maggie had seen – and saw again now – piles and piles of paper. Letters, envelopes, newspapers, leaflets, pamphlets, transcripts, bills, bank statements, handwritten memos, notebooks, photographs, instruction manuals, brochures and several high-end fashion magazines. The piles themselves were quite neat, squared-off and of even height, in a semblance of order as if – and here Maggie might have been projecting from the state of her own desk – in readiness for the big clear-out to come. Natasha's office was a garden that had overgrown, but one in which each clump of tall grass, thick nettles and strangling weeds was neatly fenced in: overgrown, but not out of control.

Natasha's instructions had been clear on one key point. Maggie was not to remove, alter or delete anything that she found, no matter how incriminating. '*Especially* if it's incriminating,' Natasha had said. The last thing she needed was any suggestion that she had removed or destroyed evidence.

Instead, Maggie's brief was to rummage through Natasha's past looking for enemies. She was to see if there was anyone with sufficient animus – a bitter ex-client, say, or an adversary she had successfully sued or put behind bars – who might plausibly have set out to make a bad situation for Natasha Winthrop infinitely worse, by finding and leaking those internet browsing histories, for example. Or even, and this was in Maggie's mind rather than Natasha's, to look for a foe so hostile they might have set up the entire thing – enticing Winthrop to kill, or be killed, by dangling the mouse of Jeffrey Todd in front of her.

The police would work their way through this material eventually. Indeed, they had wanted to do it right away. But Natasha had ensured Maggie had a clear run at it first. For the second time, Winthrop had fended off the DC Police by invoking attorney-client privilege: she couldn't possibly allow detectives to look at confidential or commercially sensitive documents, at least not before she or one of her colleagues had had a chance to go carefully through each one. Maggie was to consider this initial examination the first stage of that process.

Natasha had given her few pointers, save that the computer contained almost everything that mattered. Despite that guidance, or perhaps because of it, Maggie decided to look at the papers first. She wanted to rifle through them, just to see what was there.

The first pile yielded an invitation to address a women's organization in Pittsburgh. A letter from a client questioning a bill. A clipped article from the *New York Review of Books*. A memo from an assistant who had worked on the Congressional hearings just completed. *I've gone through the proceedings of the Church committee and can see no applicable precedent. There might be a discussion in the Iran–Contra bundle. I'll keep you posted.*

There was a handwritten note from a colleague, asking her further advice on that 'personnel matter we discussed'. A cable TV bill. The programme for a literary festival at Hilton Head, North Carolina: Maggie flicked through it to see that Natasha Winthrop was a listed speaker, down to interview a Nigerian novelist who had become a sensation.

Now she would go for spot checks, cutting into the pile at random points, telling herself that if she did that three times and each time landed upon an item of no consequence then she would declare the papers clean and move on to the digital files.

First came a birthday card. Maggie's eye went to the signature and saw that it was not from a friend or relative but 'Simon B and the Hyde Brothers team'. Maggie pulled out her phone, consulting Google to establish that Hyde Brothers was a private bank based in Boston. Confirmation of what Maggie already knew: Natasha was properly loaded.

Next Maggie went to a new stack, so far undisturbed, taking hold of almost all of it to see what lay close to the bottom. An invitation, amateurishly produced, for what appeared to be a reunion, nearly a year earlier. Not for high school or college, but for the New York District Attorney's office where Natasha had started out. The image on the front showed a blindfolded Lady Justice with scales in one hand and a martini in the other. On the back was scrawled the message, *Where it all began! See you there, I hope. F x.* The DA's office had been Natasha's first real job, after Harvard Law School and that spell clerking for the most distinguished liberal justice on the Supreme Court.

Maggie put the pile back and, as arbitrarily as she could, scythed into one last pile, the one to the right of the keyboard of Natasha's computer. She made a pact with herself. If whatever documents she came to were innocuous, she would consider this part of the exercise complete. What she found was a playbill for a production of *Turandot* at the Kennedy Center.

All right, time to turn on the machine. She typed in the password Natasha had given her – 'Pilgrim' plus a year with a couple of added symbols – and watched as the screen filled up with various folders. With a sigh, Maggie realized that here too she would not be able to read everything, but would have to dip and skim, hoping that if there was a clue to be found, she would find it.

She looked closely at the electronic folders, scanning the names. Some were labelled by case, some by client, a couple for charities on whose boards Natasha had served. She clicked first on the one that related to those House hearings that had made Winthrop's name and electrified the nation. It was a Russian doll, giving birth instantly to a dozen other folders, which themselves contained dozens more. These documents were mostly labelled by witness, including several names that had become fleetingly famous following their day in the Capitol Hill klieg lights, their hours of cross-examination forming the subject of intense cable chatter and even late-night satirical comedy. Maggie saw letters and memoranda that had been projected on screen in the hearing room, as well as briefing notes passed between Natasha and her team, charting in granular detail how best to elicit the facts from this or that witness. Maggie was fascinated by one graphic so complicated, it looked like a diagram setting out a theorem of higher mathematics. Only when she zoomed in could she see that it was, in fact, a flow chart, or rather a decision tree, setting out all the possible responses the witness might offer, and how Natasha should respond to each eventuality. The TV audience had marvelled at Winthrop's suppleness and agility as an interrogator, her calm unflappability. Now Maggie understood that that was the fruit, yes, of a keen intellect but also the most meticulous preparation. For all her aristocratic demeanour, Winthrop was no breezy dilettante. She worked.

Maggie packed the Russian dolls back together and went elsewhere, reasoning that the congressional story had played out so publicly, pored over in forensic detail by journalists, rival politicians and indeed lawyers, that there was little Maggie was going to discover in a few hours of skim-reading that wasn't already known.

Besides, there was a more fundamental matter of logic. Maggie was searching for those who might have set out to frame or entrap Natasha Winthrop. It struck her now that such people would surely have sought to act *before* Natasha could damage their cause, rather than afterwards. The only possible motive of anyone involved in the recent clashes on Capitol Hill would be revenge, punishing Winthrop for what she had already done. In Maggie's experience, that was not how such people operated. They preferred to remove a threat before that threat materialized, not once it had. If those people, whoever they were, wanted vengeance, they would surely have waited longer than a couple of weeks, and their methods, when they struck, would have been more direct.

So Maggie followed her intuition and looked around. There was a folder that related to pro-bono work, including for a group that promoted free expression. Natasha had petitioned several foreign governments over journalists jailed for doing their jobs. Maggie scribbled a few names, making a note to herself that she should check if the governments in question had ever been linked to the deaths of dissidents exiled abroad. If they didn't take out troublemakers, it was unlikely they'd take out troublemakers' lawyers.

Another folder was labelled 'Gerry'. Maggie half-formed an image of this Gerry, picturing a South Boston mafioso presiding over a family of Irish mobsters. Could that be it? Had Natasha been a lawyer to the mob? Then she clicked the file open to see dozens of electoral rolls, voting tables and large-scale maps, detailing congressional districts down to the tiniest ward. Maggie had to smile: Winthrop had been a lead member of the legal team that had sued several states over the biased drawing of electoral boundaries, also known as gerrymandering. 'Gerry' was Natasha's little joke.

Maggie kept going like that for hours, speed-reading her way through the Winthrop caseload for the last decade, seeing how Natasha had moved up through the gears, how city cases had become state and eventually national cases, how by her early thirties she had graduated to fighting fossil-fuel companies over pollution and confronting federal agencies for failing to enforce environmental standards. The Guantanamo folder was bleak, as Maggie waded through the correspondence that had under-pinned the case Natasha had made before the Supreme Court, arguing that men accused of admittedly heinous terrorist crimes had faced treatment so inhuman it amounted to 'cruel and unu-sual punishment'.

Could a former guard at the Guantanamo base have wanted to silence Natasha for her role in bringing those abuses to light? Again, Maggie didn't think so. Not least because Natasha's target had always been the US government, rather than any one indi-vidual.

More harrowing was the folder packed with testimonies of migrant children and their parents, separated at the southern border and held in detention centres. Natasha had bombarded the US Immigration and Customs Enforcement Agency, or ICE, with scores of letters, complaining about the family separation policy in general and the mistreatment of named children in particular. Natasha was one of the few lawyers who had been inside those godforsaken places, seeing children sleeping on concrete floors, toddlers denied basic washing facilities, babies sitting in soiled diapers, separated from their mothers and fathers with only other children to care for them. One letter described children in such a state of shock, 'they no longer know how to cry.'

Maggie read through a blizzard of emails between Natasha, her assistants and civil rights organizations, the Red Cross, the TV networks, the newspapers – anyone who might help those children or at least publicize their plight. Most heart-breaking were the letters back and forth between Natasha's office and the various, disconnected parts of the federal bureaucracy as she tried to reunite children, many of whom didn't speak at all, let alone speak English, with parents who had no idea where their children had been taken.

Underneath the civil language of these letters was Natasha's cold fury that officials of the US government had broken up families without keeping clear records of who was being sent where and who belonged to who. Maggie found herself reading the story of one woman who'd gone to pick up her little girl, only to be told a man had already collected the child, claiming to be her father. 'Physical and sexual abuse of these children is not merely possible,' Natasha had written in a submission to a Texas judge, 'it is probable.'

The picture of Natasha Winthrop's professional life was becoming clearer, and there was just a little corner of Maggie's mind – the part that had fought alongside, and been tutored by, Stuart Goldstein in a presidential campaign – that couldn't help but marvel at what she saw. If they could somehow get through this current . . . stuff, Natasha Winthrop would make a truly phenomenal candidate. Maggie could almost hear Goldstein's voice: *You're telling me this woman has defended little kids, fought for small towns whose drinking water was polluted, freed brave dissidents thrown into jail by evil dictators and graduated top of her class from Harvard and looks like a movie star? You gotta be kidding me. She's like a sexy Mother Theresa. Come on, Maggie, where's the catch?*

The catch, Stuart, is that she also went on kinky bondage sites, deliberately lured a man to her home and clubbed him to death. *So you're telling me she might have some baggage.*

Maggie smiled at the sound of his voice, even if it was only in her own head. Christ, she missed Stuart.

She continued in this same vein as she clicked on the rest of the on-screen files, still looking for a past act or stance or client that might serve as the explanatory motive in a plot to bring down Natasha Winthrop, but now with one barely admitted eye on the lookout for material that could work as backstory in a campaign to put Winthrop in the White House.

Maggie did not spell it out even in her own head, so it remained a thought bubbling below the surface. But as the hours went by, as she tapped and clicked at that computer, surrounded by documents – some on her lap, some arranged on the floor, some on screen – she understood that she didn't merely want to fulfil her promise to help Natasha Winthrop out of a hole. She wanted to give her a shot. Natasha might blow it; she might turn out to be a dud. God knew, that happened often enough. But if she were to have so much as a chance, she would have to clear her name – and with the deadline for presidential nominations just five days away, she would have to do it now.

Maggie came to a file labelled only 'Judith'. She clicked on that, but for the first time it demanded its own password. She tried using one of the several that Natasha had given her, but none worked. After the third failed attempt, a message popped up telling her that she would be barred from access to that document for one hour.

Judith. Was there another layer to the enigma of Natasha

Winthrop? Did this folder contain a cache of letters and notes – photographs? – relating to a past relationship with a woman? Maggie thought back to those pictures of Natasha stepping out at various Washington events, usually with a man on her arm. She thought of that day at Cape Cod, the long chat they had into the night: there had been no mention of a man. Was she hiding something about herself, pretending to be somebody she wasn't? It seemed so unlikely. Except here was a file labelled 'Judith', kept under password-encrypted lock and key. Maggie would come back to it.

Finally, she came to a file whose label she could not read. She squinted at the screen to see that the label was not in English but in the Cyrillic alphabet. She clicked it open and watched as it disgorged its contents, the screen filling with several dozen files. One was labelled with the single word, 'Remember'. Maggie clicked on it, to reveal that it contained a single email. The subject line was also 'Remember'. The recipient was Natasha Winthrop, and the sender was . . . Natasha Winthrop, though sent from a different, personal email address. It was only one sentence long:

You may know a lot, but you won't know everything.

Maggie read that over several times. It sounded like advice Natasha had given to herself, or even the kind of aphorism a less stylish type than Natasha might have embroidered, framed and hung on the wall. It would be suitably platitudinous guidance to fit any office, and yet Natasha did not have it where it could be seen daily, but only in this one file. Was this a memo-to-self, or was this perhaps a record of advice supplied by a specific client? Was it, in fact, a warning?

Now Maggie plunged in, browsing through the documents held within. They were a mixture of English and Russian, with two or three names recurring several times. One ran to several thousand pages, dense with the language of commercial contracts: all warranties, disclaimers, limitations on liability, confidentiality clauses, indemnification clauses, arbitration clauses. She tried to cut through the detail, to ascertain the most basic facts of the arrangement she was reading about. But it was impossible. She couldn't even be sure who the main parties were to this agreement. The text seemed to have been constructed by piling opaque layer upon opaque layer, each one thick not only with corporate legalese but deliberate obfuscation.

Orbiting around that text, like moons around a planet, were a clutch of others which Maggie eventually deciphered as company registration documents, locating various blandly named corporate structures in Cyprus, the British Virgin Islands, Panama and the Cayman Islands. She studied a few at random, looking for the name of an owner. Except there was no human name to be found. Instead a company registered in, say, Cyprus would give as its owners the name of two further companies, or 'LLPs', who themselves would be registered in, say, Bermuda and Belize. Finding the parents of those companies would lead to yet more mysterious corporate entities, registered in ever more exotic locations. Finding these companies was, it seemed to Maggie, like playing a childhood game of pass the parcel: each time you thought you had reached the end, you realized you had just come upon yet another layer of wrapping. The item you sought remained concealed, perhaps infinitely.

Maggie went back to that first file she had opened, with its word of warning.

You may know a lot, but you won't know everything.

Right now, Maggie thought to herself, she knew nothing at all.

In frustration, she opened a half-dozen other folders – one of which contained screenshots of messages, again in Russian, sent via ProtonMail, which Maggie knew operated out of Geneva and promised maximum end-to-end encryption – saw that they contained more of the same, then promptly closed them again. There was no way she was going to make sense of this, and certainly not in a rushed few minutes.

Finally she clicked on a file which stood out from the others because it was a JPEG, rather than a PDF or Word document. It opened up to display a photograph of a piece of paper. The picture was not casual, but carefully taken, in the style of a museum catalogue displaying a rare papyrus. In fact, as Maggie zoomed in on the image, she saw that this was not a piece of paper at all but something thicker. Words had been handwritten in solid black ink onto the white cotton of a restaurant napkin.

They were in Russian. There was a sentence, and underneath it what Maggie assumed were two signatures.

She pulled out her phone, clicked on the Google Translate app and held up the camera lens to the screen. The words wobbled and hovered for a bit, until eventually the device got a fix on them, sufficient to convert them into type. The app generated a rough, instant translation, so that magically it was an English sentence that now seemed to float on the napkin:

We agree that we own the mine and all its profits together, half each.

Was that it? Was that what all these thousands of pages of contractual minutiae boiled down to? Maggie imagined how it might have worked. Two oligarchs shaking hands over dinner, agreeing to do the deal right there and then, one of them pulling out a fat fountain pen to inscribe their agreement in cloth then handing it to lawyers in London, New York, Brussels and Washington, to turn it into a formal contract.

Was that how Natasha fitted in? Was she the Washington end of this international legal operation, doing her bit to hide the true ownership of, say, a zinc mine in Kazakhstan, wrapping it up inside a maze of shell companies and fictitious brass-plate firms in assorted island jurisdictions, the better to ensure not a cent was paid in tax?

The very thought was enough to fill Maggie with gloom. The notion of foreign, and especially Russian, influence on the US electoral process had been a battleground since the last campaign. The frontrunner, Tom Harrison, had already had to deny 'links' with Moscow, not that that had cooled the more fevered corners of progressive Twitter. They were still hot with claims that Harrison was the next handcrafted puppet of the Kremlin. According to this theory, the Russians were engaged in a classic bet-hedging exercise. Given their role in the last election, they already had the incumbent president. If his opponent in November was Harrison, then they couldn't lose. It would be puppet versus puppet, with Moscow the certain winner.

Maggie didn't buy any of that. Harrison's defects were glaring, even before he'd added to them with that creepy shoulder-squeeze-and-whisper move the other day. But there was no compelling, as opposed to flaky, evidence that he was some bought asset of the Kremlin. His record in the senate suggested he was anything but.

Still, the mere raising of the suggestion had done its work. His opponents, starting with the president, had thrown some mud and now a vague smell of it stuck. Washington was brutal like that. 'Pig-fucking' had been Stuart's shorthand for it, in memory of the legend of Lyndon Johnson, in one of his first campaigns, deciding to spread a rumour that his opponent enjoyed inter-course with pigs. His campaign manager said, 'But Lyndon, you know he doesn't do that.' To which Johnson had replied, 'Sure, I know. I just want to make him deny it.'

It was partly all this Russia talk that had fuelled Natasha Winthrop's little boomlet. She was a cleanskin, untainted by Beltway grime. If it now turned out that she had served as a consigliere to the Moscow mob, helping in what was a glorified money-laundering scheme, her electoral appeal – presuming any could be salvaged from this Todd nightmare – would be gone. She would be 'as bad as all the rest', the verdict terminal to any insurgent candidate.

Or was Maggie reading this all wrong? Did Natasha have all these documents because she was building a case against the rapaciousness of the men whose signatures were etched on the luxurious cotton of that napkin? Had she been hired by one of those NGOs that campaign for the rights of indigenous people swept out of the way by a big plant or a deep mine that destroyed the place they had called home for centuries, cutting down the ancient forest that had given them shelter or poisoning the lake that had quenched their thirst? Maggie pictured Natasha in dirty jeans and heavy boots, a film of sweat on her forehead, as she surveyed a blighted landscape, filling a notebook with the testimony of those Kazakh villagers, lamenting that their land had been despoiled and their groundwater contaminated by the arrival of a foul, polluting mine.

The trouble was, Maggie couldn't be sure. Was Natasha working with the men who had scribbled their names on that napkin, or working against them? If the former, were those men drawn from that subset of oligarchs who constituted an unofficial and dispersed opposition to the man in the Kremlin, funding dissident groups and anti-government websites, willing on the day when he would, at long last, be ejected from power? If they were, then that would explain the convoluted, arcane financial arrangements that filled the electronic folders on Natasha's computer screen: they were hiding their assets not from the international taxman, but from the long, greedy arm of the Russian state and its latter-day czar.

Or were the two dealmakers? So casual with their vast fortunes that they were happy to record a multi-billion-dollar deal on a piece of table linen; faithful allies of the Russian leader, acting as his de facto envoys to the wider world, protecting his interests and even – or so rumour had it – stashing his billions outside the country, whether in bank vaults in Zürich or luxury penthouses in Knightsbridge, ready for the day when he would need them? Plenty of the Russian super-rich performed that function. They were seen as independent men of standing in their new, adopted cities – funding a science lab in London, endowing an orchestra in New York – but in reality they were mere bagmen for the boss, able to function only until the day he withdrew his patronage.

As Maggie stared at that high-resolution image on the screen, preserving a handwritten contract as if it were a fragment of the gospels, she felt sure that, somehow, it contained the answer to the riddle that currently confronted her. If someone was indeed working to damage or derail Natasha Winthrop, the explanation surely lay here. It would hinge on the answer to the question posed by the contents of these files, but which Maggie could not yet resolve. Was Natasha the scourge of these Moscow oligarchs – or their servant?

Chapter 25

Moscow, Russia, three days earlier

One woman looked to another with a signal that consisted of nothing more than a glance in the man's direction and back again. That sent word – silent word – around the club, spoken out loud only in the changing area. 'He's in again.'

The women all knew who that meant, though the clientele at The Landing Strip included no shortage of low-lifes. Nor did the man owe his notoriety to his wealth. Plenty of oligarchs, mini-oligarchs and their well-rewarded henchmen came to this place on Prospekt Mira, handily distant from the city centre.

It was not an anonymous venue; it was not even discreet. But it was less conspicuous than some of the alternatives. Partly because it had few international customers, it was assumed that – unlike most of the sex clubs in the city, and certainly the suite of every five-star hotel – not every corner in The Landing Strip was monitored by hidden cameras. Moscow's gangster class felt unwatched, and therefore relatively relaxed, here. That was certainly true of this man.

The woman approached to take his drinks order. This was an act of self-sacrifice on her part. She'd been here longer than the other 'girls', who she regarded as too young to put in the firing line. (One, who had started only last week, claimed to be seventeen, but the woman was ready to stake a night's tips that the girl wasn't a day older than fifteen. If the man got her in his sights, there'd be no stopping him.)

She appeared at his table. She put her head up, shoulders back and her chest out, smiling her friendliest smile – safe in the knowledge that he wouldn't notice her cold, laser stare. He wouldn't be looking at her eyes.

The man was on his own, as always. Bald head, brown leather jacket, black polo neck, as always. Bottle of Johnnie Walker Black Label, as always. He tucked a hundred-dollar bill into the woman's garter, fingers lingering on the skin of her inner thigh, as always. He was sending a message: *The big shot has arrived, he has money in his pocket so he can do whatever he wants.* As always.

The woman remembered her first encounter with him. At the time, she had been glad that the man had picked her out. He was clearly loaded. And there were none of the usual warning signs: no slavering, no pawing. In fact, the man had barely seemed interested. While she performed on the stage, he had been looking at his phone.

Even when she gave him a private dance, grinding up against him, the man showed no obvious signs of being aroused. He did not breathe heavily, he did not have to adjust himself in his seat.

When he asked to have another dance in a booth, it had come as a surprise.

The man had chosen the end booth, furthest away from the bar and the stage. That was a clue, if only she had been looking out for it. But the woman's mind had been elsewhere, chiefly on the extra cash she hoped to earn.

Once in the privacy of the booth, inches away from him, she'd intensified her routine, making it slower and, somehow, more serious. As she turned and moved, showing herself to him, she remained focused on the hard currency that would soon be hers, calculating upwards from the hundred dollars he had handed her just for serving him a drink. In a moment she would unleash her signature move, one that had always paid dividends.

But she never got that far. Instead, and with no build-up or warning, he placed his hand on the top of her head and pressed down hard, as if plunging the detonator that would demolish a tall building. He stopped once he had her mouth level with his groin.

In itself that was not an unfamiliar ploy. Men often tried it and the woman had a ready response. She ducked her head out from under his hand, aiming to get back upright where she would do her finger-wagging number: incorporating the gesture into her routine, but also leaving no doubt she meant it. Done right, it usually had the desired effect, signalling to the client that he needed to back off, without humiliating him. That was one thing this woman, and all the 'girls', knew: don't ever make a guy feel small. Don't belittle or emasculate him. Because that's when he'll get nasty.

The woman had her plan but, once again, she didn't get the chance to execute it. No sooner had she got her head out from under the palm of his hand than the man connected with it again, pressing it so hard, he forced her fully onto the ground. This time he was leaving nothing to chance, gripping her skull so there was no chance of escape. He kept pressing until her cheek was on the floor.

Now he came off the banquette and, with his right hand still a vice around her head, reached for his zip with his left. When she resisted, he released his right hand for just long enough to slap her across the face, so hard she wondered if her cheek was bleeding, and then resumed his grip. After that, she did what he wanted her to do, just to make it stop.

When it was over, the woman hid herself. Cowering in the toilet, feeling the red sting of her face, she talked to the other women through the door of the stall. She didn't want to come out. She told them what had happened, warned them to stay away from him. It was nearly dawn before she dared open the door.

Later the woman talked to the woman who ran things day to day, asking that she report the man to the police. But when she gave a description of the man, the boss shook her head and her eyes hardened. 'Not this one,' she said. 'No, no, no. Not this one.'

He was too rich and too powerful. That was what she had said. 'Besides, he has the police in his pocket. We report him, *we* get in trouble. That's how it works. Sorry.' And she passed the woman a tube of cream for her face.

And that had been the end of it. He came back to the club less than a week later. The woman avoided him, but over the weeks and months that followed she realized she needn't have bothered. He didn't remember her face or the face of any of the women here, including those he had assaulted.

All the 'girls' were under strict instruction from each other, the wisdom handed down from the veterans – those that had been dancing at The Landing Strip for months rather than weeks – to the new recruits. With this man, no private dances, if you can avoid it. Never in the corner booth, if you can avoid it. No extras, if you can avoid it. And if you can't avoid it – if he forces you – don't resist. Because if you kick or scratch or punch him, then he will remember you and he will have his revenge. You've seen the picture of that girl, the one on the pinboard up by the lavatories? You know what happened to her, poor thing. May she rest in peace.

'Can I get some service?'

The woman turned around to see a new customer had arrived at a table near the performing area. The woman had been so focused on the man, she hadn't seen this one come in.

'Of course,' the woman said and took a step nearer.

Only now, no longer blinded by the spotlight aimed at the stage, could she confirm that this new arrival was a woman. Such things were not unheard of, but they weren't exactly encouraged either. The management were quite happy to have two girls simulating it on stage. But as a paying customer? That was more awkward.

The new arrival ordered a vodka and tonic, no lime, no ice. She then asked the woman to join her at her table.

The woman smiled and was beginning to explain that it was

not that kind of place when the customer took her wrist and said quietly, 'I want to talk to you about him,' and with the subtlest tilt of her head indicated the man drinking Johnnie Walker, his face alight with the glow of his phone.

Involuntarily, the woman's eyes darted left and right, checking that no one was watching. To be on the safe side, she relaxed her face into one that suggested a meaningless, ordinary customer transaction. She didn't want her brow to furrow, lest it convey either curiosity or fear, anything that might catch the man's attention. As subtly as she could, she withdrew her arm from the customer's touch, pretending to reach for her own hair.

The customer read her accurately. 'Don't be frightened. This is a trip down memory lane for me. I used to work here myself. More than ten years ago now.'

The woman struggled to believe it. The customer was dressed like a doctor or university professor; maybe a businesswoman.

'I was a student. I had bills to pay. Like you.' She paused. 'So.' Another tilt of the head in his direction. 'Is he still trouble?'

The woman gave a tight smile and a quick nod, an expression that from a distance would look like nothing more than confirmation of a drinks order.

The customer reached towards her again and, just as the woman was about to pull back, the customer placed something in her hand. She did it the way the woman's grandmother used to give her a coin on her birthday, furtively pushing it into her palm: their little secret. She didn't look down, but, through touch alone, the woman could tell she had just been handed a necklace, with a heavy, oval pendant.

'Make sure whoever's "dancing" for him in one of the booths wears this. Then, if anything happens, you call me. OK?'

The woman did not move, so the woman said it again. 'OK?'

Another nod, prompting the customer to give a wide smile of her own. 'Now about that vodka.' From nowhere, she produced a fifty-dollar bill and handed it over. When she saw the woman stash it away, the customer said – in a voice that was friendly but firm – 'In my day, we used to check the bills. To make sure we weren't getting stiffed.'

The woman did as she was told, holding it up to the light. Only then did she see that there was a phone number written on it, in faint pencil strokes. Hurriedly, she put it back, making a mental note to keep it separate from the others.

She went to the bar to retrieve the vodka and tonic, scanning the performance area. She could see that the man was paying attention now, off his phone and staring at the new recruit as she bent and turned her teenage body before him.

The woman wondered if she was meant to do it right now, somehow getting the necklace around the girl's neck this very moment. She looked towards the customer, seeking guidance. But the space where she had been sitting was now empty. She had gone, as silently and as invisibly as she had arrived.

Chapter 26

Maggie stood up, stretched, then worked her fingers, like a pianist after a strenuous performance. She had been at this keyboard in Natasha Winthrop's office for three hours straight, failing so much as to nod at best ergonomic practice. If she had been the type to exercise, pounding along the trails at Rock Creek Park or lifting weights with Dom, the go-to personal trainer among Washington women of her demographic – his client list bulging with journalists, lobbyists and State Department high-ups – now would be the moment to do it. But she couldn't be bothered with any of it: not the Lycra tops and yoga pants, not the little white pods in the ears, not the mind-bending tedium of 'Guess how many steps I did today?' *Oh, that's hard. Let me guess: I couldn't give a flying fuck.* No, as far as Maggie Costello was concerned, she had made her concession to health and fitness. She had given up the fags. Several times, in fact. Surely that was enough?

She went over to the window, thinking she could murder a

cigarette right now. She could see the lights of the convenience store on the corner opposite: it would only take five minutes. And with Uri away, there'd be no lecture about her health.

No, she would not succumb. Instead she would force herself to think through what she had seen in her online exploration of the life of Natasha Winthrop. She had been searching for anything that might explain the events of the last few days – or, if there were no hidden explanation, if Winthrop's account were the beginning and end of it, then who it was that was actively seeking to maximize her pain, not least via the contents of that package postmarked Langley, Virginia. To answer that, Maggie needed to know all she could about the woman who had hired her.

To that end, she had put aside Natasha's files and folders and taken to the internet, working backwards. She re-read the profiles that had rapidly appeared once Natasha had become the stand-out performer in the House hearings: *Washington Post* style section, *Vanity Fair*, *Esquire* and an especially glowing number from the *Boston Globe*. They offered the same outline of the résumé, retold some of the same anecdotes, quoted some of the same friends.

Then she worked her way through every mention she could find before the hearings, reports of cases Natasha had fought, statements delivered on the steps of the Supreme Court, the odd scholarly article in a legal journal or paper presented at a conference. So far, so familiar.

When she went further back, the supply began to dry. She could find only four references to Winthrop's first job, as a criminal prosecutor in New York. Twice she was merely name-checked in a court report of a murder trial; the third included a quotation from her closing argument in an armed robbery case. 'The accused showed a callous, wanton disregard for the value of human life. He poses a threat to every last one of us.' The last announced that this period in Natasha's career was over: an item on a website for the legal profession, noting that Winthrop was leaving the office of the District Attorney and entering private practice.

What was left was a gazetted note of her appointment to a highly prized clerkship at the Supreme Court and assorted bits from her time at Harvard. A story in the *Crimson*, reporting her election to the editorship of the *Law Review*, and a couple of academic articles in that journal where her name had appeared, either alone or with a co-author. (Maggie skim-read those. One was on the legal obstacles to a wealth tax and how those could be overcome, another was on – ironically enough – the pattern of sexual and racial discrimination visible in the appointment of clerks to the Supreme Court.) It was almost a relief when Maggie found a gossip item about the college ball committee, which had included among that year's raffle prizes 'a fully functioning vibrator':

Asked for comment, committee member Tasha Winthrop said, 'Don't worry, there are plenty of toys for the boys in there too.'

(Maggie imagined Stuart's reaction to that one. He'd have wanted the candidate to issue a statement: '*When I was young and irresponsible, I was young and irresponsible.*' Maggie would have suggested a tweet, featuring no more than a blushing emoji.)

Finally, she was in Natasha's teenage years. There was a picture story in the *Cape Cod Times*, proudly breaking the news that a local girl had won a scholarship to Harvard:

> *Winthrop is the sole surviving daughter of Aldrich and Tilly Winthrop of Pilgrim's Cove, and a boarder at St Hugh's Academy in Andover.*

Maggie looked hard at the eighteen-year-old Natasha, clutching her letter from Harvard, smiling broadly. Yet her eyes were doing something else, fixing the camera with an expression that was both sad and – what was it? The best Maggie could come up with was . . . defiant.

Beyond that, her birth certificate was visible online, along with a birth announcement in the *Boston Globe*. And there was plenty on the death of her parents, along with her two sisters, in a car accident in the Rhineland, where Reed Aldrich Winthrop had been serving as a senior officer with the US Air Force on the base at Ramstein. Natasha had been in the car at the time and was described in the first reports as being in a 'critical' condition. There was an account of the funeral on the Cape, held while the fifteen-year-old Natasha remained in hospital in Germany.

Maggie had gone back to the picture in the local paper, Natasha clutching her Harvard admission letter three years later. The sadness was obvious enough but the defiance made sense too: she had come through, despite everything.

There was nothing else that Maggie could see, which was hardly a surprise. Aldrich Winthrop had been posted to Ramstein well over a decade earlier; he was a colonel, holding a senior position within NATO Allied Air Command, when he died. Until her family had been wiped out, a US airbase in Germany was where Natasha had grown up.

She concluded that nothing in the public record about Natasha Winthrop shed any light whatsoever on the current situation. She had found no clear enemy, no obvious grievance. Nor had her searches illuminated in any way the Russian riddle that had been contained inside those computer files. To Maggie, it was now obvious: she would have to go back to the seam she had already mined, though this time she would be even more meticulous. Somewhere, surely, in those work files lay the answer.

The Russia file remained top of her mental list, but now she compiled a roll-call of all those who might feel wronged by Natasha and her legal prowess. It included individual CIA operatives at multiple black sites around the world, each accused of human rights abuses including torture; a group of Navy aviators charged with sexual assault; the board of a fossil-fuel company exposed as having falsified test results; a tech company that had not yet been sued by Natasha, but on whom Winthrop had already collected a voluminous body of evidence. Maggie wrote it all down: names, dates, places. (Though, in the tech case, Maggie could not quite grasp what the company was alleged to have done, let alone whether they'd done it: she would need to get Liz to give her the dummies' guide on that one.)

She worked backwards in time, tunnelling through Natasha's career as she got closer to the start of the century. When she had exhausted all the digital records, she moved to the filing cabinet – locked, but Natasha had told her where she could find the key – thumbing through hard, paper files that looked as if they'd barely been touched in more than a decade. Towards the back were records of the very first cases Winthrop had fought as a defence attorney, soon after joining this very firm.

Maggie was turning the pages – the memos to the DA, the sworn depositions, the police reports – when she came to one case that instantly stood out.

THE PEOPLE VS NANCY JIMENEZ

It stood out not because a woman was involved. On the contrary, women appeared repeatedly throughout the files, paper and electronic. But as she rushed through the document, establishing the basic facts, Maggie could see that this was the first case in which a woman appeared not as the victim of a hideous crime, nor even as a witness, but as its alleged perpetrator.

Jimenez was a single mother from the Brentwood neighbourhood of DC. She worked as a cleaner in various office buildings in northwest Washington. One Sunday night she had dialled 911 and, in a calm voice, told the operator there was a dead man in her house, lying on the kitchen floor. The operator had asked Jimenez how she knew that the man was dead. 'I just know,' she had said. 'How do you know?' the operator asked, insistent. 'I know, because I killed him.' When the police arrived, Jimenez was still standing over the man, apparently in a state of frozen shock. In her right hand was the brass candlestick she had used to bludgeon him over the head.

Natasha had argued that the man had attempted to rape Jimenez moments earlier. That he had forced her to the ground and begun 'an act of forced penetration', as the court documents put it. Jimenez said that the man had put his hands around her throat and that she believed she was going to die. She fought back and, in the struggle, reached for the candlestick. 'I didn't mean to kill him. I just wanted to make him stop,' Jimenez told police when they questioned her.

Nancy Jimenez was acquitted on all charges. The court accepted that she had killed while acting in her own defence, that her use of force had been reasonable and proportionate to the threat she faced. She walked free from the court and the first person she thanked, according to the report in the *Washington Post* – clipped and preserved in this file – was her attorney, Natasha Winthrop, then aged just twenty-four. 'This woman saved my life,' Jimenez told reporters. 'She saved me.'

Chapter 27

Washington, DC

Marcia Chester could taste her own coffee breath. If it offended her, it must have positively repelled her partner. But Allen was a subordinate sort and had never mentioned it, so Chester decided to let it slide. She could dig into her bag and find some gum, but who needed the hassle? Besides, gum made her hungry, and once the juices got moving her stomach would start to rumble. Loudly. Which was also disgusting in its own way. Best leave well alone.

Allen parked the car in one of the 'POLICE ONLY' bays outside the Office of the Chief Medical Examiner on E Street, Southwest: one of the very few perks of the job, Marcia mused. Not that anyone else was here at this godforsaken hour of the night. As she unbuckled the seat belt to get out, she considered leaving her coffee cup behind. Maybe she'd had enough for one day, given the coffee breath and all. On second thoughts, nah: in for a penny, in for a pound. She grabbed the cup and slammed the door behind her.

Inside, and to her great relief, she saw a familiar face: Dr Amy Fong. Relief because Chester didn't feel like meeting a new person and making nice, and because she knew that Fong was good and, better still, fast. There'd be no need to give her the spiel about how this was a priority of the Chief of Police and all that bullcrap: Fong would be on it.

The pathologist greeted the pair of detectives with what Chester took to be reciprocal relief: no small talk, no introductions. *Woman after my own heart.*

The familiar walk down one deserted corridor, through a set of double doors, then another and finally into an examination suite. As they walked, Dr Fong explained that the information they had had in the initial report was all accurate.

Allen seemed to take that as a rebuke. 'Sure, but we always want to see the body for ourselves.'

Chester gave Fong a brief eye-roll in solidarity. *Don't get me started.*

The corpse of Jeffrey Todd was on a gurney, suggesting it had been brought here especially for this visit. 'Talk us through it, Doctor,' Chester said.

'As you can see,' she began, pointing at the skull whose left side had collapsed, like a deflated football, 'the victim suffered a high-impact blow to the head, leading to severe contusions, shattered bone and major, fatal brain damage.'

'How many times do you think he was hit?'

'Once.'

'And with the object you've been shown by my colleagues?'

'Yes, indeed. The weight and shape of that object are entirely consistent with these injuries.'

'Anything else about the body? You know, the accused's testimony is that he had performed an act of sexual assault in the seconds before she struck him.'

'Well, as you know, there was clear evidence of ejaculation on both the victim and the perpetrator which—'

'Excuse me.' It was Allen, taking detailed notes. 'When you say perpetrator—'

'Sorry,' said Fong. 'Perpetrator of this attack. The woman. Victim, meaning this man.'

'Right. So there was semen on her clothes and on his. Is that right?'

'That's correct.'

'And I know this sounds obvious, but that semen was his? No doubt about it?'

'We've tested it, Detective,' Fong said, failing to conceal her exasperation. She glanced over at Chester who closed and opened her eyelids at half-speed: not quite as obvious as an eye-roll, but a comradely expression of shared irritation all the same. Allen was always a stickler, but he'd got even worse since the CCTV footage fiasco. After that supposed 'indistinct outline of a person opening the door' turned out to be nothing more than a shadow, he'd been double- and triple-checking every damn thing.

'So any other physical evidence on this corpse that either confirms or contradicts Ms Winthrop's account? Anything we need to know?'

'There is some of her DNA under his fingernails and some of his under hers, too, according to the police report compiled by your team. Scratches on his face, neck and hands. All consistent with a struggle. Just like she said.'

Allen took a moment to read through his notes, then looked back at Chester, signalling that he felt they'd covered the ground.

Chester too moved, as if heading for the door. Then, out of habit rather than any hunch, she asked one last question. 'Dr Fong, is there anything else you can see about this body, or about the injuries that led to his death, that might be useful to our inquiry? Anything at all?'

The pathologist paused and then said, 'I'm not sure we are talking about injuries, plural.'

'What do you mean?'

'I think he died from a single injury.'

Allen showed Chester a crinkled brow, then turned back to Fong. 'I don't follow, Doctor.'

'The fatal blow was precise. It was done very cleanly.'

'Precise?' said Chester.

'Yes. It was the right amount of force, applied to the right part of the brain.' Seeing the detectives' reaction, Fong held up her hands. 'I don't know anything more than I can see on the table. But what I can see is that whoever killed this man knew exactly what they wanted to do.'

Chapter 28

Maggie put the file down and suddenly heard the silence of the office. The hum of the computers, even those that were officially asleep, the mute vibration of the electricity ready to light up the corridors should it sense the slightest motion. In the silence, she could hear her own heart which, she now understood, was thumping.

She looked again at the file, trembling in her hand. It had to be a coincidence. Surely it was just one of those uncanny instances of history repeating itself.

But then she read the report again, individual lines jumping out at her. *'I didn't mean to kill him. I just wanted to make him stop'* . . . *put his hands around her throat* . . . *she believed she was going to die* . . . *reasonable and proportionate use of force* . . . *'I know, because I killed him.'*

Natasha had used more or less the same words about herself, more than a decade later. She knew they worked, because they had worked before. *This woman saved my life.*

Maggie thought about the woman whose home she had stayed

in just yesterday, how they had run on the beach and talked long into the night, how her eyes had sparkled with righteous anger at a world that needed fixing and her own conviction that she might be the person to do it. Was that woman capable of doing this, plotting in cold blood the murder of another human being, and doing it so meticulously that she had already gamed out her legal defence? More than that, had she actually constructed this crime as a re-enactment of a previous homicide, in order to proof it against a guilty verdict? Was this woman really capable of such cold calculation, capable too of disguising it in a cover story, earnestly told, that cast her as a terrified victim who had acted out of the natural, spontaneous instinct for survival, when the truth was there had been no spontaneity or instinct, just a deliberate, premeditated plan for murder?

Calm down, Maggie told herself. Coincidences happened; history did sometimes repeat itself. Put this story away and keep looking.

She clicked next on a file simply labelled 'Finances'. Inside were PDFs of Natasha's last seven years of tax returns, as well as related files detailing her income and expenditure for each of those years, including the related invoices and receipts. They were immaculately maintained. Maggie thought of the filing system for her own accounts at home: a pile of receipts weighed down by an unwashed tea mug on her desk. Once it became unmanageable, the pile would be shovelled into a shoebox along with anything else to do with money and then stashed under Maggie's bed. Then, with hours to go till the filing deadline, she would get on her knees, retrieve the box, call her accountant and plead for mercy. Liz had seen her 'system' once and placed her hand over her mouth in horror. Maggie had said, 'Look, I know it's a mess.' Liz had responded that, 'This isn't just a "mess", Mags. This is a threat to the integrity of the US taxation system. I've a good mind to call the fecking IRS and report you myself.'

The contrast with Winthrop's set-up could not have been sharper. Each file, labelled by financial year, contained a master spreadsheet, with tabs colour-coded by category: travel, equipment, and the like. Within those columns, each figure was a clickable link. Maggie clicked one for $1008.42 and brought up a copy of a hotel bill in Atlanta. That gave her an idea.

She scanned first through the equipment column, but could see at a glance that the figures weren't what she was looking for: she wanted a number that was roughly the same each month, and relatively low.

There.

Right first time. A click on a charge for $68.06 brought up a PDF of Natasha's cellphone bill. Five pages of it, but there on the last two was what Maggie was looking for: the itemized section, detailing each call whose cost was not already included. Maggie knew to look for it because it was the same on her own bill. On hers, it mainly showed calls to Liz's landline in Atlanta – usually the sequel to an attempt to speak via the latest app recommended by her sister, an attempt ultimately aborted once patchy Wi-Fi had rendered Liz's voice as either alarmingly robotic or so faint she sounded like a distant sprite trapped underground. That, and the occasional call to a hotel room to speak to Uri when he was on the road, venturing into red states that, when it came to cell reception, were a universe of black holes.

She was looking for the most recent bill she could find, hoping it would . . . what? Reveal a series of calls with Todd, proving that Natasha had known her victim? Or perhaps a call history with a Russian oligarch, who would turn out to be either Natasha's pursuer or her prey. Something that would explain – or at least explain better than Natasha had – why it was that, of all the rapists in all the world, she had lured Jeffrey Todd to what had turned out to be his death.

If Maggie had been hoping for a cluster of calls to a single number in a concentrated period, say, in the hours before Todd had entered Winthrop's home – and of course that was exactly what she'd been hoping for – she didn't find it. Even this most recent bill only went up to last month. There were a few numbers that recurred, often for calls lasting two or three minutes. But none in a stack, and none that obviously related to that fateful night.

Still, something leapt out. There was a number that appeared at precise intervals. Maggie consulted the calendar on her phone and saw that Natasha had called the number every Sunday evening, at roughly the same time – just after six pm – and always for a good twenty or twenty-five minutes. The area code was not one she recognized: 207. Maggie looked it up and saw that 207 was the code for the state of Maine.

Maggie thought of her own calls to Liz, not that there was any set pattern: Liz would call whenever she'd 'finally got those noisy fuckers to sleep'. If Natasha had had family, that would have been the obvious explanation: that this was a Sunday-night chat with a mother or father, brother or sister. But given Natasha had no such family, this had to be someone else. Did she have a lover in

Maine that she needed to keep secret? A married man perhaps? A woman? Judith?

That brought back another memory of Stuart Goldstein, back when there had been DC chatter about a young black governor with aspirations for a national career. 'Hmm, doubt it,' Stuart had said. When Maggie raised a puzzled eyebrow, Stuart explained that the word on the street was that the governor, though engaged to a woman, was in fact gay. Surely that was not insurmountable, in this day and age, Maggie had asked. 'I'm told that this young man agrees with you. He believes America is ready for a gay president. And he knows America is ready for a black president. He just doesn't think it's ready for a black *and* gay president.'

Maggie thought again of Natasha Winthrop, the elusively single woman who the DC gossip columns had hailed for bringing rare glamour to the famously buttoned-up Washington scene. The same question prompted by the 'Judith' file now surfaced once more. Had Natasha, like that young governor, concluded that while Americans might just about be ready for a young woman as president, it was too much to ask them to accept as their commander-in-chief a young lesbian?

She was getting ahead of herself. There would be another explanation. She looked at the clock in the corner of the screen. Approaching midnight. Too late to call the number now, though she was tempted.

What was that?

Was that the click of a door closing? She closed her eyes, an instinctive attempt to listen more closely. She barely dared move.

There! A dull thud, either a door closing again or the firm tread of a footstep. Was it in this office, or just outside in the reception area? Suddenly Maggie was hyper-aware that she was in a room that didn't belong to her, in a building she didn't know, whose quirks and creaks were unfamiliar.

Determined to take the initiative, and perhaps to retain the element of surprise, she all but jumped out of her chair, out of Natasha's office and into the open-plan area, illuminated after a second or two by the motion-activated lights.

She looked around. Nothing.

She called out 'Hello?' feeling simultaneously frightened and ridiculous.

A pause, and there it was again. The click of a door. Nearer this time.

Maggie approached the main double doors, the ones locked by a keycode, that gave out onto the reception area. Each door contained a vertical strip of glass. It meant that she'd be able to see out but also that anyone on the other side could see in.

She hung back, listening. The lights went off.

Another sound, firmer this time. Nearer still.

'Who's there?'

Silence. And then, from the other side of the door, a thud.

Maggie peered into the dark behind her. What was on those desks that she might use to defend herself? On one, she could make out the silhouette of a pair of scissors.

Gingerly, she stepped back, landing her heel first on each step, hoping to make no sound. She drew level with the desk and reached for the scissors. They were in her grasp when, suddenly and with no warning, the door was pushed open. Behind it was a man, no doubt about it, making no attempt to disguise himself, his height a match for the door. Maggie's fingers were now curled around the scissors, their metal cool against her skin. She stepped forward.

The motion, either his or hers, was enough to activate the lights and, as she raised her hand, she saw that the man just a few feet away from her was wearing drab navy overalls. Behind him was a trolley, stacked with broom, mop and a tray of sprays and cloths. He looked as shocked, and as terrified, as she was.

'Hey!' he said, uselessly.

She let out a little, and equally useless, scream. And the pair of them seemed to freeze like that for several seconds until he said, 'You scare hell out of me.'

'Me too,' was all she managed.

'What hell you doing?' She could see he had paled with fright.

'Working late. I'm, I'm . . . I'm sorry.'

He nodded, she nodded and the two of them backed away from each other, each returning to their work.

As she settled back in Natasha's chair, reassured by the presence of the cleaner just beyond the door, Maggie looked at the screen once more. It took her a while to remember what she'd been looking at and longer to make any sense of it.

Ah, Natasha's cellphone history. And the number she had dialled every Sunday night. How to turn those digits into a name? Maggie, her hands still shaking, went to one of those 'reverse phone lookup' sites but, as usual with any number that wasn't a business, it drew a blank.

Back in her White House days, this would have presented no problem. The Secret Service would have cracked this in a heartbeat. But now? Jake Haynes would have his journalistic ruses, no doubt, but given the paper he worked for, he'd have a hundred ethical misgivings to overcome before he'd agree to do Maggie this favour – and, besides, he'd be too curious. Whoever this person in Maine was, Maggie was not ready to reveal his or her existence to the media.

And yet, there had to be a way. Here was the phone number. Somewhere, in a vast unseen storehouse of data, those digits would be linked to a name and address. The question was, how to crack it. Or rather who could crack it?

Just asking the question answered it. There were probably half a dozen people Maggie could think of who would be able to extract this particular nugget of information gold from the bottomless mine of rubbish that existed online. But there was only one person who Maggie could trust with the answer, whatever it was, and who – no less important – she could call at any hour of the day or night and who, though they would shout and scream and vow never to speak to her again, would still be at the end of the phone the next day and the day after that.

She dialled the number and after five rings was delighted to hear not the abrupt divert to a voicemail message but the welcome rustle of a human being picking up the phone.

'What the absolute fuck.'

'Hi, Liz.' Maggie was whispering, imagining her sister's bedroom in Atlanta, her cramped two-bed apartment, her two young sons under their *Avengers* duvets in their bunk-beds just down the hall, hard-working and ever-patient husband Paul snoring heavily at her side, the alarm clock set to go off in no more than six hours. 'I'm sorry to call you so late, I just need—'

'You better be either dead or maimed, Maggie, so help me, God, because there is no way you can be phoning me at nearly one in the morning.'

'It's nowhere near—'

'So help me, God.'

'I'm really sorry, Liz. I was—'

'No way, Maggie.' Liz was doing that thing she always did when Paul was asleep next to her: shout-whispering, raising her voice to a furious register even as she sought to keep the volume down. 'No fucking way do you get to say you're "sorry". Because if that was even one-bloody-quarter genuine, you wouldn't have bloody done it, would you?'

'No, Liz. I wouldn't.' A tactical retreat on Maggie's part: suck up the punishment now, let it pass and then get what you came for. Trouble was, Liz had known her sister too long – all her life, in fact – to let her get away with that one. She was wise to it.

'No, no. You're not doing that thing you do. No way.'

'What thing?'

'When you let me rant and rave and you go all quiet. Not having that.'

'What do you want me to do?'

'I want you to think for one minute what it would be like to be me, Maggie. One minute. That's all I ask. Imagine being responsible for two kids who've got to be up at ten to bloody seven in the morning, and thirty kids who I've got to teach from eight thirty, and how *precious* and bloody *necessary* six hours' sleep is, if you're me. I mean, you can do what the hell you like, because no one needs you to be up to pack their fucking *Iron Man* lunch box in the morning, do they. But I need to sleep.'

Maggie went quiet, even though her sister had told her not to.

'And now you've given me the fright of my life because I'm worried something's happened to you.' A pause. 'Has something happened to you? Not that I care.'

'I'm fine.'

'Thank Christ for that. My heart's pounding, you know. Fucking thumping.'

'I'm sorry, Liz.'

'But that just makes it worse. You don't even have an excuse.' Her voice moved away from the phone. 'It's all right, Paul honey. Go back to sleep. It's nothing.'

Maggie spotted an opening. 'Listen. Liz. It'll take five minutes.' Too soon.

'I know what this is. This is about *work*, isn't it? At one in the morning, you'd wake my sleeping children to get me to do you some favour for *work*. I mean . . . you know what, Maggie? You are no different to our mother. No different at all. She was a slave to the drink, and you're a slave to the work. I've said it before and you've made me say it again: I love you, Maggie, but you're an addict. And you need help.'

That 'I love you' was encouraging. It suggested they'd cleared the water ditch and the high fence and were now rounding the bend towards the home straight. Maybe she'd have to listen to a bit more character diagnosis/assassination and then she could get to her question.

'Where's Uri? Put him on. I want to speak to him.'

'He's not here. I'm not at home.' The words hung in the air for a second as Maggie heard the cogs turning in her sister's head. 'Not like that. I'm in someone's office. Someone I'm . . . helping.'

Liz dropped the shout-whisper by a couple of decibels. 'So I was right. This is work.'

'It is. And I need something so small, we could have done it by now. I know you need to sleep, Liz. If there was someone else I could call, I would. But I need you.' Maggie closed her eyes tight: it was manipulative, Liz would see through it. Still, it might just work.

'See, the thing is, if I help you, it would be like giving drink to an alcoholic. Like literally putting a bottle of Scotch in front of our ma.'

'Oh, come on.'

'I've been your enabler too long, Maggie. It's not healthy. Not for me, not for you.'

'I tell you what's not healthy, and that's being on my own in someone else's office at one in the morning, shitting myself at every creak and thump. I want to go home. And if you do this one thing for me I can. And then we can talk about what a useless fuck-up I am tomorrow.'

A long pause. The sound of Liz resettling herself in bed, pulling the duvet over her shoulder and turning on her side, to be quieter for Paul – or so Maggie pictured it.

'One thing, Maggie. No more.'

Maggie wanted to bellow out a *Yesss!* But she knew better. Quietly and calmly, trying to do nothing that might make her sister change her mind, she said, 'It's a phone number in Maine.

I want to know who it belongs to. The name and the address. And that's it.'

More rustling down the phone. With any luck that was Liz reaching for the laptop, usually kept on the floor by the bed.

The sound of keystrokes. Then: 'What's the phone number?'

Maggie read it off the screen, still displaying Natasha Winthrop's cellphone bill. The sound of more keystrokes.

She held the phone to her ear, enjoying the sounds of her sister. In the silence, it felt like company.

After perhaps two minutes, she heard her sister's voice. 'OK, I'm sending it to you now. Goodnight, Maggie.'

'Thank you so much, Liz.' When there was nothing, she added: 'I love you.'

'I know you do.'

As the line went dead, Maggie felt a vibration in the phone. The text message was in the dead centre of the screen, a new alert.

At first, Maggie assumed her sister had made a mistake, understandable enough in her sleep-deprived state. Otherwise, the message she had sent made no sense.

The address was straightforward enough. *Pierce Pond Road, Penobscot, Maine.* But given everything Natasha had said, Maggie was stumped by the name that appeared alongside it. Natasha was a woman with no family, whose sole surviving relative, her Aunt Peggy, had died a few years ago. And yet the phone number she had dialled every Sunday at six pm was registered to a name that told a different story, a name that now glowed from Maggie's screen.

V Winthrop.

Chapter 29

Dan Benson's finger was hovering over the arrow keys, clicking through the slides. The Digital Director had sent them to him for his approval – though, tellingly, he'd sent them to Dan's personal email rather than to his campaign address. He hadn't needed to spell out why.

Benson looked at them – ads that would pop up in people's social media feeds – and had to admire their ingenuity, each one perfectly designed to reach its target audience and, just as admirable, betraying not so much as a hint of its source, or of the fact that it had anything to do with politics. Benson's favourite was the one showing a now retired athlete, a star quarterback from the 1980s, with his finger pointed at the camera, above the words: *Don't Miss Out. Guess the NFL and win $50 million.* Below, white letters on red, was a button that read simply, *Enter Here.* Who could resist that? Certainly not men over fifty who were a key demographic for the Harrison campaign. One click, and they would see the offer: guess every coming NFL game correctly and scoop the jackpot. Never mind that, as the Digital Director had explained to Dan, the odds of anyone winning that prize were one in 5,000,000,000,000,000,000,000,000. Or that the Harrison for President campaign – or rather a shell organization that would be near impossible to trace to the campaign – had taken out an insurance policy to cover that eventuality-cum-calamity.

All that was beside the point. The purpose of that ad, and the others, was to pull in people who would never otherwise click on a political message – indeed, people who had never voted before – and prompt them to reveal not only their contact details, but also just enough about themselves to allow the machines to sketch a rough, outline picture. It was a vast data harvesting programme, one that aimed to gather information on millions of Americans.

You'd be surprised how little those machines needed to go on. Feed them a few morsels of info – someone's retail habits, say, or TV viewing preferences – and the programme could slot them into a narrow demographic niche and, from there, work out with astonishing accuracy their political outlook. In turn, that would reveal what buttons – psychological and emotional – a campaign would need to press.

The button-pressing took the form of a steady drip-feed of yet more ads slipped into those voters' timelines or feeds, each one tightly tailored to that specific slice of the electorate: in the case of the faux $50 million competition, middle-aged, male NFL fans. If the ads did their job, they'd get those voters riled up and positively itching to vote. Thanks to demographic and polling analysis that assessed the political leanings of particular groups, it was barely in doubt *how* such people would vote. Getting them *motivated* to vote, that was the thing. And now, through these 'dark' ads, so customized and micro-targeted that the national media might never even see them, those people would be not merely motivated, but whipped into a state of fury that would have them up and dressed at dawn, itching to cast their ballots.

Benson was happy with this first round of ads, those that would serve as bait to lure in the unsuspecting social media surfer, tricking voters and – even better – previous non-voters to offer up their data, thereby rendering themselves nicely targetable. There were some pleasantly surprising ones, like the image of a polar bear nestled against her two cubs. *Protect her! Click here.* Once you'd clicked and signed up to 'Americans for Nature' or whatever bogus front organization the digital team had confected, you were on the list and would soon receive messages aimed at tickling your sweet spots – and your neuralgic ones too.

It was those second-wave ads Benson was interested in, the ones that would come at you via Facebook after you had, unwittingly, invited them in. These were more subtle, most not looking like ads at all. On his screen now was a message that appeared to the naked eye like a regular news story, one that had simply been 'shared'. The format matched that of a respectable news website. If you looked closely, it seemed to have been published by a newspaper called the *Seattle Telegraph*.

Natasha Winthrop says men should apologize before they speak

Presidential hopeful and lawyer Natasha Winthrop has suggested men should begin every sentence with the words "I'm sorry", to make amends for centuries of "male oppression" of women, it emerged last night.

Winthrop, who far-left activists are pushing as a rival to long-time frontrunner Tom Harrison, made the remarks at a recent, closed-door meeting of supporters. "Women have suffered for thousands of years. And who's made them suffer? It's men. Now, I'm not asking for the earth. All I'm asking is that men at least acknowledge what they've done. And I mean every man, every time they open their mouth."

The lawyer-turned-politician went on to suggest that if a man is talking to a woman or group of women, he should first utter the words, "I'm sorry."

"It should become a habit. Like a reflex. So that even when no women are in the room, when it's just a bunch of guys, they start with an apology."

Asked at what age this practice should begin, Winthrop said that she was open to further discussion on the matter. "Obviously it should be compulsory for all males over the age of fourteen. But maybe we should do this for every male baby and toddler, from the moment they learn to talk. So that it becomes truly ingrained. We'll know we've made progress when a male child's first words are, 'I'm sorry.'"

Benson had to admit it had been artfully done. The little evasions were relatively subtle. No specific time or place was given for the event where Winthrop had supposedly made these remarks and not many would know that the *Seattle Telegraph* did not exist. It would hit the outrage nerve directly, prompting many – maybe even most – of the carefully targeted audience who would see it to hit the 'Share' button in their fury.

But, he wasn't sure. Was it too much? Did it lack the requisite kernel of truth, or at least the plausible lie, that helped such stories grip the imagination and start spreading? Also, he didn't love the reference to Harrison in the second paragraph. Any journalist saw that, they'd immediately know who'd paid for it. They might as well put Harrison's signature on it.

He scrolled to the next one, which was a variation on that same theme: same format, same bogus source.

Natasha Winthrop says women should receive reparations

Presidential hopeful and lawyer, Natasha Winthrop, has called for men to pay women "reparations" to compensate for centuries of "male oppression" of women, it emerged last night.

Winthrop, who far-left activists are pushing as a rival to long-time frontrunner Tom Harrison, made the remarks at a recent, closed-door meeting of supporters. "Women have suffered for thousands of years. And who's made them suffer? It's men. Now, I'm not asking for the earth. All I'm asking for is a stipend, perhaps two or three thousand dollars a month paid to every woman over the age of sixteen and funded by every man of the same age."

The lawyer-turned-politician went on to suggest that the law could stipulate that no woman should be allowed to share their reparation money with a male, whether that male be a husband or son. "This money is women's. No man should be allowed to get near it . . ."

It was ludicrous, of course. As obviously, laughably, false as could be. And yet he knew that would present no obstacle. The fake news stories that had shaped the last couple of campaigns were equally outlandish, and that had slowed their progress not at all: they had taken flight, soaring into the social media stratosphere. The key, Dan had learned, was that what such stories lacked in literal truth they had to make up in *emotional* truth. They needed to hit voters where they hurt.

Old-school political operatives thought that meant targeting a rival candidate's weak spot. Your opponent had once, as governor, failed to support the death penalty in a specific case, commuting the sentence of a man with learning difficulties: ergo, they were soft on crime. Your opponent spoke French: ergo, they were effete and unpatriotic. Easy. That, Benson suspected, was the political style of his new boss. For Harrison was nothing if not old school.

But that approach rested on a misapprehension. It wasn't the weakness of your rival you needed to target. It was the weakness of your *voters*. It was *their* insecurity, paranoia or lack of self-esteem you had to home in on, ruthlessly.

The 'I'm sorry' and reparations posts were not bad in that regard, playing on male fears of emasculation. But they were a little direct, a tad on the nose. Which was why Dan preferred the messages he looked at next.

The first was a short video. It showed the hands of a white man in a plaid shirt – you couldn't see his face – holding a letter. The voiceover made clear that it was a job rejection. As the hands scrunched up the letter, the voiceover intoned: 'You needed that job, and you were the best qualified. But they had to give it to a woman because of a "gender quota".' The phrase was all but spat out. 'Is that really fair? Natasha Winthrop supports gender quotas. Tom Harrison believes jobs should go to the best person, whoever they are.'

Benson smiled at that. The homage to campaigns past was clear, and the messaging effective. He could see that one working.

He looked at the next suggestion, also a video, which once again focused on a pair of hands. Except this time they were a woman's: the nails were painted a strong red. The hands were holding a phone, thumbing out a text message. As she tapped away, the voiceover said: 'Natasha Winthrop killed a man. She says she'd never met him before. But now we know she sent him secret messages before he came to her house. What did those messages say?'

Interesting, but Benson's gut told him it was wrong. It was somehow too literal. Besides, he felt sure there were plenty of Harrison's target voters who would admire anyone who had killed a man, especially a bad one: no point reminding them that Winthrop was tough.

Next came the simplest offering so far. It showed a Photoshopped image of Natasha Winthrop, altered so that she was in the pose of a schoolmistress, wagging her finger. There were only four words.

Meet the new boss

Dan absorbed his own instinctive reaction, a fleeting, barely conscious moment of recoil. He told himself it was not peculiar to him, certainly not a weakness of his, but rather an instant, unmediated response that would be common to most men confronted with the image of a bossy woman.

He skipped to the next image, which the Digital Director had called 'The first wife'. Again, there was a Photoshopped Natasha, this time standing in a kitchen, hands on hips, her face folded into a scold. Her expression conveyed: *What time do you call this?*

Benson had to smile at that. He remembered the focus groups he'd witnessed the last time his party had chosen a female nominee. When male voters, especially older ones in blue-collar jobs, were on their own with a male moderator, they admitted that the candidate reminded them of a hectoring teacher, an imperious new manager tasked with shaking up their factory or office, or, most damningly and revealingly, their 'first wife'.

In that case, the female candidate had been older and an established figure of authority. But the digital team apparently reckoned that those factors were secondary to the more basic one: that there were only so many ways men could see a woman with power, even one who was in fact young and new to politics. Hence the gambit that had resulted in these images: to cast the young and beautiful Natasha Winthrop as a nagging, joy-killing harridan.

Benson's colleagues had clearly given this some thought, because they had presented him with options within options. There were, for example, two versions of the 'Meet the new boss' image. In one, Natasha was wearing dowdy, schoolmarmish clothes while her face had been subtly altered. Her lips had been redrawn to expose more of her gums, the teeth enlarged. Her nose was bigger and her eyes smaller and uneven.

The other version showed Natasha wearing her own clothes – a tight-fitting, thin-strapped black dress, showing plenty of skin – with her face intact, her eyes sparkling, even if her mouth was no longer fixed in that *People* magazine smile but resting instead in an expression of rebuke. Her body was still moulded into the same, imperious shape as the first version, her finger was still wagging, but her looks were intact.

The effect was unnerving and confusing; Dan felt it himself. And if he did, so would most of the men who would see this image scrolling across their screen. He was simultaneously attracted and repelled and – was this his therapist talking or him? – attracted *because* repelled. Or should that be repelled *because* attracted?

He was staring at the alternative the team had generated for the 'first wife' image, still feeling the same, contradictory, destabilizing sensation. There she was, the gorgeous Natasha Winthrop, absurdly recast as a moaning housewife. It left the male mind torn and conflicted, not sure whether to move towards what it saw or away from it. The loins were stirred, but the brain disapproved. One part of you knew that this person was your enemy, the other desired her. Which only made you resent her more.

Benson sat back in his chair, impressed with his colleague. He'd known the Digital Director was savvy with the technology, a whizz when it came to algorithmic patterns and social media data tracking. In fact, one of the inducements to joining Team Harrison was the assurance that the campaign had bought for itself a tech advantage that would guarantee it an edge over its rivals. He remembered the smile on the face of his soon-to-be boss at the hiring meeting, as Doug Teller said proudly, 'Dan, I'll spare you the details, but when it comes to technology this campaign has a secret weapon that will revolutionize digital warfare.' Teller hadn't spelled it out – 'No chef ever gives the recipe for his secret sauce' – but Dan took it as read that the secret weapon was the Digital Director himself.

While he had never doubted that man's online prowess, he hadn't credited him with such a grasp of human psychology. He seemed to understand what underpinned male hostility to women, and to have tapped into it quite ruthlessly. It made Benson think more highly of Tom Harrison. He'd appointed this digital guy and of course he'd had the vision to appoint Benson himself. Maybe he really did have what it took to be president.

Chapter 30

Washington, DC

For the duration of the journey back to her apartment, two thoughts had jostled with each other for primacy in Maggie's mind. Though 'thoughts' might be flattering at least one of them. The first was the conundrum that had been dropped in her lap by her sister's (reluctant) sleuthing skills, the unexpected two-word resolution of the mystery of the Maine number that had cropped up often and regularly in Natasha's phone bills: V Winthrop. The other was the prospect of a warming glass of malt whisky.

The two were linked in that only when she was seated at her own table and sitting in her own chair, with a swig of Ardbeg stinging in her throat, did Maggie believe she'd be able to solve this puzzle. She was in that exact position now, and yet she kept coming back to the same basic contradiction.

On the one hand, Natasha had been insistent that her family were all dead. Not only had her parents and sisters been killed in that car crash back when Natasha was a teenager, but the woman who had raised her was gone too. Maggie remembered the conversation they'd had on Cape Cod, when Maggie had blundered into mentioning Natasha's Aunt Peggy. *Died a few years ago, I'm afraid.*

Had Maggie misheard that somehow? Had she got the wrong end of the stick?

No, Maggie's memory of that exchange was still sharp. She could hear Natasha's voice: *I do miss her* terribly *though, as you can imagine.*

Perhaps there was another 'V Winthrop' close enough to Natasha that they spoke every Sunday evening, and yet who was not her great-aunt Peggy. Maggie supposed it was theoretically possible, though it seemed vanishingly unlikely, not least because Natasha had been clear: she had no living relatives. So who, exactly, could this Victor or Veronica Winthrop be?

Maggie heard a rattle from the bathroom, metal on metal, like someone fiddling with a lock. A second later there was a creak of wood.

She sat bolt upright, her senses prickling. She was conscious of her eyeballs moving from side to side, like antennae twitching at the unexpected presence of another creature. All her energy, the blood in her veins, seemed directed towards her ears, straining to pick up any further sound, to decode it for more information.

A beat, then another beat, then another. As quietly as she could, she rose to her feet and moved away from the table and towards the kitchen, willing her feet to make no sound.

As she assessed what was available – there was a large knife in the cutlery drawer, but opening it would be too noisy – she heard a loud thud from the bathroom. Her brain processed that sound along with the others and decided that a man had come in through the bathroom window. It would have been difficult but, thanks to the exterior iron staircase that served as this building's fire escape, not impossible. A parallel stream of thought, running along the borderline that separated the conscious from the sub-conscious, was regretting that she did not own a gun. Uri had wanted her to do it, to keep it by the bedside – *I would recommend it for anyone, but you, given the work you do: it's crazy that you don't have one* – but she clung to her view that a firearm in the house would only make her more vulnerable. Take this moment, the one that was playing out right now in both split-seconds and a weirdly drawn-out, treacle-like slow motion: would she really want to introduce a gun into this situation, running the risk that if she aimed it at the intruder, he might grab it, turn it on her and, in the panic, it would be her not him who would end up shot?

All of that passed through Maggie's mind in less than a hundredth of a second, or so it felt. At the same time, instinct had made a decision for her, prodding her to reach for the knife block that sat on the counter and remove the heaviest blade, one with a serrated edge. That too entailed a risk, she understood that: she could be providing this man, whoever he was, with a tool he might not have. If he disarmed her, she could be supplying him with the murder weapon for her own death.

That calculus sped through her in the time it took to blink. Same with the question of whether to march towards the bath-room and ambush the intruder or lie in wait for him here. The element of surprise, compared to the greater room for manoeuvre offered by the larger space she was in now, set against the ability to hide – all these factors she weighed up and against each other in a splinter of a second. And through it all, she heard another quieter thud and then another – the footsteps of a man who had come to get her.

She tucked herself in behind the return on the open kitchen, before it gave out to the corridor leading from the bathroom. She hadn't decided what she would do or how she would do it, but a kind of animal reflex, seizing authority from her frontal cortex in an internal, neurological coup, had put her there. Now she awaited further instruction from her instincts.

It came when the bathroom door creaked open. She moved out, knife glinting, standing not in the narrow span of the corridor, but with the space of the kitchen to her right. What she saw sent a flood of terror flowing through her, the fear a physical substance, like a toxic, yellow chemical gushing into her bloodstream.

Before her was a man two inches taller than her, dressed only in black, his face covered in a black ski mask. He stood still, as if adopting a combat stance in a martial arts class. The fixedness of his pose, its rigidity, made Maggie wonder if he too was shocked, even frozen, by the sight of her.

'No knives,' he said, which added surprise to her alarm. She had not expected him to say those words, in a flat, uninflected American accent; she had not expected him to speak at all. Somehow that helped. He was no longer an undifferentiated threat, a masked intruder. He was now *specific*. She did not have to repel an abstract menace. She had to defeat this individual person, vulnerable enough to have his own voice.

She too adopted a kind of simian posture, her hands hanging by her side, drawing attention to the knife in her right hand. Just as she was contemplating her next move, and without warning, he thrust out his right leg and, in a single, accurate, darting movement, kicked the blade from her grasp. She heard the knife skittering across the wooden floor behind her.

'Like I said, no knives,' he repeated, in such a way that she had her first, subconscious intimation of what was happening.

Now, emboldened, he stepped forward and grabbed her by her wrists. Without delay, she raised her knee sharply upward, so that it pile-drove into his balls. He reeled backwards, his hands clutching at his groin, towards the bathroom door through which he had just emerged. Maggie followed him as he tottered back, eventually pushing at his shoulders with both hands, her palms flat. Using all her strength, it was enough to make him lose balance and fall backwards, hitting his head on the wall as he went down.

She was searching for another weapon, wondering about the razor in her bathroom, when she instead dashed back down the corridor to retrieve the knife. She had taken the first step and then the second when she felt herself plunging downward, landing hard on her knees. He had pulled at her ankle.

Now, without getting up, he crawled until he had caught up with her, letting his weight fall on top of her, his groin pressing into her backside. He placed one hand over her outstretched wrist and was attempting to pin down the second.

The sensation of his proximity to her, and what it threatened, filled her with a rage she had rarely known, which metabolized first into will and then into strength. She moved to raise herself, to throw him off her back, like a horse ejecting an unwanted rider. Somehow, she found the might to do it and, once he was off, she sprang to her feet.

She got as far as the knife, but overshot, accidentally kicking it forward. She could feel him getting up, moving towards her. She wheeled around to face him. She could hear her own panting, and feel her features contorted into a mask of complete fury. She loathed this man with a hatred so pure it was physical.

Instinct made her want to kick him in the balls once more, but some inner voice of restraint warned her of the risk: he might catch her leg before it reached him, then use it to pull her down again. She felt her right fist turn into a ball and understood that her body had decided for her.

She all but ran at him, holding up her left palm like a traffic cop. It was a decoy, distracting his gaze from her right arm, which now launched a single hard jab at his jaw. Except he jerked his head upward and out of the way, so that her fist landed hard in his throat.

Through the mask she could see his eyes widen, as he let out a dry, rasping noise. She seemed to have hit his windpipe.

She worked hurriedly now, anxious not to lose advantage. She grasped his head in both hands, as if holding a watermelon, and with no ceremony rammed it hard into the wall. He slumped down, and she moved with him, her hands still on his head, crashing it into the wall a second time. Now he crumpled.

For a second or two she thought she'd killed him. For an insane second, she wondered if this man was in fact Jeffrey Todd, and if she was about to re-run the events at Natasha Winthrop's house four nights earlier. But then she saw his chest rise, and heard a lowing sound come from his mouth.

She darted back along the corridor to pick up the knife, then into the kitchen where Uri had somewhere stashed a ball of rope. (He'd had a notion about constructing a washing line on the fire escape.) Knife in hand, she opened first one drawer, then another, looking up every other second at the doorway: she feared the man would be back, standing there, revived and arisen, his eyes blazing. This time, he would be determined to finish her off.

She should call the police, she knew that. And yet she also knew what that would mean: delay as she explained the situation, more delay as they headed over here. There was no time for that, not while this man was just a few feet away. To say nothing of the risk that the police would do to her what they had done to Natasha, that they wouldn't believe her, that she would end up the one accused. She had rammed his head very hard into that wall.

Now she came to a third drawer, filled with dishcloths, reels of Scotch tape, old power cables, a defunct computer charger. She slammed it shut. He would be stirring now, recovering his strength . . .

She flung open a cupboard. Saucepans, cheese grater, hand-mixer. Then another: dustpan and brush, vodka, a kite she'd bought for when the nephews visited. *Come on, come on.*

There was a rustle and another low moan from the corridor. She moved, with her knife, and peeked into the corridor: he was still there, though now he was stirring. She went back in and there it was, on the counter the whole time. She remembered now: Uri had given up on the washing line and put the rope there. Maggie had not moved it in three weeks.

Now she grabbed it, and a second later was standing over the man who had broken into her house. She considered shoving his head into the wall one more time, just to be sure. But then she imagined his corpse in this room, and that thought horrified her even more than the sight of him, breathing noisily now. So she bent down, used the blade to cut off a section of rope and, as swiftly as she could, tied his hands together. Then she tied them again, tugging at the rope to test her handiwork. She did the same to his ankles.

Now she stood back up to full height, planting her feet into the floor to steady herself. With the knife in her right hand, held about six inches away from his throat, she gripped with her left the man's ski mask. She held it for a moment, like a waiter about to lift a domed, silver cover off a dish, and then, swiftly, she pulled it off.

Revealed was the face of a man in what she guessed was his early thirties. He was white, clean-shaven, with features that were somehow childish. She understood why he wore a mask. Without it, he was not a man to fear.

The act of exposure had startled him, forcing his eyes wide open. Maggie used that as her cue to shift round so that she was standing directly in front of him. She gave him a second to flex, to realize he had been restrained and then, as if in resignation, to resume leaning, sideways on, into the wall.

She was about to begin her interrogation when he surprised her by speaking first. His voice was slurred, as if he'd woken from a hangover. Or been concussed.

'Is this your thing?'

'What?'

'This,' he grunted, using the failed movement of his hands to indicate his current situation, bound from top to bottom.

'What do you mean, "my thing"?'

'This why you got me here? You get off on this shit?'

'What the hell are you talking about?'

''Cause I gotta tell you, I don't.'

'You just broke into my house. You. Not me.'

'No one "broke" into anything.' He was slurring badly. She wondered if she had inflicted brain damage. Or broken a couple of teeth.

'Well, actually, they did. You broke into this apartment.'

'So you changed your mind, is that it? Decided you didn't want to go through with it?'

'Listen. I'm about to call the police. You can save all this bullshit for—'

Now his face was that of a panicked child. She wondered if he was even younger than she thought. 'No, no. Please no. Not the police. I've got a job. I'd lose my job if this came out. No way.'

'You're a fucking *rapist*. You think I give a fuck about your *job*?'

'No way. It's not rape when you consent. You don't get to—'

'*Consent?* What the fuck?' She could feel the fury rising in her throat. 'You burst into this house wearing a ski mask. There was no consent.' She was conscious of the knife still in her hand.

'Once you're on the site, that's consent.'

'What?'

'Everyone knows that. Once you agree to the terms of that site, that's the consent right there. Don't believe me, go check. As soon as you gave your information and checked the box, that was your consent.'

'What box? What?'

'The site. You know, where you signed up.'

'I promise I don't know what the fuck you're talking about.'

'Let me get my phone.'

'No way.'

'All right. Look, it's in this pocket.' He used his chin to indicate a breast pocket. She could see the bulge, under a Velcro flap.

Gingerly, she got nearer.

'Go on,' he said. 'I can't do anything. Just pull it out.'

She flipped the flap and brought out the phone, handling it carefully, as if her fingers were tongs. 'All right,' she said, taking two steps back. 'What's the code?'

She followed his prompts, opened the phone, clocked the picture of the attacker with what she presumed was a girlfriend, and then did as he instructed – going into his browser, set in 'Private' mode, rolling through the tabs until she was in the right place.

The page took the form of a low-spec message board, formatted like a website from the turn of the century. All words, no pictures. 'Keep scrolling,' he said.

And then, without further instruction from him, she found it. There in black and white was her first name and her precise street address.

'What is this?' she said.

'It's a . . . forum. For, er, you know. Like-minded people.'

'What kind of people?'

He was colouring around his neck. 'People who, you know.'

'No, I don't know.'

'It's for people who share rape fantasies.'

'Jesus Christ.'

'So you didn't post on there?'

'No, I fucking did not.' Maggie reached for a kitchen chair. She needed to breathe. 'You mean, men who want to rape someone and women who want to be—'

'—who *fantasize* about being raped. No one is actually raping anyone.'

'You're just forcing women to have sex with you.'

'It's role play. I play a role. You – you know, the women – play a role.'

'So that's why you said, "No knives"?'

'Yeah. It can get kind of dangerous, once knives are involved. Things can go wrong.'

'You don't say.'

'It's sort of a rule. In the community.'

'Community? Christ alive, you're not making a quilt.'

He gave a grimace of pain.

'And you saw my name and address on there and you thought that meant I wanted to play out a rape fantasy?'

He nodded. 'That's kind of the way it works.'

'Why me?'

'What?'

'Of all the listings on there, why did you come here?' Her breathing had barely settled. She still sounded as if she'd run up three flights of stairs.

'It'd only just gone up. I like the fresh listings. I mean, everyone does. But I'm really on it, so.'

'Did you just say, "fresh listing"?'

'You know, a new person on there. And you sounded very hot in the description.'

Maggie looked again at the phone. She was struggling to navigate her way around the very dense website. Her name and address had been embedded in what looked like a customized spreadsheet. Now she saw that that information was in a box, and that alongside it was another which read: *Mid-thirties, slim, fit, long auburn hair.* She felt a dull nausea stir in the well of her stomach. It meant someone, someone who knew her well enough to describe her and give her home address, had doxxed her – placing her personal details online for all to see – but, much worse, had offered her up to be raped, or near as damn it. The idea of it sickened her, her body placed on a slab for these sick losers to feast on. *Fresh listing.*

Then a new thought came, one that made her guts rebel.

'How long did you say this has been up?' She gestured towards the phone.

'Not long.'

'How long?'

'Maybe a few hours.'

'Because you're quick on the new material. But if you saw this, someone else will have seen it, right?'

He gave what she thought looked like a guilty nod.

So it could happen at any moment, another entrant through her bathroom window, some loser dressed up like a Provo volunteer playing Jack the Ripper.

'How did you manage to get in?'

He looked towards the bathroom. 'It was like I expected.'

'What? What do you mean, "like you expected"?'

He sighed, resting his head against the wall. He looked exhausted. She had, she realized, beaten him quite badly.

'Oh, I get it,' she said. 'The women leave their bathroom windows open, is that it?'

He said nothing.

'And mine was open?'

A tiny, weary nod.

'And if it'd been closed?'

'That might have been, you know, part of it.'

'Jesus.'

'I'd have turned back. But some guys would—'

'Have forced it open, because it might all be "part of it", all part of the fun?'

Now she wondered. Had she left that window open? Or had someone not only put her details on a rape site, but also broken into this apartment, leaving it primed for her faux rapist? She tried to think, spooling back to the shower she had taken in that room earlier today. If the room had got too steamy, she might have opened a window. On the other hand, this time of year, she'd surely have closed it . . .

Either way, it wasn't the main question. What mattered was

that someone had, deliberately and maliciously, set her up for what would have been an horrific, deeply traumatic experience. She looked again at the man who had let himself into her home, his hands and feet now bound, his head apparently throbbing.

'Normally, when you do . . . this,' Maggie said. 'If a woman resists, what happens?'

He paused, reluctant to answer.

'Tell me, for fuck's sake.'

'I keep going,' he whispered.

'You what?'

'I keep going. It's what you expect. That's all part of it.'

'So if I'd been scratching and kicking at you, screaming for you to get off me, you'd have—'

'Kept going. Yes.'

'Even if I'd said stop.'

'Absolutely.'

'Is there not a safe word or something?'

'Sure. And if you'd have used it, I'd have stopped.'

'Jesus Christ. And what is it, the safe word?'

'You don't know it?'

'Of course I don't bloody know it, you stupid bastard. I didn't put myself on your rape club thing; someone put me on it, remember? So go on. The safe word.'

'It's the name of the president.'

'Seriously?'

'Seriously.'

Very suddenly she decided she wanted everything about this episode to end and for this man to be out of her home. She was about to hand his phone back to him when she hesitated. She punched in the code one more time, saw the screen light up and then took a couple of screenshots, which she promptly forwarded to her own phone, taking care to delete her details from the 'Sent Messages' queue on his device. She noted the web address for the gross rape fantasy forum, then took a look at his emails and texts, jotted down his address and number, and finally dropped the phone back in his pocket.

'OK. These are the terms. I will cut this rope and let you go if you immediately do whatever it takes to remove me from that website, forum, thing.'

'I think only an admin can—'

'Well, find the admin and tell them. You get me off that thing right away. Within the next thirty minutes. Or else I will have the police on you so fast, your employer . . .' She consulted her scribbled note. 'Oh yes, Voltacity Systems of Reston, Virginia, won't know what hit them.'

The remaining colour drained from his face.

'Do we have a deal?'

He nodded.

'Good. One last thing.' She went to the table to retrieve her phone, came back and took three pictures of the man trussed up like a Thanksgiving turkey in her hallway. 'Just in case Voltacity are not sure if I'm telling the truth.'

She then moved forward, cut the rope at his ankles and, knife still in her hand, said quietly: 'Get out. Now.'

He struggled to his feet and she repeated, louder this time, 'Get out!'

Once he was standing, his face adopted a sheepish expression she found simultaneously ridiculous and loathsome. 'OUT!'

He raised his hands, a supplication to be untied.

'Deal with that yourself, you pathetic bastard,' she said. And, with a final shove, she pushed him out the front door. He could wander the streets like that, for all she cared.

She closed the door behind her, went to the bathroom to close the window, then contemplated her apartment. She didn't want to lie on her bed, because lying down was now associated with the scumbag who had been here just a moment ago; it was associated with what he had wanted to do to her. She didn't want to sit on the couch, because to sit in comfort felt wrong: nothing about her felt comfortable. She looked at her kitchen, where four drawers and cupboard doors were still open, and she could think only of her panicked search – how long ago was it?

So she sat instead on a simple, hard chair. She looked at her fingers, which were cut and scratched and trembling. She heard her own breathing. She wondered if crying would make her feel better. Or screaming or drinking. But she chose sitting and staring.

And slowly, in the silence, a resolve formed. To get out of this apartment, to get as far away as possible from it. And to find the person who might unlock at least one part of the riddle that was Natasha Winthrop.

FRIDAY

Chapter 31

Back in her campaign days, Maggie Costello was one of the few people on the team who actually enjoyed the endless hours on the road. And, by 'on the road', she did not mean generic travel but specifically being in a car, ideally at the wheel, gobbling up mile after mile of asphalt, watching it get swallowed up in the hood as she crossed the great, wide continent. She assumed it was because she was an outsider, because she had grown up on a small island in the Atlantic, that motoring across the surface of vast America enthralled her while the native-born barely glanced out of the window. For her, to touch the face of this new world was a wonder.

She was glad the thrill hadn't left her. The flight to Portland did the job, ninety minutes in the sky a good antidote to staying in an apartment that had been soiled by the intrusion of that man. Up in the air, she had felt the shudder of it still lingering on her skin. But renting the car and hitting the road, she at last felt it recede. She wound down the windows, forgiving the autumn chill, hoping the frigid air would prove too inhospitable for those memories to survive.

This part of the country was new to her. She had driven into every corner of New Hampshire of course but rarely ventured further east. The road from Portland offered the familiar pleasures of New England, the place names that alternated between the old country – as she powered along I-295 and then I-95 she saw signs for Durham, Bath, Wales and Manchester – and the world that had come to America to start anew: Lisbon, Poland, Dresden. So much of it was empty: immense tracts of farmland broken up by stretches of trees turning to myriad shades of gold, russet and auburn, interrupted by the odd hamlet, river or town.

Maggie kept the radio on. At the start of the journey, she could still catch the New Hampshire stations – she heard one ad for Harrison half a dozen times – but the signal soon petered out, giving way to the usual mix of Christian, country and talk. She found a public radio station playing classical music and let it drift over her.

Fresh listing. The phrase appalled her, but it was also useful. It meant whoever had unleashed the fantasy rapist on her had only just done it. Which meant there was a good chance that whatever had provoked them into action had only just happened. As she drove, she went back through the preceding hours, focusing on her visit to Natasha's office and the files she had rummaged through. Had someone been aware of her snooping? Had she stumbled on an unseen electronic tripwire, causing such alarm that her invisible adversary had decided to set her up for a violent sexual assault?

She'd been driving nearly an hour when she saw it, a road sign that reminded her why she was here and who she was dealing with. A few miles before the turn-off for Route 3, the road offered a turning in the other direction, west on the 202 to a place called Winthrop. A reminder that Natasha was the descendant of the New England aristocracy. If she had the confidence of a woman raised to believe her family owned the place, that's because, around here, they did.

But Maggie was not going to Winthrop, tempted though she was to look around. She was heading further east, past Liberty and on towards Belfast, to where the great land mass of America began to run into the Atlantic, dipping its toes into the vast, cold ocean. The coastline became jagged, all spits and spurs and peninsulas that would eventually be marked by a Canadian flag before giving way to the cold, endless water. The last stretch took her around a natural bay named for her destination. She had reached Penobscot Bay.

She pulled out her phone and looked again at the text Liz had sent her, giving her the name and address of V Winthrop. Nearly twelve hours had passed since that night-time call to her sister, waking her as she slept. Maggie had got an earful, but she hadn't been treated to the usual diatribe. *Why the fuck can't you keep regular hours, like a normal person? Why can't you live a regular life like a normal person? Why don't you marry Uri, have kids and stop trying to save the world?* In some ways, she almost regretted that the fusillade hadn't come. It had been the backbeat of their relationship for so many years, she'd grown used to it. In a way, she found it a comfort. She still mattered enough to Liz to infuriate her.

Maggie thought of Uri, filming on the other side of the world. He hadn't given up on her either. And yet what Liz hadn't said this time – hadn't needed to say because she'd said it before and Maggie always knew what her sister was thinking – gnawed at her all the same. She loved Uri, and he loved her. They had been through so much together. And yet they were not sleeping in the same bed or even living in the same city. They were apart and Liz's voice in her head was clear as to the reason why: *Because you want it that way, Maggie. Don't give me that bullshit about 'We like it' or 'It works'. It works for* you, *Mags. For you. That poor man would marry you tomorrow if you'd let him. But you just keep pushing him away.*

Her phone said her destination was still a few miles off, and yet the signs had welcomed her to the town of Penobscot, incorporated in 1787. She drove for a bit longer, waiting for a cluster of houses or shops or even a stop light, just to confirm she had arrived. She came across a sign directing her to the town hall and eventually approached what appeared to be a home, built in the old colonial style: white clapboard, three storeys, perfectly symmetrical with a front door in the middle and a single window on each side. It might have been made from gingerbread. Above the door hung a simple, handpainted sign whose font suggested the 1930s: 'Penobscot Municipal Building'.

Maggie parked outside, grateful for the chance to breathe real air and to stretch. She approached the door and saw that, though there was a light on, a handwritten sign had been taped to the window:

Back soon!
Sally

The notepaper confirmed that Sally was the town clerk.

Maggie put her hands on her hips and looked around. A couple more houses, signposts for the fire department and an elementary school. There was a mini-market down the 175, at least according to her phone. She didn't fancy cold-calling on V Winthrop, at least not right away. Sounding out the locals seemed like a smart idea, or at least a bit of displacement activity she could tell herself was legitimate.

She jumped back in the car and drove the short distance to the spot on the map. The phone had got it wrong. This was no mini-market, but a fishmonger-cum-takeout-stand, a wooden hut with a Pepsi sign on the roof that suggested the 1950s and three window counters, offering lobster in sea water, stuffed clams and smoked mussels, root beer and milk shakes and your body weight in fries. As Maggie got out, a fleeting picture drifted into her head unbidden: she saw herself here on a summer's evening, sitting at one of the picnic tables with Uri, looking out over the water. She enjoyed the image and let it linger. To her surprise, it expanded, as if the camera lens was pulling out, and now she could see there were children at the table. They must be Liz's boys, she thought. But there was no sign of her sister. And then, as if to shatter the illusion, another uninvited image floated behind her eyes: of the man in the ski mask, coming through her bathroom window.

Maggie approached the counter, peering at the chalkboards like a diner studying the menu.

Eventually a woman – middle-aged, wearing glasses that might have been ironically chic on a twenty-year-old but which were clearly worn in earnest – emerged clad in an apron and took up her place at the first window, so that Maggie had to move over to her, even though no one else was there.

'What's better today, the smoked haddock pâté or the crab-meat?' Maggie asked.

'Depends what you like.'

'I like both! What's freshest?'

'Everything's fresh here.' The woman looked over Maggie's shoulder, as if she were pressed for time.

'Well, why don't I take both. And I'll have a root beer while I'm at it.' Maggie smiled and looked for change. 'Guess it's all pretty quiet here just now?'

The woman nodded and said, 'Locals keep us busy enough.'

'Oh, I bet,' Maggie said, smiling wider still. She'd known so many women like this in Ireland: hard to crack at first, but once you broke through, they'd chat to you like a favourite auntie. 'They must be here all the time, reputation like yours.'

'You heard about us then, did you?'

'Just drove a few hundred miles from Portland to come see you.'

'You serious? Just to come here?'

'Reviews are incredible for this place. You've got a following!'

'Well, we do our best.'

'Truth is, I was happy to come by. I'm visiting someone out on Pierce Pond Road. Not too far from here, is it?'

'No, you're almost there. Who is it you're visiting with?'

Maggie had anticipated this question but had not come up with an answer she was happy with. The problem was one of gender. She did not know if V Winthrop was a man or a woman. So she answered, 'Oh, the Winthrop place,' and then immediately asked for more detail on the chowder recipe, asking if it was true that the clams were better in Maine than in Massachusetts.

The woman seemed to buy it too, resting her hands, one on top of the other, on her belly, as if settling in for a chat, before deciding this most complex of questions could only be settled by giving Maggie a taste. She found a small styrofoam cup and ladled in an espresso's worth, handing it to Maggie for approval.

The broth was warm and soothing, and, as Maggie turned around to gaze at the ocean, she felt a sensation to match the image she'd had before. She could taste a vacation in this place, wandering around with Uri at her side. Sharper still was the taste of the very idea of vacation, of relaxation, of being somewhere without pressure, where the only decision was what you might eat that evening, and where you could actually be interested in the difference between the clams of Massachusetts and Maine, rather than using feigned interest as a ruse to win someone's trust. She couldn't remember the last time she had lived like that. She knew Uri wanted to, but she could barely imagine it.

She turned around to see that the counter was empty, the woman gone. Perhaps she was collecting the pâté from a storage fridge round the back. Maggie peered in and could hear the woman's voice, coming from what was surely some sort of office area. And then she heard it.

Not the words, those were indecipherable, but the tone.

Instantly recognizable, it was the sound of a voice lowered, a furtive phone call. Instantly, Maggie understood.

She rushed to her car, switching on the engine and screeching off in a matter of seconds. The phone said Pierce Pond Road was just two minutes away. For someone committed to making a getaway, two minutes would be plenty. Maggie kept her eyes on the oncoming traffic: any car that swept past her could be V Winthrop, making a dash for it.

Maggie replayed the encounter with the woman at the seafood place. It was the mention of the 'Winthrop place' that had triggered the change. That was when she had become friendlier, readier to chat. If Maggie had been in her shoes, that was exactly what she would have done. Hide your reaction, stall for time and then, when the moment presented itself, make a quick call to the Winthrop residence, and tip off V Winthrop that someone was onto him or her.

As Maggie powered along the road, with its view to her left of what the signs told her was Hutchins Cove, she worked through what that had to mean. That either this V Winthrop was a recluse, whom the locals knew to alert should his or her privacy ever be at risk or, more simply, that Winthrop had something to hide, and had won the collusion of the locals in keeping his or her secret.

An SUV sped by, driving almost as fast as she was. There was barely a moment to take it in, but Maggie registered a youngish white man at the wheel. She thought about wheeling around and giving chase, but instinct told her to keep driving forward. It had only been ninety seconds; there was a chance that V Winthrop was still there, at the house.

Maggie turned right onto Pierce Pond Road, instantly slowing down. She didn't want to announce her arrival any more than she had to. There were no more than a few houses, hundreds of yards apart. She glanced down at the note she had made in Natasha's office, checking the house number. She drove a bit further, worried that she was now going suspiciously slow. She imagined V Winthrop watching her from a hiding place, waiting for her car to pass, then stealing away unnoticed.

Finally, she was near enough to pull over and stop. She closed the car door quietly.

The house was old and wide, made of white timbers and grey painted shutters. There was a gentle smell of lavender on the breeze, a last gasp before the fall. Crawling and gnarling around the windows was a wisteria, thinning in the cold.

Maggie knocked on the front door. She noticed an old plate on the left-hand post, with a space where the name should be. It was blank. Though when she looked closer, she could see scratch marks and the trace of an outline where it had once been. The name had been removed.

She knocked again, more firmly this time. Still nothing. She leaned rightward, to look into the window. The curtains were drawn. The room to her left was not obscured, but it was dark and empty.

Had she really driven all this way, only to be foiled at the last moment? She was furious with herself. She should have come here straight away, using her only advantage: surprise. Instead, she had surrendered that, blabbing away to the first local she met. Such a basic error. And to think Winthrop was in that car, already steaming west on Route 1 by now. She hadn't even got a plate number. Who was he, Maggie wondered. An ex-husband of Natasha's perhaps? Even a current one who, for whatever reason, had to be kept quiet? Maybe if—

There was a noise from inside. Maggie looked upward, girding herself against attack. Reflexively, she took a step back, away from the door. Another noise. Then another, then a footstep, then another, each one getting nearer. Until, at last, the door opened and Maggie came face to face with a ghost.

Chapter 32

She was tall, elegant and with eyes so blue they seemed to pierce the air. If Maggie had to guess, she'd have said mid-seventies, though as she held her gaze, she wondered if this woman was, in fact, as much as a decade older. Truth was, it was hard to tell. Maggie had talked about it with Liz often enough: growing up where they did, hardly anyone lived to be really old. Even their nan had barely seen seventy. Maybe it was the drink, as it was for their ma, or the diet or something. Whatever the explanation, Maggie had not grown up meeting many people over eighty.

And the ones she had certainly didn't look like this. This woman's back was so straight, she looked positively aristocratic, if not regal. Put a tiara on her and she could have walked out of one of those British costume dramas that Liz lapped up.

Her hair was white and her cheeks had a blush of colour, hinting at bracing morning walks and fresh air. Her eyes carried a sparkle that was whimsical and somehow curious and which reminded Maggie immediately of Natasha.

'Can I help you?'

Maggie paused, unsure what to say, unprepared for this moment, despite hours of flying and driving and endless time to think. Only then did she notice that the woman at the door was wearing a coat. 'Are you going somewhere? Could we perhaps walk together?'

The woman smiled, a tight, steely smile. 'I don't think so.' And she now pushed past Maggie, towards the car – a battered station wagon, with fake timber panels.

Maggie could hardly get in the car with her. What was she going to do? Start pursuing her in her own car? She could hear Uri's voice. 'You got into a high-speed chase with an octogenarian? Seriously?'

She would have to make her move right now. She caught up with the woman as she was unlocking the driver's side door. Maggie called out: 'Natasha sent me here.'

The woman ignored her. Maggie could see, from the angle of the car door, that she had time to utter perhaps five more words before this woman would be gone.

'I work for Natasha Winthrop.' She paused. Maggie approached, until she was just a yard or two away. The old woman was in her seat, but hadn't closed the door. She was holding the belt, about to click it into place.

'It's true. I'm not a journalist. I don't work for anyone else. I work for Natasha. She's in trouble and she asked me to do what I can.'

'And who are you exactly?'

'My name is Maggie Costello. I work in Washington.' From the look on the woman's face, she could see that that was insufficient. With a hint of surrender in her voice, she said, 'I'm . . . I'm kind of a troubleshooter.'

'A troubleshooter? Is that a job?'

'It is for people who need me. And, right now, Natasha needs me. She asked me to help. And I'm trying, I really am. I've come all this way, because I think you might be able to help me help her.'

They held each other's gaze for what, to Maggie, felt like ten or twenty long seconds, Maggie looking down, this woman – V Winthrop or whoever she was – craning to look upward, still holding her seat belt. Her eyes revealed nothing, except the intense act of assessment. She was judging Maggie, deciding whether she merited trust.

Eventually, she released the seat belt and exhaled. 'All right,' she said. 'We shall have tea and then I shall make a decision.'

The house was modest and defiantly timeless. Maggie could see nothing in it that might not have been there in 1985. There was a TV set, but it faced no chairs and was set at an angle that suggested it was looked at only rarely. The furniture was worn, the arms of the main sofa threadbare, the stuffing visible. On the walls were faded prints – country scenes, a racehorse – and antique maps. There were books everywhere and no computer.

Maggie had her head cocked to one side, reading the spines – the *Federalist Papers*, a biography of William Penn, a Walt

Whitman anthology, the Brontë sisters – when her host returned to the room, carrying a tray with, as promised, tea. She took the armchair, and gestured towards the sofa for Maggie. Behind her was a window, looking out onto a paddock, fringed by red maple trees on both sides, arranged like sentries.

She didn't pour the tea straight away. She let it brew a while, as Maggie's nan had done. 'So you're here to get Natasha out of trouble, is that right?'

'That's right.'

'And you thought it would help her to come here?'

'Yes.'

'Does she know you came here?'

'No.'

'Why not?'

'Because . . .' Maggie hesitated, before deciding to tell the truth. 'Because I wasn't sure she would allow me to come here. Because I suspect she isn't telling me everything. And yet if I'm to help her, I need to know everything.'

'So if she didn't tell you, how did you know to come here?'

Again Maggie hesitated, and again she opted for honesty. She had nothing else.

She explained about her search of the office, the phone records, the recurring number traced to this address. That last detail prompted a raised eyebrow. 'This is an unlisted number.'

'I know,' Maggie said, glancing downward in an involuntary show of contrition. 'I have a sister who is very skilled. With technology.'

'I see.'

'She connected the number to this house and this house is registered in the name of V Winthrop.'

'Yes.'

'And yet, Natasha told me that her Aunt Peggy died long ago and that, after that, she had no family.'

The woman said nothing. She neither nodded nor shook her head, nor closed her face in a deliberate and forced show of inscrutability. (A move Maggie had seen plenty of politicians make when confronted with awkward facts, an almost animal reflex of self-protection, like those underwater creatures who turned themselves into a rock, camouflaged and unmoving, when a predator approached.) On the contrary, she held her gaze, looking intently at Maggie as if listening closely, waiting for her to say more. Almost anybody else would have spoken, to fill the void. But Maggie was practised at this. In a staring contest, she had learned not to blink.

Finally, the woman spoke. 'To be clear,' she said. 'Natasha gave you access to her office?'

'Yes.'

'And that included her computer passwords?'

'Yes.'

'And her telephone records, her bills and so on – they were all there, on that computer?'

'Yes.'

Now the older woman sat back, almost visibly digesting this information, a vein by her temple twitching slightly, as if to denote active processing, the way the lights on a computer used to flicker when the machine performed a particularly challenging task. She then smoothed her skirt, her palms moving from her thighs to her knees, and cleared her throat.

'Natasha is a very careful young woman. She tends not to make mistakes. But nonetheless she gave you access to her computer, and allowed you free rein to find a path here.' She cleared her throat a second time. 'To find me.'

Maggie said nothing, not wanting to emit so much as a noise that might make this woman change her mind.

Finally, she stood and offered Maggie her hand. 'My name is Virginia Winthrop. I'm Natasha's great-aunt. Everyone calls me Peggy.'

Chapter 33

Penobscot, Maine

After that handshake, the temperature instantly increased by two or three degrees. As Ms V Winthrop transformed into Peggy, her shoulders dropped and she talked at twice the previous speed. She was solicitous now, insisting that Maggie eat something after 'such a frightfully long journey' and positively fussing around her, as if hosting not a stranger but her own great-niece on a rare and precious visit.

It was the accent that struck Maggie most, an even more pronounced variant of the Brahmin inflection that so distinguished Natasha. While Natasha had made the odd concession to modernity, the occasional vowel flattened out by exposure to television, Peggy spoke in a voice that was surely unchanged since the 1930s, a voice redolent of ladies' colleges and country houses, of lacrosse tournaments and New England estates as old as the republic.

Maggie peppered her with questions, learning that as a child

Peggy had been 'thin as a peg – hence the name', and that she had moved to Maine over a decade ago, 'once Natasha was out of college and making her way'. Peggy had spent her childhood vacations at Pilgrim's Cove. When Maggie raised a quizzical eyebrow, she explained that it had been vacations only because the rest of the time she had been at boarding school. Maggie dipped her head to signal, *Of course. Just like Natasha.* The school had been on what Peggy called 'the mainland', meaning the bit of Massachusetts that wasn't Cape Cod.

She had been raised as one of two siblings, her older brother Reed inheriting Pilgrim's Cove when he turned twenty-one. 'He was the eldest and he was a boy, so that's just the way it was. I didn't question it for a moment.' Reed had had only one child, also Reed but known by his middle name of Aldrich, and so Aldrich had inherited the house when his father had died. 'He barely had time to enjoy it, poor soul. He was posted to Germany when the children were tiny and then . . .'

'The accident?'

'Quite.'

'And what about Natasha? When she came back from Germany – after the accident, I mean – she'd have had the house to herself. That must have been strange.'

'Which is why I was there with her. I'd always had a small workman's cottage on the estate. But of course, once Natasha was there I moved back into the main house.'

'So you raised her?'

'Well, she was at school most of the time, of course. And then off to college.'

'Sure, but when she was there, it was just the two of you.'

Peggy gave a small nod, which Maggie took to be a gesture of old-fashioned modesty. 'We got on rather well. I don't mind telling you I enjoyed those years very much. As you have probably guessed, I never had children of my own.'

Maggie smiled back and felt a wave of shame at her next question. She was aware that it would hurt and yet there was no way around it. At least no way that Maggie could see.

'Your relationship was very private, I think.'

Peggy got up, nominally to refresh the teapot. She called out from the small kitchen at the end of the corridor. 'You'll stay for supper, I hope?'

Maggie sighed. How nice it would be just to relax for once, to sit and talk to someone without plotting the conversation as a game of chess, to enjoy being cooked for by a sweet old lady who, though she might as well be a different species from Maggie's nan, was at least cosy and welcoming. How lovely it would be to settle into this sofa and let herself relax, maybe even doze off after that flight and the long drive.

But that was not how it worked, not for her. She had to stay focused, plotting her next move, her antennae at attention, alert to even the subtlest morsel of information. At this moment, that meant making another attempt to breach a defence Peggy had shored up securely. Maggie had made an initial approach a few moments ago, which the older woman had repelled early, so now she would have to approach from a different angle.

Maggie followed her host into the kitchen, offering to help as she watched her remove various items from the fridge and a

SAM BOURNE

larder. Keeping her voice as relaxed as she could, she said, 'I'm guessing you haven't seen Natasha's place in Washington.'

Peggy ignored the question, stooping to retrieve an enamel baking tray from a low cupboard. Maggie would have to try again.

'She's kept you out of view. And don't get me wrong,' Maggie said hurriedly, as if to snuff out an objection Peggy had lodged, though Peggy had still said nothing. 'Smart move for anyone who might run for president, keep everyone you love out of harm's way.' No reaction. 'But the thing is, she hasn't just started saying it. She's been saying it for several years, long before this presidential talk got cranked up. It's there in those magazine pieces and profiles.'

She watched Peggy's face, hoping for a sign of curiosity or even confusion. Maggie longed for the woman to say the words, to ask the obvious question. To just make it a little bit easier for her. But Peggy was now immersed in pots and pans and chopping boards and her message was clear: *If you have something to say, you're going to have to jolly well say it.*

'You see,' Maggie began. 'Natasha tells people, and has done for some time, that she has no surviving family.'

No reaction.

'She includes you in that.'

Not so much as a look.

'She told me that her Aunt Peggy is dead.' A pause. 'That you are dead.'

Maggie held her breath, as Peggy slid a dish into the oven and then stood back to full height, one knee clicking loudly to mark

274

the occasion. She looked over at Maggie and said, 'While that's cooking, why don't you come into the drawing room. There's something you should see.'

Maggie followed but warily. A chill came over her which she associated with fear, before she told herself that the very idea was absurd. This woman, who said she was Peggy – but, come to think about it, had offered no proof – this woman was, given the chronology she had set out, not far short of ninety; she posed no physical threat. And yet, here Maggie was, in this desolate spot on the Atlantic coast in mid-November, far away from anyone, with a woman who, if she was telling the truth, had seemingly colluded in the lie of her own death.

Peggy was reaching for a book, stretching on tiptoes. A dancer, Maggie guessed, back in the day. She pictured her some eighty years earlier, long sessions at the barre at boarding school. *On the mainland.*

Peggy grasped hold of a battered volume that, on squinting, revealed itself to be *Moby Dick*. Maggie imagined an evening ahead of literary readings, from which Maggie would be expected to divine some coded lesson. The thought made her impatient, irritable. She was about to say something, to declare that she'd had enough tiptoeing and that, if she were to help Natasha, she'd need some concrete answers, when she saw Peggy stretch once more. She was sending her hand back into the space which had, until now, contained the story of the great whale.

Her face was taut with concentration as her fingers probed for a second or two, her eyes opening wide on discovering her quarry. She took a deep breath and pulled out a book that was smaller than the Melville, though larger than a regular paperback. It had a stiff cardboard cover, bearing a blue marble pattern. It was a notebook.

'Here,' Peggy said, handing it to Maggie. 'You can be the second person to read it.'

'Did you write this?' Maggie said in a whisper.

'No. Not me. I read it. But I didn't write it.'

'Did Natasha write this?'

Peggy smiled, as if amused by the improbability of such a suggestion. 'No, not Natasha. Someone else entirely.'

Chapter 34

My name is Mindy and I am nine years old. I live in Little Rock, Arkansas. Actually I don't live in Little Rock—more on the edge of Little Rock just before it stops being a city and becomes fields and farms. If Little Rock was an actual rock our house wouldn't be in the middle of the rock it would be kind of part of the moss on the outside.

I've lived here since I can remember though I have maybe one or two memories from before. I live here with my mom and my dad and my brother Paul though I call him Paulie. Paulie is older than me.

When I say that their my mom and my dad and my brother maybe I should explain something about that. They weren't always my mom and my dad and my brother. When I was born I had a different mom and she tried to look after me but she couldn't so she gave me to this family even though they didn't know me and I didn't know them. They were called my foster family and I was not going to stay with them forever maybe just for a year or two but now they are my family and a letter came in the mail saying that I am now theyre daughter and my name is the same as theyres.

I love my dad because he's a plummer and he fixes stuff and sometimes he lets me join in when he and Paulie play with the ball out in the yard. And once there was this basketball hoop and he put me on his shoulders so he and I were really tall and we could dunk the ball real easy and Paulie got mad. I love my mom because she brushes my hair and when I was little, she read stories to me before sleep. She also makes amazing pie only sometimes because we don't have much money but my favourite is apple but sometimes also peekan. I love Paulie as well because sometimes I can't fall asleep and I like knowing that if a monster came they would be scared of him because he's older than me and bigger.

That is enough for today. I will write in this book every day I promise.

Maggie closed the book and looked again at the cover. Pencilled on the front were the words, *The Diary of Mindy Hagen*, along with a few childish doodles that had faded. She flicked back inside and smiled as she saw that young Mindy's resolve had not lasted long: her next journal entry came much later. The ink was black now rather than blue and the letters were less round.

I am sorry diary that I did not come back when I said I would. I have been busy at school and also playing soccer for the team (yesterday we won three to nothing and I scored!!). But there is something on my mind and I'm not sure who I can talk to about it. Definitely not my Mom or Dad and definitely not anyone at school even though I think Lisa might understand but I don't want to.

I don't even want to write this down and I'm scared if someone finds this but I don't know what else to do. After I have written this page I am going to hide this book where no one can find it.

So P and I share a room and his bed is in one corner and mine is in the other and normally he goes to sleep first and I'm the one who is still awake. So a few weeks ago I was getting into bed and I noticed he was looking at me funny. I got into bed and didnt think about it but I must have fallen asleep because I woke up in the night. Maybe it was an hour later maybe it was much less, I couldnt really tell. But I woke up because I heard a noise. Kind of like a shuffling sound or like rustling.

I immediately looked over to his bed because thats what I do when I'm scared and normally he's there and I feel OK. But the bed was empty and he wasnt in it. And then I looked up and I realized he was standing right there right next to my bed and and. I dont want to say but I was scared and he told me not to say a word about what he was doing and about what I had seen and that if I said anything to Mom or Dad then he would kill me. And I was scared and my heart was beating so fast I didnt say anything and then he put his hand over my mouth and all I could think about was where his hand had been and I didnt want it near my mouth and he leaned in so that his face was real close and he said Dont scream. Swear you wont say anything. Swear. Swear. And my heart was thumping so loud and I didnt like his hand on my mouth and I couldnt speak with his hand there I was gagging but he made me say it and so I said I swear.

He went back to his bed and I could hear the rustling noise again and I think I know what he was doing but I didnt want to imagine it and I was scared and I had bad dreams and in the morning I went to school. The teacher asked me to read the story to the rest of the class because she said Im a good reader and for a while I didnt have to think about what happened because I could think about the story and later when we did math I could think about that because I could do all the sums even without really trying. We played soccer and when we got changed I thought about what had happened and I didnt like taking my clothes off because I was imagining him looking at me.

Mom and Dad think I'm doing my homework but I did that real quick *so I am doing this instead but I need to stop before he gets back. He's at football practice but when he gets home I need to make sure this is hidden away somewhere he would never find it. I dont want to fall asleep tonight maybe if I can keep myself awake I can make sure he doesnt do it again I'll just be looking and listening all night like a bat or a hawk whose always watching and never blinks.*

Maggie looked up from the handwritten pages and surveyed the small guest bedroom where Peggy had invited Maggie to rest after her 'long travels' and to read the journal in peace. The walls gave off the very faintest hint of must. It wasn't unpleasant. On the contrary, it was familiar, reassuring. It reminded her of staying the night at her nan's.

She was reading the journal on a narrow single bed. Again, it was old-fashioned, if not downright ascetic: no duvet, or comforter, as they called it here, but rather a sheet and a fairly rough blanket. Given that Aunt Peggy was a Winthrop, a family with serious money, it seemed to be making a point. Something about the virtues of modesty and restraint, of old money wearing itself lightly.

Was this where Natasha stayed on her visits here, a grown woman, an accomplished lawyer, curled up in a single bed as if she were still the teenage niece? The funny thing was, Maggie could picture it.

But that still left an obvious question. Why would Natasha lie about her one surviving relative? Why would she go out of her way to say to Maggie and to everyone else that her beloved Aunt Peggy was dead?

Maggie had assumed this journal would contain some kind of

answer. But this story – while unsettling – shed no light at all. Was this a child whose case Natasha had taken up? Would the denouement of this tale be a plea from Aunt Peggy? *And you see, Maggie, it's girls like Mindy that my niece wants to help. That's why she's running for president.* Maggie remembered the Tuesday deadline. There was so little time.

Resisting the urge to flick to the end, conscious that Peggy had removed this notebook from a hiding place, that she had shown it to no one else until today – *You can be the second person to read it* – Maggie went back to the diary. She saw a clear break, a change in the handwriting that suggested Mindy had left a long gap between entries, that she had grown older.

Dear Diary, I've missed you. It's been two years and ten months since I picked you up. You've been buried in the . . . well, you know where you were. I don't have to tell you to keep that place a secret, because you don't say a word about anything. You're the best kind of best friend. I trust you.

So you probably know what's been happening but I'm going to write as much of it down as I can. I wish there was someone I could tell. Someone else, I mean. (No offense.) Sometimes I think about my birth mom and whether I could tell her. I try and picture her face, imagining what it would be like to talk to her. I imagine her voice, and when I imagine it, it's kind of soft and soothing, like a lady in one of those ads for Thanksgiving gravy or for soap powder that smells so nice you hold the blanket next to your cheek even though I don't think she really talks like that. I don't know how she talked, I don't remember her voice at all. Or her face. And I don't have any photos. But P once said she was a junkie—he kept chanting "Your mom's a crackhead, your mom's a crackhead"—and even though I pretended to ignore him, and did that little smile I sometimes do to show that it doesn't bother me, I can't get that out of my head. And sometimes I imagine her like one of the addicts on Summit Street, her skin covered in spots and so thin her bones show. Maybe she's sleeping outside or maybe she's dead.

Anyway, I've got off the point which is that I'm going to tell you because there's no one else I can tell. It's about P. I just read the last thing I wrote in here when I was ten and it made me sad because I was so shaken up back then about what had happened, and now I'm like, well, yeah, of course you were shaken up, you were only ten, but also, come on, that was nothing compared to what happened afterwards.

I was right about what I thought he was doing to himself, standing over me, next to my bed. He would have been fourteen then, when I was ten. I told myself then that maybe I had got it wrong, that maybe he was having a nightmare or like sleepwalking or something. You know, like he was doing it without knowing? I kind of wanted that to be what it was, I guess.

But then it happened another time and then once more. And the next time, he didn't hide it or look embarrassed. He said that same thing again, that if I said a word to Mom and Dad he would kill me. He made me swear. And I promise you, if you'd heard him, you'd have known he meant it.

So I had to just let him do it. I tried to pretend I wasn't there, closing my eyes and imagining I was somewhere far away but he made me open my eyes. He wanted me to look. He wanted me to keep looking until he "finished". That's what he called it. I was scared of it, I would turn my face away when it happened. But when I did that, he slapped my face and made me look.

That went on for a few weeks, every night he'd do it. I dreaded night time because I knew it was going to happen. One time Mom was telling me it was past my bedtime and I needed to get to bed, and I didn't want to go and I began crying, and I think P must have thought I was about to say something because he gave me this look, like a glare, and I swear I thought he was going to kill me that night.

Instead, he punished me a different way. Now I didn't just have to look while he touched himself. Now he made me touch him. He made these noises, kind of like grunting, when I did it and I hated it so much, I tried closing my eyes and pretending I was somewhere else, that my hand was touching something else, but he told me I had to look.

After that, it got worse. I think it was kind of my fault because when I got a bit older, like when I turned twelve, my body started changing and that made him even more crazy. He would stare at me when my Mom and Dad were around, just looking at my chest and stuff. I tried to hide from him, kind of to cover myself up and hunch over, but he was always staring at me. Every night in our room, he'd stare at me and then try to touch me and when I said no, he would put his hand over my mouth or he would pin me down on the bed and whisper in my ear while he was doing things to me. He'd say, "You make even a little sound and I will take your eyes out with a fork." And he'd say other things, about knives and about other parts of me, that I don't even want to write down.

And while he was saying these things he'd be doing things. It would hurt so much, but he'd put a pillow over my mouth so that no one could hear me. One day I was gagging from, you know, and Mom must have been up and heard the sound of me coughing, because from outside the door she said, "Are you all right in there, Mindy?" I wanted so much to say "Mommy, come in here" or "Please help, Mom" or just "Help" and for a second I was about to. I was on the verge of doing it. But all he had to

do was glance at me—he didn't even have to glare—and I knew that he
would kill me if I dared say anything.

Also I was ashamed. I didn't want Mom to see me like that. I know she
would know that P forces me to do it. But it would get him into so much
trouble if Mom knew what was happening. She would be so mad at him.
They would send him away or maybe even go to jail or something and this
whole family would be ruined. She'd be crying and he'd be crying and it
would all be my fault. My fault for telling, my fault for having this body
that makes him this way.

Maggie looked out of the window, at the cold, grey sea. She
was finding this unbearable. She knew of course that child abuse
happened, just as she knew that there were men and boys who
preyed on underage girls for sex, and that both horrors happened most often within families. She *knew* all that: how in this
world could you not? But that didn't mean she forced herself
often – or ever – to look at the reality of what that meant,
not to really look at it. This poor girl, Mindy, was demanding
Maggie's attention, demanding she stare into the abyss. The
truth was, Maggie had always avoided doing that, skimming
past the news stories, turning down the radio, finding the pain
of it too intense. Now, with Mindy's diary in her hands, Maggie
had no escape.

But why was this diary in Peggy Winthrop's home? A thought
came in swift reply. Perhaps this was a charity case, embraced by
this Brahmin family as part of their patrician duty. Maybe Peggy
was going to ask Maggie to help in some way, lending a hand to
a foundation endowed with the great Winthrop fortune. *I'll help*

you to help Natasha, but first I want you to help me and these terribly unfortunate girls.

And yet, the journal had been hidden. No one, apart from Peggy herself, had read it before. If this was a case study, why the intense secrecy?

Maggie was becoming impatient for an answer. That, coupled with her reluctance to digest any more of the agonizing details, made her skim through the next paragraphs, which, she could see, detailed in the sometimes plain, sometimes bewildered language of a young teenage girl, her further abuse at the hands of her adopted brother. It seemed Paulie, or P, repeatedly raped Mindy, coercing her through both actual violence and the threat of it. And all of this took place under the roof of the people Mindy regarded as her parents. A vulnerable young girl who had kept this torture secret and, if anything, blamed herself for it.

Maggie stopped at an entry written soon after Mindy had told her diary that she had turned fourteen.

Today I saw something that shocked me so much and I still don't know what to do about it or what to think about it. What's even weirder is that I don't know what to feel about it. I just feel numb. The one thing I know is that I have to tell you about it. I've been waiting for this moment, when I could be alone with a pen and with you so I could just get it all down.

So I was going back from school and now that P has finished at school I walk the last bit on my own. I didn't mind, I quite like having time on my own. But then I remembered that I'd left my math book at school and we have a test tomorrow so I had to turn around and get it. Normally I'd only ever go the street way, by Chalamont, but this time, because it's like summer, I thought I'd take the shortcut, through the woods.

So I did, and I got the book from school and then I took the shortcut again, and this time it was like after five and as I was walking I could hear the sound of voices. But not like the voices of people having fun. This sounded different.

Something made me stop, just by the dip where the old abandoned wagon is, where P always used to play when he was little. I was by this tree, kind of looking down into the dip, with this completely clear view. And there was P. And he was with Helen, from my class.

It took me a second or two, because at first I thought maybe they were fooling around, but it was obvious: he was—Oh, God, I can't even write it down—he was . . . doing to her what he does to me. He was forcing her. She was kind of screaming, but he had his whole arm across her mouth, like a gag. And he was using his other hand to pin her arm behind her back. She was in such pain, because he's really strong, and he pushed her down onto her knees and then he forced her to, you know, in her mouth, and he was slapping her face at the same time. Like he does with me. There was worse stuff, but I can't even . . . I don't want to write it down.

I didn't say anything. I should have done, I should have screamed or called for help. But it was like I was stuck there, my legs nailed to the ground. I couldn't move.

And I had the strangest feeling. Because for the longest time, I'd been thinking that maybe—I don't know how to say this—that maybe what P does is sort of normal, that maybe this is just what brothers do with their sisters, even though no one else ever talks about it? Or maybe no one else does what he does, but that's because of me, because of something I do, that makes P like that.

But now there was Helen. When I saw him gagging her and twisting her arm, I suddenly felt, I don't know, but it was kind of like relief, because I thought it's not just me who makes him this way. If he does this to another girl, not even his sister, then maybe it's him that's the bad one, not me. I'm not explaining it very well.

And then I realized that if it's not just me he's doing this to, then someone has to do something. Because he could keep hurting people, not just his family.

I was thinking, maybe I should tell the school? But P doesn't go to school anymore. He's working now, as an apprentice in the shop. I really want to talk to Helen, but then I'll have to admit that I saw her and she'll feel so ashamed—I know she will—and what if she tells P that I saw, because she might do that, and then what would he do to me? Or I could go to the police, but then he would kill me.

I don't know what to do, which is why I wanted to come to you, the friend I trust most in the world. But telling you doesn't solve anything.

There was a change in ink colour, and then, though it was not clear how much time had passed, another line had been added:

I think there's only one thing I can do. I'm going to have to tell Mom and Dad.

Chapter 35

Washington, DC, one day earlier

'Guys, listen up. Now, I'm going to leave all this to you experts here – you know this stuff better than me – so I just wanted to say a few very general things, before throwing it over to you all. First: thank you – thank you for coming today. Not easy to cut an hour into the kind of schedule I know you're working.' Here Senator Tom Harrison leaned in towards the flat, grey, starfish-like device at the centre of the boardroom table, a speakerphone designed for conference calls like this one. 'I'm looking at you, California. And you, Arizona. I know this is a horrible hour of the day for you, so truly, I'm extra grateful.' He leaned back. 'But all of you, seriously, I know you're putting your backs into this campaign and I appreciate it.'

There was some grateful nodding. Watching, Dan Benson dutifully joined in. But he also kept an eye on the couple of staffers, both senior, who remained impassive. That could just be their rank: they didn't need to suck up. But it could also be a mild signal of dissent, their way of registering that this meeting was happening because things were not all well. And that that was not their fault.

'Second,' the candidate continued, 'we're here because we're in a very unusual situation. Normally, you're in a race with the candidates who've declared their candidacy. But this time, there's a lot of interest about someone who has not declared, but who might. True, this someone has only, what, three working days to jump in before the deadline for nominations? Also true that this someone has no political experience and has never served in elected office – which used to be considered a negative in this business, but heck, things have changed.' There was just an edge of bitterness, which even the folksy delivery and whitened-toothed smile could not conceal. 'Even more unusual, this potential candidate is not currently free but is in *custody* awaiting trial for homicide. So, all in all, a real strange situation, even wilder than my first race for county commissioner, which was about one hundred and thirty years ago.' More polite laughter.

'So I'm going to sit back and listen as you geniuses kick this around, work the angles. Like I say, I'm just a kid from the South Side. You're the experts. I want to hear how you see it.'

As campaign manager, Doug Teller assumed the right to speak first. The presence of him, Greg Carter and the candidate himself attested to the significance of this gathering.

'All right, I just want to stress that both the content and fact of this meeting is strictly confidential. When the senator has completed two full terms in the White House, and this gathering is mentioned in the memoirs, then and only then will any public reference to it having taken place be forgiven – and maybe not even then. There were no papers circulated in advance of this meeting, there is no PowerPoint presentation and none of you will write any notes. You've all left your cellphones with the team on your way in. Sorry that we're behaving like paranoid Stasi assholes, but that's what a poll lead of three points, forty-one to thirty-eight, does to ya.'

Dan Benson registered the ripple that went around the room. As Director of Comms, he'd had advance warning of the poll numbers Teller was referring to, but most hadn't. He could see the faces falling, behind each pair of eyes the same question, one he had asked himself: *Have I just tanked my career by jumping on a ship that is holed below the waterline?*

Teller had seen the same look. 'OK, before you all start hawking your résumés around the Hill, let me clarify. That's not the headline figure. Basic horse race, voting intentions, the senator is still nineteen points ahead. Nice fat lead. But when you look underneath the hood, it's not so pretty.

'Our big issue is gender. We do fine when you ask registered party supporters who they'd prefer as the party's nominee for president. But you know my view. At this stage of the cycle, you ask that, it's basically a quiz question. We might as well be asking, "Who have you heard of that is running for president?" With name recognition in the high eighties, the senator's always going to win that one.

'But with prompts, once we start suggesting names, things look very different. Strip out don't knows, make it a head-to-head, Harrison versus Winthrop, and the senator's lead is down to eleven points among all voters. He leads by nineteen among men. Among women? It's just three. That's not a gender gap. That's a gender chasm – and we're falling right into it.'

With that, Teller did not throw to Greg Carter, which would have been the natural progression down the chain of command. Instead, he gave a nod to Ellen Stone. Teller was no fool. He understood that this was a message that couldn't be delivered by a succession of men. Ellen took her cue and began to speak.

'We've done qual as well as quant on this, and we're getting the same message. Our initial assumption – and the assumption, we understand, made by all the campaigns as well as by the media – was that once Winthrop was formally charged, that would burst the bubble. Among men that is clearly true: her numbers are low; among white men lower, among white men who didn't go to college, lower still.

'But women see this completely differently. In focus groups, we're hearing women describe her as a "political prisoner", as a "champion" of women, and all lining up behind the idea that there's more to this story than they're being told. Big numbers across all sectors, white women, black and Latina women, non-college – every one. At several groups, women said, unprompted, that they wouldn't just vote for her, they would *volunteer* for her.'

'And this is a woman currently in jail.' It was Teller, leaving no room for misunderstanding.

'The stuff about the dating sites and BDSM hurts her with older women, but nowhere near as much as we'd assumed before going into the field. And in other categories, many just don't believe it.'

SAM BOURNE

'Don't believe what?'

All eyes turned to the head of the table, where Tom Harrison himself was sitting. No aw-shucks folksiness now; he was all business. That three-point lead among women, within the margin of error and against a novice whose name recognition had stood at zero a matter of weeks ago, had got his attention.

Ellen now addressed him directly. 'They don't believe the police case against Winthrop, Senator. That she had somehow plotted to kill this man in cold blood. The dating sites, the messages, the browsing history – they shrug it off.'

'I don't follow.'

'In the groups, they mention fake news a lot. It's become the go-to for any story or facts you don't like.'

'So they think this is fake?'

'Well, Senator, they kind of *want* it to be fake, which we've discovered is very close to *believing* it to be fake. They move between either contesting the facts or saying those facts don't matter. So either Natasha Winthrop didn't go on those BDSM sites or, if she did, it doesn't take away from what happened eventually – which is that she killed a serial rapist and suspected murderer.' Ellen checked her notes. 'The same phrases come up again and again. "She did the right thing, even if she did it the wrong way." "She brought that man to justice." And this one, "Sometimes you gotta take the law into your own hands." In one group, in Tucson, a participant described Winthrop as a "superhero".'

Dan Benson watched the senator pale, no mean feat given his perma-tan. Spotting it too, Greg Carter – often the good cop to Teller's bad cop – stepped in.

'There is a flipside to this. Men are *very* uncomfortable with Winthrop.' Now it was his turn to check his notes. '"Ball-breaker" comes up a lot, as you can imagine.' There was a snigger, its precise location impossible to pin down, its volume somewhere between inaudible and imperceptible. Carter was turning pages on his notebook. 'This is from a voter in Kentucky. Male, fifties, non-college. "I know you're not meant to say this, but if it's true that she was on those dating sites and asked that guy over to her house – well, you know, she kind of asked for it." Also, "If you're president, you've got to control your feelings. This woman sounds like she was out of control. I'd be frightened with her finger anywhere near the nuclear button." That was in Ohio. All of those voters prefer you, Senator, by a country mile. The trouble is—'

'I know what the trouble is. I know what the goddamn trouble is.' On the second 'trouble', Harrison brought his fist down on the table, with such force it made the KeepCups and Chilly's Bottles jump. 'The trouble is, men don't like this woman, but women *love* her. And there is no way to win the nomination of this party – the nomination for the presidency of the United States, I may remind you – by being on one side of a sex war, gender war, whatever. No way. I know this party and I know what it's capable of. If this party fights itself, it will be *vicious*. There'll be no coming back from it. I've seen our party divide on race before – before some of you were born – and we're more than capable of taking lumps out of each other on this too. Believe me.'

A silence fell on the room. For four or five seconds no one

dared speak. Only Teller had the rank to do it. 'Sir, I agree that these findings are serious.'

'You're goddamned right they're serious! I've been in elected office for more than three decades. This woman comes from nowhere and she's already within *three* points of me?'

'That's only among women,' Ellen said quietly.

'I know that. But think what she can get when she's not behind friggin' bars, people!' More silence, not least at the shock of seeing the usually smooth, avuncular demeanour replaced by a behind-the-scenes persona few outside the senior staff had ever glimpsed. 'Do we seriously not have any oppo on this wom— this person? Nothing? I mean, why are we not dumping twenty tons of horse manure on this lady? Can't we use that thing we've got, the Imperial whatever-it's-called that we've spent so much dough on?'

Teller shot the senator a look, a glare whose unmistakable purpose was to shut him up. Or at least get him to swerve away from the subject. It seemed to work.

'Opposition research. If we have any, surely now is the time to use it.'

'While a police inquiry is underway—'

'Yeah, I know the rules, Greg. But didn't we all learn four years ago that the rulebook is gone? Finished. Kaput. Maybe you missed it, but there was a guy who won the last election by putting the rulebook in the shredder. It's done. It doesn't exist any more. We can't wait for the police to do their thing. "Let due process run its course." No, sir. OK, maybe it goes our way and the DC Police charge her – though judging by these numbers, even that won't finish her off. But what if they don't? What if they release her, cleared of all charges? Huh? You think about that little scenario?

'No, my friends. We cannot afford to sit around, looking at numbers any more. We need to know everything about this person. She can't have just come out of nowhere. She'll have a record, somewhere: things she said that she shouldn't have said, things she did that she shouldn't have done, people she knew that she shouldn't have known. Three points, folks! Three goddamn points. We need to take this little lady out, and pronto.'

With that, the senator collected up his papers, rose to his feet and headed for the exits, at least three aides, Ellen included, leaping from their seats to leave with him.

Those left behind all looked to Teller, waiting for a lead. Dan Benson noticed that the campaign manager swallowed hard before talking, the prominence of his Adam's apple briefly testifying to his anxiety. When he spoke, there was a tiny wobble to his first word which he rapidly covered. Everyone was thinking the same thing: for a campaign manager to be chewed out by the candidate in front of the entire team had surely left Doug Teller's authority in pieces. Still, he forced the sentence out.

'You heard what Senator Harrison said. We must take Natasha Winthrop out and we must do it soon.'

Everyone understood that as the conclusion of the meeting and Dan moved towards the door in silence with the rest of them. On his way out, Teller caught him, grabbing him by his elbow. Dan turned around sharply.

'So, guess we've got our instructions, Daniel.'

'Yep. Clear as day.' Benson looked at his elbow, noting that Teller's hand was still there.

'One point that may not have come through. Winthrop herself is doing nothing right now. She's in a cell, yes?'

'That's right.'

'So some of our focus will need to be on those who are acting on her behalf.'

'You mean surrogates, social media, all that?'

'No, I don't mean that. I mean something much more specific than that. Or rather some*one* more specific. Someone who is working hard as we speak in the service of Natasha Winthrop. No names, but if I say Washington's go-to troubleshooter, you'll know who I mean.'

Chapter 36

Thank God that is over. That was the hardest twenty minutes of my life. Actually, the twenty minutes was not so bad. But the waiting and the build-up, oh my God, that was just the worst. Worse than for any test or exam ever. Mom even noticed, the way I couldn't eat anything when I got back from school. "Something's up," she said. "What is it? I can tell."

But I wouldn't tell her, obviously. I wanted to wait till Dad was back, so I could tell them both at the same time. I knew we wouldn't have long, just that gap between my Dad getting home and P coming back from his shift.

As soon as Dad got back home, I came into the kitchen and said I needed to talk. I could see my Mom looking worried. My Dad looked relaxed at first, until he saw my Mom and then he looked worried too. What is it? he said and I was like, can we just sit down? And I sat at the table and I kind of waited till they took out a chair and sat down too.

I just said, It's about P. And my Mom instantly said, Oh thank the Lord, I thought you were going to say you were pregnant.

That kind of threw me a bit and I said, It's about things P does to me.

My Dad said, What? Something about the way he said it made me think he kind of knew. I don't know why but that's how it seemed. My Mom was just quiet. Sort of waiting.

P does things to me. He's been doing things to me since I was ten. Touching me and making me touch him.

What? My Dad said again.

He forces me, I said. He forces his —but I couldn't say it. Not when it came to it, I couldn't say the actual word. I don't know why, but it had something to do with not hurting their feelings, which I know is insane, but that's the only explanation I can think of.

I don't believe it, my Mom said. I just don't believe it.

It started when I was ten, I said. But it's worse now, I said. What he does is worse. It got worse when I was eleven and worse when I was twelve and worse and worse. I could see how shocked my Mom was and so I sort of stopped, but it was such a relief to be saying the words after all this time. I kept on talking, telling them about Helen and what I'd seen, until eventually my Dad raised his hand and said, "OK, Mindy. That's enough." I think he was worried that it was upsetting me to say all these things, even though it actually felt like taking big rocks out of a backpack you've been carrying for years.

They told me to get some rest, to go to bed. Though when they said "bed", I think I saw my Mom kind of make a face.

I'm sitting on my bed now listening to their voices. I can hear them talking and sounding upset, maybe angry. P's coming home soon and I know this sounds crazy, but I'm scared for him. I keep picturing them throwing him out of the house, into the dark and the cold and him sleeping in the car or at the workshop or something.

I'm a bit worried about writing this right now. I keep looking at the door, because one of them is bound to come in here to talk to me any minute now, and I don't want them to see what I'm doing. I feel so bad for them. This must be a big shock for them too.

Oh my God, I can hear something. It's my Dad on the phone. Wait there.

OK, I just cracked open the door and heard him talking to Helen's Dad. I couldn't hear much but he must have asked him what happened. Oh God, this is getting really serious. What if they call the police. I don't want him to go to jail, I just want him to stop.

I'm going to stop now. I'm just going to sit by the window and wait till P gets home.

I'm writing this under the covers, pretending to be asleep. It's hard to see, because I've just got the light of my torch, like a cone of yellow on the page. It's quiet now and I don't really know what's going on.

I heard P come home like maybe an hour ago. Mom and Dad were waiting for him, and they started talking to him immediately. I could hear my Dad doing that thing he does when he's angry, like his calm voice which shows he's not calm.

I thought P would start shouting and throwing things, but his voice sounded calm too. That's so weird, it's kind of scary. Because it means things are not normal, something different is happening. I keep imagining that the police are about to come and take him away and it's all my fault. I should never have said anything. And now the police will know that he did the same to Helen and probably Helen's Dad wants to kill P and he'll have to go to prison far away for his own safety, like they say on the news.

I'm so stupid, stupid, stupid. I should have kept my mouth shut. I've ruined someone's life.

I must have fallen asleep. I woke up just now and it's quiet. P has not come in here. They must have told him he's not allowed in this room ever again. I wonder if he's sleeping on the couch or maybe the police came and took him away when I was asleep. Maybe he's in a prison cell right now, with those chains around his legs and handcuffs. Oh God.

It's twelve hours later now and I am not at home.

I am in the house of someone I don't know. They gave me some food to eat—mac and cheese—and showed me to this room. There was a small towel on the bed and a little bar of soap in plastic. I don't think I can really explain what's going on. All I can do is start at the beginning.

I came down in the morning and could see that P had slept on the couch. He was gone though. Maybe he'd had to go to work early. Mom and Dad told me to sit down at the kitchen table. They had rings under their eyes. I felt sorry for them.

Dad began, while Mom looked down at the table. I thought: she feels so bad for me, she can't even look at me. She's ashamed that this happened to me under her roof. She feels she let me down. I began to say, It's not your fault, Mommy, but my Dad raised the palm of his hand, like a traffic cop and I realized he wanted to tell me what was going to happen. I was hoping they would tell me that P would not go to prison but that maybe he would live somewhere else.

Mindy, we need to have a talk, he said. OK, I said.

We've spoken to Helen's parents and they've spoken to Helen and she said that nothing like this happened. Nothing at all.

I didn't know what to say. But then I said, But he told her he would kill her if she said anything. Just like he said to me. He always says that. He says he'll put a knife inside my—

Listen, Mindy. This has to stop. I know this can happen with girls your age. Maybe it's all that time you spend in the library, all these books and stories or stuff on TV, maybe your imagination has been running away with you. Maybe you've been reading dirty books that you shouldn't have. But making stuff like this up about your brother—

I'm not making it up!

Helen's parents were shocked when I called them. Very upset. Weren't they Carole?

My Mom nodded.

Course they were. They said straight away, Helen's not that kind of girl.

What?

Even having to talk about that kind of thing on the phone—

What do you mean, that kind of girl?

Now my Mom said something. She said, The kind of girl who goes into the woods with a boy.

And I said, But he forced her. That's the whole point. He forced her. I saw it. Just like he forces me.

We don't believe you.

That's what my Mom said, just like that. We don't believe you.

I made this sort of stammering noise. Words didn't come out. Just this sort of croaking, stammering noise: er, er, er

My Dad carried on. I don't understand why you'd make up something like this, Mindy. Is it for attention? Don't Mom and I give you enough attention?

I felt this weird sensation. It was different to anything I'd felt before. Like all the blood was flowing out of my head and my brain, like someone had hit a switch to power down a machine. I imagined how I must look, I imagined my face turning white, and then the flesh and skin falling off it, like a speeded-up film of a corpse becoming a skeleton, until I imagined I *was just this set of bones sitting opposite these two other people. I couldn't say anything.*

Now Mom spoke. These are terrible things to say about anybody, Mindy. Terrible things. You can't just make up things like this, accusations. What if we'd believed you? What if Helen hadn't told the truth? Think of what that could have done to Paulie. He's loved you like a sister all this time, and you say these terrible things. He was so shocked when we told him about it when he came home last night. He was stunned that you could have said what you said.

I was feeling kind of numb but that went through me like an electric shock. I tried to say, What do you mean, like a sister? Like a sister? I thought I was, I thought . . . but I couldn't finish it, I couldn't say the words.

I expected myself to cry, but my body was still powering down. Whole parts of me were shutting off, as I sat there. I could hear ~~my parents~~ —I could hear Jim and Carole's words, but they sounded like they were underwater or coming through the wall of the house next door, or as if I was listening from the bedroom.

But it's true, I heard myself saying. It's true that I saw him do those things to Helen. And it's true that he did those things to me.

I got up and began to unzip my jeans. I was going to pull down my underwear and show them how and where he'd done it—I thought they would be able to see it—but my Dad grabbed my arm and said, Stop that right now, young lady. And I heard my Mom, I mean Carole, say, She's very disturbed. She's got something wrong with her. She needs help.

I was just saying, It's true, It's true, over and over again. I still wasn't crying, but that was only because my body wasn't working.

We know Paul, my Mom said. We know who that boy is. We know what he is and what he isn't. He's our own flesh and blood.

And that was when my soul left my body. That's when I floated out of Mindy, and was just hovering above, like one of those dead people who's not quite dead yet, looking down at these two people and this girl, Mindy. They were strangers to me, but that wasn't the weird thing. The weird thing was that they were strangers to each other. Mindy was still calling them Mom and Dad, but they didn't think Mindy was their daughter. That had been her mistake all along. Of course they believed P and not her. P was their son, and she was just a guest in their house.

Now the voices were even harder to hear, like they were on TV with the sound turned down. I think my Mom—I mean Carole, Carole, Carole—was saying I carried that boy for nine months or something like that.

I don't remember if I stood up and then my Dad—Jim, I mean, Jim, Jim, Jim—said, Your mother and I have spoken and we think it's best for everyone if we end this arrangement, or if it was the other way around. Maybe first my Dad, I mean Jim Hagen, said, We think it's best for everyone if we end this arrangement and then I stood up. Maybe that came first. I don't remember.

Mom said things like We've called the fostering agency and There is an emergency fostering service but none of it really went in. I think she said You need help and She needs help a few times too. I've just remembered one other thing as well. She said, I thought of you staying with Aunt Chrissie but that's not a good idea, not with Matthew being in the house. (My cousin—not my cousin—Matthew is seventeen.) I wanted to say, Why would I say anything about Matthew? He's never hurt me. The only person who ever hurt me is P. But no words were coming out.

And so I'm here. In a house in Briarwood that belongs to an Emergency

Fosterer. A woman who has children stay here for a few nights when they've been kicked out of one place and waiting for the next one. Someone told me not to feel too bad, it happens quite often. She didn't really talk to me. She just showed me the bedroom, and the small towel and the soap in plastic and pointed at the bathroom down the hall. There are little signs everywhere telling me what I'm not allowed to do. Like, No talking after 9.30pm and Lights out at 9.45pm.

I don't like it here. I would say I want to go home, but I don't want to go there either. Which I guess means I have no home.

Maggie rubbed her eyes. The journey here had taken its toll, but it wasn't that that was making her tired. It was the agony of this young girl, the cruelty of her treatment at the hands of this 'P' who she had wanted to love as a brother and, most heartbreaking of all, the response of her parents. Or rather the people this little girl had considered her parents. Maggie found herself worrying for Mindy, for the damage these wounds would have inflicted on her. She thought of herself and Liz, still reeling in their thirties from the experience of growing up as the children of a mother who drank too much. She instantly heard her sister's voice, rebuking her. *Say it, Maggie: alcoholic. Not 'drank too much'. Alcoholic. The first step to defeating it is naming it.*

Maggie smiled, imagining the conversation she and her sister had had a thousand times, usually after Liz had come back from a session with her therapist. But whatever had happened to them – and Maggie refused to believe that her mother's condition was to blame for her being, as Liz always put it, 'an adrenalin junkie with a Messiah complex' – they did at least have each other.

Now and at the time. Poor Mindy, alone in this ordeal. In fact, so much worse than alone, because Mindy had believed she had a mother and father who loved her and would surely protect her. Maggie had read the diary: she saw how Mindy unself-consciously regarded this man and woman, Jim and bloody Carole, as her actual parents. *A letter came in the mail saying that I am now theyre daughter and my name is the same as theyres.*

Mindy had been rejected twice over, as a baby and as a fourteen- or fifteen-year-old. Maggie remembered what it was like to be a girl that age: the awkwardness, the burning, hot-cheeked embarrassment, the self-doubt, the self-criticism, the insecurity. And that was how it had been for Maggie, who had her nan, her sister and, on good days, her ma. What must it have been like to endure all that alone, to have been abused and then cast out by the only family you'd ever known?

Maggie felt her spirits sinking. She worried where this was heading; she was afraid she knew. In a rushed moment, to confirm her darkest expectations, she turned to the last page of the notebook. It was blank. She flicked through the preceding pages to find it, the last page covered with words, and her eye went immediately to the last line and there it was in neat blue biro ink, confirmation that this story had ended exactly as Maggie feared it would.

Mindy Hagen is dead.

Maggie snapped the book shut. This was what she had dreaded: that she had been reading an extended suicide note, inscribed over several years, written in real time. She felt a surge of sudden anger towards P, his parents and, unjustly she knew, towards Aunt Peggy. How dare that woman put her through this, making her read this terrible, tragic story – and for what? Mindy was dead, and none of this took Maggie any closer to helping Natasha. None of this explained what she was doing here, in the middle of nowhere, in a cold bedroom in an isolated house on the wrong side of the Atlantic. She wanted to be far away from here, back in Ireland, back when she was Mindy's age, back when the world was, if not simple, then simpler than this.

She moved towards the door, determined to find Peggy. She was touching the door handle when something made her look back, eyeing the journal lying there on the bed. She had done it too; she had abandoned Mindy, like everyone else in her life. She hadn't even let her tell her story, rushing to the denouement, cutting to the chase, as impatient as a Washington official who, presented with the text of *Romeo and Juliet*, or *Anna Karenina*, would demand the Executive Summary.

She turned back and, penitent, resumed her place in the journal of Mindy Hagen. She'd only read a few lines when she was caught by a sentence that was wholly unexpected.

Today I went back to the library. I saw something that gave me an idea. It's a crazy idea but I'm going to do it. I think it might be my only chance.

Chapter 37

Penobscot, Maine

Glued onto the page was an item cut neatly from a newspaper. The headline immediately made Maggie's skin tingle.

US MILITARY FAMILY KILLED IN CAR CRASH
Parents and daughters left dead in Germany collision
A serving US Air Force colonel was killed on Tuesday along with his wife and daughters in a road traffic collision near the Ramstein Air Base in Germany.

A military spokesman said Reed Aldrich Winthrop III, 48, Matilda Winthrop, 45, together with their daughters Annabel and Lilibeth, died from their injuries. The family were evacuated from the scene to Landstuhl Regional Medical Center, but the four did not respond to emergency treatment and were declared dead on arrival.

The youngest person involved, 15-year-old Natasha Winthrop, is unconscious and in a critical condition, according to the spokesman. He later said that her life was in grave danger.

> *Paying tribute to Col. Winthrop, the senior ranking officer at Ramstein declared him to be, "One of the finest airmen of his generation. He was a proud and talented aviator, wholly devoted to the Air Force, to his country and to his family. Our thoughts and prayers at this time are with Natasha Winthrop, and we wish her a full and speedy recovery."*
>
> *Contacted for comment, Miss V Winthrop of Pilgrim's Cove, MA, said only that her "prime concern is the welfare of my niece Natasha" and that she was in touch with the authorities in Germany.*

Maggie gazed at the wall, her skin turning colder with each second. She felt a shiver form around her shoulders, then shudder down her back. She closed the book and marched out the door and into the living room. It was empty, closed up for the night. She looked into the kitchen, similarly quiet.

She checked her watch. Quarter past ten. But that wasn't going to stop her. She took the stairs and saw a stretch of light under the door. Allowing herself no time to change her mind, she knocked on the door loudly – too loudly for the house guest of an elderly lady at this time of night.

'Yes?'

'It's Maggie,' she said, redundantly.

A pause. Maggie pictured Aunt Peggy on the other side of the bedroom door, weighing up her options, thinking it through. Eventually, the older woman said quietly, even sombrely: 'Come in.'

Maggie turned the doorknob warily. Intruding into this woman's bedroom felt wrong and awkward. She would rather have had this conversation downstairs, a fair distance apart.

Aunt Peggy was in her nightgown sitting up, her back propped against two pillows placed vertically, her hair pinned up. She would, Maggie saw now, have been a beautiful woman back . . . when? She didn't know how old she was, whether she was Reed Winthrop's older sister or younger or why she apparently had no children of her own, or even if she had ever been married. In truth, she knew nothing about her. But she believed she knew one thing – the thing that mattered.

'I've read the diary,' Maggie said, standing at the end of the bed.

'All of it? All the way to the end?'

'I read enough.'

'Ah, well that depends on—'

'I read up to the moment when "Mindy" sees the report of the deaths of the Winthrop family. I think I can work out the rest.'

'Can you, though, Maggie?'

Aunt Peggy resettled herself in bed. Maggie caught a whiff of night cream. Peggy nodded towards an old leather chair in the corner. 'Why don't you sit down?'

Maggie wanted to say that she was more comfortable standing, that she was not in the mood for a bedside chat, that she just wanted to get to the bottom of all this and to do it right now. She could feel the fury rising somewhere between her chest and her throat, her anger at being strung along like this, at being duped. Who did these people take her for?

But she also knew that the fastest route to the information she needed did not include a detour over whether she should be standing or sitting. Best to comply and let this woman start talking.

Grudgingly, like a teenager in a strop, she moved towards the chair and then, in a small and equally juvenile gesture of defiance, moved the chair closer towards the bed. *I'm not going to sit where you tell me to sit.* Finally, she sat.

'Good. I wanted you to read it in her own words but—'

'Whose own words? Mindy's? Or Natasha's?'

'I wanted you to read it in her own words, but I can see you're impatient.'

'You're bloody right, I'm impatient. I think you've been leading me a merry dance. And not just me, for that matter.'

'Please, Miss Costello. Just listen.'

Maggie leaned back, and put her hands on her lap. *All right*, the gesture said, *I'm listening.*

'Good,' Aunt Peggy said, with the patient condescension of an elementary school teacher, which she might well have been. 'So you've seen the news report of the car accident, in Germany.'

Maggie nodded.

'Well, as Mindy records in her diary, that gave her an idea. She had a very small amount of money, a tiny amount from working a few hours every Saturday. But early the next morning, while the temporary foster mother was asleep, she collected her things and crept out of the house. She took a bus into the centre of Little Rock and walked again until she reached the Greyhound bus station. From there she took a bus to Boston. Remember, this was a fourteen-year-old girl, who'd never been out of Arkansas. And she did this on her own.'

Maggie said nothing.

'I think often of that journey. Thirty hours on that bus, a girl on her own. Mindy was very pretty, and she had been used for sex since she was ten years old. Men can detect that, I think. The bad ones. I wonder what she had to fend off during that journey. I imagine her trying to sleep, not sure if it was safe.' She paused and looked towards the curtained window. 'Knowing it wasn't safe, is more accurate.'

The silence held for a moment or two, as both imagined that journey. Maggie kept her gaze fixed on the older woman, as other memories began to encroach. Of childhood stories at her nan's house; of sitting close to the bed in her mother's dying weeks. Maybe it was being perched at the edge of the Atlantic, in far eastern Maine, but Ireland had felt strangely close since she had got here.

'From Boston, she could afford one more bus. After that, it was hitchhiking. At night. I dread to think what price she might have paid for some of those rides. And then several stretches on foot. But somehow, two or more days after she crept out of that house in Little Rock, she turned up at Pilgrim's Cove.

'Of course, the staff didn't want to let her in. This waif off the streets, with her peroxide-blonde hair and that southern accent. After that journey on the bus, and hitchhiking and Lord knows what else, she looked a terrible mess. I dislike the expression "trailer trash" very much, but I'm afraid that is what she looked like.'

Maggie nodded, not in agreement but to confirm understanding.

'It was only fortunate that I was out in the garden. I remember it as if it were today. I was pruning my favourite Falstaff roses:

beautiful, dark crimson-red flowers. They bloom continuously, you see. I found them a great consolation, in that period.' She paused at the memory. 'I heard the commotion for myself. The head gardener was arguing with her, telling her she couldn't come in. But she was asking for me by name. I remember, that's what struck me as odd. She knew my name. And she was clearly not a reporter or anything like that, though we had had one or two of those in those days. That much was obvious.

'I put down my secateurs and wandered over. I still had my gloves on. I remember hanging back, lurking really, behind the birch tree, observing this little scene. I don't think she could see me, but I could see her.' Aunt Peggy gave a small smile, her eyes far away. 'The determination on that face. She wasn't screaming, but she was loud. And forceful. She didn't touch Henry – the gardener – she didn't push her way in or anything like that. She didn't need to. It was quite clear, she would stand her ground. Whatever it took.'

Maggie cleared her throat, about to speak. But if that was meant as a cue, Aunt Peggy didn't take it. Maggie could see that Peggy was no longer in this room. She was in Pilgrim's Cove, in that garden more than two decades ago, watching this fourteen-year-old force of nature.

'Eventually I approached, and asked what was going on. Instantly, Mindy looked at me. And – this is the strangest thing – the moment I looked into her eyes, I knew instantly. It was as if I knew the whole story. Everything that had happened, everything that would happen. I knew what she would ask, and I knew I would say yes.'

'What did she ask?'

'She asked to come inside. We sat at the table under the white oak. Henry brought out some lemonade, and she drank a full glass and then another. He brought out some food too, and she devoured that. I don't think she'd eaten for twenty-four hours. But I knew that wasn't what she was there for.

'Straight away, she said, "I've come here to make a plea." It was clear she had planned very carefully what she was going to say. No doubt she had rehearsed it in her mind, during that long journey. A lawyer making an argument.' Another smile. '"I've come here to make a plea," she said. "I hope your great-niece, Natasha, lives. I hope she makes it. But if she doesn't, then give her identity to me. Don't register her as dead. Give her identity to me."

'"Why on earth should I do that?" I said. And she handed me that journal you've been reading. Right there and then. I sat and read it at that table in Pilgrim's Cove, with my gardening gloves on my lap. While she sat opposite me.

'When I finished it, at the very same point you've reached, as it happens, I looked at her. And she looked back at me and we said nothing for a full minute or more. And then she said, in that southern accent of hers, "Let me start a new life, Miss Winthrop. Let your family's name live on. Let something good come out of all this horror."'

Maggie could not speak for a while. Instead, she kept looking at Peggy, trying to read in those eyes the calculations that the woman would have made more than twenty years earlier. Newly bereaved, having lost her nephew and almost all his family, what would she have made of Mindy Hagen, the girl washed up on the Maine shore like a creature from another world? How would she have looked at her? Maggie pictured the older woman, assessing Mindy, sizing her up, deciding whether her story was true. The fatefulness of that moment, a moment that would change both their lives forever. The weight of that decision and the reverberations that would be felt for years to come – the decision to perpetrate a lie, to replace one life with another.

But Peggy did not meet her gaze. She was far away, her eyes glazed with memories. Maggie had so many questions to ask, but none of them felt right for the quiet, intimate atmosphere that now filled this room. What had happened to the real Natasha Winthrop? Did she get buried somewhere else, separated from her family? Was her body still there in a plot in Germany, or perhaps on Cape Cod, alongside her parents and sisters, unmentioned on a tombstone recording the deaths of four Winthrops when it should have been five? How had Peggy got away with not registering the death of her great-niece? Perhaps the death *had been* registered, but only in Germany and not in the US. Maggie had heard of such cases: it was a loophole undercover police officers had used to construct false identities, taking the birth certificates of children who had died abroad and so left no record of death. Or maybe the explanation was simpler than that, the oldest explanation in the book, in fact: maybe Peggy Winthrop had got her way, and been allowed to cut crucial corners, because she had money.

But those questions just fed other ones. How on earth had

she turned Mindy into Natasha? It would have been a transformation worthy of Pygmalion. Mindy had turned up at Pilgrim's Cove in late June. Peggy would have had only the summer to teach her how to speak like the orphaned daughter of a New England WASP, the scion of a *Mayflower* clan with a long, officer-class pedigree in the US military, in time for the new term at boarding school. It would have been a completely daunting mission.

Except Mindy would have had several crucial advantages. First, Maggie remembered what teenage girls were like: their focus was, always and forever, themselves rather than anyone else. If a new girl turned up claiming to be an expat orphan, no one would have looked too deeply. Second, the young were nothing if not adaptable. Maggie had known people at university who'd changed their accents in a week, let alone three months. Third, if Mindy Hagen was tough enough to have dragged herself from the outskirts of Little Rock, Arkansas, to Pilgrim's Cove, Massachusetts, with nothing but one scrap of newspaper, twenty-odd dollars and a hunch to go on, then washing the dye out of her hair and the southern out of her accent would not have been beyond her. She was resilient and clever, her diary was evidence enough of that.

Above all, though, Maggie could see now that Mindy was never going to fail. Because that day, over glasses of lemonade in the garden, this fourteen-year-old girl would have become the project of Virginia 'Peggy' Winthrop. Earlier, Maggie had wondered why Peggy had never had children of her own. Now she understood that that was the wrong question. For on that summer afternoon, aged – what, sixty, sixty-five? – she had at last given birth. Not to a baby, admittedly, but to a new person all the same. One armed with the name of a great-niece who had just been taken from her, one who would ensure that that branch of the family tree would not shrivel and die, but would live on, one with the grit and determination to bring glory to a dynasty that dated back to the birth of the republic. A new person called Natasha Winthrop.

Maggie looked at Peggy and could picture the two of them, together that day and every day thereafter – both alone and both lonely, both without families of their own, united in grabbing a little piece of life from the death and pain that surrounded them. What a bond that must have been. No wonder Natasha called her every week. She was her mother and father, her brother and sister, her sun and her moon. She had given her life.

And now, without really planning to, Maggie spoke out loud. 'The thing I want to know is,' she said, almost surprised to hear a human voice after all that silence. 'Why did she say you were dead?'

Peggy did not snap out of her reverie; she did not speak straight away. She moved her head slowly, as if emerging from deep rest. A slight smile formed on her lips as she said, 'What was that, dear?'

'Why did she say you were dead? She made a point of it, when we met. She's said it in interviews too. Very insistent: "I have no one left." "My last surviving relative died several years ago." Why would she do that?'

Peggy smiled at that too, as she smoothed the sheets that were covering her. 'It's the same reason we agreed I should leave Pilgrim's Cove and disappear here a few years ago, once she was sufficiently established to take over the house. It's easier to keep a secret if there's no one left to tell it.' She twinkled and then added, 'It worked too. Neither of us ever breathed a word.'

'Until today.'

'Until today.'

Maggie got up and made for the door. She was about to leave, when a last question came to her.

'Did Natasha ever mention someone called Judith?'

'Who, dear?'

'Judith. Did Natasha ever mention that name to you?'

Aunt Peggy brought her forefinger to her mouth, as if thinking. 'Was that the name of a friend of hers?'

'I don't know.'

'Recently or in the past?'

'I don't know that either.'

'Hmm. I'm sorry, but it doesn't ring any bells at all. At college I think she had a friend called Julia, who she mentioned once or twice. But no Judith.'

'OK.'

'I'm sorry not to be of more use.'

Maggie went back to her room and collected her things. It was November and the idea of driving through the night along empty, sea-swept roads in such a remote part of the country made her heart sink. Staying inside in the warm, hiding in that single bed even for just a few hours, appealed much more.

But she knew she had to leave. Now that she understood who Natasha Winthrop was, she knew exactly where she had to go.

Chapter 38

Chicago, Illinois, one day earlier

Afterwards she would think: what if I had left a minute later? Or two minutes earlier? What if I had missed that subway train and got the next one? None of this would have happened.

But somehow that had been the moment she decided to leave the bar just off Franklin Street. That precise moment. She'd been thinking about her exit for at least twenty minutes. She hadn't wanted to make it obvious, by checking her watch: the international sign of boredom and a desire to get away. Thankfully, these days, you could disguise it. You just had to pull out your phone and pretend to be checking a message: no one had to know that your eye was on the clock at the top of the screen. But maybe her colleagues were wise to that. Maybe they did it themselves.

Besides, she had done the statutory hour. Surely there was a law written down somewhere that said attendance at a colleague's leaving do was compulsory for sixty minutes, voluntary thereafter. She had complied in full. From now on, she was free to make a getaway.

The awkwardness was the excuse. She could not claim, as some of her co-workers could, that she had children to put to bed: she had no children. Nor could she cite the needs of her 'other half', as her colleagues regularly did: she had no 'other half'. There was no mystery about it; that was who she was in the office: the single, middle-aged woman. Her workmates knew too that her family lived on the other side of the country, so there could be no invoking of an elderly mother who needed accompanying to a medical appointment early the next morning. All that left was, 'I've got an early start in the morning.' The flaw there was that, first, her colleagues knew that Carolyn Savito had no work-related reason to have an early start in the morning and, second, 'I've got an early start in the morning' was second only to checking your watch as an unambiguous sign that you'd had enough of drinking white wine with your co-workers and wanted to go home.

In that sense, the minute of her departure was preordained. And so she had put on her coat, said her goodbyes, accepted with a smile the borderline mocking remark of Glenn in Development – *Ooh, somebody got a better offer!* – and headed out to walk the three blocks to catch the Red Line. She had not seen the man on the platform who, according to later police reports, had latched onto Carolyn Savito at that point, if not earlier. He didn't get into her carriage, but the next one along: he positioned himself near the end, by the connecting door, so that he could 'keep an eye on her'.

He watched as she scrolled through her phone, reading a couple of articles, and kept watching as she leaned back, resting her head against the glass and closing her eyes for a minute or two. He watched as she collected her things at North/Clybourn Station and when she got up to get off at Fullerton.

He followed her through the turnstiles, keeping about fifteen yards back, and up the stairs to street level. His eyes stayed fixed on her as she turned right on Fremont, where the pedestrian traffic dropped sharply. That was his cue. Once there were fewer people around, that was the moment to increase the pace and narrow the distance.

Perhaps thirty seconds passed before she became aware of him. Was it the sound of his footsteps becoming nearer or that sixth sense that every woman develops soon enough, of a man getting too close? Afterwards, she would decide it was the latter: that she felt his presence before she heard it.

She glanced over her left shoulder and understood the danger immediately. Chiefly because he did not look away, or have his head in his phone, but met her gaze. Maybe there were some places in the world where a strange man walking behind you, and then failing to look somewhere else when looked at, would not be a danger sign, but Chicago was not one of them. She quickened her pace and so, unmistakably, did he.

Now the calculations began. How much further did she have to walk to reach her building? Was it better to press on till she got there, or should she seek some alternative refuge, aiming to duck into a bar or restaurant or convenience store? Trouble was, these were residential streets. There was nothing on her way home, unless she broke from her usual route and changed course. But if this man had been watching her, studying her from a distance after work each night, he would know she'd improvised. What was more, it could lead her into new danger: she might accidentally head down a dead-end street. Should she break into a run, or would that be to discard the one advantage she had: namely, his presumption that she did not understand the threat he posed?

She was approaching the left turn, the last one she would need to make. This, she decided, would be her pursuer's final chance to prove his innocence. If, when she turned off, he kept on walking, she would know it had been a false alarm: he'd have confirmed himself as a weirdo who didn't observe the usual social cues, but he wouldn't be a rapist. But what if he made the turn?

Her feet did the work, controlling themselves well, she thought. They didn't convey the panic that was making her chest thump, that was making her light-headed. They were acting the part of a normal, self-assured woman walking home from work. With no instruction from her, they turned left.

A combination of her peripheral vision, her ears and her sixth sense told her he had made the turn with her. Now her heart thumped louder. She was perhaps two minutes from home. She began calculating and then instinct took over. Her legs decided to run.

As soon as she did it, she knew it was a mistake. There was no one on this street to see her, to realize that she was in danger. She could hear him running too, the thud of his tread on the sidewalk no louder than hers, but heavier, the vibration of each step palpable to her. It was obvious: he would catch up with her soon enough. She was too far away to get to her front door before he caught up.

She increased her speed, the memory of running at pace on school sports days coming back to her from decades earlier. Any second now he would outstrip her, pulling her down to the ground or grabbing her by the back of the neck.

And then, the very second she thought of it, she felt it — as if the imagining had willed it into reality. A hand brushed past her shoulder. It must have been a lunge at her, his first attempt, a hopeful arm stretched out.

From somewhere she found a new reserve of energy, enough to make her run faster still. She cursed the bag on her shoulder and these ridiculous shoes . . .

That's when it happened, at such speed and in such a blur her brain could not process it. She suddenly heard a new noise behind her, a commotion, a scuffle. She kept running, only daring to turn around three or four seconds later. What she saw astonished her.

Her pursuer was no longer running. Instead, he himself had been grabbed, by a gang of four figures, all clad in black, who now surrounded him. Carolyn assumed they were police. But then she saw them bundle the man into the back of a black minivan that was waiting, its side door open, by the kerb. His arms were flailing as they shoved him inside, but he couldn't land any blows. He was outnumbered. He kicked out once, making contact with one of the four who let out a strained yelp. A second later he was in the van, the police, if that's who they were, piling in after him.

The door slid shut and the van immediately went into a turn and sped off, in the opposite direction.

Carolyn watched it all from perhaps thirty yards away. She was panting; her lungs felt like they were bursting. But though she was desperate to put her hands on her knees and catch her breath, or even crumple in an exhausted heap on the ground, she remained standing, staring at the same spot, even after the van had gone. Because it had turned around, she never saw who drove it. She never caught the licence plate. All she could tell the police afterwards was that there were no markings on the van at all. And, now that she thought about it, there were no markings on the uniforms of the four who had apprehended him. Nor did she ever see their faces. They seemed, she would say in her sworn statement, to be wearing ski masks.

The van drove a circuitous route, turning right and right again, doubling back, then making a loop, and repeating similar moves at intervals. That, along with the radio tuned to a metal station playing at close to full volume, filling the vehicle with tearing, serrated sound, to say nothing of the blindfold, seemed to do the job, ensuring the captive had no idea where he was being taken. By the time they reached their destination, the four captors, together with the driver, were confident that their hostage was suitably and sufficiently disorientated. He would know nothing more than that he had been bundled out of the van twenty-five minutes after he had got in it, and that after just a few paces outdoors he had been led downstairs, below street level.

He couldn't see it, but he was in a basement, consisting of a concrete floor and empty, unplastered walls. There was next to nothing in here, besides a table, two or three hard plastic chairs, some metal tools, a computer, a loudspeaker and several yards of cabling. The room was cold and damp, a barely visited underground store. The captors kept their ski masks on, so that they were unrecognizable even to each other.

The man's wrists were still cuffed behind his back, secured by the cable-ties his captors had attached seconds after ambushing him just off Fremont Street. Now he was shoved down onto one of the chairs and his wrists tied again, this time to the back of the chair. His ankles were manacled by locked metal chains to each other and to the legs of the chair.

He didn't call out, or rather he didn't call out with words because he had been gagged, by means of a red ball attached to a leather strap buckled around his head. He had been making muffled sounds since the start of the journey here.

Now a pair of hands unbuckled his trousers and, with some effort, given the way he was seated, pulled them down. The hands did the same to the underpants. The clothes gathered around his ankles, as if he were sitting on the toilet. He was still blindfolded.

Now a voice addressed him, over a loudspeaker.

Do you know what it is like to be touched against your will?

The voice was not human, though not quite robotic either. It sounded metallic and distorted. The captive made no sound.

Do you know what it is like to be touched against your will?

The captive produced a grunt.

Now there was a sound of activity as two of the figures in

black approached the chair. One of them was carrying a thin cord, somewhere between string and rope. The texture was rough.

Calmly, like a doctor conducting a medical examination, a hand reached for the man's scrotum, identifying one testicle and separating it from the other. Next, the hands moved to tie the cord around the individual testicle, pulling the string to test that it was secure. The man let out a cry, but again the sound was muffled by the gag.

Now the second figure held the man down by his shoulders, while the first took a few paces back, cord still in hand. The captor, the one who had tied the initial knot, jerked on the cord, producing a long, protracted howl from the captive, although once more the sound was stifled by the ball in his mouth.

Do you know what it is like to be touched against your will?

Even as the metallic, distorted voice – unnaturally deep, like a record played too slow – filled the room, the sound of the howl lingered in the air. Whether because the captive was continuing to cry out in pain or because the original noise was reverberating, like the sustained note of a piano, in this dank, empty basement, it was not easy to tell.

The robotic voice, dull and expressionless, spoke again.

Even though you are making the sound of pain, we think you want it really. So we will carry on.

There was another tug on the cord, pulling, so that it gave the man the sensation, or the fear, that his testicle was about to be separated from the rest of him. He was bellowing into the gag covering his mouth. Tears were streaming down his face.

Even though you are crying and begging for us to stop, we will carry on.

The pull was so hard this time that the man made a gasp, which was followed by silence. One of the captors wondered if the testicle had been removed, if the captive had been castrated. Liquid was pooling around the chair. The captor stepped forward, to check if it was blood. It turned out to be urine. The captor concluded that, in his terror, the man had wet himself.

The captor bent down and loosened the cord. The captive let his shoulders slump in a gesture of relief. But the captor did not move away. Instead, the rope was now reapplied to the man's penis, tied hard around the base, so that it cinched it, like a belt around a waist.

He let out a high squeal of pain.

We think you are saying no. But no sometimes means yes.

The captors repeated the previous drill. One pressed down on the captive's shoulders, while the other moved away a few paces until the cord was taut. Finally there was a sharp tug, generating more muffled noises of agony.

You are protesting. But we don't care about your pain, because this is what we want. What we want matters more than your pain.

The captor pulled the cord several times, until the man moaned rather than howled. Eventually two of the captors came forward and untied the cord. The base of the captive's penis was circled by a deep red welt, ringed with blood. His penis was flaccid and limp, a piece of useless flesh. Now the voice spoke again.

Do you know what it is like to be touched against your will?

This time, and with apparent great effort, the captive made

a weak nod of his head. He murmured something that seemed like assent.

There was a pause for ten or eleven seconds. Then the voice sounded once more, through the loudspeaker.

You know what it is like to be touched against your will.

Another pause. A feeble nod.

But you do not yet know what it is like to be violated.

There was a dull silence in the room. The captors looked at the captive, trying to detect a reaction. One captor met the eye of another. The voice spoke again.

You do not yet know what it is like to be violated.

Now the same two captors stepped forward and, while taking care to ensure the captive's hands and ankles remained immobile, they untied him from the chair. They then pushed him off the chair, so that he fell forward, landing on the ground on his knees. One captor took the chair away, while the other shoved at the captive's back. He fell further forward, so that he was now on the ground on all fours, like a dog. His trousers and underpants were still bunched around his ankles, though now they were soaked in urine, the underwear especially.

You do not yet know what it is like to be violated.

He was trying to cry out. Though the gag was stifling the words, it was clear from the pitch of the sound he was making that he was pleading for mercy.

One of the captors now nodded to another, who went over to the table where several objects were arranged. Wearing latex surgical gloves, the captor picked up one of them and moved towards the captive. Once again, the first captor held the man down by his shoulders. It was becoming hard to hear over the gagged screams. It crossed the second captor's mind that the captive might soon vomit into his gag, which would cause choking and asphyxiation. Nevertheless, the captor assumed a kneeling position behind the captive and did what had to be done.

It took several minutes. The work was hard, requiring physical effort, not made easier by the sounds emanating from the captive, which resembled those of a pig in an abattoir.

Now the metallic voice spoke.

Do you know what it is like to be violated?

Visible underneath the leather strap that held the ball gag in place was the matted tangle of his hair, now drenched in sweat. He made a noise that sounded like 'Yes'. But it was feebly quiet.

Even as the other captors stood around, watching, the second captor remained at the task. At one point, the captor returned to the table, coming back with a new object.

Do you know what it is like to be violated?

Another 'Yes', more emphatic this time.

That was the cue for the captors to derig the basement and pack up. As they did so, their captive remained in the middle of the floor: bound and gagged, on all fours, naked from the waist down, his genitals exposed and wrecked, his clothes soaked in urine and much else.

He began to squeal again, doubtless anxious that he was about to be left here, cuffed and manacled and unable to escape.

Thanks to a raised hand from their leader, the captors understood that they were to remain still for a minute or two, to allow their captive's fears to deepen. His crying and bleating grew louder. Until, on a signal, they lifted him to his feet, covered him in a blanket, guided him up the stairs and, once the coast was clear, pushed him back inside the minivan which was waiting kerbside.

They repeated the previous journey, the same circuitous route, the death metal soundtrack, the nauseous loops and false turns, until some thirty minutes later they were back on Chalmers Place, the small side road just off Fremont Street where he'd been apprehended.

The van came to a stop, engine idling. The door of the vehicle slid open. Now, as one, the captors spoke to their captive. For the first time, he heard their voices. In chorus, they uttered the three words which they had agreed in advance — and which they knew would complete his humiliation. That done, they shoved him out onto the sidewalk, pulled the door shut and sped off.

He remained there, shivering in his nakedness, his wrists and ankles still restrained, gagged by a gimp ball, until a couple emerged from one of the brownstones. At first, they giggled at the sight of him: they assumed he'd been the victim of a bachelor party prank or perhaps that he had been turfed out of a BDSM dungeon, where he'd been an otherwise willing participant. When they caught the whiff of urine, they assumed he'd got so drunk, he'd let himself go. They never for one moment imagined him as the victim of a sexual assault.

As he sat there, shivering in the autumn cold, processing the three words his kidnappers and torturers had spoken, a question began to throb through his brain. Once he got someone to loosen this gag and break these cable-ties, should he report what had happened to the police? Or did self-preservation dictate that he keep this humiliation, this violation and shame, to himself?

Chapter 39

Some breaking news now, out of Chicago. Important new details concerning an incident last night, in which a man was violently assaulted and left for dead — police sources telling CNN in the last hour that the man involved was a convicted rapist. Detectives in the city are pursuing the theory that the assault was a 'copycat' of the lethal attack on Jeffrey Todd, for which Washington lawyer and possible presidential candidate Natasha Winthrop is currently in custody. Remember, the clock is ticking for Winthrop. If she wants to enter the race, she needs to get out of jail, clear her name and get running. Just two working days to go now till that registration deadline.

Reporting live for us now, from Chicago: Kaine Braw. Kaine, lots for us to untangle here. What's the latest?

Chip, major developments tonight. As you know, Chicago Police say they were called to this street corner in the Lincoln Park neighbourhood last night, after a man was reported to be lying in the gutter in a state of what police are calling 'severe distress'. They say he had suffered 'extreme, aggravated sexual assault', with some details that are too graphic to share on this network.

But the big news came just a few minutes ago, with the naming of the injured man. He's convicted rapist Nicholas Corey, who recently completed five years of an eleven-year sentence for rape, winning early release four months ago. Law enforcement officials tell CNN that this was the second time Corey had been paroled following a rape conviction, this second release coming despite objections from his victims and their families. Questions there for justice officials and the Governor of Illinois over that parole decision. Also significant perhaps: at the time of that second conviction, the judge accepted that there were perhaps dozens of rape cases that had not been brought and in which Corey was the prime suspect, the judge ruling that those additional cases should be taken into account during sentencing.

And talk tonight, Kaine, of a possible connection with the Winthrop case.

Well, no formal connection alleged as such, Chip, but the revelation that this man is a convicted rapist has sparked talk tonight of the uncanny parallels between the two cases. Both situations, if you will, centre on a known rapist who, for whatever reason, was still at large, on the receiving end of a violent assault. Now obviously Natasha Winthrop is currently accused of murder, because Jeffrey Todd was found in her home, apparently bludgeoned to death. This case, very different — Corey is still alive — but what sources are telling CNN is that police are exploring whether this might be some kind of revenge attack on Corey, perhaps even a copycat of the Todd killing. Or at least an attempt to copy the Todd killing.

And what do we know of what happened?

Details are still emerging—

Of course.

But it seems that Corey may have been snatched off this street and taken away in a black minivan to an as yet unknown location. Eyewitnesses on the seventh floor of the apartment building just over my left shoulder, Chip, tell CNN that they saw a black vehicle fitting that description pull up sharply and suddenly, at around nine o'clock last night. They saw four men dressed in black, wearing ski masks or balaclavas, jump out and grab a man, bundle him into the vehicle and speed away. Then, several hours later, another sighting of an apparently similar vehicle on this same street, shortly before Corey was found by police. So the working theory right now – and we should stress, these are unconfirmed details at this stage – the working theory is that Corey was taken away, assaulted and then brought back here and dumped. With some suggestion that whoever did this might have been following the lead allegedly set by Natasha Winthrop, taking the law into their own hands.

Kaine Braw reporting live from Chicago. Thanks, Kaine, and of course more on that as we get it. Coming up: the Kansas high school hockey team who might just be revolutionizing the sport . . .

SATURDAY

Chapter 40

On days like these, Maggie Costello had to remind herself that
her time had once been consumed with faraway border disputes,
meetings with foreign ministers or mediating between warring
parties in distant civil wars. She had come to this town as a
foreign policy specialist, years of experience as a UN mediator
under her belt. Now here she was, sitting in a waiting area at
police headquarters, in downtown DC. She doubted any of her
former colleagues at the State Department or White House had
ever even passed this building, let alone stepped inside. They
inhabited the Washington she used to inhabit, the Washington
of 'the administration', of think tanks and book launches, of
network TV bureaux and cocktail receptions. You could live
in that Washington and barely touch this other one, the urban
Washington of police stations and potholes, of elementary schools
and shootings on the local evening news. Maggie knew that was
true, because she'd done it.

She flicked through a discarded copy of yesterday's Metro section, abandoned on the black vinyl-covered bench by whoever had last been unlucky enough to sit in this waiting area. But she couldn't concentrate on the newspaper. She was exhausted from the long drive that had brought her here, a thirteen-hour marathon from deepest Maine to DC, interrupted only by snatches of sleep in the rental car in various gas stations and parking lots, the seat reclined, a scarf across her eyes – and the door locked.

Still, the drive had given her the chance to think about Mindy, who through force of will had turned herself into Natasha Winthrop, the Brahmin girl with a Katherine Hepburn accent. How daring, how ingenious, to realize that if you're going to live a lie, then make it a big one. She could have posed as a regular daughter of the American suburbs, the child of Anywhereville. Instead, she had recast herself as a member of the 0.01 per cent, the oldest elite in the country. The idioms she'd have had to learn, the verbal inflections, the dress codes, the etiquette, the mannerisms of a tiny tribe, its ways all but unknown to anyone not called Bunny or Muffy or who didn't have a surname as their first name.

Yet it was also so insane as to smack of genius. Because it was the grand deceptions that worked best. Perhaps it was easier to disguise an accent shaped by southern poverty in the strange lilt of upper-crust Massachusetts than it was to sound like just another Midwesterner. If Mindy had done or said anything strange, wouldn't most outsiders have put it down to a peculiar tic of the *Mayflower* set, rather than a tell-tale vestige of the trailer park? If you were going to cross sides in the class war, best to run all the way behind enemy lines, rather than be left exposed and vulnerable in no man's land.

And then Maggie would remind herself that young Mindy – alone, rejected, abused and desperate – had scarcely made a choice at all. The story she had glimpsed in the newspaper, that she had stumbled upon in a library in Arkansas, her refuge from the daily abuse at the hands of P, that story was about the tragedy that befell the Winthrops. If the crash had happened to the family of an accountant in Delaware, she would have turned herself into their daughter and be that person now. She had been drowning and grabbed for the only available piece of driftwood. It just so happened to be a piece that would turn her into the heiress of a fortune comprised of money so old it might have borne George Washington's fingerprints as well as his face.

Maggie had interrogated herself too, wondering why she had suspected nothing. She rated herself a good judge of character and she had spent serious hours with Natasha, and yet she had to be honest: she hadn't had the slightest clue. Was that because she was a Dubliner whose ear was deaf to the nuances of the language and mores of the American elite? It couldn't be that: no native-born American had ever caught Natasha out either. Maggie thought of Aunt Peggy, hidden away in that sea-sprayed cottage in remotest Maine. What a brilliant, gifted teacher she must have been. What an accomplished, thorough operator too, ensuring that there was not so much as a stray document anywhere – neither here, nor in Germany – that would betray their secret. What delight she must have taken in this child, whom she had rescued from violation and cruelty and who, in the process, had rescued the Winthrop family from oblivion. That pact the teenage girl had dreamed up had worked, more effectively than either of them could ever have imagined. *Let your family's name live on. Let something good come out of this horror.*

'Maggie Costello? Miss Costello?'

Maggie had almost forgotten herself, sitting here, her eyes shut for what she had thought was just a few seconds. But now she saw a woman standing before her, her face weary, her hair greying, her expression impatient. Next to her was a man younger than her, with concern etched on his forehead. He was casting worried glances at his boss, an angst Maggie recognized from her own past alongside various senior officials – the fear that your superior was about to ruin everything by saying the wrong thing.

She followed the pair into a room identified as an 'interview suite'.

'Hold on,' Maggie said, pointedly not sitting down even as the others did, gesturing for her to do the same. 'This is not . . . I mean, I wanted to come in for an informal chat. I'm not author-ized to have a formal—'

'Cool your jets, sweetheart,' said Marcia Chester, apparently the detective in charge of Natasha's case. 'No need to get all fucking ACLU. Apparently your social life is so bad, you want to spend your Saturday morning having a chat with us. Which is convenient, because we're so sad, we want to talk to you too. Everybody's unhappy, everybody's happy.'

'This won't be recorded?'

'Nope.'

'No signed statements?'

'Only if you have something to say and you agree to sign it.'

'But that would be a whole separate process?'

'Exactly.'

'With lawyers present?'

'If you say so.'

'All right.' Maggie could feel the tiredness at the back of her eyes, trying to tug her towards sleep. The light in this room was unbearably bright.

'So.' It was Allen, pen hovering above a yellow legal pad. 'You said you had something to ask us.'

Maggie had planned this conversation during the marathon drive, but she hadn't gone back to it. She'd allowed herself to think of other things, so now she had to scramble to remember the play she had plotted.

'As you know, I have been contracted to work for Natasha Winthrop.'

They nodded.

'I am not a lawyer, but I am seconded to her team and therefore am covered by attorney-client privilege.'

Chester sighed audibly, looking first to her nails, then to the wall, painted a dull magnolia, scuffed by time and, it seemed, recalcitrant interviewees. She could tell Maggie was stalling.

'I believe we may have useful light to shed on Jeffrey Todd.'

Neither Chester nor Allen reacted.

'Relevant to this case.'

Allen cracked first. 'What kind of light?'

'I'm not going to share that yet, not while the details are

SAM BOURNE

unconfirmed. Though naturally, we'd be open to sharing whatever we discover with the prosecution in due course.'

Now, as planned, Maggie reached into her bag and produced a file, a document wallet that she kept on her lap and only partially opened. She leafed through the papers, without ever taking one out and ensuring that none remained visible. Crucially, she did not make eye contact. She spoke again.

'The records we have relate to the period before Mr Todd's change of name.'

Now she glanced up, as briefly and casually as she could manage. She hoped her voice betrayed no quaver, that they couldn't hear her heart, which was beginning to thump.

There was no reaction from either Chester or Allen. They were just waiting for her to say more.

Now she placed some papers on the desk, though she was careful to do so in such a way that even an upside-down reader, like her, would not be able to make out anything at all. She cleared her throat, as much to steady her own nerves as anything else. Now she flannelled some more.

'We believe this goes to the pattern of conduct, the record of past behaviour that will be germane to this case. Clearly, recent events have shown that Mr Todd had a history of sexual assault, rape and murder and that will inevitably be part of the defence. For the sake of completeness we want to explore the history that pertains to the period in which the deceased was not known as Jeffrey Todd but under his birth name.'

Now she looked up again, meeting Chester's gaze. What she saw emboldened her. Or rather what she didn't see. There was no demur; not so much as a furrowed brow or quizzical look passed between the two detectives.

She pressed on, willing her own voice to give nothing away, to sound as if what she was saying were routine, even dull.

'What we have in mind is the period when Mr Todd was known as Paul Hagen. We believe that will buttress our contention that . . .'

She carried on speaking, more padding and faux legalese, as she saw Chester eye her warily. But Detective Allen was now rummaging through his own files, looking for a document which he produced and laid on the table, as if to refresh his memory. As he read, and only glancing up once, he said, 'So you're talking about the period prior to the family's move to Glasgow, Kentucky?'

'That's right,' Maggie said, a rasp in her voice close to giving her away.

Allen now leaned in to examine the document in front of him, suggesting he'd found what he was looking for. 'Paul Hagen of—'

He glanced over to Chester, seeking authorization. She gave a tiny nod.

'Paul Hagen of Little Rock, Arkansas. Right?'

'That's right,' Maggie said. 'That's exactly who we're talking about.'

Chapter 41

She'd been in the car for perhaps thirty seconds when the phone started ringing. She glanced at the dashboard screen and, although it didn't flash up the name, she recognized the number: Liz.

Maggie thought about answering it; for a second her finger hovered over the 'Accept' button. But she was too wired to speak to her sister now. Already almost delirious from tiredness after that marathon drive, she now felt as if ten thousand volts had jolted through her system during that conversation with Chester and Allen in the police suite. She was at capacity; there was no room for any more input, not even a chat with Liz.

Paul Hagen of Little Rock, Arkansas.

So it was confirmed. The man Natasha had killed that night in her Georgetown home was her childhood abuser, the older, adoptive brother she had once loved. The name on the death certificate was Jeffrey Todd. But he was Paulie. He was P, the nightly intruder into her sleep, into her bed, into her body.

As Maggie stopped at a red light on Seventeenth Street, in her half-hallucinating state she could almost see how it might have unfolded. The Hagen parents deciding that the business with Mindy and with her friend at school – Helen – was a shadow they needed to escape. Maggie wondered if it had ever been admitted out loud, between the parents and their son, or whether it remained one of those secret facts that can sometimes exist in families, understood but never acknowledged. *Paulie, your mother and I have been thinking. Maybe it would be best for everyone if we made a fresh start. A completely new beginning, far away from here.*

As for the name change, the detectives had filled that in. The paperwork had been filed not in Arkansas but in Kentucky, about a year after the family had moved there. The last existing records for Paul Hagen revealed him to be the subject of an informal police warning, following a complaint from the principal of Barren County High School in Glasgow, Kentucky: Hagen had been accused of following a female student, aged thirteen, home from the school and was said to have initiated a sexual assault on her on a secluded part of the nearby Trojan Trail. Unfortunately for him, but very fortunately for her, he was disturbed by a jogger who saw the incident and asked the girl if she needed help. Paul insisted the two of them were just 'fooling around' and the girl refused to press charges. The change of name came soon afterwards.

Maggie imagined that too, Hagen's parents realizing – too late – that the young and vulnerable Mindy had been telling the truth. That was if they hadn't always known, even if they couldn't bear

SAM BOURNE

to admit it, even to themselves. So now they resolved to wipe the slate clean, ridding their son of a past that could catch up with him. Had they worried especially about Mindy? Did they realize that she was a person of uncommon strength? That she had disappeared from Little Rock, leaving not a trace behind, but that one day she would want her revenge?

Another incoming call from Liz. Maggie pressed 'Decline': she needed time to think.

Somehow Natasha had worked out that, like her, P had taken on a new identity. God knew when it started or how she had done it, but she must have watched the newly minted Jeffrey Todd from afar. In the internet age, that would have suddenly become possible, whether by lurking, anonymous and unseen, on his Facebook page or just alerted whenever his name was mentioned. Maggie could picture Natasha at her screen, monitoring her one-time brother, reading of the arrests, the collapsed trials, the near-misses. The former Mindy Hagen would have seen that 'Todd' lived as an adult the way he had as a teenager: as a cruel and violent sexual predator.

How easily it must have become an obsession, as Natasha saw him evade justice again and again, just as he had when she was little more than a child. Even as she was mastering the law, persuading judges and juries through her command of the system, she would have been consumed with rage that the system seemed powerless in the face of this one criminal: the man, the boy, who had filled her young nights with terror. No wonder she had hatched a plan to administer justice herself, if that was what it took: luring him to her home where he would

346

be caught in the act, once and for all brought to book for the brutal rapist that he was. Except that the plan had gone horribly wrong.

The phone rang one more time, just as she was turning into Massachusetts Avenue. At last, she surrendered.

'Hi, Liz.'

'Mags, listen. Where are you?' Her sister seemed to be panting.

'I'm in DC. Don't tell me you've taken up running?'

'Where in DC?'

'I'm on my way home.'

'Don't go in.'

'What?'

'Don't go in.'

'I don't understand.'

'Listen, were you in Maine yesterday?'

'Yes. How do you know that?'

'In somewhere called—' She could hear her sister fiddling with her phone. 'Penobscot?'

'Yes, how the fuck do you—'

'And you rented a car from Portland airport?'

'Yes. What is this, Liz?'

'Have you been on Twitter lately?'

'Yes. No. I mean, not that much. I was driving mostly.'

'And you never search for yourself, do you? You stopped looking at your mentions, didn't you, after the whole White House thing?'

'Please, Liz. What the hell is this?'

'Pull over and then look up a hashtag. It's #FindingMC. It's a spillover from Gab.'

'That far-right thing?'

'Have you pulled over?'

'Hold on.' Maggie parked up. She could feel another wave of exhaustion building up, ready to crash over her. Her heart was beginning to pound. That edge in her sister's voice, she'd heard it before. It came when she sensed danger.

'All right, I've pulled over.'

'So someone started it on Gab. Anonymous account, identified only with the male symbol. You know, the circle with the arrow?'

'Started what?'

'Some kinds of "men's rights" activist. From there it spread. There's a whole movement online. Anyway, it was a call-out, asking people to look out for you and post pictures of you, wherever you're spotted.'

'Jesus.'

'I know. It's completely sick. It's like mass surveillance by social media. But it's taken off. People have been sending pictures of you . . . Shit.'

'What? What is it?'

'There's another one. Were you just at the . . . what is that?'

'What?'

'DC Police headquarters. Were you there seven minutes ago?'

'Yes. How do you know—'

'There's a picture of you, getting into your car. It's stamped nine forty-one am.'

'Christ. And does it say anything?'

'People are putting up the picture, and then the hashtag. FindingMC.'

Maggie put her head in her hands. She was trying to think, but the lightness was rolling in and out like surf on a beach. She desperately needed to sleep. Finally, a question she had been trying to formulate came to her. 'What did it say, the first tweet or whatever?'

'I think it's the first, I can't be sure. But if it is, hang on, I've got it open on another . . . Here, the original message on Gab said: "Fellow warriors, mark the face of this woman. Her name is Maggie Costello and she is covering for a man-killer. You are invited to spot her in the wild, then post pictures of her. Use the hashtag FindingMC." That last thing is all one word, FindingMC.'

'And now it's on Twitter?'

'Kind of a spillover, yeah. Still mainly on Gab. Bit on Facebook as well. Maybe Instagram. TikTok. There was some video of you, buying fish or something from a stall?'

'What?'

'Seafood. Like from a shack. In Maine?'

'Yes, OK. Jesus, Liz, there was no one around when I did that. Video, did you say?'

'Like, twenty seconds. No sound. Too much wind. Wobbly picture, like it had been done on a phone with maximum zoom. Could have been taken from a car. Or anywhere really. The thing is, Mags, what's this about? Why would they be doing this?'

'I'm sure you've worked it out. You saw what they said. "Covering for a man-killer."'

SAM BOURNE

'I sort of guessed when you got me to look up that number. So it's true. Jesus. You're working for—'

'Yes. That's who I'm helping.'

'She killed that man, right?'

'She was defending herself from a known rapist and murderer, Liz.'

'So why would all these men be on your case?'

'Why do you think, Liz? Because these men think it's OK for men to rape women. They think men should be *allowed* to do it. They're angry that someone stopped them. They see a woman and a rapist, and they side with the rapist. That's what's going on here. You just need to open your fucking eyes, Liz.'

There was a moment of silence, far worse than the response Maggie would have expected. Her sister would normally snap back, *Well, don't bite my fucking head off, you daft bitch*, but now she said nothing. Another wave of pure fatigue, coloured bright white, crashed over Maggie's head.

'I'm sorry, Liz. I'm just so exhausted. And frightened. I'm sorry.'

More silence. Then Maggie spoke again.

'What should I do, Lizzie?' She could hear the smallness of her own voice.

There was a rustle at the other end. Maggie wondered if her younger sister was reaching for a tissue, to wipe away tears. Then she heard her.

'Oh God.'

'What?'

'Where are you now?'

'I'm on Massachusetts and—'

'Are you parked near a place called Au Bon Pain?'

Maggie looked through her windscreen and saw nothing ahead or on the left. But then, directly through her right window, she could see the name of that lunch place. She was parked right in front of it.

'Yes.'

'OK. Two pictures of you parked outside it have gone up in the last five minutes. You're wearing that zip-up jacket.'

'Jesus.'

'Fuck, there's another one.'

Maggie scoped the area, eyes left and right, trying to search out a man aiming a phone in her direction. 'So someone's watching me right now?'

'Not someone, Maggie. The pictures are from different angles. It's several people.'

Maggie hit the lock button on the car door. She could feel her heart beginning to bang. 'I'm going to drive home.'

'How far away are you?'

'Maybe five minutes.'

'OK. Stay on the line. I might have an idea.'

Maggie pulled out slowly. She was scanning the sidewalk, looking at the faces of the people walking past, especially those holding phones. Now she shot a glance to the other side of the street. It must have been from there or thereabouts that at least one of the photos Liz had described had been taken. What about that guy, looking straight ahead, staring even—

A car horn screamed through the air and straight into Maggie's central nervous system. Reflexively, she slammed on the brakes. The horn didn't stop, because as she had pulled out – staring at that man across the street, rather than watching the road – she had come within an inch of ramming into a Subaru advancing in the next lane. He'd come to an emergency stop and, clearly shaken, was now glaring at her. He opened his door and got out, coming towards her for a confrontation. She had to make an instant decision.

She hit the gas and pulled away, leaving the man to issue a cloud of 'Fuck you's as she sped off.

'Are you still there?'

'Yes, Maggie. I'm still here.' A pause. 'Please try to drive safely. Tell me when you're nearly there. But don't get too near. There might be people waiting for you. Park a block away.'

'Really?'

'Make that two blocks away.'

'They know my home address?'

'They might do.'

Maggie remembered the intruder, the fantasy rapist, who knew where she lived thanks to that sewer of a website. She hadn't told Liz about that episode, and not only because it would have revealed who she was currently working for. She had held it back for the same reason she withheld so much about her working life from the only person in the world she truly regarded as family: because it would have terrified her. Still, if her address was known on that forum for rape freaks, it was bound to be known to whichever crazed incel bastard had started this online hunt.

She parked the car one block east and one block north of where she lived. She looked left and right, and then upward, at the windows of the first-floor apartments. One woman moving potted plants on a narrow roof terrace; nothing else.

'OK, I'm walking now.'

'All right. So Maggie, I need you to open Twitter.'

'For fuck's sake, Liz. I'm not going to start tweeting.'

'Trust me, Maggie. It's not tweeting. Put me on speaker and hit the "Compose" button.'

Maggie opened the app and had to look for the 'Compose' button. Truth was, she had almost never posted a tweet. She was a 'lurker'. She would hang around, reading other people's tweets, 'monitoring the debate', as they used to call it in the White House, but rarely making a peep. She preferred it that way.

'That sort of feather quill thing?'

'That's it. Press that.'

'OK.'

'You're not there yet, are you?'

'One block away.'

'You've pressed the quill thing?'

'Yes. I've done it.'

'Now, Mags, can you see an icon that looks like a camera? Bottom left, but not the very bottom?'

'OK.'

'Hit that. What can you see?'

'It's showing me my feet as I walk.'

'Good, so the camera's working. Now, can you see two words at the bottom of the screen?'

'Yes. "Capture" and "Live".'

'Exactly. Only when you're ready, I want you to hold the camera up in front of you, so that it's showing the street ahead. As close to your head as you can, so what it's showing is your point of view. Have a go at that. Don't press anything! But just do that.'

'All right.'

'Can you see it?'

'Sure.'

'Like you're the camera. Whatever you're seeing, it's seeing. Yes?'

'Yes. Now what?'

'Where are you?'

'About a hundred yards from my building.'

'Good. When you're ready, take a deep breath and hit the "Live" button. That will cut me off, so you won't be able to hear me. But I'll be following you on Twitter. How many followers do you have?'

'I can't remember. Hardly—'

'I'll check. OK, that's good. Nearly fifty thousand. You got that huge lift after the whole White House saga. Even better, lots of media people follow you. Fuck, that senator follows you. Whatshisname, Harrison. So they'll be watching. You ready?'

'Not really.'

'Make sure no one can see exactly where your apartment is, OK? Keep the picture generic. It's their faces we want to see. Not the building number. Got it?'

'Got it.'

'Remember, when you're ready, press "Live". Bye, Maggie.'

Maggie ended the call and shoved her right hand, still gripping the phone, deep into her bag, so that it wouldn't be seen. She kept on walking.

Perhaps twenty-five yards stood between her and her home when she saw the first one. He was younger than she was expecting, pale and acned, a student who looked as if he'd only just started cooking for himself, not graduating beyond beans straight from the can. She saw him do it, raising the phone, snapping her, then fiddling with the buttons. He was very clearly posting a picture of her.

Ten yards now and she could see a man loitering by the front door, as if he were a maître'd poised to greet guests at his restaurant. A half-second later, she clocked the phone in his right hand, which he now raised to his face and *click*. He was white and, she'd have guessed, in his early fifties.

As she got nearer, she saw that there was another man perhaps two doors down. Now that he had seen her, he too was advancing, also holding up his phone. There was some movement to her right. She swivelled to catch the sight of a fourth man crossing the road: bearded, hipsterish, wearing a black beanie. Once he had reached the kerb, when he was no more than a few feet away from her, he raised his phone to chest height and took her picture.

At last she was by her own front door. With her left hand she began to rummage in her bag for the keys, but her right was still holding her phone and she didn't want to let go.

SAM BOURNE

So now there were four of them, four men who had somehow acquired her home address. Now, wordlessly, they moved towards each other, forming a huddle, a phalanx with the oldest man facing her. They were blocking her path, standing between her and her front door.

The hipster spoke first. Politely, in a voice that suggested he was simply confirming a dinner reservation, he asked, 'Maggie Costello?'

The older man didn't wait for an answer. He said, 'So you're the bitch working for that whore who killed a man.'

The hipster picked up from there. 'Don't go crying rape now, sweetheart. Just because we want to fuck you up doesn't mean we want to fuck you.' Maggie noticed his right hand was balled into a fist. She didn't need Liz to say it, but she heard her sister's voice in her head all the same. *Now.*

She pulled the phone out of the bag, held it up and, though her fingers were trembling, pressed the button marked 'Live'. She spoke.

'Hi everyone. This is Maggie Costello. And this seems to be the welcoming party that's come to greet me at my apartment in Washington, DC.' In the frame were two of the quartet, acne boy and the middle-aged guy. 'You may have heard – these men clearly have – there's a hashtag doing the rounds, encouraging people to take pictures of me wherever I am and to post them online. I think it's meant to intimidate me.'

The youngest, also perhaps the quickest to grasp what was happening, looked aghast and then, a second or two later, silently moved out of shot. He began walking down the street,

356

rapidly breaking into a jog. Maggie was tempted to call after him, but instead kept her focus on the three who were now in the live picture. Unexpectedly, the bottom of the screen began to be dotted with small, floating hearts, rising like bubbles in an aquarium.

'So, guys, how about some introductions?'

Reflexively, the oldest of the trio lunged forward, trying to grab the phone from her. He succeeded in pushing her arm down, so that the camera was now aiming towards the ground, but he didn't prise it from her grasp. She knew it was still on, beaming its sound and pictures to whoever was watching. The only viewer she could think of was Liz.

'Sorry about that everyone,' she said, aware how bumpy and uneven her voice sounded, as if she'd just come in from a run. She was nervous. 'Seems one of our guests is a little camera-shy.' As she spoke, she raised the camera again, so that, wobbling and jerky, it showed the three men. One of them had his face obscured by his own phone; perhaps he was filming her filming them.

'So how about those introductions? Let's start with you,' she said, focusing on the hipster. Now, in a short, sharp move that caught her by surprise, he sent his arm towards her, his hand giant as it filled the image on her phone. Instinct accounted for her response. Still holding the phone in place, she kicked out. Aiming only for his shins, she struck something softer. The howl that she caught on camera confirmed instantly that she had struck him hard in the genitals.

There was a sound over her shoulder. She wheeled around

to see that two more men had arrived. She caught them mid-signal, as they were gesturing a plan of attack to the other three.

With strained jollity, she said, 'Oh look, two more want to join the fun. Hi! Let's wave to all the people watching.' She made a wave of her own, her hand oversized in the foreground. 'Seems we have several thousand followers watching this, live. Hey, you . . .' She was addressing the tallest of the new pair. 'Seems a few friends over at the DC Police Department have joined us. Oh look, and the FBI. How cool is that? They're all watching us.'

The taller man spread his fingers across his face in an attempt to hide himself. The second of the new arrivals turned and sprinted away.

Emboldened, she spun around and focused on the man in his fifties. 'So you want to tell me what this is about? I think our audience wants to know.'

'You're working for a goddamn murderer. Natasha Winthrop killed a man in cold blood!'

For the first time since Liz had called, Maggie had a thought that went beyond self-preservation. She was thinking about Natasha and whether, by doing this, Maggie was inadvertently providing a platform to those bent on harming the woman she was meant to help. She also knew she'd be doing Natasha no favours if she simply cut the feed at this moment.

'So what were you planning to do to me? Were you planning on coming into my home? What were you men going to do to an unarmed woman in her own home?'

Now he stepped forward, so that Maggie instinctively recoiled.

His face filled the screen, covered in white stubble. His nose was latticed with tiny purple veins. 'This is what you want, isn't it?' He seemed to be addressing not Maggie, but the unseen audience. 'A world where a woman can kill any man she wants. Just like that. You just cry rape and any man is fair game. Open season. Well, we won't let it happen.' Now he leaned in even closer, so that his breath was near enough to mist the lens, and bellowed: 'You will not DESTROY US!'

With that, he turned and marched off. Maggie looked around, confirming that he had been the last; the others had all gone. She saw a man on the opposite side of the street quietly put away his phone. Perhaps he had planned to join the party but, once he saw what was going on, thought better of the idea.

She held up her phone, clicked the button to reverse the shot, so that it was now her face in the frame, and said, as wearily as she'd ever heard herself, 'Thanks for watching.' Then she clicked the button to cut the transmission. The device revealed that, at the close, she'd had nine hundred and sixty-one viewers. She had lied when she had spoken of thousands, but clearly there had been an audience. People would stop in the street to watch a fight: why would social media be any different?

A couple of neighbours now appeared – Maggie guessed they had seen or heard the commotion and waited to see how it played out before getting involved – to check she was OK. One offered to call the police, an offer which, largely to avoid the hassle, Maggie declined. She checked once more, left, right and all around, found her key and let herself in.

Normally she felt only relief when she got home after days

on the road, especially when she felt she had evaded danger. But not this time. It was not just the confrontation outside, though that had shaken her. It was what had happened the last time she was in this apartment, the man who had broken in through the bathroom window, the man who thought he could force himself on her, or pretend to, which, because she hadn't known it was a pretence, amounted to the same thing.

She approached the blind and, with as small and subtle a motion as she could manage, she separated the slats to look outside. Two men, both in their twenties she reckoned, were on the sidewalk opposite. They seemed to be conferring. One was showing the other the screen of his phone. Then, as she knew they would, they looked up, to indicate her apartment. Instantly, she stepped back, hoping to be invisible, though she was not hopeful: the tremor of the blind had surely given her away.

Her need for sleep now was overwhelming; her body was screaming for rest. And yet, she knew there was too much adrenalin flooded through her system for sleep to come easily. She was familiar with that sensation: exhausted to the core, but her nerves still crackling with electricity, throwing off blue sparks.

That would fade eventually. It always did. But still she feared rest would be out of reach. It was thanks to those men outside, and the others that were bound to follow – the men who had not yet had word of the live Twitter transmission, or who had heard about it but did not fear it, men who were still acting on the initial call-out: #FindingMC. It had been on the phones of aggrieved men all over America by the sound of it; in Portland airport, in bloody Penobscot, for Christ's sake. To think that in every corner of this huge country there were 'men's rights activists' imagining themselves heroes for hunting down a single, unarmed woman.

Every corner of America, all the way to her front door. That's why she couldn't rest. Her home was no longer a haven. She wanted desperately to soak in a hot bath. But she knew her eye would forever be on the window where that would-be rapist had climbed in. She wanted to slip into bed and under the covers. But she knew she'd be thinking about the men down below, on the street, looking up, waiting. She'd feel their eyes on her. Her home was no longer a refuge. It was no longer hers.

The phone was ringing. She reached for it and felt relief to see the name on the display. She and Liz spoke only briefly, just long enough for Maggie to reassure her younger sister that she was now safely indoors – and also to let her know the full picture. There seemed no point holding back now; Liz had seen for herself the danger Maggie was in. So Maggie told her, as concisely as she could, about the intruder who had broken in and the online forum where he had found her address. Liz was shocked and livid, but audibly did her best to contain it. She knew her sister didn't have the strength for that now.

Once the call was done, Maggie fell onto the sofa and put her head in her hands. She thought of the older man on the street outside, the one who had shouted in her face. *You will not DESTROY US.* She thought of the man who had broken into this apartment. She thought of Senator Harrison's hands squeezing her shoulders. She thought of P and what he'd done to the child who had once loved him like a brother. Their faces blurred into each other. And like that, with her coat still on and anger bubbling through her veins, she drifted into fitful, exhausted sleep. But even then, in her dreams and nightmares, her subconscious began to grope towards what she had to do next.

Chapter 42

Bangalore, India

What was his last thought? Was he even capable of thought by then? His captors hoped so. Though they had tormented him – no, though they had *tortured* him – they had taken pains to ensure he remained conscious, that he could still hear, that he could still process information. There was one important fact they wanted him to absorb.

They looked at him now, his ankles chained, his wrists cuffed, his mouth gagged. They surveyed the battered, mutilated state of his genitals, pulled, beaten and twisted. They beheld his nakedness, his degradation.

They had confused him about his location, blindfolding him as soon as they snatched him off the street, bundling him into a van and driving him through choked streets in circles. But they wanted there to be no confusion about their motivation. Through the last eighty minutes, behind the steel door of this lock-up garage on the outskirts of the city, they had spoken to him at intervals throughout. Not in their own voice, of course, but by means of a distorted, electronic voice, as recommended.

They had reminded him of his past crimes, the most recent of which was just last week – not to mention the sexual assault that had been underway when they had picked him up. They recounted the scooter case, when he and three friends had spotted a young woman – a doctor – on her way home from work. One of the men had been tasked with deflating the scooter's tyres, then running off. The other three watched as the woman struggled with the useless vehicle before they approached, offering to help. They then dragged her to a patch of wasteland away from the road, where they were joined by the fourth man – the one who had let down the tyres. There, on that patch of dirt, weeds and garbage, they had repeatedy raped her, each one taking turns, sometimes simultaneously, using her as if she were a doll designed for their satisfaction. When they were sated, they strangled her and dumped her body under a bridge. They soaked it in petrol and watched it burn.

He had been bailed while waiting to be charged for that crime, and while free he had raped again. Somehow, he evaded justice for both. And those were only the most egregious incidents. He had been assaulting or raping girls and women for years. His neighbours knew it; the police knew it; the dogs on the street knew it. But he was still a free man.

All of this information was conveyed to him in that pitiless, metallic voice, while he howled and moaned as his testicles were twisted and as a thick, alien object was shoved inside him. Occasionally the captors would ease up on the punishment, anxious not for his safety or wellbeing – they did not care about that – but out of concern for his consciousness. They needed him to absorb what they were about to tell him.

In the last of these periods of respite, as he kneeled, whimpering and blindfolded, on all fours, the captors gave each other the signal they had pre-agreed. Their faces still covered, even from each other, they now formed a square around him, so that he was equidistant from each of them. The captor who had been using the voice-distorter to address the captive had moved away from that device. Another nod and then all four, in unison, said the same three words.

Did they hear a gasp from their captive? Afterwards, when they discussed it, two said they had. The others were not so sure. But there could be no doubt. He had heard what they had said and he had understood it.

That cleared the way for the final move. As agreed, all four of them had in their right hands a section of lead pipe. These weren't exactly the same length, but close enough. They took a step forward, so that they were all within striking distance of their target. They raised their right hands and then, on the arranged signal, they came down hard, the four heavy pipes simultaneously striking a different part of the man's skull.

Despite their fears, the effect was instant and complete. It was clear he was dead, what remained of his head lolling forward, loose and lifeless.

The captors began to pack up, moving efficiently, untying the man and zipping him into a mortician's body bag, ready for transportation and disposal. As they worked, they drew satisfaction from the fact that the last neural information that went through the rapist's cerebral cortex consisted of three words he would have known were true, for they were spoken by voices that could not help but confirm the statement they had uttered. The last three words he heard were:

We are women.

Chapter 43

This is the BBC World Service, you're listening to Newshour. *To India now – a country that some say is in the midst of an epidemic of rape. At an extraordinary press conference earlier today, police in Bangalore said they believe a vigilante gang may be active in the city, hunting down notorious rapists. They're basing the claim on security camera footage that showed the abduction of a man with multiple convictions for sexual assault, and on the fact that that man's body was found brutally mutilated hours later. What's more, some are linking the crime with a highly publicized act of so-called vigilante justice an ocean away. We're joined on the line now by our South East Asia correspondent Randeep Tripathi. Randeep, what more can you tell us?*

Well, Tim, one statistic tells the story. In India one rape is committed every fifteen minutes. Women's groups here have long argued that not enough is being done to tackle the problem, despite some horrific cases that have outraged public opinion. But now some are wondering if ordinary Indian citizens are taking the problem into their own hands. It comes after that footage emerged, as you mentioned, suggesting an infamous rapist in Bangalore had been snatched off the streets.

Now, these CCTV pictures, which have been playing on a loop on some of India's news channels, appear to show the dead man – who is currently not being named for legal reasons – in the act of committing assault against a woman. The quality of the pictures is quite grainy, but what they appear to show is the man walking behind a woman, suddenly pouncing to grab her by the neck, bringing her to the ground and then, if you will, the first stages of him forcing the woman to perform a sex act.

At that point, an unmarked black vehicle pulls into the shot. Four masked men, four masked figures, jump out, they bundle the man inside and take him away. And, as you say, a few hours later his dead body was found in what police say was a 'horrific' state.

And to reiterate, Randeep, that's sparked talk of a possible vigilante movement in India. What can you tell us about the link some are making with a similar episode far away from India?

That's right, Tim. You might remember reports yesterday of a similar incident in Chicago in which a past sex offender, apparently also apprehended in the commission of a sex crime, was also snatched off the street, also in a black vehicle, also by masked figures, and also dumped close by a few hours later. In that case, the man was found alive. But some here are wondering if what happened in Bangalore is a 'copycat' of that episode in Chicago. Social media is buzzing with what is, for now, a conspiracy theory, but the BBC understands that the authorities in Bangalore are 'exploring' the parallels and have 'not ruled out' any line of inquiry . . .

Maggie's eyes were still shut, but she was awake. Slumped on the couch where she had fallen asleep, she could feel a film of sweat on her face and a foul taste in her mouth. She had no idea how long she had slept or what time it was: the BBC playing on her phone was no good, because it kept on saying it was whatever o'clock Greenwich Mean Time. Had she set her alarm, was that why she was hearing the World Service? She couldn't remember.

She was hazy too on what she had just heard. She reached for her phone and, squinting through half an eye, she saw that she had dozed for several hours. She opened up the BBC app, rewound thirty seconds and listened again to the last chunk of that report from India.

. . . apparently also *apprehended in the commission of a sex crime, was* also *snatched off the street,* also *in a black vehicle,* also *by masked figures, and* also *dumped close by a few hours later.*

She sat up, the gears in her mind turning over slowly. She headed for the bathroom, to splash some cold water on her face, glanced up at the window, remembered why she didn't want to be in this room, thought about food, headed for the kitchen, opened a cupboard and wondered, not for the first time, if it was too early in the day for whisky.

Now she reached for her laptop. She didn't know what she was looking for, but she knew it had something to do with that India story and the one it referred to, in Chicago. Something not quite right.

She looked up the Reuters account of the Bangalore incident, which contained a few more details. The report said the man's skull had been 'smashed to a pulp' and quoted a police spokesman saying the dead man had been 'violently sodomized' with objects that had caused serious injury.

Now, on a new tab, Maggie looked up the *New York Times* account of the Chicago abduction. She skim-read it – the black vehicle, the masked figures, the past record of sexual assault and rape, the 'victim' dumped back where he'd been picked up. Obviously there was no mention of injuries to the head: he had been found alive, after all. There the parallels ended. That the two incidents were not identical made sense, even if one were a copycat of the other. The vigilantes of Bangalore only had to be inspired by what happened in Chicago; they weren't following an instruction manual.

And yet something nagged at Maggie all the same. Something about the Chicago incident and the way she first heard about it. Where had she been? She just needed to remember where and how she had heard about it. Come on, think. *Think.*

Now it came back to her. The parking lot of a Subway on I-95, between New York and Trenton. She had pulled over for her second or maybe third stop of the night drive down from Maine and she was listening to the radio. Except it wasn't a radio station. It was one of those digital stations which played the audio from cable news. She could picture herself leaning against the car, a cup of foul coffee and a grotesque, too-soft tuna sandwich resting on the roof, while CNN played on the car speakers.

. . . a man was reported to be lying in the gutter in a state of what police are calling 'severe distress'. They say he had suffered 'extreme, aggravated sexual assault', with some details that are too graphic to share on this network.

Too graphic. Now her mind was turning over at double speed. She quickly checked the *New York Times* website and read their account of the same incident. There was no extra detail she could see that had not been reported on CNN, but there was a reference to 'circumstances so disturbing', police sources were reluctant to divulge them on the record. She thumbed out a text to Jake Haynes at the *Times* bureau. Time to cash in the remaining credit left on her account in the favour bank.

Quick chat?

Thank the Lord himself for Haynes's hunger for news. He called back straight away.

'Hey, Jake. You got two minutes?'

'For Maggie Costello, I got three.'

'So this is not strictly speaking a DC story. But it might feed into a DC story.'

'Feed in?'

'Eventually.'

'This about Winthrop?'

'I'm not sure yet.'

'Not sure? OK. But when you *are* sure—'

'You'll be the first to know.'

'Sounds good. OK, shoot.'

'I need to ask something about a *Times* story written out of Chicago.'

'OK.'

'It's the story about the rapist dumped on the street.

Apparently there were some details that were "too graphic" to be published.'

'We said that? "Too graphic"?'

'CNN said it. You said something about "circumstances so disturbing".'

'Sounds like us. So you want me to find out what those extra details were, and then tell you.'

'You're a doll.'

'Byline on the story?'

Maggie told him the name that had appeared on the *Times* report, hung up and paced. It was only a hunch, she told herself, as she paced some more. Only a hunch. Only a hunch.

After ten minutes, the phone rang again. On the screen, the name she wanted to see: Jake Haynes. Her index finger trembled over the 'Accept' button. She was still so exhausted.

'Yeah,' she said.

'I'm fine, thank you, how are you?'

'Sorry, Jake. Go on.'

'So this took me a while. The newsroom in New York is up to their eyes in a big story, but I finally got what you need. Are you near a bathroom, because you may want to throw up. First, the guy was found bound and gagged, with one of those red gimp-ball things in his mouth. You know, leather strap around his head.'

'OK.'

'Second, his genitals had been, like, totally abused. Balls pulled and twisted, penis really damaged. And the main thing was, he had been . . . I don't know if this is quite the right term, but . . . he'd been anally raped.'

'Right.'

'I'll spare you the details, because, believe me, they are gross. But the point is, it involved, you know, objects.'

'Objects?'

'Heavy objects. Thick, heavy objects.'

'Ouch.'

'"Severe and lasting damage", apparently.'

'Jesus.'

'So that's why we didn't put it in the paper. And neither did anyone else. Police shared those details on background only. Kind of see why.'

'Yep.' Maggie was still pacing. 'All right. Jake, I owe you.'

'No, I think officially I still owe *you*. That was the story of the year.'

'Story of the decade, you said last time.'

'Ah, but maybe *this* will be the story of the decade. Lead to it, I mean.'

'We live in hope. Thanks, Jake.'

'And you'll let me know, right?'

'If there's a story, you'll get it first.'

She hung up and went back to the computer, to that Reuters piece. It was still there, that crucial line, saying the dead man had been 'violently sodomized'. And the report was explicit: he had been violated by means of 'objects that had caused serious injury'.

Now she opened a fresh tab and did a Google search that made her shake her head in disbelief. Had it really come to this? She typed in the words, 'Chicago rapist abducted anal'.

Plenty of stories appeared that included the first three search terms but not the fourth. The ones that offered a match for all four related to stories from long ago or, in one case, to a review of a movie shown only in a single arts cinema in Brooklyn.

The rest of the results page linked to accounts of the incident in Chicago and she skim-read them all: no reference to anal rape or sodomy or anything of the kind. She did word searches for every possible term. Nothing. She closed down the tabs and pushed away the machine, satisfied that no one besides her, a handful of reporters and the Chicago Police Department knew precisely what pain had been inflicted on that man.

Which left a question. If the Bangalore attack was a copycat inspired by what had happened in Chicago, replicating most of the key details – down to the masks, the colour of the van, the modus operandi – how come the vigilantes of India had copied an element they couldn't possibly have known about, an element that had never been made public? What if the one episode was not a mere copy of the other, one day apart, but something very different?

Maggie got up, paced around, walked into the kitchen, eyed up the bottle of Ardbeg, walked back into the living room, then back into the kitchen. At one point, she kneeled on the floor to pull open the bottom drawer, almost unconsciously rummaging through it before she realized what she was doing: looking for a packet of cigarettes she had hidden from herself months ago, around the time she promised Uri that she had given up, once and for all. No joy.

She went back to the table and her laptop. That too, she knew, was displacement activity, if of a slightly more rarefied kind. She needed to think through the question that was turning over in her mind. The two episodes – Chicago and Bangalore – were more similar than the public accounts of each let on: how come?

By way of procrastination, she checked Twitter. It was obsessing about some celebrity story that had just broken, involving a major network TV executive accused of sexually coercing a junior employee. The primetime news anchor of that same network had posted a single emoji – showing a green face, poised to vomit in disgust – above a link to the story.

This was not helping. She wanted more information on what had happened in India and on the streets of Chicago. She needed more detail, however 'graphic', that might shed light on whether the echoes between these two incidents were coincidence or—

Hold on.

Was this TV thing the breaking *New York Times* story Jake had mentioned? Maggie went back to the puke emoji tweet, then clicked on the article and, sure enough, it was time-stamped as posted a matter of minutes ago. She skimmed the first few paragraphs.

Album is said to have grabbed, groped, harassed and assaulted female employees for decades. One source, speaking on condition of anonymity to safeguard her own position at the network, said: "Marty regards women in the news division as his own personal all-you-can-eat buffet. He's had the same MO for years: the invitation to do 'extra work' for him at his summer house, outside regular hours. Then, before you know it, he's in the shower, butt-naked, asking you to join him. Or he's in his bathrobe, expecting you to take care of business. Pretty much every woman in news has been through it. It's kind of an initiation rite."

The Times *has learned that disciplinary proceedings have been launched twice against Mr Album in recent years, only to be abandoned on both occasions due to lack of evidence. Documents from the second of those two inquiries, seen by the* Times, *include a letter from Mr Album's attorney urging that the complaints be dismissed as "a classic case of he-said, she-said to which there can never be any resolution".*

These latest revelations seem set to have a different impact, chiefly because they come accompanied by video evidence. In the recording seen by the Times, *Mr Album can be seen grabbing an employee, more than forty-one years his junior, by the hair and forcing her into a sex act. He can also be heard pressuring the employee, a recently-hired subordinate within the news division. At one point, the woman is heard crying as she explains to Mr Album that she "was just here doing my work". He replies, "Don't cry, baby" before he is seen pulling her head by the hair towards his private parts. She can be heard letting out a yelp.*

The Times *has spoken to the employee, and confirmed that she is the woman in the video. She has corroborated the video, which she says she recorded herself, through covert use of her smartphone. She co-operated with this investigation on condition of anonymity.*

Jesus Christ. Everywhere you looked, if you could bear to look, it was there. How many men were like this Marty Album, regarding women as an 'all-you-can-eat buffet'? Lots, it seemed. More than Maggie had realized. She remembered what Natasha had said, that night on the Cape. How rape was, in effect, no longer a crime. *If society essentially shrugs its shoulders at a certain act, then it is signalling that it has made a decision. And the decision in our society is that, most of the time, a man is permitted to force a woman to have sex with him. It is tolerated. Like smoking weed at home. Or hitting eighty on the interstate. Technically a crime, but not really.*

At the foot of the *New York Times* report, there was a link to 'Related Stories'. Maggie wanted to click away from the page; she wasn't sure how much more of this her spirits could take, without plummeting. But some part of her brain, not wholly obvious to her, was whirring now. She clicked on the most recent item, a report out of London from just a few days ago.

It told how a top restaurant chef, an emerging celebrity in Britain, had been accused of sexual assault. A UK newspaper had revealed a pattern of bullying behaviour: he had engaged in 'constant harassment and cruelty'; on one occasion, he had asked a pregnant colleague to allow him to drink her breast milk. The chef had now been suspended from his own restaurant, after his financial backers pulled the plug. 'The key development came this week, when a lawyer for an unnamed kitchen assistant sent investors a video which showed the chef forcing himself on the young employee. The video has been confirmed as genuine, a secret recording made by the victim of the assault.'

Her brain was still in a haze – from lack of sleep, mainly, from the jolt of being surrounded by those men outside her front door, by the fact that her own home no longer felt safe – but somehow, through the blur, an idea was taking shape. Less than an idea, fuzzier than that. It was an intimation of an idea, an inkling.

She forced herself to go back to where this started. She knew the dangers of a descent into an online rabbit-hole, especially when you were all but tripping with fatigue. First move, climb out of the rabbit-hole and come back to the surface. Next, remember how you got there. Which for Maggie meant recalling the question that had seemed so sharp in her mind a matter of moments ago.

Through the fog, she dragged it back to visibility. It was the curiously similar tortures inflicted on the rapists of Chicago and Bangalore, alike in ways that were never made public, in ways that made it almost impossible for one to be a copycat of the other. How had that happened?

Drained as she was, desperate for a proper sleep as she was, Maggie knew there was only one person who could settle that question. She grabbed her bag and her keys and headed out the door and into the night.

Chapter 44

'We need to get out in front on these rape stories.'

'I don't think we want to use the word "rape".'

Dan Benson sighed, turning to Ellen Stone, the one woman in the room and the one woman on the team. Christ, if karma wasn't paying them back for being so testosterone-heavy. After the sisterhood crashed and burned so badly with the first female nominee, it became tacitly acceptable within the party to 'appoint whoever was best qualified for the job' – which was understood by the consultant class as, 'Go back to hiring men'. The stigma had gone out of it. Like, *We tried it, it didn't work, let's go back to winning elections.*

But boy, right now, did that look like a mistake. Again and again, Senator Tom Harrison was being cast as the sexist dinosaur, a clumsy, clunky, goofy dad or even granddad who was perennially on the wrong side of history. Natasha Winthrop was behind bars, for Christ's sake, and still she managed to seem more in touch, more in tune with the times, than him. And now this.

'All right, OK. Let's call it "sexual assault" if that makes you more comfortable.'

'Doesn't matter what makes *me* feel comfortable, Dan,' Doug Teller said, his voice split between octaves of irritation and condescension. The only thing missing was a hint of apology for dragging them in here on a Saturday night. 'It's what message we want to convey to voters. We call it the estate tax, our opponents call it the death tax; our opponents win. Given the candidate has been a close personal friend of Marty Album's for the last thirty years, I don't think we want to say that that close personal friend is guilty of *rape*. It's all in the framing: estate tax, death tax. How you feel about it depends on what you call it. We *know* this. We have the data that *proves* this.'

'You talking about the Imperial Analytica thing?'

Teller glared at him, part reprimand but also part surprise, a look that said, *How the hell do you know about that?*

'It's OK, Doug,' Benson said. 'The Digital Director gave me and Ellen a briefing. It's in the vault, don't worry. But good to know we've got state-of-the-art software on our side. Not that it can help us out of this particular situation.'

Teller was looking down, rubbing an eyebrow between thumb and middle finger. Whether his despair was over the breach of secrecy relating to the campaign's hiring of the Imperial Analytica data-mining company or because of the Album issue was not clear.

Benson carried on. 'So, Doug, what would you have the senator say? "I'm saddened to hear that my long-standing friend has paid *unwanted attention* to his colleagues"?'

'No, I'm not saying that.'

Ellen jumped in. '"My friend has been accused of inappropriate conduct towards his co-workers."'

'I like "accused". That could work.'

'"Inappropriate"? Are you kidding me? "Inappropriate" is wearing a tie at a barbecue. "Inappropriate" is checking out your girlfriend's mom.' He felt himself getting a look from his right. 'Sorry, Ellen. Holding the intern's head and forcing her to suck your cock is not "inappropriate". It's sexual assault.'

'But not rape all of a sudden?'

'OK, that isn't, Doug. But the rest is! Have you seen what's in the *Times*? I mean, have you actually read through the detail of these allegations?'

'Allegations. That's the key word in that sentence, Dan. The only thing they have evidence for is the blowj—' Now Doug shot a guilty glance at Ellen. 'The oral sex act.'

'No, Doug. That's the only thing they have *video* of. There's plenty of evidence. Sworn testimony from dozens of women.'

'Which he denies.'

'Listen, seriously. Between these four walls. Our phones are outside. Is your worry that this story will somehow implicate the senator?'

'Let's not do this here.'

'We're the senior staff of the campaign, Doug. If not here, where? Is the senator implicated in this story?'

'I'm not going to answer that.'

'Oh, for God's sake.'

381

'Except to say, Harrison and Album have been friends for a long time. Weekends, summer homes, trips to the Caribbean.'

'The whole nine yards.'

'Yes.'

'So you are worried?'

'There will be some who will try to drag his name into this story.'

'And will they have reason to?'

'The point is, people can allege what they like. Doesn't mean there'll be evidence. But: they were friends. They vacationed together. If Album gets a bucket of shit poured over his head, some of it will splash onto Harrison's shoes.'

Ellen furrowed her brow and then said, 'Which might be all the more reason for him to get out in front of it. Distance himself from it. "I've known Marty Album—"'

'Martin. Or Mr Album. Don't make it pally.'

'Dan's right, Ellen. Mr Album.'

'All right. "I've known Mr Album a long time, and yet he kept this dark side hidden from me, as he did from so many others."'

'That's good.'

'Bullshit, but good.'

'Keep going.'

'"I naturally condemn some of the appalling behaviour we've read about in recent days. I won't prejudice any legal proceedings that might ensue by saying any more. But above all, my heart goes out to the women who are hurting. Be strong. Have courage".'

Dan smiled. 'That's great. We should get that written up. He's doing a sit-down today with the *Des Moines Register*, isn't he? He can do it there.'

Ellen, smiling at the praise, said, 'We want video, don't we? Maybe save it for *Morning Joe* tomorrow?'

Now Doug came in, breaking up the party. 'I like it too, Ellen. Definitely worth working up. My only note is that it could be a little . . . strong.'

'Strong?'

'That language. You know: *condemn, appalling, hurting*. Little strong, is all.'

'Doug, is there something you're not telling us?'

'Just that the senator is a loyal friend. I'm not sure he wants to be the guy who kicks a man when he's down.'

There was a pause. Dan and Ellen exchanged looks, before Dan theatrically placed his hand over his mouth, like a child who's accidentally given away a family secret.

'Oh my God, I get it! I'm so sorry, Doug. Seriously. I should have realized. You're worried that if the senator hits Album, then Album will hit back! And – it's OK, you don't have to say what it is – but you obviously think he's got some ammo. You don't want to make an enemy of this guy, because he's got some *kompromat* on the senator. Is that about right, Doug? Is that about the size of it?'

'I think we should move on.'

'Doug?'

'Ellen, work up some language that we're all comfortable with. Some words the senator can use. Give us some options. Now, I'm really sorry, guys, but I need to get to another meeting. Glad we could do this. Thanks, Ellen. Thank you, Dan.'

Chapter 45

Maggie was relieved to see that both the dongle and keypad combination still worked. No one could have blamed Natasha Winthrop's law firm for locking their colleague out: she was, after all, sitting in a prison cell, charged with homicide. Perhaps no one had thought to do anything about it.

As silently as she could, Maggie took the elevator, punched in another few numbers and let herself into the open-plan office, mercifully empty on the weekend, and, finally, Natasha's room. She sat herself at the computer, powered up the machine and typed in the password.

While she waited to be logged in, she glanced at her phone. Nothing back from Liz yet. Counselling Maggie to be patient, her sister had said in a rushed text sent while making supper for her boys, *I'm a computer geek, not a fucking miracle worker.* After all this time, Maggie still had no idea what magic Liz performed when she set to work with a keyboard and mouse, and therefore she had no clue how long it would take. All she knew is that she had asked Liz to look into the Gab post that started the #FindingMC exercise in mass surveillance, and at the subsequent posts that had propelled it far and wide, beyond Gab into Twitter and elsewhere. At the same time, she had also forwarded the screenshots she had taken of that rape fantasy forum and her entry on it. *'Mid-thirties, slim, fit, long auburn hair.'* *Flatters you a bit*, Liz had said, by way of confirmation of receipt.

Now the screen was filling up with the assorted folders and files that Maggie remembered from her last visit. She barely knew where to begin, as she clicked and opened the various documents, almost at random. There was the Russian folder, even its name, in Cyrillic characters, opaque to Maggie. She opened the others – personal correspondence, invitations, bills, the phone records that had led her to Aunt Peggy. She saw again the files of Natasha's cases on Guantanamo and child separations at the border, alongside multiple environmental lawsuits.

Maggie went back to the Russian file and found once more the document that consisted of just a single line, apparently emailed from Natasha back to herself.

You may know a lot, but you won't know everything.

It might have been Natasha speaking, addressing Maggie from the other side of the computer. And there was no denying it: it was a statement of the truth.

Maggie didn't even know what this vast Russian file related to, not really. Some kind of contract, contained on that signed napkin, but the rest of it? She had no idea. She looked again at the file name, copying and pasting the word into Google Translate. It came back stumped, asking: *Did you mean . . . ?*

Embarrassed by her ignorance of an entire alphabet, not knowing what each character represented let alone what the word meant, Maggie copied the letters on the screen onto her pad, slowly drawing each one rather than writing them down. She had no idea what word was in front of her.

Maggie tilted back in her chair and let out a big sigh. What was she looking for, really? She hadn't even spelled it out in her own mind, telling herself that she would know it when she saw it. Some connecting thread that would tie together what she had seen and heard today. Like one of those dot-to-dot drawings that she and Liz used to do on idle Sunday afternoons back in Quarry Street, taking pleasure as the picture materialized before their eyes. Maggie had been doing this long enough now that she trusted herself to recognize the pattern once it was in front of her. She just had to find it . . .

But she had so little to go on. An intuition, nothing more. She pulled Natasha's yellow legal pad over towards her and made a list:

Chicago
New York
Bangalore
London

That was all she had. Less than an inkling.

Maggie used the search function on Natasha's computer and typed in 'Bangalore'. Nothing. She tried India next, which brought a slew of files on a pollution case Natasha had fought against a multinational company based in Chennai. She searched a few of the documents for 'Bangalore', but apart from the corporate address of a tech company tangentially involved in the case, there was nothing.

She began drumming her fingers on the desk at high frequency: no rhythm, just pure stress. Was this pointless? Was she running down a blind alley?

Now, warily, but armed with the passwords Natasha had given her, she logged into Natasha's email account. The inbox filled up, mainly with bulletins from assorted media and political organizations as well as recent messages of solidarity and support, usually titled 'Thinking of you' or 'What can I do?'

In the search field, Maggie typed in the single word, 'Bangalore'. Eventually eleven messages appeared and she clicked through them, doing a word search on each one. A Daily Beast email, promoting a feature about life in a call centre was the first. There was another from the *Guardian* – this time pushing a story about a Bangalore healer who had become a local cult figure – and one more from one of Natasha's clients. It included that document Maggie had just seen, relating to a tech company registered in the city.

The next one was different. It was clearly personal. The subject field consisted of a date and an exclamation mark: *September 20!*

It was a group email, with Natasha one of the recipients. It had been sent by a woman called Gargi Amarnath and it read:

Can't wait!!! I wanted to get the earlier flight but I may have to fly later. It's a nightmare getting out of Bangalore at that time, but wish me luck. I'll come straight from the airport.

The rest was more back and forth about timings, venues and arrangements for what was clearly a long-planned get-together last autumn. There were seven people on the list, including Natasha. They were all women.

The wheels were beginning to turn. Maggie now copied Amarnath's name and pasted it into Google.

There was a string of what seemed to be quite technical entries, in which a G Amarnath was listed among several other names. Clicking revealed these to be court judgments.

A few more clicks and then, at last, a longer piece in the *Bangalore Mirror*. Not quite a profile, it explained that Amarnath was a much-admired lawyer who had made her home in the city five years earlier, after moving there with her husband, a tech entrepreneur. *Raised in the US, she practised in New York before setting up with one of Bangalore's leading firms* . . .

Now Maggie went back to the email and scribbled down the names of the other recipients. She Googled the first name on that list and saw that that woman was still doing what Amarnath had done: working as a lawyer in New York City. She was attached to a high-powered law firm, specializing, according to the corporate website, in 'workplace issues'.

Maggie's hands were beginning to tremble. She was joining the dots.

Now she typed in the fourth name and was jolted to see that, just as she thought a pattern was emerging, here was a new dot far outside it. Like the others, Elsa Sjogran was a lawyer but she was not based in New York, Bangalore or London but Stockholm.

With no confidence, Maggie searched for Sjogran's name along with the words 'rape' and 'Stockholm'. Nothing that made any sense, just a couple of items from several years ago about a bill going through the Swedish parliament. But then Maggie swapped the word 'rape' for 'sexual assault' and a fresh list appeared. One was an AFP item from a few days earlier in The Local, apparently an English-language website for Swedish news.

> Housing minister August Granqvist was arrested by Stockholm police last night in connection with an alleged sexual assault at the site of the law firm charged with handling his financial affairs.
>
> Police had been called to the offices of Bolund, Eriksson and Sjogran after hours, by a partner at the firm, Elsa Sjogran. She told police she had walked into the office to find the minister "sexually assaulting" a junior colleague. She said, "I was an eyewitness to the attack. And used force to stop it going any further. I have given a sworn statement to the police and my colleague will be pressing charges."

Adrenalin throbbing through her now, Maggie went back to the email recipients list and worked at double speed, copying, pasting and searching each name until she had established a full list. All lawyers, all either directly involved in recent cases involving sexual violence or based in the places where such cases had happened. What's more, each incident had a crucial element in common: the women had taken action.

In New York and London, they'd used cameras to record their abusers, whether a top-ranking news executive or a five-star acclaimed chef. In Stockholm, an eyewitness had seen the crime as it was performed, an occurrence which Maggie knew – from what she'd read and from what Natasha had told her – was vanishingly rare. How had she put it? Most cases never came to trial and, if they did, the chances were high they'd end in acquittal. When it came to rape, the vast majority got off. *For the obvious reason: there are never any witnesses. Except the victim, of course. 'He said, she said.'*

These women, on different points of the globe, had upended that logic. They had made sure this crime, almost always unseen, was witnessed. It must have required meticulous planning, relying on foreknowledge of men known to be sexual predators. In the case of the TV honcho, Maggie could see exactly how that would have worked: hadn't that *Times* story said that the man was notorious, using the same MO every time? It wouldn't have been too hard to tell the newest intern to be summoned to the boss's summer house on Long Island, to make sure her phone camera was switched on. They must have done the same with the chef in London and with the latest scumbag to be revealed by an online search, an oligarch in Moscow who got his kicks raping and beating lap dancers. In Sweden, the method had been different – involving an eyewitness, rather than a camera – but the principle had been the same. What sacrifice those young women had had to make, allowing themselves to be prey in the pursuit of evidence that would, once and for all, convict these predators. Maggie wondered if they had fully known what they were letting themselves in for, whether they had consented easily or had

had to be persuaded, whether they had been victims or heroines or, as so often, both.

What didn't fit were the incidents on the streets of Chicago, where a known rapist had been tortured and dumped on the sidewalk, and Bangalore, where an abuser had faced similar treatment with an added sanction: death. Maggie underlined the names of the women on the email list who lived in those two cities. Why had they taken things further than the others? What linked these women in the—

Maggie got to her feet and suddenly, as if directed by a hidden hand, attacked one of the piles of papers she had rifled through on her last visit here. *It's here, I know it.*

At breakneck speed, she was turning over papers: letters, magazines, invitations, texts of speeches, PowerPoint presentations, one after another. Once she got to the bottom of the first pile, she was drilling through the next, powering through the paper, until, close to the bottom, there it was. Just as she had remembered it.

A home-produced invitation for what appeared to be a reunion. The date confirmed that it had taken place nearly a year earlier. It was a gathering not of schoolmates or college pals, but of colleagues from the New York District Attorney's office. Maggie recognized the image on the front; it had lodged in her mind at the time: a blindfolded Lady Justice with scales in one hand and a martini in the other. And there was the scrawled message on the back: *Where it all began! See you there, I hope. F x*

F. Maggie went to the list of names and there was a Fiona Anderson. Google established that she worked now in Moscow, but just over a decade ago she had worked in . . . the office of the

District Attorney in Manhattan. One of the others was a Caroline Secker, who apparently still worked in that same office. *Caroline.* Maggie remembered the conversation that night at Pilgrim's Cove, as Natasha described the colleague who had kept a close, almost obsessive eye on the sexual predators eluding justice. *Caroline liked to have someone she could vent to, at the end of a long day. Feet on the desk. Glass of vodka for her, whisky for me.*

Maggie sat back in her chair and studied the invitation, drilling into those handwritten words as if they might yield the secrets of this group of women who had worked together all those years ago: Gargi, Fiona, Elsa, Caroline, Natasha . . .

Now back at the keyboard, she typed all seven names into one search field and hit return. There were only a handful of references that brought up all seven. The first on the list was from two years ago:

Criminology, justice and reform: an international colloquium
Emory University, Georgia, February 23–25

Maggie scanned the list of participants. She counted off the seven women, listed either as speakers or attendees. Natasha had presented a paper on whether the planet itself should be granted rights under international law; Gargi had appeared on a panel on indigenous people and pollution.

Maggie clicked out of that entry and went to another meeting of lawyers and scholars in Paris three years earlier. There they all were again. Elsa had delivered a keynote address on 'The law and gender'.

The third entry scored five out of the seven names: no mention of either Winthrop or Anderson. It was a paper published eighteen months earlier for the *Yale Law Review*, co-authored by three of the women, with the other two cited in the footnotes. It was on the problems of prosecuting rape. Even in a skim-read one paragraph stood out:

> There is what we call "the evidence gap". In sexual crimes, there may be copious amounts of physical evidence of sexual interaction, for example, bodily fluids, hair, DNA and the like. There may be a similar abundance of evidence of physical struggle — scratches, blood, DNA under the fingernails. And yet even that will not be considered determinative, not if the accused is running a "consensual rough sex" defense, a line of argument that has become increasingly popular in what the authors contend is an age of freely available internet pornography. Uniquely, perhaps, rape is a crime that is almost never witnessed. Witness evidence is decisive in the prosecution of many forms of crime, including violent crime. But not in crimes of sexual violence. By their nature private, away from the gaze of other people, these crimes fall into an "evidence gap". Once there, and further beset by the numerous other obstacles that exist in rape cases, prosecution becomes difficult, conviction vanishingly rare.

The article ended on a question:

> The legal community must ask itself whether the evidentiary threshold for such crimes is set in such a way that it can only seldom be cleared, thereby rendering prosecution functionally impossible. Has the law

served, in effect, to have decriminalized all but the rarest instances
of sexual violence?

Her name might not be on the paper, Maggie thought, but that was Natasha's voice. Maggie had heard her make that very same argument by a crackling fire in Cape Cod.

Now the dots were in place, the lines between them forming easily. A group of women who had worked together more than a decade ago, and who had stayed in touch ever since, had all arrived at the same conclusion. In the DA's office, they had been different ages, Natasha among the youngest. But for all of them, it seemed, these had been formative years. Working together as prosecutors, discovering together how hard it was to act against men who had forced themselves on women and girls, they would have watched as one rapist after another walked free.

Maggie imagined the late-night conversations after work in New York. The same conversation continuing years later, over martinis into the small hours in Atlanta or Paris, fending off other conference delegates who wandered over to join in, these women huddling together and slowly, slowly thinking: *What if there were another way? What if we were to fill that evidence gap? What if we could help women fill that gap themselves?*

Dotted all over the world, they had activated their mission at roughly the same time, equipping soon-to-be victims with the equipment and skill to capture their abusers in the very act of rape – and so bring them to justice. Information would not have been hard to come by. After all, one of their number still sat in the New York Prosecutor's office, in touch with counterparts everywhere: Caroline with her 'comprehensive' files.

And yet something had changed. Jeffrey Todd had ended up dead on Winthrop's floor, and two men had been tortured and mutilated, one of them fatally. They had begun as a small, tight-knit network of female lawyers committed to justice. They had ended as a revenge circle – and Natasha Winthrop, who had killed her rapist ex-brother with a single, precise blow to the head, was at the dead centre of it.

Now a half-memory slowly rose to the surface, the hint of a fact that she hardly knew she knew. Maggie went back to the Spotlight button that allowed her to search the entire computer. She typed in a single word.

Judith

Once again, that folder came up on the screen. She tried opening it and was blocked once more. It remained locked and impenetrable. She didn't bother guessing the password, but the machine did tell her that this folder contained several megabytes of data. It was no empty shell.

Now Maggie dredged up that semi-remembered fact. To check it, she brought up the browser and entered a few key words in the search field. Confirmation came in a second or two. *Of course.*

There, filling the screen, was a stunning Renaissance painting. It showed two women pinning a man down on a bloodstained bed, one of the women thrusting a knife into his neck. The man was nearly naked, the knifewoman full-breasted, her neckline plunging and low. The painting was *Judith Slaying Holofernes*, apparently the work of a seventeen-year-old woman from seventeenth-century Italy.

The entry explained that this was a depiction of the possibly apocryphal story of the Israelite heroine who had beheaded an Assyrian general: the general had intended to rape Judith, but she killed him first. Next in the search engine's list of offerings was a blog post, headlined: *On women fighting back, in art – and in life.*

Now Maggie stared at the closed folder named 'Judith', locked and sealed. She looked from that icon to the picture of the avenging women and then back to the folder – and she knew with complete certainty what kind of secrets were kept within.

Chapter 46

Maggie tried to transfer the 'Judith' file to the memory stick she produced from her bag: she'd get Liz to see if she could break into it. But the folder was wise to that trick. It had been encrypted in such a way that it refused to be dragged onto the stick, skipping back to the desktop each time Maggie tried. Luckily the Russian file was less resistant.

Next, she went back to the computer to check one last thing – whether Natasha had met with any of the other women in the lead-up to the death of Jeffrey Todd. She began typing, but now no letters showed up on the screen.

She tried to click again on the browser, just in case she was stuck in another application. That didn't work either. She shook the mouse, but still it refused to respond.

Meanwhile, the cursor was moving around the screen. She had seen this before: sometimes it happened if the batteries were running low on the mouse or, occasionally, if there was interference from her phone. She took the phone off the desk and put it on her lap, but it was no use. The cursor was whizzing around, apparently with a mind of its own.

Now she saw that its movements were not random. The cursor was closing down documents one by one, clicking shut the various files and folders Maggie had opened. Eventually, it went through each of the search tabs she had opened, the details of Gargi in Bangalore, the academic papers written by Fiona, the conference webpage for Emory University, removing each of them from display. Soon, most of what was on the screen had been removed, clicked into disappearance. Just one document was left and it remained open, the cursor dragging it into the centre of the screen and, after another click, expanding it so that nothing else was visible. The whole screen was filled with a single message, aimed at her.

You may know a lot, but you won't know everything.

Maggie stared at it a while and then tried to click it out of the way. No good: she had lost control of the machine entirely.

The cursor blinked at her, defiant. And now it typed new words, below that sentence of Natasha's. Each letter appeared only slowly, as if the keys were being punched one finger at a time, by a child.

If
I
Were

You

I

Would

Get

Out

Now

And then the computer screen went dark.

Maggie threw everything into her bag, leapt out of the chair, flung herself upon the door and headed for the exit. She pulled at the door handle, but it wouldn't open. She had forgotten the green exit button, big and shaped like the head of a mushroom, at the side of the door. She pressed her entire palm against it, but there was no click of response. There was no sound at all.

She gave the button another nudge and then another. Nothing. She yanked at the handle, as if that would make any difference, as if the door might have changed its mind.

She turned back into the open-plan office, looking for an exit, anywhere.

Just rows of desks and windows that, given the floor they were on, did not allow themselves to be opened at all.

Her skin was beginning to crawl, the need to get out urgent and desperate. Her phone began to ring. *Not now, not now.*

Maggie broke into a jog, as she headed for the opposite corner of the work area. As she got closer, she could see there was a door unlike the others: it did not lead off into a personal office. Could this be a fire exit?

She turned the handle and, to her relief, it moved. She pushed and a second later the light came on, revealing that she had walked not into a stairwell, but a stationery cupboard.

Maggie turned around and was back in the open-plan area, looking at every sealed window and realizing there was no way out. In desperation, and in the full knowledge it was futile, she ran back to the door that had been electronically closed off. Perhaps, a small hopeless voice told her, this was just a system error that had corrected itself. Perhaps the door would open now.

She got there, pressed the green button and, of course, it didn't work.

Now Maggie took a closer look at the door. There was a handle, but one that didn't turn. It was fixed, there solely to be pulled once the lock was released.

Her eye moved all around the doorframe, as she looked for any kind of mechanism that could be sprung manually. She squatted down by the handle, squinting into the gap between the frame and the door. But there was nothing there; the handle was dumb, there was no normal lock that you could start tinkering with. Not that Maggie would know what to do, even if there were. In the house in Dublin, growing up, when she and Liz were forced to fend for themselves – which was often – odd jobs usually fell to Maggie. She'd had to learn her way around a toolbox and she still knew one end of a screwdriver from the other. But this was not bleeding a radiator; this was in a different league.

Now her gaze settled on the left-hand side of the door, and two metal hinges. She squatted down to look closer at the lower one. The two parts – one attached to the frame, the other to the door – were held together by a long, vertical pin. On this one, the pin was peeking out just enough to be visible. Speculatively and with little confidence, Maggie tried to get her fingers, still cut and scratched from her encounter with the wannabe rapist, around the top of it and pull.

It was near impossible to get a grip on it, or to get her fingernails under the head where she might find purchase. A brief moment of encouragement came when it moved just a bit, but her next efforts were in vain. She applied so much force to her fingernails as she sought to grip the pin-head that, when her finger slipped, the metal of the hinge sliced the skin of her index finger, drawing blood.

Only then did she have the obvious thought. If she couldn't pull the pin out from above, why not push it out from below? She lay down, her head on the floor looking up, to assess it. Now she knew what she needed.

She sprung up, and all but sprinted back into the working area. She started checking out desks, rummaging through several of them to find what she was looking for. There were pencils, but they were too thick. There were promotional ball pens, marked with the logo of Gonzales Associates, but, when she opened them up, their innards were plastic. She needed something more old school. She headed back into Natasha's office.

On the desk was a china pot, like a mug without a handle, decorated with a line drawing of what seemed to be a bucolic English scene. It contained pencils, two fountain pens and exactly what she was searching for: an upmarket ball pen. She unscrewed it and, to her relief, there it was: a metal refill, thin but tough.

Her phone buzzed again. She looked at the screen. A number appeared, but it made no sense: 0-000-000-0000. The message, however, was unambiguous.

Out.
Now!

She ran back to the door and, lying on her back, pushed the pen refill upward into the slot. She pushed and felt the slightest give. Now she pushed as hard as she could and heard a click.

But the pin had not popped out. The refill had snapped under the pressure, breaking off at the nib, coating her fingers with thick, viscous ink. A drop landed on her shoulders.

There was no time to go back to Natasha's desk. She would have to use what she had and damn the mess.

Now she turned the refill around and, holding it by its leaking, inky end, inserted it once more. This worked better; the bottom of the refill better matched the dimensions of the pin. A focused push and she could feel the pin give. A little more, a little more and, pop, it was out.

There was the second hinge to do. Maggie tried to stretch upward, and though she was tall enough to touch it, her outstretched arm couldn't get the precision or pressure. She darted into the working space and grabbed a chair, wheeling it into position. She climbed up and onto the seat, wobbling as it swivelled.

Now she stood, feet planted wide apart on the moving seat,

the leaking metal refill in her stained hand, attempting to repeat the manoeuvre she had performed on the lower hinge. She pushed up, then pushed some more, trying to ensure the seat she was standing on did not start spinning. She felt the pin move a smidgeon, then a tiny bit more.

A half-second later, she was knocked backwards, off the chair and flattened onto her back, smashed in the head by the full weight of the door, which now lay on top of her. She remained there for a second or two, brain throbbing, wondering if she could even move. She could see nothing, except the wood in front of her face, but even that seemed to be spinning.

With great effort she shoved the door to one side, so that it slid off her, landing on her right. The pushing of the pin inside the hinge must have worked, but she'd been an idiot: she should have realized that once the pin was out, there'd be nothing holding the door in place.

As quickly as she could, she got to her feet, though it was not fast. She wiped her nose on the back of her hand; it came back bloody. She staggered her way to one of the desks, where she helped herself to a box of tissues. There was a lot of blood and her nose felt painful and tender. She wondered if it was broken.

There was no time to check. She reached for her bag and walked through the now-doorless archway. She pressed for the elevator, but was not surprised to see that the indicator did not light up and that nothing moved. Whoever had taken over Natasha's computer and locked the door had clearly hacked into the building's entire system.

But not, Maggie reckoned, the fire escape. She looked for the sign for the stairs, just off the elevator lobby, knowing that no building in DC or anywhere else was allowed to have electronically controlled access to the fire escape; it had to be open even if everything else failed. And it was.

Maggie rushed down the stairs as quickly as she could manage, her face, her nose, her head all throbbing in unison. Finally she reached the ground floor, where she saw the emergency exit. A push against the horizontal metal bar and she was out, back into the cold of the outside world.

Panting to catch her breath, Maggie pulled out her phone. There was the missed call from a few minutes earlier: Liz. There was a string of texts too, most of them variations on *Call me right now*. Maggie pressed the button.

'Liz?'

'Mags. Thank fuck. You need to get away, get somewhere safe.'

'I know.'

'Seriously. These people are powerful. I don't know what you've got into, but whatever it is you need to get out.'

Maggie thought of these women, the connections they had, the power they wielded in cities across the world. One of them was a plausible candidate for the American presidency, for God's sake. They had power and, as Chicago and Bangalore had proved, they were also ready to be utterly merciless.

'I know, Liz,' she said quietly, sniffing back the blood that was still trickling into her throat. But her sister was barely listening.

'I've been going through the stuff you sent me, and that Gab thing. It was brilliantly done – spoofed EXIF data, cycling devices, machine translation, the works – but here's the thing. There's a common path between that and the listing on the, you know, rape site thing.'

'The listing of me, you mean?'

'Yes. I think they both came from the same source.'

Maggie all but rolled her eyes. 'Of course they came from the same source. Someone is trying to take me out, Liz. Either get me raped or scare me off. The point is—'

'The point is who. Exactly. So they trace back to an operation which seems to work by spinning up synthetic personalities, using them to seed authentic identities on the major social networking platforms – or just buying dormant ones from a grey-market hacker, of course – and then activating them as needed to engage in co-ordinated inauthentic behaviour.'

'Liz, English!'

'Sorry, sorry. It traces back to a troll farm. In St Petersburg.'

'Florida? Or Russia?'

'Russia. I think. Hang on, let me check.'

'Jesus, Liz.' Maggie was watching two men on the opposite street corner. They had been talking to each other. They were now looking at her.

'Yes, Russia. Definitely.'

'You've traced these threats to there?'

Maggie thought of Fiona Anderson, working out of a swanky international law firm in Moscow. Could she be the hidden hand behind all this? Would she really unleash a would-be rapist and an army of alt-right stalkers and incel maniacs on another woman, just to stop the truth about the revenge circle coming to light?

The thought appalled her. And yet she couldn't, in all honesty, dismiss it.

'They all trace back to an office in St Petersburg. St Petersburg, Russia. It's dressed up as some kind of academic institute, but here's the thing. That wasn't the end point. I kept on finding this strange connection, like a pathway, between that institute and a company based here in America. In fact, it's based in DC.'

Maggie felt her skin go cold.

You may know a lot, but you won't know everything.

'Mags? Are you there?'

'I'm here.'

'I think it's that company that's behind these attacks on you. I think it's them who want to stop you.'

'Who are they?'

'They're incredibly secretive. They're a tech company that hardly anyone knows about. They're trusted with all these security contracts and, you know, they're based in DC. So there's lots of conspiracy theories saying they must be deep state.'

'What's their name?'

'They're called Imperial Analytica. Big international reach, been involved in elections in Australia, India, Britain, Germany, Latin America. Everywhere.'

'And they have a connection with Russia?'

'I can't be one hundred per cent sure.'

'But—'

'But that's what it looks like, yes.'

Maggie was trying to think. She could feel the vein in her temple throbbing. 'Liz, how's your Russian?'

'It's shit. You know it's shit. I gave up after one term.'

'You're right. It's shit. Look, see if you can make sense of this anyway. I'm going to send you a picture of one word right now. Text me back what it says.'

Maggie hung up and, as her hands trembled, she reached for the yellow pad she had stashed in her bag. She found the page where, like an infant tracing a map she didn't understand, she had copied the Cyrillic letters that Natasha Winthrop had used to title the folder packed with thousands of contracts, documents and that single sentence. *You may know a lot, but you won't know everything*.

She took a picture of the word and texted it to Liz.

Three dots appeared under her message, the sign that Liz was typing a reply. Come on, come on.

A message arrived.

It's not a Russian word.

Then another.

It's in Russian characters, but it's not Russian.

Please, Liz. Come on.
And then a single word appeared.

Imperial.

Chapter 47

By Jake Haynes, New York Times
WASHINGTON

A US-based data-mining company employed by the presidential campaign of Senator Tom Harrison has links with the Kremlin, has engaged in illegal hacking of US citizens' social media accounts and appears to have been involved in a campaign of violent harassment targeting a former White House official, according to documents seen by the New York Times.

Washington-based Imperial Analytica is revealed to have been involved in a practice known as "micro-hacking": breaking users' passwords to raid their supposedly private data, from credit card details to the content of confidential direct messages. While rival companies simply "scrape" data from publicly available online sources—Facebook posts, tweets and the like—Imperial's micro-hacking allowed the Harrison campaign's digital data team to target US voters with greater precision than ever before.

"That's our secret sauce," one Imperial official is quoted as saying in correspondence with Harrison campaign officials.

The cache of documents also reveals that Imperial Analytica functions as a front for a secretive company based in St Petersburg, Russia. Hidden in a labyrinth of offshore shell companies, the corporate structure's ultimate owners are two oligarchs with close ties to the Kremlin. Analysis of data patterns reveals intense traffic between Imperial's head office in Washington, DC, and the St Petersburg operation. According to one expert analyst consulted by the Times *for this report, "Imperial Analytica and Russia are linked by a strong, thick neural pathway. Whatever the Harrison campaign knew would have been known, instantly and in real time, in St Petersburg. It's a safe assumption that such information would have been of great interest to the company's friends in the Kremlin."*

Evidence has also emerged that Imperial Analytica directed a dirty tricks operation against a former White House official, Maggie Costello, now advising indicted Washington civil rights lawyer Natasha Winthrop as she faces a homicide inquiry. Ms Costello was the victim of a "doxxing" attack, in which her home address was published online, leading to a break-in by a violent intruder on Thursday. A call on alt-right social media platform Gab, urging users to track Ms Costello's movements and post photographs of her, can also be traced to Imperial and to its undisclosed parent organization in St Petersburg.

Speculation as to the motive for the targeting of Ms. Costello centers on Ms Winthrop who, the Times *understands, was working on an investigation of the Russian tycoons behind the St. Petersburg operation. "They feared Natasha Winthrop was about to expose them and their illegal online activity," a source familiar with these events said on condition of anonymity. "They were especially worried about her increasing political profile. Their preferred outcome was Winthrop behind bars, unable to investigate further." The timing of the attacks on Ms Costello suggests they were designed to halt her efforts on behalf of Ms Winthrop.*

Though there is no suggestion that the Harrison campaign was itself involved in the operation directed against Ms Costello, the campaign's links to Imperial Analytica have caused concern among allies of the senator. His spokesman said: "Like any nationwide campaign, Harrison for President has employed hundreds of outside contractors, organizing everything from catering to transport. We of course keep all our contractors under constant review, as we try to spread our message of a fairer, stronger America."

Imperial Analytica declined all requests for comment, referring the Times instead to their legal representatives . . .

For the second time Maggie scrolled through the article on her phone. Jake had let her know only at the last moment about the added dimension to the story, but still she could hardly believe it. When they'd met so that she could hand over the memory stick loaded with the 'Imperial' folder that had been on Natasha's computer – ingeniously labelled so that it would be unrecognizable to any software searching for the word 'Imperial' in either the English or Russian languages, since it was in neither – she thought she was giving him a story about a US data company with links to Moscow, with a side dish of violent stalking of a former US official, namely her. But she should have realized from Jake's reaction that there was far more to it than that.

He'd been interested from the start, of course. 'If it comes from Maggie Costello, then you've got my attention.' And he nodded in all the right places as she explained what she had: international firm, links to Russia, micro-hacking. He'd smiled when she told him of her surprise on discovering that the 'mine' referred to in that contract-on-a-napkin on Natasha's computer was not digging for zinc or iron ore, but data – often of the most private, intimate kind. He'd been appropriately appalled at her recounting of Liz's discovery that the Gab threat against her, and the fantasy rapist, traced back to the same point of origin, to say nothing of the act of cyber-intimidation inflicted on her in Natasha's office.

But it was when she uttered the words 'Imperial Analytica' that he had sat bolt upright. She understood now what should have been obvious then: that Jake and his team had already been looking at Imperial and its 'secret sauce', ever since a *Times* reporter got word that the firm had been hired by the Harrison campaign. What Maggie brought in clicked together with what he already knew to form an explosive story.

She looked around the waiting area, its blank walls deliberately austere and inhospitable. How long had Natasha been here now? To think that Natasha could have got out if she had wanted to; bail was negotiable, even if expensive. Maybe she thought the politics played better with her jailed: the optics screamed 'political prisoner whose destiny is to lead her country'. Or maybe it wasn't as much a hardship for her as it would be for almost anyone else. After all, Mindy Hagen had endured far worse.

Maggie's phone vibrated, a text from Jake linking her to a

Reuters report that Imperial Analytica had 'suspended trading' after a police raid on their offices in London. Maggie was halfway through sending a reply when an officer appeared, giving Maggie a sullen raise of the eyebrow that signalled it was time for her to come through.

She was taken into an interview room and asked to sit on a hard, vinyl chair at a plain wooden table. Another wait and then, eventually, Natasha was ushered in, guided to the chair on the other side of the table, as if this were a police interrogation. She looked thinner, but not gaunt. Dressed in plain grey, prison-issue sweats, she nevertheless held herself straight: head up, shoulders back. She was still in absolute command of herself.

'Maggie, it's very good to see you.' The cut-glass accent. It sounded different now, odd. It induced in Maggie a fleeting sense of admiration, the way you marvel at watching a familiar actor make themselves sound, say, Danish. 'I hear you've been working terrifically hard on my behalf. I am *so* grateful.'

Maggie wanted to say, 'It's OK. You don't have to pretend any more.' Or even, 'Hello, Mindy.' On her way here, she had considered both options. But all that came out was a line she had not prepared, or even considered. She said, 'I've been to Maine.'

'Good for you,' Natasha said. 'It is so beautiful up there. Stunning in the autumn.'

'I met Aunt Peggy.'

'Ah.'

'She told me everything. She showed me the diary.' It seemed wrong to refer to Mindy's journal as 'your diary'. Easier to tiptoe around that.

'Ah.'

'And I know about Judith.'

'I see.'

They sat in silence for the best part of a minute, each second slow and full.

'Might I ask how you found her? Peggy, I mean.'

Maggie looked down at her hands, feeling a brief blush of shame, even though she knew it made no sense. 'Phone records,' she said. 'Your bill showed her number.'

Natasha gave a tight little smile, but her eyes seemed to glitter with sadness. 'Ah, the Sunday phone call. My one weekly moment of weakness.' She looked to her side, as if reluctant to let Maggie see her eyes. 'You see, Maggie, none of us can live entirely without family.'

'I understand,' Maggie said, instantly regretting the word. 'I mean, obviously I don't *understand*. What you went through. But I see what you mean about family. My sister drives me around the bend. But if I couldn't speak to her on the phone, I don't know . . .' She heard her own voice trail away.

She cleared her throat and tried again, on a different tack. 'Can we talk about Todd? Paul.' She saw Natasha visibly recoil at the mention of that name. 'How long were you following him?'

'Following him?'

'Monitoring him.'

Natasha sighed and sat back in her chair. 'In my head, *forever*. Not a day went by. Even at St Hugh's, even when I was studying and learning lines for the school play and being invited to parties and getting into Harvard and becoming "Natasha Winthrop", every day I remembered. Actually, that might be the wrong word, because it implies an act of the brain or the intellect. But it was rather more physical than that. My *body* remembered. Does that make sense? Every day. Actually, every night. Every night when I got into bed. Every night when I *get* into bed, my body remembers.

'But my brain became better at, if not quite forgetting, then putting it to one side. Compartmentalization, though that is a frightfully ugly word. Natasha is good at that. Better than Mindy.'

Maggie smiled, but for a reason she couldn't quite explain she felt her skin shiver.

'And then I was at the DA's office. In New York. I'd been there a matter of months and one day a photograph comes through. That's perfectly routine, by the way, there'd be dozens of them: law enforcement agencies in other states or cities, asking for help in locating a particular individual. New York would get more than most, for obvious reasons. You know, "Nashville Police Department has reason to believe that a John Doe might have fled to New York City." One of those. Except the picture was of . . . him.

'Different name. But the face. It was obviously him. Wanted for sexual offences. Dragging a woman into scrubland and assaulting her. I'd seen him do that, of course. As you know.'

Maggie nodded, guiltily.

'I didn't do anything, naturally. But I kept an eye on the case. Contacted our counterparts in Nashville or wherever it was on some *wholly* spurious pretext, just to hear what was happening. And, as night follows day—'

'He got off.'

'Exactly. "Lack of evidence." Even though I knew, and his victim knew, and *he* knew, and his parents knew that he was guilty.' She shook her head at the injustice of it. 'Well, after that, once I knew his name, it was not too difficult to keep tabs on him.'

'So when did you decide to take things . . . into your own hands?'

'It wasn't like that, Maggie. There was no *moment*, if that's what you mean. And certainly not while we were all there, working in that office. Naturally, one would notice it in the course of one's work. We all did. You couldn't *not* notice it: it was the most clear, undeniable statistical trend. Of every hundred rapes committed, less than one— I'm sorry, you've heard that lecture. You don't need me to go over it all again. So, yes, we would talk about that in the office. At the water cooler. Over a glass of wine after work.'

'You and the other women? Elsa, Gargi—'

'No, this is my point. Generalized moaning, yes. But the *idea*, as it were, did not come until many years later. We were at a conference. In Atlanta, I think it was.'

Maggie nodded.

'Initially, it was only three of us who were down to attend. Then Fiona suggested that we should seize the opportunity, make a reunion of it. So the others came too. The very first day, we'd all sat through an *extremely* tedious paper by a criminologist – male – and afterward we were saying, "Everyone is missing the obvious here." And we came up with a phrase for it: "the evidence gap".'

'Yes, I read the paper.'

'So you know. And that was all it was going to be, I think. A paper. But then we met up at another one, can't remember where – we used these conferences as an excuse to get together – and began talking. "It's not enough to have identified this evidence gap. We need to *fill* it." I think that's when it started.'

'"It" being "Operation Judith"?'

Natasha offered a smile of admiration, as if impressed. 'As it happens, that's the very name I gave it. Just in my own head. No one else. "Operation Judith".'

'Judith beheaded her abuser.'

'Yes.'

'So when did that idea come, then? Not just to get evidence against these men, but to—'

'Oh no.' Natasha looked aghast. 'That was never the *plan*. No, no, no.'

'But you called it "Judith".'

'Yes, but only in the sense that Judith took *action*. She stood up to her rapist, she refused to be a victim—'

'By *killing* him, Natasha.'

'I didn't *plan* it. You have to believe me, Maggie. Look, you now know what happened to me. You know who I am. You know what I endured.'

'I do. Which is why I can understand how you longed for revenge. Anyone would feel exactly—'

'Not revenge. *Justice*. The distinction matters, Maggie. The distinction is everything. Why do you think I became a lawyer? I could have been anything. Done anything. I was top of my class, at St Hugh's and at Harvard. Did I ever tell you I was offered a job in television news before I'd even graduated? Vulgar to say so, but I had very many options. Yet it was always going to be the law. The law was my destiny.

'And then I saw it fail, Maggie. Again and again. And I watched him—'

'Paul?'

Another recoil, just on hearing the name.

'I watched him doing it to other girls. What he had done to Mindy. That poor child.' Again, and no less involuntarily, Maggie felt a shudder pass through her. 'But,' Natasha continued, 'that was never a *plan*. I watched him, I monitored his movements and, slowly and with the other women – though of course they never knew what you now know – the idea took shape: to lead him into a situation where he would commit the crime and be *seen*.'

'A solution to the evidence gap.'

'Precisely.'

'And yet, he's now in a morgue.'

'Because it went wrong, Maggie!' Natasha slammed a fist down on the table, prompting the officer on guard to step forward. She resumed in a whisper. 'Look, I won't pretend that I didn't dream of doing exactly what I ended up doing that night. My *body* dreamed of it. That painting of Judith? Mindy saw it for the first time in a library in Little Rock. She must have stared at it for an hour at least, that first time. She kept going back to it, after school. The power of it. The rage. The *justice*. She loved it. *I* love it.

'But it's a fantasy, Maggie. That's all it ever was. The plan was to get a much more satisfying revenge. The best revenge there is: justice. Think of it. Imagine how perfect it would have been if he'd have known that it was Mindy who brought him down after all these years, Mindy who banished him to a tiny cell for the rest of his life. But he never had any idea. Even that night, when he was poking and jabbing and touching . . . he wouldn't have known. It would have been just meat to him; another hole. He wouldn't have remembered. Not the way she remembered.'

'She?'

'Mindy. But he never knew it was her in that house in Georgetown. She never had a chance to tell him.'

Maggie shifted in her seat. She wanted to look away.

'It went wrong, Maggie. The plan was for others to be there to witness the crime and to apprehend him. But the plan failed.' Natasha paused. 'I never meant to kill him. I wanted him to be *caught*.'

'So how, Natasha, do you explain this?' Maggie produced printouts of the Chicago and Bangalore stories and spread them out on the table between them. Natasha skim-read them and said, 'I didn't know about the Bangalore case. That's news to me.'

'What do you think happened?'

'I don't know.'

'Take a look. We both know there are – do you have a word for each other? – I don't know, let's use "Judiths". There are Judiths in both those cities. Gargi went to live in Bangalore—'

'I know who lives where, Maggie.'

'Look at the dates on those stories.'

She peered forward and then said, 'I see.'

'Do you? Because all I can see is that these abductions and torture, and *murder* in the India case, happened after Jeffrey Todd – Paul – was found dead on your floor.'

'Meaning?'

'Meaning that I think your killing of Todd acted as a signal to the other women. Whether you intended it that way or not, the Judiths took it as a cue. "Right, we're not just collecting evidence now. We're taking this further. We're taking the law into our own hands. We'll be prosecution, judge and jury – just like Natasha was in DC."'

Natasha was silent for a while, studying the printouts in front of her, checking the dates, then checking them again. Finally, and quietly, she said, 'I can see how this looks, but . . .' She didn't complete the sentence. Then she looked up at Maggie, and held her gaze for a while.

'You know, I haven't spoken to any of them – the women – since it happened.'

'Since what happened?'

'"Todd". No contact. There was no way to do it. And it would have been too risky.'

'Phone records.'

A small smile. 'Exactly. But I can see the implication.' She nodded towards the reports on the desk. 'It's possible that you're right.' Another pause, her reluctance to draw that conclusion expressed in the silence. 'Perhaps they read my action as some kind of signal. But that was not my intention. Not ever.'

'And is it likely they would read your action that way? I mean, were you, in effect, the leader?'

'I don't know that I'd put—'

'I assume you were. Because you are, Natasha.'

'I am what?'

'A leader. A natural leader. It's why, if you run for president, you might even win. And I don't say that lightly.'

Natasha said nothing.

'Which is why this question matters. Did you decide on a change of strategy? Did you decide that the Judiths should be like Judith, and torture and violate the men who violated them?'

Natasha held Maggie's gaze and then said softly, 'Maggie, I kept things from you, that's obvious. The same things I have kept from everyone, my whole life. But what I said to you that night on the Cape is the truth. I cannot live in a world where women and girls are treated as objects that can be seized and used for the pleasure of men. And yet, as of this moment, that is precisely the world we both live in. The law allows it. Justice is meant to be blind, but it is turning a blind eye to this particularly horrific crime. It is saying, not in principle but in practice, that it is not a crime at all, that we tolerate it. And I cannot tolerate that.

'And now you know why. Because inside this clever, accomplished human rights lawyer who you and others think could be president is a different person whose soul was stabbed a little bit every day for four years, six months, two weeks and three days. That person is a child, Maggie, who never healed. Not really. I carry her around in me and I still have to protect her.

'I kept her hidden from you, because she needs to stay hidden.

Sometimes – often actually – Mindy hides from me. But every-thing else I have said to you is the truth. I wanted "Todd" to stand trial. I wanted that very much. Mindy wanted it. But, in the moment, in that split-second, I understood that I needed to defend my life. That's what I did. No plan, no plot. Just an instinct for self-protection. That instinct is strong in me, as you may have seen. But that's all it was, a spontaneous, life-or-death decision. What the others did, I can't speak for them. But it's important to me that you believe me.'

Maggie looked hard at the person in front of her – at the two people in front of her, according to what Natasha had just said. She looked and looked, searching for an answer.

When you heard someone say that they were a good judge of character, what, Maggie wondered, did that really mean? Surely it meant that you took a good look at someone, looked especially perhaps at their eyes, and you listened for some voice inside you that said yes or no, thumbs up or thumbs down. And you had faith in that voice and you decided to take a leap.

Maggie had got that call wrong in the past, sometimes at great cost. She had allowed her heart to be broken, more than once, because she had got it wrong. But in the end, what else was there? What other voice could you listen to, if not the one inside you? And what kind of life would it be if you never took that leap?

She leaned forward intently, narrowing the distance between her face and Natasha's. She rested her elbows on the table and her chin on her fists. 'I want to believe you, because I know what happened to you and I know it's true. And I know that you were denied justice.' She paused. 'So here's what I want.'

Natasha nodded, like a dutiful schoolgirl about to receive her homework. And for the first time, Maggie thought she'd glimpsed Mindy Hagen, right in front of her. She felt her heart squeeze.

Maggie cleared her throat. 'I want you to get a message, through me if necessary, to the other Judiths. Say that the killing has to stop. That this is not what you intended, that this is not what you want.'

Natasha gave another nod.

'Second, I want you to give a TV interview and tell the truth about what happened that night in your home.'

'OK.'

'And in that TV interview, I want you to say who you really are. I think you need to tell the story of Mindy Hagen, and the life you have made for yourself. If you run for president – and there's still time, just – it will come out eventually. It has to. But even if you don't, I think it's the only way you can live. I learned that myself recently: that in the end you have to tell the truth.'

Natasha smiled. 'Are you speaking as a political adviser or as a therapist?'

Maggie smiled back. 'Both.'

'Can you imagine what the great American public would make of that? The press? They'd say I'm a total fraud. That I've been living a lie.'

'Not if you told them the story you told me, through your diary. They would be moved. And they would applaud your courage, your resilience, your honesty.' Maggie heard Stuart Goldstein's voice in her head. *That Mindy thing is a killer backstory: trailer park kid from Arkansas gets herself to Harvard, are you kidding me? Much better than being some silver spoon princess from Massachusetts. Besides, Massachusetts is in our column already; Arkansas would be a gain.*

But all Maggie said out loud was, 'Your story is authentic, and that's all that matters in politics. That you're true to yourself. But first you have to admit who "yourself" actually is. Including admitting that to you.'

'And if I do all that?'

'Then the revenge circle stays between us. No one will ever know. The women in Chicago and Bangalore will be safe; so will the other Judiths. I will keep your secret.'

Once again, Natasha examined her own hands for a while, the same hands, Maggie thought, that had tried and failed to fend off the touches of a boy she had loved as her brother. Natasha was wrestling with the same decision Maggie had, wondering if she should dare take the leap.

Finally, she reached across the table and shook Maggie's hand. 'OK,' she said. 'Deal.'

MONDAY

Chapter 48

This is Meet the Press Daily. *For our full hour tonight, in-depth insight and analysis of last night's sensational NBC interview with presidential hopeful Natasha Winthrop, the civil rights lawyer accused of homicide in what she says was an act of self-defense against a violent rapist.*

Gotta begin with you, Katty. We've both been in this town a long time, have you ever seen anything like that?

No, I have not. (Laughter) You've got me there. I know 'unprecedented' is an overused word in the news business, but seriously: there is no precedent for what we witnessed last night. I mean, let's just start with the optics—

Right, that is something else—

There she was, this is a woman who aspires to be president, and she is interviewed in what was very clearly a prison, wearing prison fatigues and – this is what is so extraordinary – it kind of worked.

I know, this is—

It looked like something you might see in a developing country – you know, the leader in waiting, jailed by the regime, granting a rare interview from her prison cell.

It was stunning.

Stunning! And it reinforced her message that she is somehow a political prisoner. That she is in jail for daring to take a stand on violence against women.

And what about this strategy of full disclosure: how do you think that worked for her?

Well, she just laid her cards on the table, didn't she? She explained that, yes, she did know the man who violently attacked her; that she had been following his case for many years, tracking his skill in evading justice again and again; and that she devised this scheme to ensure that the next time he tried to rape a woman, there would be evidence. I mean, that was a compelling case.

Let's take a listen to that part of the exchange:

'You did not plan to kill him?'

'Absolutely not. I had plans in place that would ensure I was safe and he would be caught. Lester, those plans went horribly wrong. I was playing with fire and I got burned. I ended up in this place, having to defend myself. But my word, that was the last thing I would have planned.'

That's the interview from last night and you found it persuasive?

I found it brave. I found it honest. I found it moving. But it doesn't matter what I thought. Just listen to the American people. Polling overnight shows that—

Let's flash that figure up. There we go.

Sixty-eight per cent agree or strongly agree that Natasha Winthrop was telling the truth, with a similar number saying all charges against her should be dropped—

That was before word came from the prosecutor's office in DC

428

saying that the homicide charges would indeed be dropped, on the grounds that 'there is no realistic prospect of conviction'. Sorry, I interrupted, go ahead—

Well, Chuck, as you can imagine, this is the number that's got people in DC excited. 'Should Natasha Winthrop enter the race for President of the United States?' Sixty-four per cent saying yes to that question. Now, clearly, that's not sixty-four per cent saying they would vote for her, but especially in the light of Tom Harrison's decision to suspend his campaign over those Russia and hacking stories—

Maggie muted the TV. She wanted to focus on which dress to wear. With Uri on the other side of the world, she was reduced to propping up her phone on the bathroom shelf and posing in front of the lens while Liz assessed her outfits via FaceTime.

'Turn around again.'

'I've already done that twice.'

'I'm just trying to work out if it's the dress or just that your arse has got bigger.'

'Not being helpful.'

'Believe me, I really am being helpful. You don't want to go in there looking like Sister Agnes in her gym pants.'

'Liz, I don't have time for this.'

'Seriously, though, do you remember the arse on that woman? It had layers. Like the ice sheet in Greenland. Like it had its own ecosystem or something. What are you doing?'

'I'm taking it off.'

'Why?'

'Because you said my arse looks like it's the size of Greenland.'

'I said, I wanted to *work out* if it looked like that.'

'What about the black trouser thing?'

Eventually, Maggie got herself dressed and out. It was a party for Natasha's release, but it was also very clearly not only that. Parties in Washington, DC, were rarely just one thing: a senator would host a silver wedding party for six hundred of his closest friends eighteen months before a presidential election and every guest would greet each other with the same two words: 'He's running.'

Once Maggie arrived at this do, at a restaurant on Washington Harbour, its lights twinkling on the water, she saw nothing to alter her view. The room was full of journalists from Axios, the *Post* and Politico, congressional aides and, strikingly, the leaders of the key national women's organizations. For a party thrown together at just a few hours' notice, it was impressive.

Maggie got herself a drink, fended off the attentions of a former State Department colleague, now divorced, and was soon chatting amiably with Jake Haynes of the *New York Times*.

'Thanks again, Maggie,' he said, raising his glass. 'Took Harrison out with one strike.'

'That was all you, Jake, remember. I didn't even know he was using Imperial Analytica.'

'And we didn't know the company was basically a Russian front operating like a gang of thugs.' He raised his glass again. 'You see, that's why we're the perfect team.' He gave a smile which Maggie suspected was an attempt at being flirtatious.

When Maggie offered zero response, he said, 'That interview was something, huh?'

Maggie assented that it was, though what she was thinking about was what she had been turning over in her mind for the last twenty-four hours: namely, all the things Natasha did not say on television.

Yes, she had confessed to knowing of Todd, to having followed his case. But when asked why she had singled out this rapist of all rapists, Natasha had shown the interviewer the same dead bat she had shown Maggie at Pilgrim's Cove a few days earlier. She made no mention of Little Rock. And not so much as a hint of Mindy Hagen.

Maggie had thumbed out a text: *What about our deal?* But she had not sent it.

She wanted to think some more, especially about one question she had not got to ask when they'd met in the DC jail. It was simple. Natasha had thrown open her entire life to Maggie, allowing her to roam through her files, paper and digital. She must have known it would lead to Penobscot and to Aunt Peggy, and indeed to the Judiths. Why would she have done that?

Of course, Maggie knew the official answer: Natasha wanted to know what in her work might explain, and ideally identify, the enemies that were out to get her. But she had risked Maggie probing much deeper into her past. Why?

Someone was dinging a glass, calling for silence. An actor was on stage, a box-set favourite who, Maggie knew, Liz would be swooning over but who Maggie struggled to name. He was delivering a long paean of praise for '. . . the champion of civil rights, role model to our daughters, warrior queen . . .' but Maggie was barely taking it in. She was thinking about her question.

A snatch of conversation came back to her, from when she'd been trying to persuade Peggy Winthrop to talk to her.

Natasha is a very careful young woman. She tends not to make mistakes. But nonetheless she gave you access to her computer, and allowed you free rein to find a path here. To find me.

Maggie hadn't probed that too deeply at the time; she'd been glad just to have her foot in the door. But now she wondered if the aged Aunt Peggy had understood what Maggie had missed: that Natasha had wanted Peggy to be found. Which meant she had wanted Mindy to be found.

Now Natasha was onstage, basking in the applause. A chant picked up: *'Run, Tasha, run! Run, Tasha, run!'*

She was smiling and modestly gesturing for the crowd to pipe down.

How easily Peggy had handed over the diary. No resistance at all. She had volunteered it.

'Run, Tasha, run!'

Why would Natasha Winthrop want to be found, and then agree to do a set-piece TV interview only to say nothing, only to keep Mindy hidden?

'Thank you, everyone. Your support means so much to me.'

Maggie watched Winthrop the way Stuart Goldstein would have watched her. There was no denying it. She was quality 'horseflesh', to use the word Stu deployed when assessing candidates like animals at a livestock market. Crisp, clear, compelling. And beautiful. A thirty-something lawyer with no experience of elected office; a rape victim accused until today of murder; a (supposed) WASP from the East Coast elite, it was mad to think of her running for the White House – and yet it was also possible.

Natasha came down from the stage and was instantly mobbed. Maggie hung back, waiting for the scrum around the candidate-to-be to edge towards her. As it got close, Maggie moved towards it, until the two women were face to face.

Over the din, Maggie said, 'Great speech, Natasha.'

Natasha shouted back. 'Thank you so much!'

'Interview went well.'

'Yes! Thanks for your help with it.'

Several looks passed between them, an expression that said *Not here* from Natasha, and a *Don't worry* in reply from Maggie.

'There's something I'd like to ask you, Natasha.'

'Great! Why don't we fix up to meet?'

'It'll only take a second.'

'Hi!' Natasha shook hands with a woman in her sixties who held up her phone, requesting a selfie. Maggie waited for it to be done and then, as Natasha tried to move on, placed her hand on her wrist. As if to say, *Stop*.

'I want to know why you wanted me to find out.'

'Find out?'

'About you.' Maggie's eyes said: *Don't make me spell it out.* 'Why?'

Natasha paused, then took Maggie's hand. 'Because you're the very best, Maggie. The best.'

'That doesn't answer my question.'

'Oh, it does. I knew that if there was any possible way to find out about me, you'd find it. And you did.'

'I don't follow.'

'You'll remember that the man I once thought of as my father was a plumber. Before installing a pipe, plumbers test it. They send water down the pipe, and check to see if any comes out where it shouldn't. That way they know in advance if there's a hole where they might spring a leak. Well, you, Maggie, found the hole. And now I can patch it up.'

'What? How?'

'Those phone records, for example. Not too difficult to make those go away.' And there, once more, was that look of pure ice that Maggie had glimpsed in Cape Cod. It had sent a chill through her then and it did so again now.

Maggie suddenly thought of Great-Aunt Peggy, out in the middle of nowhere on the distant Atlantic shore. She'd moved there a decade or so ago, she said. Was the truth that Natasha had banished her saviour to the very edge of the country once her career was up and running, the better to keep her secret safe? So many thoughts were tumbling through Maggie's mind, but the words that came out were: 'But, but . . . I know about it now. The story is out.'

'Not at all.' Natasha squeezed Maggie's hand again, and moved her face closer still. 'Because when I say you're the best, I don't just mean that you're good at your job. Though you are. I mean that you're *good*. You're a good person, Maggie. I know you won't betray me, just as you won't betray those other colleagues of mine. What did you call them? The "Judiths". So ingenious. And I certainly know that you won't betray Mindy. Not after everything that happened to her.'

Now a man pushed through the throng, arms outstretched

for a hug, which was duly offered. In tow were what Maggie assumed was a wife and three daughters, all clamouring for a selfie with the woman of the hour. Within a second or two, they had jostled Maggie out of the way and Natasha was swallowed up and gone.

A waiter arrived with a bottle of champagne, clad in a white napkin. He moved to top up Maggie's glass, but instead she handed it back to him. She headed for the exit, receiving a little wave from Jake Haynes, who was shouting into his phone, on her way out.

Outside, by the water, the throb of the party behind her, she caught herself breathing heavily, almost panting. Natasha Winthrop had played her good and proper. She'd made Maggie do a pilot run for the opposition research that she knew would come her way if she ever sought the presidency. If someone somehow gained full access to all her records, what would they find? Maggie had provided the answer.

As another chant erupted and spilled out from the restaurant – *'Run, Tasha, run!'* – Maggie thought once more of the story Natasha had told again and again, to her, to the TV interviewer, to the nation. How she had acted spontaneously, to defend herself from a violent attacker.

But did Natasha's plan really go wrong that night? Or did it, in fact, run like clockwork? Did she only ever want to see 'Todd' – Paul – the brother who had abused her so cruelly, arrested and convicted? Or did this woman who had lived two such different lives – keeping each one hidden from the other – set out to kill a man in a premeditated, cold-blooded act of revenge? And if

SAM BOURNE

Natasha Winthrop, who might now be on her way to winning the most powerful office in the world, had done that, was she right or wrong to do it? Should Maggie keep her secret, or expose it?

In the glittering night of a Washington autumn, as the cheers and chants drifted over the harbour, Maggie realized with a dizzy kind of sickness that if there was an answer to any one of those questions, she did not know it.

Acknowledgements

This is a novel, but it is rooted in a bleak set of facts. The conviction rates for rape are as appallingly low as Natasha Winthrop says they are, with the picture in Britain as grim as it is in the US. In India, one rape is indeed reported every fifteen minutes. The episodes of sexual harassment and assault, whether set in New York, London or Stockholm, are based on victims' accounts that are anything but fiction: I feel deep admiration for their courage in speaking out, and great gratitude to the journalists who recorded their stories.

I'm also indebted to the many lawyers and experts I spoke to for this book, starting with my *Guardian* colleague Alexandra Topping who has written so powerfully in this area. Julie Bindel, a veteran campaigner on the issue of violence against women, was both patient and generous in sharing her insights. Hadley Freeman and Rachel Burns were kind enough to read an early draft, both offering characteristically shrewd advice. I also want to say a special word of thanks to the poet and writer Lemn Sissay, who talked to me with great candour about his own experience of rejection at the hands of a foster family he had loved.

Once again, Alex Hern, tech guru for the *Guardian*, was an astute guide around the digital realm, while the indefatigable Rob Evans advised on the tricky business of false identity. Gary Copson and Kate London allowed me to benefit from their huge experience of police work. I am grateful too to my old friend and legal sage, James Libson.

There is a posse of comrades who have helped me before and helped me again. My thanks to Steve Coombe, who is unwaveringly generous with his expertise in matters of security and tradecraft, and to Jonathan Cummings for his frankly uncanny ability to uncover even the most elusive fact.

I could not be more grateful to the team at Quercus for their patience and wise counsel, with special mention to Jon Butler, Stefanie Bierwerth, Laura Soppelsa and Hannah Robinson: I feel lucky to be in their hands. Rhian McKay has the keenest copy editor's eye in the business, Sharona Selby offered a proofreader's eagle-eye, and Viola Hayden at Curtis Brown provided some very perceptive advice.

The origin of this novel was a brief news item spotted by my agent and friend Jonny Geller: he continues to be the rock that I, like so many writers, rely on.

Lastly, a word to my family. Sarah, Jacob and Sam bring constant love and joy into my life. Whatever gloom there might be in the wider world, they make our home a place of sunshine and laughter. I cherish them more each day.